1959

1959

A NOVEL BY

Thulani Davis

GROVE WEIDENFELD
New York

Published by Grove Weidenfeld
A division of Grove Press, Inc.
841 Broadway
New York, NY 10003–4793

Published in Canada by General Publishing Company, Ltd.

Library of Congress Cataloging-in-Publication Data

Davis, Thulani.
　　1959 / by Thulani Davis.—1st ed.
　　　　p.　　　cm.
　　ISBN 0-8021-1230-7 (alk. paper)
　　I. Title.
　PS3554.A93779A615　　1991
813′.54—dc20　　　　　　91-24548
　　　　　　　　　　　　CIP

Manufactured in the United States of America

Printed on acid-free paper

Designed by Irving Perkins Associates

First Edition 1992

10　9　8　7　6　5　4　3　2　1

For Ella Baker
& the Old Man
this little light

Namu Amida Butsu

1959

The way I hear it, when nomads move on from one of their weathered, disassembled villages, the animals often return to forage where there was once food, and to curl up on the hot barren land right where they once slept in the sun outside the dwelling of a human being. A child of such a line once described to me how these nomads talk to each other over the long stretches of savannah now turned to desert, how they can make themselves heard by means you would call supernormal. My tribe never practiced any magic arts, but storytellers all, they cling very close to my ear and tell softly what I have forgotten or have never known. Slavery dropped them in one place and there they stayed, amid the swamps and tobacco fields of the plantations they knew and then in the slave-built camp that became a town. When, a hundred years later, the town was razed, as if to erase the minds of those who tried to claim it, all the sounds and voices of the place were torn free from where they were sheltered.

The authorities didn't need any cranes and steel balls to gut the African heart of the town of Turner because it was so small, so fragile, and so freely built—without plans or any sure circumstance in mind except to enjoy ordinary days out of bondage. Folks knew it would all be met day by day. In the face of the uncertainty of freedom's first days, knowing only the dailiness of all the past, the people built no monuments. A few bulldozers could take down their ancient wooden bungalows sitting close to rosebushes and dandelion weeds on the low-lying seashore.

Those who took it down would never know that this spit of land was where the first ship bringing slaves to America stopped and dropped anchor long enough to put ashore an ailing African woman, presumably to die. It's a meaningless bit of history but I claim her with my laugh, knowing she probably lived, knowing she was mad as hell. I imagine her as the vehicle, the way we all got to this particular corner of Virginia. They called her Angela. I call her Gambia. I've claimed her as kin, first of my line. I've watched the storms build off her shore. I've walked her beach.

Those who took down the old places that were once our quarters would never know that homes were built four and five times on the same plots of earth where newly freed Africans had dug their garbage pits and tossed all the broken clay pots or glass or anything that could not be burned for fuel. Down came the house my great-grandfather had built, and the one next door his son had put up and two on the other side built by slaves who'd run from Nat Turner's lynch mob, and others built by men who'd promised to fight for the Union if somebody would give them a rifle. And down came the bridge where poor folks fished and the docks where crab pickers kept rowboats tied up along with the metal baskets used to catch hard-shells. Down came the little cottages surrounding Victorian mansions, homes where all the mansions' laundry was done. While the mansions were kept as part of the town's history, the history itself was ripped up and set loose to cry through the cracks of boarded juke joints and hair salons in tacky storefronts.

None of us had anything much that somebody would save. The signs of slavery had been buried as worthless, and finery was hard to come by. Still, the new municipal building, the parking lots and garden apartments could not revive a place that had died when all the front porches were turned over and all the buried treasures were unearthed. The old socks and flat tires, the broken picture frames and lye pots, the slave "dog tags," the Sunday school certificates and stillborn babies and broken promises shared their secrets when the nights seemed so quiet and a thin fog sat low in the sea-level streets. They were all coming loose that year, when hairline cracks were beginning to show through the years of plaster, when floorboards soaked in the flood of '57 began to warp under our feet. I still return to root and forage. Sprouts still appear, seemingly at random, where the ground was turned over. In places where old hands pruned the mint and plucked the honeysuckle stems, the plants grow back without structures to cling to or the appreciation of children's hungry fingers. We used to wander, sneaky and laughing, literally eating the backyards of women who shooed us away once they spied us snatching the berries or fighting over split ripe figs. Creeping onto a farm, we hunkered down in the rows and ate the tomatoes right off their spindling branches. We knew where everything was growing. I am the last of my line. I return to curl up in the sun there because I know the sound of the birds, the smell of the tide when it has gone out.

1

BILLIE HOLIDAY died and I turned twelve on the same hot July day. The saddest singing in the world was coming out of the radio, race radio that is, the radio of the race. The white stations were on the usual relentless rounds of Pat Boone, Teresa Brewer, and anybody else who couldn't sing but liked to cover songs that were once colored. My cousin Marian and I talked about that for a while sitting on the porch, till it got boring because we talked about it every day in the summertime when, naturally, we heard a lot of radio. White radio was at least honest—they knew anybody in the South could tell Negro voices from white ones, and so they didn't play our stuff.

You could tell Billie Holiday's shattering tones from anybody's on the planet. We could not sing anything she sang, Marian and I. We didn't even really understand it. Billie Holiday was in the faces of grown women, in looks we didn't stare at too long. My cousin and I spent summer days together at my house or roaming around because everyone had to work. My old man went off to teach his summer school class at Turner, the Negro college down the street, and my brother had a job house painting. We settled for singing Tina Turner, and Mickey and Sylvia. My father told me they used to say twelve was the age of reason. So just before my birthday I had forced my father to deliver me to a beauty parlor, where I had my braids cut off, and I had started wearing flats. Maybe that was why on my birthday I was allowed to go out with a boy for the first time. His name was Dallas and I liked him.

That day Marian and I sat on the front porch watching the cars go by, and singing "Love Is Strange." The harmonies were off, way off. You could whine 'em out like country and western. We usually spent a lot of time on my front porch, which was open and wrapped around two sides of the house sitting on the corner of Nahemsah Lane and Union. The views were excellent. "That's Cassie's boyfriend, Jack Dempsey," Marian said, as a dark green Chevy with fins passed. She was two years older and knowledgeable about all things when it came to the kids in the high school.

Cassie had been one of her baby-sitters. Everyone seemed to have been one of her sitters. Now that she'd more or less outgrown them she spoke of them as equals, as if they'd gone to the elementary school together. Since I never had baby-sitters because I had a brother, I never knew anything, not about the high school girls, or anything they were supposed to have to tell. "Jack Dempsey is a football player." With a dumb name, I thought. I preferred the name Champion Jack Dupree—I'd heard it on the radio. Champion Jack Dupree. Now *that* was a name I'd give my kid, a star's name.

"We'd better get going," I said. The heat smacked us as we stepped off the porch of my house. We were sweating before we had left my yard and got to the road. We took Union toward downtown. Marian lived on Liberty behind the main drag, Raleigh Street. Her mother, Maddie, was supposed to be back from one of her vacations—Haiti, I thought my old man had said. Cousin Maddie, it had dawned on me, seemed to be going to places I wanted to hear about.

"I want to ask your mom about Duvalier."

"Who?"

Now it was my turn to play smart. "Duvalier, the dictator. Papa Doc Duvalier. Your own mom went to a country with a dictator and you don't even know it. I mean, do you know anybody else who went to a country with a real dictator?"

"No. And I can't say I ever cared either. Besides, I don't think they have any dictators in Atlantic City." Marian started cracking up.

"Atlantic City? I thought she went to Haiti."

"Nope. That costs too much money, she said."

"Well, last year she went to Cuba."

"They had some money last year from Dad's uncle."

This fact of Maddie going to Cuba had haunted me because I had only just gotten interested in dictators and I had missed getting the details last year, like if Maddie saw Batista, or any guerrillas. It was one of the aggravations of school that I was constantly finding out about these things that I could have been wondering about before. But I hadn't missed Cuba, no one could, because the white folks were so upset about it. It made them crazy, like Little Rock. Cuba broke all the rules. I really didn't know anything about what it was like there. What I heard about was cha-chas, conga lines, glass-shiny dance floors, and swarming ship docks piled high with bales no man could carry—sugarcane, tobacco, coffee, cocoa. A mixture of Xavier Cugat and geography class. When I tried to envision the place now, in 1959, it was still a huge emporium, a roiling market of raw goods and battering rhythmic tongues, blown up from the drawings of slavery in my schoolbooks, except that the raggedy devils lazing on those bales had cut machetes loose on the fancy suits. As I saw it, there were no cartoon Negroes in Cuba. And besides that, every time I thought about President Eisenhower, Fidel Castro was like Marlon Brando. Ever since the winter when the crowds shouted, "Fidel, Fidel," as he marched out of the hills, and revolution had followed Maddie's very footsteps out of the hotel, I wanted to know about her vacations. Atlantic City was not what I meant though. Even Marian had been there. She'd already told me all about it.

From the swinging screen door on the open rear porch, Maddie Alexander, who was not in Haiti or Atlantic City but in her slacks and slippers, spied us with a critical eye. As soon as we hit the door she grabbed us for close inspection. "Willie," she said to me, "it's not even the middle of the day and you're a sight already." I thought I had concocted a pretty tough hairdo that day. Marian and I had been experimenting with Dippity-Do and *Hairstyle* magazine for my date. "Get my hairbrush," she ordered, and Marian, throwing up her hands, scooted out for the brush. Maddie had a mighty grip. If she got ahold of any part of you, the rest would suddenly follow. She took out the hairpins and stiffly brushed my whole head back. "You look terrible. What is all this mess in your hair? It's a shame your mother isn't alive to show you how to take care of yourself. I'm going to tell your father he has to take a closer look at you in the morning." This always got my goat. She continued to yank and brush until order was restored, twisting the hair tightly into a new ponytail.

I had only come to visit, but I knew already I'd not only get to help with the chores, but would be getting a bath and some borrowed clothes that were either too big or too tight. "I'm glad you-all showed up. I can use some help. The beds upstairs could use your attention." The house was still as a church, and when we went up the bedrooms were all dusted and just mopped. No maracas or straw sombreros. Just two swimsuits hanging in the bathroom and one or two bottles of suntan lotion. No French perfume. Duvalier, Batista, names running in place in my head, like a cha-cha. Batista, Duvalier, Pa-pa Doc! When they were on the news you could tell something wasn't being told. Hell, look how they talked about Negroes in code. You had to know what they were really trying to say because there was so much they didn't say. We moved from room to room and changed the beds.

"Why do you think people go to Cuba?" I asked.

"To rumba," Marian said.

"Well, what about Haiti? Sounds like an awful place to me."

"The water there is aqua blue, isn't it?" she asked.

"Yeah, I'd like to see that."

"I think Maddie doesn't care where she's going as long as she can dress up."

At least that was one reason to go somewhere that was hotter than Virginia and vacation around dictators. And even if it was Atlantic City, it must have been lah-di-dah and fine, I thought, because Maddie liked glamour and glow.

Maddie Alexander, who preferred to be called Madeleine, was a very stylish person. She had clothes tucked away in store boxes all over their house, high heels in every shape and color, and a dresser covered with bottles of Revlon nail polish and atomizers of perfume. Her clothes drawers were bursting with intricate, delicate things that were never seen, like slips, garters, and negligees. Marian and I used to like just to grope through her gloves, which were practically the only items we could try on, and admire the neatly boxed purses she left in Marian's closet. Maddie was much more complicated than my mother had been when it came to being feminine. She was always

11

changing things about how she looked, nail color, hair, dress styles. My mother had had simple tastes and wore only rouge and lipstick. She got up in the morning and brushed her hair into something plain and simple. And Marian's mom believed in clubs: Madeleine belonged to two Negro women's clubs, one sorority, and one of those clubs for parents of children who should, by virtue of class, associate with one another. She was always being "active" in something women did in groups. On summer evenings at home she'd put on a pair of tight black pants, a halter, and her high-heel mules and sip cocktails to the bounce of Jimmy Smith.

"C'mon, let me show you girls how to dance," she'd say after we'd done the dishes. "You're never going to catch a boy if you don't know how to dance when you go to parties." And so, we'd have impromptu jitterbug lessons on weekend nights before her company came by, or after school if a party was coming up. She gave pointers on cha-cha and slow dancing too, including tips on how to keep the boy from pressing too close. Her idea of a good catch for us would be some kid who came by wearing a suit, got straight A's, and was devoutly Catholic. She wasn't Catholic or even terribly religious, she just thought a nice Catholic boy wouldn't be grappling every time she left the living room. She always kept her eye out for those little bookworms, and then Marian and I would have to discover their hidden problems. Maddie burst in.

"Girls, what are you doin'? You don't look like you're working too hard." She hurried us through the job.

"So, what did you do on vacation?"

"Went to nightclubs."

"When you went to Cuba did you see Batista, the dictator?"

"No, honey, I don't think I even saw a monument. Why?"

"I'm doing research."

"Well, I got something for you to research, young lady." She shuttled us into the bathroom and shut the door. "Get those sweaty clothes off and clean up," she called through the door.

"What do you do at a nightclub," I asked Marian, "just dance a lot?"

"You smoke cigarettes and get your picture taken looking like you're having a great time. And you get drunk. My folks go to nightclubs all the time when they go to Atlantic City. The Club Harlem is their favorite."

Cousin Maddie and Bill were Count Basie fanatics. My father wouldn't think of going to a nightclub; at least I didn't think so, because I'd never seen him dance. He said he danced whenever he put on his tux to go to a Bon Frères Club ball, but then, he said he played football and ran track. My father, Dixon Tarrant the college chemistry teacher, had never even run for class president, much less track. An aching-bones former athlete he was not.

"Sounds like fun if there's handsome guys there." I wrapped myself in a towel and looked in the mirror. I could see myself smoking a cigarette in a red evening gown. Bare shoulders.

"Well, you don't have to worry about Dallas taking you to any nightclub tonight." She laughed. "Where are you-all going, anyway?" I had my mouth open to answer when the door opened again and Maddie put folded clean clothes on top of the hamper.

I whispered. "I don't know. And I don't want your mother to hear about it or she'll probably call Dixon and tell him not to let me go."

"You got that right. She thinks your father's too 'permissive.' I wish my parents would get permissive for just a couple of days. Well, you're probably not going anywhere. I mean there ain't nowhere to go around here." We looked at each other nervously.

"Nope," I said.

"Some back road."

"Oh God."

Marian laughed again. "Maybe he's slow, he looks slow." We cracked up. "Cassie's mother told my mother that she thinks Cassie might have gotten pregnant."

"Oh God, now you tell me that! How did they do that?"

"What do you mean, stupid, 'how did they do that?' You know how they did that. They've been going together since they were sophomores, two whole years!" I told Marian that I'd heard you get pregnant when you sleep with a man.

"Well, they sure weren't asleep!" Marian cracked up. "No wonder you ain't nervous about your date. I was wondering if you were just cool or what. They were in his *car*—you know, the one I showed you this afternoon. They go out in the car together, and I guess they went too far. It happens when you go too far! You know, like when he gets your clothes off."

"Oh God! I don't want nobody foolin' around up under my slip and stockings and garter belt. How gross."

"You don't wear stockings and garter belts yet."

"Well, I would if it was winter."

"Right. Knowing my mother, she'll have me going out on a date in anklets—five years from now."

WHEN DALLAS came to pick me up he sat on the porch with the old man, probably answering questions. I left my room with clothes all over the bed because I'd had to change a few times before getting the outfit that "struck all the right notes," as I'd told Marian. What that boiled down to was a black straight skirt, as usual, sleeveless top because it was hot, and sweater in case the place was air-conditioned. Ponytail. I wore flats with bare legs. It was too hot for stockings and I didn't own any.

I was glad he was being interrogated outside. We never kept the living room too neat or polished. All the cushions of the couch looked as if they were dying unless you fluffed them up hard and then didn't walk near them. Even foot vibrations would make them start sinking. Four years after her death we still couldn't keep things straight. All the sleek black modern furniture she'd picked out usually needed dusting, and her old piano usually had sheet music all over it from my lessons, and my schoolbooks on top of it. If it weren't for the fact that my brother and I weren't too neat, the house would have looked like a shrine to my mother, her handicrafts and art books all around, only pictures she had chosen on the walls, baskets of her old sewing materials still sitting around. My father just never went through any of the stuff to throw it away. After throwing out her cosmetics and giving away her clothes, he didn't have the heart to go on.

What I heard through the screen door was that Dallas and I were supposed to go roller skating at the colored rink, where a local radio DJ was going to play the records. His brother would drive us. I didn't say anything but I was wondering if I could skate in a straight skirt. When I stepped out they looked sort of sweet. Behind his eyeglasses the old man's face was deep coppery red from the summer sun. He sat stout and content in his favorite spot on the front porch getting the breeze and breathing in the heavy fragrances from his lush garden. After working in the garden, he was clean and scrubbed and cool, with his thinning hair brushed back and lightly oiled. After dinner he would sit out in the dark with pipe or cigar, then most nights go in to read. People frequently dropped by to sit and have a drink because they knew he'd be out there. This was Dixon at his most serene. Dallas should never have been so nervous because it was the one time of day you'd have to go some to get the old man riled.

15

Dallas, who was slim and caramel colored, and very clean and scrubbed himself, looked as if he were sitting on a pail of crabs, as if he were trying not to actually sit at all. Dallas could be real handsome if he smiled more, but he was usually serious, and even the old man's attempts to make him laugh were not going over well. The old man said that was why he wasn't too worried about me being out with him; he didn't seem fun loving enough to be trouble. I thought pretty much the same thing. I knew what the "trouble" ones looked like. In the car I realized Dallas and his brother weren't too concerned about skating. We stopped to pick up a girl his brother was dating and took the long way around, following the shoreline toward the next town, where the rink was. The older two in the front seat ignored us and we ignored them. No one was offended.

There were creeks and inlets ripping up and around the town of Turner like veins—Little Creek, Big Creek, Curl Creek, Magnolia, Tomahawk. Actually, they were all part of the Turner River—which we just called "the creek." The town was built around the opening of the river, which was narrow but deep and spilled into the Chesapeake Bay. About a mile inland from the river's mouth Turner's fishing wharves gave a curved shape to the center of town. We went over the small stone bridge that connected the wharves and the old town on the west side with the farms and beaches looking out at the Chesapeake on the east.

The sun had not yet set, and we could see the fishermen tying up boats and putting in for the night. The early settlers of the place had learned shellfishing from the Indians and then left it to their slaves. Blacks became oystermen and fishermen, and they still hauled in the catch on the fishing boats and crab dredges. In the canning houses behind the docks, black women were fish filleters and crab pickers. When the work wasn't bringing in enough for a family to eat, you could see folks fishing for porgies or eel on the creek.

There really wasn't anyplace a boy could take a girl. There was a colored bowling alley in an old Quonset hut, where boys set up the pins, and one segregated movie house. We could get take-out snacks at Shorty's little drive-in place, or go to somebody's house. If you were very careful about nobody seeing you, there were some places you could walk on the beach. These things didn't matter much, since being with a boy in a car seemed clearly the most exciting thing you were going to do anyway. Going somewhere was gravy. We drove around to the quiet boulevard where the rich folks lived and the whole bay opened into the sky.

The biggest houses had been built right on the shore in slavery times, with private boat docks at the end of footpaths from their front doors. Up the nearby James River the houses sat barely visible on high cliffs, with wooden stairways zigzagging down through the brush to the docks. In those days a rich farm near the Chesapeake with deep river in the front yard could import provisions directly from the Caribbean or anywhere—sugarcane, Carolina rice, pineapples, slaves. Now only a few little skiffs were tied to the docks. When the big money had gone, many of the piers were allowed to rot into the tides. Some old houses wound up with mounds of oyster shells on the lawns and pieces of long-dead clammer hulls pounding against the moorings.

The summer night smells were blowing in through the car windows so loud I felt as if I could talk myself into being in love with this boy who put his arm around me but barely spoke to me. We talked some about school and then we talked about places we might go someday. Sometimes he talked like the boys in love comics, saying he liked me and that was about it. Most of the time he talked about whatever else he could think of. When I tried to tell Marian what it was we said on the phone for so long, nothing came to mind. Finally everyone in the car agreed to pass on the skating—I mentioned my skirt—and we drove around some more. We stopped for snacks and then drove on again. As we rode down the winding, dank, and overhung roads I was wondering if I was going to kiss the guy, and if something else transpired should I just have a fit or what? The roads, so familiar in the day, became totally strange to me in the dark. The tiny houses had disappeared, leaving only their driveways. The night's humidity and our sudden freedom to be out alone merged in my mind as a craving, a hunger. For what, I was not sure.

Near my house but not in front of it, the car stopped, and Dallas and I got out. At first he became talkative as he moved on me. He kissed me twice, trying to get his tongue in while I thought I was supposed to be pursing my lips. I was not really thrilled. After the river it seemed anticlimactic. I did think it would be worth trying again though, if we could be out in that miasma that had made me feel completely unhinged.

To my embarrassment, my dad and Mrs. Boteler were sitting on the porch. They didn't seem the least bit interested in my arrival. They were serious. She was like an aunt to us, and ever since my mother died she had taken to sitting the old man down and telling him how to raise us. My brother and I rather liked it when Dixon didn't get any advice and just went along without really knowing what he was doing—that way things were always open to discussion. With Mrs. Boteler there was only a right way and a wrong way, and children were to be told, not asked. I just looked and nodded and went in. I went upstairs to the old man's room, where the phone was, and called Marian and told her nothing had happened to me when I got kissed. She was just as puzzled as I.

Once in my room, I crawled out the window of my bedroom and sat on the porch roof to find out what was so delicate. I was very surprised to hear Lillian Boteler mention Cassie's name. Her son, Coleman junior, ran around with my brother Preston and it seemed he'd told her something about them going to visit Cassie and another girl over on Ulysses Grant Street.

"Apparently last Christmas the boys were seeing a lot of those girls."

"Is that so?" the old man was saying, obviously totally in the dark as to what she was getting at. I could hear him trying to sound interested. I could smell his pipe. People were always telling him where his kids were. I couldn't even get over the bridge to the dime store without getting a call from him when I got back. Right from his office on the campus he'd know I was standing in front of Woolworth's, "looking like you were waiting for something," as he said. I used to go into town to cool off. Marian would come from her house on Liberty Street, behind Raleigh, and meet me in front of the Woolworth's and we'd "shop"—which is to say we looked around—in the air-conditioning, or take a bus to the next town and shop.

Preston too had lots of little adventures that no one knew about. He told me that summer that he had gone to a Holy Roller baptism by the river. It was another of the many things I was astonished to know was going on in Turner. He said he had gone to this storefront church before to hear the music and it was really good, so he went back to go to the baptism because he thought it would be interesting. Preston had a lot of interests: chemistry sets, rhythm and blues records, girls, swimming, exploring, and recently, gospel music and Daddy Grace. At seventeen, he was practically the town anthropologist.

But the girls Preston visited were all daughters of Dixon's friends. We hardly knew anyone who lived on Ulysses Grant Street. It was a lane with a boulevard-size name, a rough, narrow little half street downtown near where Marian lived. Ulysses Grant had just inserted itself between Raleigh and Lincoln streets and grown. Unpaved and rutted, it was short and ran about the length of two blocks, from Lafayette over to Bolden's Corner. The houses there were tiny three-room timber shacks set up on concrete blocks, with tentative porches and irregular grass. A few old outhouses were still standing back in the brush among the chickens. I had been to Ulysses Grant with Marian, because we had some friends from school who lived there, but hanging out there was not on the approved-activities list.

Cassie lived in a rambling low-set house at the near end of Grant. It had what I imagined to be gables, having been added on to at various times and in several directions. Like most of the houses in the neighborhood, it was a hundred years old, with floors that warped and a porch that was getting close to sea level. But it was nicely kept and always warmly lit in the evening. Ancient Victorian glass lampshades of fading tulip yellow made the wide-open house seem cozy.

Mrs. Boteler also seemed to know that Cassie was pregnant, a fact that had her quite alarmed. Since Dixon had never heard of the girl, he was still straining to get the point.

"Dixon, I don't know if one of our boys could be responsible, but if it should be so, it will be a terrible thing."

"One of our boys?"

"Yes, Preston or Little Coleman. That's who I'm talking about, Dixon."

"I can't imagine that, Lillian."

Neither could I. I also couldn't imagine the old man talking to Preston about getting someone pregnant. *Much* too personal for Dixon to be discussing. Mrs. Boteler was staring crossly at the old man, I could just feel it. Like several of the other women of my father's generation, she usually wore her whitening hair pulled back in a serious-looking bun, and looked over her glasses at you when she wished to drive home a point. She had gotten heavy in the bosom and hips but must have had a tailored, schoolgirlish look when she was young. Her crisp, prim appearance and northern manner must have been a bit off-putting to her southern neighbors, though they may very well have simply credited the whole effect to her sallow ivory skin, straight hair, and light eyes. She could seem very severe, and a little lipstick was her only admission of vanity.

"Now, listen here, Dixon Tarrant, it's time you started think-ing about these things. The kids are growing up. And it would be just terrible for one of these boys to be ruined by something like this."

"I thought it was the girl who was usually ruined." She did not laugh. "I mean it would be unfortunate for both of them, but what are we supposed to do? From what you're saying, I'd say we don't even know if they were dating these girls."

"Well, you should start by finding out. Then I would suggest we do nothing. We have their futures to think about. These boys are going to college, and you can't let Preston get tied down with trying to take care of some poor girl who can't keep her skirt down, if you'll forgive my bluntness." The old man wouldn't like that a bit. Dixon's chair squeaked as he shifted his weight.

"Well, these boys may be going to college, but I have to live in this town." His voice was slightly higher—he was getting mad now. "I can't turn my back and pretend my son didn't know the girl if he's responsible. If he's responsible, he will damn well deal with it. I sure don't want any grandchildren around here for *me* to keep, but that's not the point. That girl won't have a chance in hell to raise that child right if she's trying to make it by herself. I couldn't leave any child of my son's out there without a pot to piss in or a window to throw it out. I don't care if it's illegitimate or not. To hell with that!"

"Dixon, don't raise your voice. The whole house will hear."

"I don't care if they do."

"Look, that child's got a mother, and if she'd been doing her job her daughter wouldn't be pregnant and still in high school. Let her deal with it. Besides, I hear that girl had some regular boyfriend that she was seeing. There's no need for us to be involved at all. You just better tell your son to mind what he's doing. If you don't want to tell him, I will do it for you. I'm certainly going to tell Coleman I better not ever hear any more about him dating on the wrong side of town. These boys have to be told what's expected of them."

"Hmph. I'll talk to the boy. I'm going to tell you again, though, I don't much like the idea of you suggesting that they wipe their hands of a thing like this. You make your bed, you lie in it. And I'll tell you, Lillian, frankly, this just doesn't sound like you. You've never been wound up quite so tight about anything like this. Hell, you know we've seen kids get pregnant before."

"Dixon, sometimes I feel as if I'm coming apart at the seams. You get right up to the brink of letting these kids go and be gone and so be it, and they start to try your nerves. I don't know if they know what they need to know to be out in the world. Seems like ever since they got ready to get out of high school, they got dumb and crazy like my husband. My son and yours."

"Well, that's true."

"I just want to keep a grip on my boy a little longer. He doesn't seem ready, not one bit ready."

"They're not going to get ready, either, Lillian."

"How did you get so sanguine about it?"

"I'm getting old. That's all. Just realized there's not much I can do. I'm not sure I ever did do much."

"Oh, Dixon, please. Old! You still got women chasing you. Shit. You just lazy."

They got up and she said good night and stepped off the porch. He continued to sit there till long after I crawled back inside. I tried to imagine if Mrs. Boteler thought we'd never have to see the could-be grandchild because he or she would always be across town. The whole thing seemed preposterous, but I was scared to mention it to Marian. I decided to wait to see if Preston would talk. The next day all I got out of him was yes, he'd seen Cassie, but only a couple of times and it was none of my business because I was just a kid, stay out of it.

A few weeks later, Cassie and Jack Dempsey were necking in the dark green Chevy. They had parked by the river near the old mansions. Jack Dempsey got out and headed for a nearby car to ask for a light for a cigarette. The man in the car, who was white, was frightened when he saw this young black football player coming his way. He reached over his girl and into the glove compartment, got his gun, and shot Jack Dempsey dead.

IN AUGUST it was just too hot to work. That's what I tried telling my father, anyway. It was doggishly hot and june bugs were laying siege. Around the neighborhood bugs of all kinds seemed to attack the pulpy meats of fallen figs and neglected peaches, sometimes dragging the remains near the back steps where they were a hazard to humans. For several days gnats bombed in from all directions, a sign that the wind wasn't moving at all. No wonder the early settlers decided to move upriver to Jamestown after trying to land in Turner's swamp. It must have frightened those poor Englishmen to death. Cicadas were hatching themselves all over our yard, a thousand tongues clacking at night, a thousand translucent corpses in the morning. The front lawn was like a potter's field some August days, covered with rows of hard brown shells, ridged tubes lying scattered about like miniature catacombs an ant could run through. It was as if in late summer everything living took off its outer skin and lay inert in the coolest place on the earth or, like softshell crabs, in the smooth mud. Within days, the air reaching the soft, inert body would cover it like an unguent, just enough for the creature to move, perhaps to a genuine death at the hands of curious children. There were squalls almost every afternoon, but they brought scant rain and no relief. Every morning and evening we had to water the garden. "It's hotter than the hinges," I told the old man. "Where the hell did you get that?" he asked. I told him I'd heard this redneck say it in town, "hotter than the hinges of hell." He sucked his teeth. "Lose it," he said.

The old man missed nothing. Teaching was not his occupation, but the way he lived his days. Gardening was his favorite subject. To hear him tell it there was a system to everything, or at least a pattern. Gardening required one to remember the needs of each kind of plant and the cycle it lived in. He simplified cooking to a matter of reading and measuring; mathematics, he said, was about patience. He concocted home remedies for our illnesses, some from chemistry know-how, some from folk recipes. For sore throats he dished out gargle made from bottles that said DON'T SWALLOW and simply said, "It'll be fine, just don't swallow." Once, terrified of making a speech at school, I told him I couldn't do it.

"Do you have something to say?" he asked. "That's it, then. That's what it's all about. The essence of the arrangement is that you have something to say that the audience doesn't know. As long as you have faith in that premise, you go on."

24

When it came to work, he resorted to a grab bag of well-used lines about "character building" and his own childhood of seeming hard labor. He taught me to play poker rather than tell me what lies the men were yelling about when he and his friends got the cards out and closed the sliding door to the dining room. He dragged me to the local potter's shop so the man could show me how my mother had made the bowls and figures sitting around the house. He would never mention that he did this because he himself did not know how it was done. He later lugged home an extremely small firing oven that the potter was probably throwing out, and told me if I wanted to make some things out of clay we could "fire" them.

Dixon Douglas Tarrant was basically a nineteenth-century character who was lucky enough to be young in the 1920s. It was then that he met my freethinking mother, when she came to Turner College to teach. He'd gone north to college on a scholarship during World War I and worked the railroads in the summers. When he came back to settle down he met Leigh Stanley, who, he said, was upsetting the school inside of a week. Leigh thought the Negroes running the college were stuck in the past, and she was a believer in all things modern—modern dance, modern dress lengths and hair lengths, modern art, modern lampshades. For starters, she thought, the school ought to teach modern dance and modern music, and failing that, at least they could teach black students something about black music and black dances. She eventually got her way on some of it, but not until she befriended Dixon, who thought she had beautiful legs and who smoothed some of the ruffled feathers around the school.

Leigh told Dixon he should marry her, and he did, but she never realized that even though he was crazy about her, he'd never met a woman who didn't put in three hours getting dinner together and most days cleaning house. She never got it together to be what Dixon imagined. When she died, he realized that in her own way she had been doing what he had expected. For the first time he began to express his limitations openly. Finally he noticed that he knew how to set a table and cook eggs, that he did know how a bed was made from his days on the pullman trains. So he started from there. And he repeatedly remarked that what a Tarrant didn't know, he or *she* could find out, and once she got the hang of it, nobody was gonna do it better. That, he said, covered everything.

And so he taught homework, dart throwing, badminton, whist, gardening, model trains, what to do with dandelion greens, or how to cook a Smithfield ham and how to know if the savory flavor was just right—everything except, in my case, fishing. That was asking too much, he said. He also taught his own skeptical brand of religion. When I got into trouble a few years back with Mrs. Taliaferro's sister-in-law the Sunday school teacher for asking how exactly Jesus could change water into wine, he told me that the Bible didn't necessarily mean that he changed it *literally*, like from water to wine, "but please don't tell Miss Taliaferro I told you that. I don't want that woman calling me. Just nod your head or something when she's talking. What you think about what she's saying is your business."

IN THE middle of the month we heard our first serious hurricane was heading up from Florida. Once the season started I would hope for a real good one, a storm big enough to stop everything and shut folks up in their homes with makeshift meals and maybe even a flood like the ones they sometimes had before I was born. In Dixon's photo books people rowed around town in boats, and it took days for the water to subside. Dixon, who was mildly obsessed with weather observation, made storms seem more interesting than dangerous. When Hurricane Erla had gotten within forty or fifty miles of the bay, he drove me and Preston down to the docks where the ferries came in and the old steamboats once moored. We drove through the eastern end of town beyond our house, where once tobacco fields stood around a village made of barrel staves and other scraps from the great war machine that had fought there. Now it was a black township with poor white fringes, a place of weathered bungalows with sand in the front yards. The ferry docks wrapped around an old Civil War fort perched on a narrow spit of land jutting into the bay, surrounded by churned-up waters. As we cruised out the spit toward the piers, a smattering of rain tried to fall, but hard winds blew it inland across our car window.

"Did I tell you about your grandfather Charles living out here during the Civil War?" Dixon asked. He was pretty sure he had, but every time he saw the fort his mind traveled to a time he'd missed for being born too late. He was like that about the world wars too. Ruefully he would say, "Too young for the first one, too old for the second."

"Grandpa was just a boy, wasn't he?"

"Yes, just a boy. His father, William Walker Tarrant, rounded up all his children when their master ran off. They were at another farm round here somewhere. Anyway, they took refuge out here. But my old man talked about it as if he remembered it, all the fighting, troops moving in and out, hauling big guns with wagons. When I was a boy he had me down here with him working, building the hotel. He was a mason, you know."

"Yeah, I know, and he worked white."

"That's right. I told you that, huh? Like the hotel, that was a white folks' job, of course. Right across the road there was the first house they ever lived in, real tiny thing. I ought to take you

27

in that house sometime. Well, I don't even know if we *can* still go in there."

We rounded a corner after the last pier and came upon the back side of the hotel. The bricks came back to him row by row as scenes of his old man scowling and scolding him as a boy to work like the men, and get the rows just right. It was starting to really blow and a police car passed us headed for the last dock, but there was a certain order to Dixon's stories, a certain logic to his reminiscences that would not be broken, not by the storm, or the cop, or the fact that no one who wasn't wearing a uniform was out because the hurricane was getting close.

"You see, your great-grandfather William Walker got away first, here to the fort, when the contrabands first started running. Then he brought his family here. They had never been together before—can you imagine that? It's something to think about, isn't it? They'd never been together. And he kept them all in the little lighthouse where he had gotten some work. There it is; you can barely see it now, can you? The trees have grown so thick around it now. When I was a boy there was not much around here, just one or two houses for the commanders."

A right turn put us on the point, in front of the resort hotel and facing the steamboat dock, a huge rectangle jutting out into the sea. The water was high and roiling and the Coast Guard had already blocked off the wooden wharf from the road. The men were hoisting sandbags on top of one another against the open spaces where the bay might rear up and kick hell out of the Halifax Hotel.

And the old landmark could just as well have drowned for all most black folks cared; its dense high walls of shrubbery and striped canopies were keen reminders of how white folks liked to be shuttered in from the rest of us. It didn't matter a damn if Charles Walker Tarrant and other black men had built it. All the folks who ever came in the back door and made the beds would just as soon see Erla drag the cabanas out to Cape Hatteras. Neither Dixon nor his old man had been in the place. We didn't say a word to the white men at the barricade. They eyed us curiously as we stepped around their trucks and stacks of bags to get to the seawall. They might have warned us off, but Dixon waved at them as if it were any summer afternoon and turned his head so as not to hear anything they might say.

"The tide might come up ten feet from where it usually is," he said, "and it hits so hard it could crack this wall." He pointed at the cement barrier holding in the fort's grassy lawns and cannon battlements. The rain was blowing in sheets now and the rush of the salt spray was becoming frightening. Water sprayed through the cracks between the boards on the wharf, and the one-room ferry terminal was getting battered from above and behind, from all sides and from below. Dixon slipped away into the great wonder of it all, took the air and water as if it matched him element for element, cell for cell, the water no more than another skin, another shirt. Wherever it was that he let himself disappear, it was a place beyond reason, beyond any explanation for taking his kids into a storm. He did not fear the moment; if he could have stayed, he might have remained till his entire skin was blown and washed away, till the thought of thought was gone and the flesh was new.

Deep within the wind was a whistle too faint to catch, really, a frightening high-pitched sound from nowhere. Salt spray stung my face. The boards moved and wheezed the way they did when a boat slammed into the moorings. We were on the rough sea, sails unceremoniously dropped. The wire stays whipped against the masts with a stinging sound and the boat was heeling.

The ringing was far off in the buoys that rocked from side to side. The little nun buoys closer by leaned way over and dipped their heads to the waves. The Coast Guard men shouted orders to hurry and Dixon turned from his meditation, announcing that it was time to go. Back in the dark Buick we drove home nearly silent, the reassuring clack of windshield wipers breaking up the sheets of water on the window and the view of the town, which by now lay in harm's way.

"By the time they left the lighthouse, most of the town had been burned down by the Union troops. After that, William Walker and his family lived in a horse barn near where we live now."

"Oh yeah. Where's that?"

"It's gone now. It was on the waterfront too, down on the farm where the college is. Then he built a house on Liberty Street and his sons built all around the house."

"Where Grandma lives now?"

"No, that's the one my old man built, the one I grew up in. William Walker lived next door where your uncle Robert used to live. And before World War I, your uncle Lucius lived on the other side. Everybody lived together, and as the family got bigger they just built around William Walker on the land he had. That was the way people did then."

"How come you and your brothers didn't do that?"

"Just didn't work out that way. When the old man made us get out of the house to work, most of us just kept going."

On the front porch at home we counted the seconds between thunder and lightning and measured the distance. My brother Preston was an old hand at the storm business, and he stood out with us in his raincoat, letting me get the weather lessons without interfering. Dixon showed me the barometer falling, the instrument being overwhelmed by the obvious. He periodically announced that Erla was nearly overhead and brought another piece of porch furniture indoors.

The shutters started banging on their hinges, crying and

thumping, until we clamped them down. We got all the candles and candle holders out of the pantry and lined them up, replacing the burned-down candles with new ones from a box tucked away in the china cabinet. Pretty soon the lights would go, and maybe the phones. The three of us fixed some fish and leftovers and watched the weatherman on TV track the course of the storm up the Carolina coast.

"You know, if a storm comes up while the local black fishermen are out," interjected Dixon, "they may stay out there, depending on the tide and the storm's direction. Not a hurricane like this, of course, but most of the smaller ones come from the west toward you, and as they come you'll see the white men's boats going in. Usually the boys and I are trying to get in too," he laughed. "But the old Negro fishermen will tell you, 'It's going to blow over and miss you,' and they just keep fishing. In fact, the fish might be jumping into the boat in a high tide out there. It'll get good just as that storm appears. It's the damnedest thing how they know when it's safe, but I've seen it work. I even went and looked in the books to see if anybody had studied this. It's the damnedest thing, but those fishermen risk their lives every day on their own rules about the tides."

He went on in an awestruck tone about how no science book said anything about the connection between a storm's direction and the high and low tides.

"I've never seen them go wrong with it," the science teacher said, "never." The rain came down in thick walls into the streets and fields. The lights got shaky and finally went. We in Turner, sitting at sea level, would flood quickly.

For days after it was cool and wet. Even the linens got soggy from the dampness. A pale green fungus soon appeared in the cracks of sidewalks and old stone walls. Life seemed to be starting over in places where it wasn't supposed to be growing.

The trees and fields looked ragged and glistening. Oaks we couldn't climb for two summers suddenly lay at our feet, their highest mysteries to be broken off in our hands. All the children prowled through the green litter and split wood, relishing the smell of the insides of trees. We sopped our clothes in the wet scattered leaves like biscuits in gravy. Savoring our own good luck to live in places with lightning rods.

MY NOSE was in the flower garden. I was supposed to strangle the weeds and bring them out of the damp earth. They'd gone crazy since the rain. The scoundrel weeds. My father tried to console me about this humbling little job by telling me how his dead sister, my aunt Fannie, used to tend the family garden. Tuberculosis saved her, I would think. Fannie had great aspirations. Anybody who grew up with seven brothers would. I was thinking about the asparagus around the other side of the house. One foot deep in the sandy stuff. They have to start life real low.

There were no weeds on that side; the pebbles in the sandy soil kept them down. I had once taken a flying leap into that gravel trying to push the swing as high in the air as the boys did. My body lurched forward and I lost my grip. The rocky patch at the end of the house cut me from head to foot. My brother Preston and the other boys laughed as I went screaming in the back door, knowing that for weeks the story would be etched into my face. If I had had more than one brother and his friends to contend with, I would've been hauled away from home in a white jacket.

Fannie was one of the characters from my father's stories that stayed close to me. She was in my dreams sometimes, and what he didn't tell I filled in for myself. Fannie was best remembered by all her brothers, it would seem, for having convinced the family to give up the Baptist church and become Episcopalian, and for how she died. They said she was always trying to give them some class. She was a very pretty, slim woman, coppery like my father, with nearly black hair and her mother's high cheekbones. According to my father, Fannie just "never warmed up" to the idea of marriage. The only good thing about it, she used to tell them, was that she'd only have to clean up after one man instead of eight. She just assumed she'd never have children. Their mother, Louisa, indulged her because she was her only girl, rarely saying anything when Fannie complained that she wanted to be able to leave town like her brothers. Their father, Charles Tarrant, had more or less announced to each child that he could not afford to keep them at home once they hit the age of twelve or fourteen, except for Fannie.

Fannie went to the depot when any of her brothers were coming or going, just so she could stroll onto the train and see all the other colored folk traveling from further south or up north. Sometimes she would ask a young man to take her on the long buggy ride down to the steamboat docks on the bay side so she could see one of the steamers that came in three times a day from up north. The folks emerging from the whites-only upper deck or the colored section on the lower deck were the finest-looking people she'd ever seen. As they strolled off toward waiting buggies or the fancy new Halifax Hotel with the wide striped awnings, she coveted their luggage and their freedom. Fannie didn't dislike the pretty little fishing town of Turner, it was just that by the time she was fifteen, it seemed to her that Turner's rivers and bays, billowing out into the Atlantic, were an invitation.

My father was her little brother, to whom she confided her dreams. But he betrayed her once by siding with the old man, who said she could not go out with them for a day of fishing.

He was only eleven then, but he had gone out in the boat with old man Brown down the street that summer and they had discovered a dead body floating near the mouth of the river. They had had to lash a rope around the neck of the bloated carcass and bring it back to the docks. Dixon had thrown up all the way from the smell. Now, acting much older, he told old man Tarrant that a young lady should not be taken out in a fishing boat. What if something like that happened? The old man didn't think much of his reasoning but simply considered women too much trouble when a man was trying to do some serious fishing; young boys, he said pointedly, were bad enough. She stopped telling Dixon anything one day when she realized that he was getting to the age when he too would leave home.

I often tried to get him to tell me about his sister's trips to see minstrel shows, which he said she snuck out every night to see when they were camped in town. Dixon tired of trying to re-create old gags he'd never seen himself and always began with a prelude about the evils of fascination with the stage, and especially with blackface coon shows. It was an old instinct in him, a fear that, without much provocation, any Negro could revert to doing what survival had trained his grandparents to do, to "play" Negro. It was not just the brown faces on *The Ed Sullivan Show* that made him worry. He had been forced to sing spirituals before they would serve him his dinners in college, he and two other boys who had never sung in public in their lives. He knew it pleased the whites to remind themselves they had brought a darky out of the jungle into higher learning, even if they had to withhold his food to do it. Far from having to play Negro to become famous, one might have to do it to eat. In either case, Dixon thought, it should not come too easy. He'd sung some spirituals he thought he'd made up, his Negro repertoire not being very large, his voice being pretty bad, and his four years of college being pretty long. Minstrel shows, he said, well, the first thing about them was that they were in a different language. It was a hungry language and all the words were a complicated code that grew more and more intricate. And all the words said, "I'm a fool, but I'm not a fool," or "I'm just here and I don't understand but I know *exactly* what is going on." But all the words put together really only meant, "Feed me," or "Let me live."

The minstrels were still coming around in the first years of this century. Some of the clan living in the compound, like William Walker, who'd turned ninety, and his oldest sons, Charles's elder brothers, had more recollections of slavery than of freedom. They refused to let anybody patronize any so-called "ole-time plantation entertainment." None of it was real to boot, they said, even if the troupe was colored, and especially if they said they were "gen-u-ine." Louisa said it made folks look ignorant, and anybody sitting there laughing was igno-rant too. Even though all the Tarrants liked to tell stories about far-flung kin outwitting masters, for the most part slavery was something Charles and Louisa Tarrant talked about behind the doors, as if it were something the children shouldn't know had ever happened, at least not to them.

William Walker used to chide his son Charles about forget-ting slavery. He always said, "The good thing about the race is that we only live in the present, but it's the bad thing about us too. Every child has to find out for himself that nobody thinks he's a human being without proof that is extreme." Charles gave up arguing because the old man would get loud and tell him how he went to the white man's court to get his wife and children out after buying their freedom and the white man told him point-blank, "You may say they are wife and children to you, but they are property still. Possession is nine-tenths of the law. What, Mr. Tarrant, do you possess? They are not in your possession, they have never been in your possession." Every Tarrant who had ever sat at the table with William Walker knew the judge's speech, or Grandfather William's version of it, like a blues song passed down the hands on the levee. "Nine-tenths of the law, Mr. Tarrant. And what do you possess? How exactly did you come to stand in my court, Mr. Tarrant? How exactly did you come? How did you come to possess yourself, Mr. Tarrant? How exactly did you come?"

William Walker's voice would boom across the parlors of his house and he would eyeball Charles and say, "Fruit of my loins, before Jesus I swear, and I know you to have served the first ten years of your life before the cross, and yet you will forget. You will let your children forget and that girl there, Louisa, was only born after they sawed the anklets off her mama. She never had sense enough to thank God she would never wear them herself. I saw her mama one time. Louisa don't believe that; she thinks I'm just old and crazy 'cause she thinks nobody knew 'bout her mama. Well, let her think what she wants. You-all live in the world like it's new." His preaching tirades scared everyone in the house into silence for hours. Louisa used to say the old man wouldn't have been so bitter but he lived too long.

There was something to that. In the third month of the Civil War, three slaves had escaped to a Union fort near Turner and had been declared "contraband of war." By July, almost a thousand runaways were there, including William Walker, who probably didn't have far to run since twice a week he sailed a boat for the white folks that passed right by the fort. In August, local rebels burned Turner down to keep it out of Union hands, and the planters fled. William Walker got a wagon and fetched his mama off one farm and his wife and children off others and made it for the flat wooden bridge in Turner that crossed over to land declared federal and, for Africans, "free." Black people were camped out everywhere for miles, from the bridge down to the fort—in peach orchards, dairy pastures, on sandbars and oyster bed beaches. In each camp, all the women wore dresses that were identical in cut, if not cloth, mass-produced by slaves on each plantation for the hands living there. Most wore kerchiefs tied to the back of the head, and many still had aprons around their waists. Only the grown men wore shoes. Old covered wagons stripped of their cloth crept along carrying the elderly and the tiny. Dozens of men walked alongside with bundles stuck on sticks and all the clothes they owned piled on their bodies in layers to lighten the load. For as far as the eye could see, hobbled, ragtag, old, and young African slaves and their American children were crowding all the narrow routes onto the fort's little peninsula.

As the war ground nowhere in Virginia, and Union troops had to move west and north, the runaway slaves built "Slabtown" on the "federal and free" side of the creek and then moved back across the wooden bridge into the heart of Turner. There behind Raleigh Street, and right where the Tarrant home would stand on Liberty, they built the Grand Contraband Camp, a tent city that became the town. And there they were when the war was over and the white folks returned, outnumbered and crops dead in the ground. The contrabands built First Baptist, Zion Baptist, and elected leaders. There were no more paterollers—plantation night riders—chasing them down, no more curfews. The life had been harsh from the beginning, and more homeless folk appeared each year, but the life was theirs. Working tobacco meant going past every fragile plant every day, pulling the bugs off one by one, living with a black gum in the pores of your body. They were fighting to hold ground in the face of bosses who paid black laborers five dollar a week and charged newcomers twenty a month for rent. The old-timers saw the grand dreams grow humble like the wages and elections; everything slipped from the grip but the land where their cabins and houses stood, and the streets the contrabands had named after the liberators. But in 1896, the year Fannie was born, white folks came back strong with a piece of trash named Jim Crow. It was then, at eighty-four, that William Walker Tarrant began to feel too old. He was not much impressed with the new century. The lynchings adding up each month told him Africans would have to be harder and yet more Christian than he had it left in him to be. And then he let it go.

I OFTEN pictured Fannie sneaking out of the house at sunset, heading up the blinding white street to the minstrel tents. Dixon did a poor imitation of the shows he'd only seen Fannie reenact. Fannie, he said, was the expert. She had a set of bones she'd found left behind one time when they struck the tents. Bones were loud clappers made from thin pieces of wood, with pencil-thin cylinders in between. He thought she played them masterfully, coaxing intricate rhythms out of the palms of her hands. The first show of the season was usually on a placid, hot Memorial Day weekend when a big crowd could kick off the summer. They started the shows at sunset. At that time of the day Liberty Street would have an eerie glow, set off by the oyster shells paving the road. The sun's setting light spread up and down the street as well as across the sky, putting everything in between in silhouette the way sunset on a river turns trees on the shore suddenly dark. Bristling clean and bright in the morning, the street at night was no longer a poor folks' street of white wooden cottages, but a glowing avenue leading from the sun to the creek.

Between Ulysses Grant Street and Lincoln, and bordered by Lafayette's broad cobblestones, as you headed toward Bolden's Corner, was an open field where shows like the Rabbit Foot

Minstrels set up the wiggle. It was smack-dab in the middle of the old camp, and a good spot to catch a black worker coming home to the neighborhood. On the farthest end of Raleigh Street were the storefronts belonging to the colored barber, tailor, hairdresser, and undertaker. The last stop was the colored saloon, always called by the current proprietor's name. All day long vendors would ramble up and down the streets hawking fruit and vegetables from the seats of their wagons. Others rumbled by slowly with rough-hewn ready-made clothes and the new machine-made shoes, fashioned with indifference to the matter of left or right or size. While most folks went to the pier for fish, crab vendors knocked on kitchen doors with cooked crabs wrapped in parchment. By late afternoon they were trundling home with loud empty wagons, the wheels crashing against the oyster shells packed in the streets.

The razzle started just before the sun set, and went on till the shooting stars appeared and the money ran out. When the Good Foot Tent Show or the Christy Minstrels came to town, Fannie unbraided her hair and gathered it up into a Gibson to look older, pinned a brooch at the neck of her high-collar blouse, and got out a shawl. She took her little drawstring cloth purse with whatever change she had, and a neatly wrapped package to look as if she were on an errand. Slowing down as soon as she began to hear the warm-up music, she tried to look as if she were just stopping to take a peek. When the performers emerged, she sidled up to a gap in the tent flaps to see. Twelve men appeared grinning, with shiny black faces, bright eyes, and white circles around their mouths. They looked strangely grand in their tired long black dress coats, white vests, top hats, and white gloves. They announced a quartet, and as the custom went, *five* men rose and sang a mournful harmony about a sweetheart who died young. The other performers turned their backs to the audience and stood with their arms crossed. As the song ended, the twelve struck a unified pose, flashing their white gloves and white smiles. They sat in a semicircle on twelve tree-stump seats. The men moved like dolls animated by bad spirits. Mr. Interlocutor, the brains man on the gags, took the middle seat; the end men played tambourine and bones. In the middle on either side was a banjo picker. When the end man clacked the bones, it cleared Fannie's head like hollow laughter.

TAMBO
Mr. Interlocutor, are ye 'fraid of lightnin'?

INTERLOCUTOR
(*Chin high, eyes lowered, looking haughty.*)
Not part-i-culahrly. And from what I see, many's the darky seeking a little lightening.

TAMBO
You oughta hab seen Bones the other day. We was out in the country for a walk when a turrble storm arose.
(*Fearful grimaces all around, except for the middle man, who listens for the rest of the story.*)

BONES
It made my *hair* stand on end.
(*White fingers sticking straight up from his head.*)

INTERLOCUTOR
That's one way to get it straight.

TAMBO
We took shelter under a tree.

INTERLOCUTOR
You surprise me.

TAMBO

Well, scarce were we 'neath the boughs o' dat tree dan de lightnin' flash and strike a fruit tree standin' jes' by, and sliced it to bits.

INTERLOCUTOR

(*Snidely to the audience.*)
That's probably as close as you come to getting some jelly.

TAMBO

Y-a-s sir, den Bones begin to cry, and he gits down on his knees (*acting it out*) and says, "For heaben's sake, do somethin' religious."

INTERLOCUTOR

And what did you do?

TAMBO

(*Innocently.*)
I passed him the hat and asked for de contribution.

INTERLOCUTOR

You know, Tambo, I don't believe you could git no lighter.

BONES

(*Puzzled.*)
I b'lieve that is a conundrum, sir.

INTERLOCUTOR

(*Mocking him.*)
Only to de coon what's dumb.

With a flash of all teeth and a flip of the tails, the twelve whisked out on a wave of laughter. Next came the "wench dancer," a female impersonator who shook and wiggled to the banjo rhythms. She ground her hips in her shiny dress and walked a big, bowlegged walk. She was so shameless, Fannie turned her back to the tent and only peered sideways through the flap, thinking maybe if somebody saw her she wouldn't look like she was looking at any such lowdown mess. But she was looking, and wondering too. The tambourines and bones started shaking and the whole crowd roared. Then the guitars and banjos plucked out the melody of a local favorite, an old-fashioned marching dance tune called the "Contraband Schottische," dedicated to Major General Benjamin Butler. The tune was greeted like an anthem in Turner because so many of the old-timers had actually found rescue with General Butler at the "freedom fort." She tapped her foot, but Fannie much preferred the "Gentlemen Coons' Parade," which at least was funny. When the cakewalks and rags started, everyone jumped up and danced. A few would cakewalk down the sidelines, and people outside the tent who did not pay to go in would practice their steps, improvising acrobatic leaps as the music pounded. The night ended with a contest of the buck-and-wing, and only the old ladies were left in their seats. The jubilation in the place made Fannie feel crazy, and she loved it.

She waited around the back to get a glance at the real women who performed, wearing rather short garments made out of gaudy materials that you couldn't even buy for lining in town. Sometimes they sang these moanin' kind of songs, about men mostly, or leaving their sweet mama, never to return. The songs talked about a life that sounded wretched, but to Fannie it was heartbreaking and exhilarating too. Coming back up Liberty in the dark she would try to swagger her hips like these knowing women. "Well, I'm goin' away, baby, / won't be back till fall. / Goin' away, baby, / won't be back till fall. / If I find me a new man, / I won't be back at all."

For weeks after they left town she would walk the streets hearing rags, trying to imagine what women did who left home, other than sing the blues. She would go to the fish market or the dry-goods store, trying to see them as a visitor might, or to see how they might look to her if she were just returning from someplace vast like Chicago. Fannie never figured out where to put all her strong feelings, and she saved her secret swagger for a young man she took a liking to that year when she was fifteen.

Her brother Lucius brought home this slim, handsome fellow from Arkansas who wore a moustache and was always elegant in his short-jacket suits and boaters. Vernon Taylor had worked the railroads just about everywhere, and he told her he'd known women who worked as nurses, librarians, running businesses. She liked Vernon because he took her seriously. At the same time he scared her because he was like a compulsion in her life—his caresses made her feel more driven than her dream of going off into the world somewhere. If he so much as ran his hand down her neck, she got breathless.

She would pretend she was one of those blues singers as she walked with him over the flat wooden bridge in town and looked down at the creeks and lagoons winding their way up toward the moon still low in the sky. They would walk down by the shore on the other side and sit on a stone wall behind one of the marinas. She would let him undo all the buttons of her waistcoat and blouse, then all the little tiny fastenings of her chemise. Her feelings rushed open inside her like a beast bursting free of a cage. Finally she would force herself away from him, telling herself, "He's going to leave, and he won't be here next week, or even next month." Vernon never promised her anything, and she didn't ask.

He told her that each time he left they should say it was over. He didn't want any girl waiting for him. So for two years that was their agreement, no letters and no promises. Each time he visited they went out as if for the first time. The arrangement suited Fannie just fine because she had made some plans of her own. Vernon thought that what with the war on in Europe, if America got in it she'd be able to sign up to help the soldiers. Perhaps so, she thought, and decided to bide her time.

Whenever Vernon came to town he brought along for the old man a bottle of good whiskey, some Cuban cigars he'd gotten off a high roller on one of his trains, and a copy of the *Boston Guardian*. Charles Walker Tarrant would enjoy this last item for weeks, reading it aloud as he did the daily paper every day at luncheon, and passing it around to all his friends to show what enlightened Negroes in the North were doing. Mr. William Monroe Trotter's newspaper made it a habit to take on that first son of Virginia, Mr. Booker T. Washington. Not a paper in the state—Negro or white—would dare to print the kinds of criticism of Washington that were Trotter's meat and potatoes.

Charles Walker Tarrant, like his father the contraband who could read and write, favored education for Negroes above all other routes to full citizenship, but lately he'd come to see that white folks would pass any kind of law to crush Negroes and keep them down. With the years of lynchings, blacks had learned they had to keep their hunting rifles in the bedroom. Trotter just didn't trust white folks, so the old man always liked to see what he was saying. Tarrant couldn't understand Booker T. Washington's looking the other way on political issues, discouraging folks from demanding their rights. Since 1903 Charles Walker had had to stop going in places he'd gone in all his life. He said it was a short step back into slavery. He framed a *Guardian* cartoon of the great Negro leader doing a buck-and-wing surrounded by a circle of white minstrels. He looked at it and remarked with funereal seriousness, "The most famous colored men of our time are all entertainers."

Fannie taught at the Negro school down on the old Morgan

farm on the other side of the creek. It was the only occupation her father would approve. A large one-room cabin, the school had been named after an abolitionist who had helped in some way already forgotten. Children of all ages came there in their knickers and pinafores, all with the same high-top boots and serious faces. There were two teachers, four or five black-boards, framed pictures of the American Founding Fathers and of slaves, and a piano for singing. They taught reading, writing, history, arithmetic, laundering, gardening, grooming, and whatever else they knew about survival and propriety.

When Fannie was free she stayed in her room reading books, and each day she would tell her students something interesting she'd read the night before. But her real mission in all the reading was to stay out of sight, almost as if she thought she could get her parents to forget she was there and stop looking over other people's sons for her to marry. She had firmly decided to avoid that and wait for the war, ever since she crept home one night from a tent show by way of the backyard.

She had heard a woman crying in the dark and soon realized it must be her mother since she was the only other woman in their house. As Fannie had her skirts halfway over the fence, there was no going back. Louisa turned in shock, but then turned back as if she didn't care.

"What's wrong, Mama?" she asked, quiet as she could, and nervous because she'd hardly ever seen the woman cry.

"I'm having another child, girl."

"Oh, Mama, it's not that bad," she said, thinking maybe it could be a girl, which would be at least a little better.

"Leave me alone, Fannie. Go on in the house. Tomorrow I'm gonna want to know exactly where you been."

Fannie crawled into bed with a book she'd found in the house; it was about Antarctica, and though it seemed strange, she was more fascinated with it than any book she'd read in

45

years. One of the boys had become interested in polar explorers after the papers carried the accounts of Matt Henson, a colored man, going with Admiral Peary to the North Pole a couple of years back. So she returned to her place in the darkness with the crew of a ship trapped in antarctic ice.

TAMBO
Mr. Interlocutor, are you afraid of silence?

INTERLOCUTOR
Never seen any call to be scared of a little peace and quiet.
(Laughter.)

TAMBO
Bones, tell Mr. Interlocutor about your brush with silence the other day.

BONES
Well, it wasn't exactly silence. I was running down the street singing a raggy tune to myself and then I forgot the song.

INTERLOCUTOR
What's so remarkable about that? Your mind never was a work of art.
(Laughter.)

BONES
I forgot who I was. I was just walking down a blinding white street, in a flimsy dress and red shoes. Everything was distant and all I could hear was a groaning, scraping sound like when ice rubs against ice, or how you imagine an earthquake coming. Like sitting in the darkness for months and months listening to glaciers move. I couldn't catch my breath. I could see some people dimly, sitting on porches, rockin' babies, but I didn't know them. I was trying to scream above the scraping sound so they could hear me.

1959

TAMBO

You were like a one-eyed cat peepin' in the seafood store.
(Laughter.)

BONES

The rockin' chairs moaned on the wooden floors and everybody looked
away.

INTERLOCUTOR

What is it that a young girl looks for, and does not wish to find?
(Laughter.)

TAMBO

A hole in her stocking.
(Laughter.)

Louisa never asked her a thing the next day. Fannie went out to see if the garden needed watering, and check if any of the tomatoes had turned reddish yet. She stopped dead at the door and made a little gasp. Every flower, every tiny bush, tomato plant, every cuke, collard, pepper, even each wild dandelion had been pulled from its roots. All the work of spading and digging that spring, and all the little just-budding vegetables, had been mauled into ruin. She raked everything into a heap and made a compost pile, covering the good buds with leaves. At dinner she announced that the family would have to get vegetables from the wagon because mites had infected everything. Her mother never looked at her. The baby was the seventh boy, and for a while Fannie, who was kept at home most of the winter with a persistent cough, told him her stories. It was 1914 and no Americans were in the war.

2

ON NIGHTS after Erla, when the thermometer had crept back to 105 and stayed, and the mosquitoes had bred in the dampness by the millions, I thought that what we needed was another hurricane, especially when the old man started running us through his paces with a fury all day. Dishes after breakfast, water, weed, spade, mop, and scrub. The heat came down on us like a pressing iron. If we moved an inch, sweat rolled from everywhere and my muscles were dead weights. Relief came at lunch when the crabman knocked at the back door with fresh deviled crabs wrapped in wax paper and reeking of hot sauce. An avid gossip, he was an emissary from the old neighborhood across the creek, carrying word on his bicycle pushcart from Raleigh Street, Ulysses Grant, and Liberty, where Grandma Louisa lived. Titus was so old he was almost a visitor from the other side, never changing in the least from year to year. He was never seen during the week. On Saturdays, though, he was seen by every Negro household in every corner of town.

"Yes, sir, Mr. Tarrant. I was to your mother's this morning."

"That's fine, Titus. Glad you looked in on her. How're the crabs this week?"

"Big ones this week, sir, and the crabmeat is sweet. You'll see."

"Well, gimme a half-dozen."

"Half-dozen it is. That'll be a dollar and a half, Mr. Tarrant."

"Titus, prices are getting pretty high."

"Yes, sir," the old man laughed. "You always say that. They been the same two years now. Maybe you oughta buy 'em from the white folks."

"Naw, Pops, I ain't crazy."

Right behind Titus came the boy with the *Journal and Guide*. The Negro newspaper had a front-page story on a possible school integration plan. There was also a full-page spread comparing colored schools to white. Some folks who had gone to the city councils in three towns asking for the schools to be integrated two years ago were making progress in Turner. The schools in the paper were worse than the Negro schools in Turner, Carver Elementary, Ida B. Wells Junior High, or Booker T. Washington High. Every town with a Negro high school seemed to have named it Booker T. It seemed as if Turner, of all places, should have had a Nat Turner High. Of course, this was a joke in the South, where Negroes couldn't even name what white folks had abandoned. The whole business of suing to integrate the schools was a mystery to me because the Supreme Court had said the schools should be desegregated back in 1954. But nobody did it. Except Little Rock. Even after all the mess with their governor telling President Eisenhower no, he wasn't going to do it, and the troops going into Little Rock and taking the nine kids to school, the only thing that happened in Virginia was that our governor said no thank you too.

"Imagine these white people calling the public schools a 'dual school system,'" Dixon said.

"What's that?" I asked.

"You know, the schools were supposed to be 'separate but equal.' When white folks are trying to make it sound nice they say what we have is a 'dual system.' Look at this," he said, thumbing through the pictures of dilapidated schools in the *Journal*. "That's what started the whole thing in the first place."

"Started what whole thing?" I asked.

"The suits to end segregation that went to the Supreme Court."

"Oh, yeah. I know."

"Negroes in different places were suing to get their 'separate but equal' schools fixed up so they were equal. Crackers didn't even want to do that, so as things went on Negroes went to court with the position that you can't get equal education in this system. The colored school in Ocwamseh still has outdoor toilets. Some of these are no better than the school I went to—not as good."

"The one-room schoolhouse?" Preston asked.

"Yes, and not such a bad place when I think about it. At least it was clean."

"Izat where Fannie taught?"

"Izat? Who taught you to talk like that, Willie?"

"Is that where Fannie taught?"

"That's where everybody taught and everybody went to school. Me and Fannie and all your uncles. Well, young lady, looks like things might be very different for you, though, very different."

"What do you mean?"

"I mean kids your age will probably be the first to go to integrated schools around here. Looks as though they're going to try for it here," he said, finally looking up.

"Try for what?" I asked.

"School integration."

"To put us with the white kids?" Preston grabbed the paper and began studying it.

"That's what integration means, but probably not anytime soon at the rate we're going. We only have one Negro on the Board of Education."

"Would that mean white kids would be coming to Wells and be in my classroom?"

"No. It would most likely mean some of you, just a few, would be going over there to Patrick Henry Junior High."

"A few of us? That's like Little Rock!" I was horrified.

"Yes, Katherine, like Little Rock." He only used my given name when he was running out of patience, or it was important. Little Rock, which I'd seen on the television, was the worst thing I'd ever seen in my life. The white people came after those kids like animals every day. The mobs of crazed housewives and men yelling, "Lynch them, lynch them," outside that school were the first crackers I'd seen out being like folks said crackers were. Worse. Little old ladies spitting on schoolgirls. Nobody would ever want to go near people like that. Little Rock was like realizing colored people were really living in the redneck fun house—you step in a doorway sometimes and out come the ghouls, real ghouls who'd make no difference between killing you and scaring you to death. In Little Rock they came out every morning, prompt, standing ready by the hundreds. Any fool knew there had to be lots of people like that across town waiting to leave their ironing and soap operas and jobs and babies to come out and kill. The old man just looked at me and raised his eyebrows as if to say, "You never know."

"Well, who's going to come in here next, the insurance man? You-all get back to work out there. You still got a long ways to go around that yard."

Dixon forgot all about the pregnancy across town and got on the horn to find out if this integration business was serious. The school year was getting ready to start, and he knew nothing would happen right away—*and,* he said, he knew they would *never* start with a high school like they did in Arkansas. All three Negro schools in Turner were loaded with distant cousins from Prince Edward County. People there had sent their kids to towns all over where they could stay with a family and go to school. The trouble had started there years ago when a girl in the tenth grade had organized all the Negro kids to strike the school. Prince Edward County had just closed *all* their schools to keep from desegregating them. In fact, when he thought of that he muttered to himself, "And they won't integrate here either." So, one thing was sure: if it came, integration was going to reach out for kids at Ida B. Wells. They were too scared of Negroes to bring willful high school kids across town. But it was white parents that worried Dixon—he'd seen them on TV yelling for blood in Little Rock. They were real. He called Madeleine, who likely would know what was up. She was always in the middle of all the talk.

Maddie usually did know. She took it as a point of pride that she should be involved in what certain folks were doing. That meant lawyers, teachers, and folks who might have dealings with the school board. But most Tarrants didn't bother with finding out what other folks were up to, or "cultivating" friends—they pretty much stuck to the ones they already had. So Madeleine was bitterly criticized by Dixon for everything from social climbing with professional Negroes all over the state to just plain gossiping. But he always called her if he needed to know something about somebody.

What did Madeleine know about the integration? Not much. Mrs. Brown, whose husband was the lone Negro on the

Board of Education, said that the board had made integration conditional. They had to test all the students in the colored schools first because several members doubted that colored children could compete with white children due to a "lower level of intelligence." Mr. Brown said they could simply look at the available testing scores, but the board believed it best to have new tests administered with their supervision. Perhaps the Negro teachers had been "overzealous" in preparing their students for the previous tests.

Madeleine was incensed. Her voice came across the kitchen from the phone. When she got annoyed she talked slower rather than faster and her diction became painfully precise. "They give our schools the worst materials to work with, and then if the children do well in spite of that, they're suspicious. If we send *our* children over to *their* schools, you *know* who the little *savages* are going to be."

"Of course. That's what's got me worried, Maddie. I'm not sure I want to send the kids over to a place like Patrick Henry. Those crackers are liable to want to hurt somebody."

"What can we do, Dixon? We have to press forward. At least we have to act as if we're prepared to go through with it. It's the only way our children will get something better, have a chance to compete. I thought you, of all people, Dixon, would want to fight this one."

"Sure, if *we* could fight for it, but is sending the kids over there to do it the only way?"

"Seems so. I know what you mean, Dixon. And what if the teachers won't teach them? What if they don't get anything better out of it?"

"If they were mine they'd be coming home."

"Well, let's wait and see, Dix. The board has all these ideas about testing and picking a few guinea pigs. It may not be our problem in the end."

"Are they planning to watch every Negro child in the town of Turner?" Dixon was getting frustrated.

"I guess they're going to try. But I doubt it will actually get any farther than that."

THAT EVENING Preston shined his loafers with the tassels, slapped on the Aqua Velva, left the collar button open on his shirt, and split before anyone could find out where he was headed. Naturally I had to wonder if he'd gone over to Ulysses Grant Street, yet I was inclined to dismiss the whole idea. It was obvious, first of all, that he was too young for Cassie. On the other hand, Preston was cute, in the pretty-boy way. But then he dressed like a college kid, not like the slick pretty boys with their high-waters, tight black socks, and close-cut hair with the part on the side. Jack Dempsey had been more like them, even though he wasn't skinny like most of the cool boys. They didn't go out for athletics—they went in for wine.

When he'd left, I went in his room to play some 45s. I laid the Elvis Presleys to the side—that was his stuff. I stuck pretty strictly to the old and fast ones. "I'm searchin' . . . searchin' every whiiiitcha way . . ." Actually, Jack Dempsey had been really cool. It was obvious Cassie would have liked him, everybody did. She must be heartbroken. I'd seen him outside the high school, even in the paper. He had a *Quo Vadis* cut and wore a black leather over his varsity sweaters. And even though I thought Preston could be cool, he was still Preston, too nice to be really cool. He wasn't ever going to be really cool, just like I knew I wouldn't ever really be cool. Too straight. And as for me, there was just too much stuff I didn't know. I was always late on the pickup. Like when one of the kids told me Dootsie Burleigh's sister Martha let anybody do everything. I knew that to be cool I shouldn't ask what everything was. I sort of knew what everything was. But were there a *lot* of things involved in everything?

Preston's record collection wasn't keeping up. He hadn't gotten my new song, "Personality." I could pull it out at the record store and take it in the booth and listen to it, but I almost never had money when I got to go down there. The Coasters and Chuck Willis would do. I practiced the stroll back and forth to "Betty and Dupree" in his room. Everybody had been doing the slop, but this new line dance was on TV, and now it was the thing. Black kids made the stroll look colored, better than on *Bandstand*. We put an easy rock on it, like a walk with a dip, casual— the same as we did with all the dances.

At a dance, the cool boys were casual too, standing against the wall like they hadn't noticed a dance going on. And they never moved when they danced, slow or fast. On a hard bop each one struck a different pose, maybe holding his hat in the crook of his arm, and with an indifferent look he would twirl the girl through constant turns only moving his wrist.

But since the boys mostly preferred the slow songs and were very picky about partners, the girls would watch to see them step out of the shadows and play the lover. Any one of them would slow drag with a cigarette in the corner of his mouth, inches from the girl's mohair. On something like "Since I Fell for You" they'd put a lock on you with almost no sway. Somehow you or he or something would be moving, barely.

If it was "For Your Precious Love" and the boy fancied he could sing, low bass notes would vibrate in your ear. All the boys seemed to think they could sing that one, and that singing it was going to loosen a strap or something. They'd get one knee up under the hem and press against your straight skirt. If the skirt was short enough it would slip up. Then it got hotter than the hinges. With each grind your thighs would become sex weapons blowing away his cool.

Hunched up in the middle of Preston's bedroom clutching Preston's pillow, I could remember dancing with Dallas or Ronnie Brown, who was very sexy. But then too, I could see Reuben King in his loose-fitting blue-gray rayon shirt bending his knees in a low grind around Tonda Roberts. His silvery-buttoned cuffs were riding on Tonda's butt. Tonda had more nerve than anybody in the seventh grade. Finally, embarrassed at myself, I gave up and started prowling through Preston's desk just on GP.

He had a few letters from friends and I read them all. One was from Coleman when he was away with his parents somewhere last spring. He seemed troubled about Cassie. They'd done a few things, but "not everything." There it was again. What should I do? Go tell Dootsie's sister Martha everybody says she'll let anybody do everything, so she could tell me just what's "something" and what exactly is "everything"? As a fallback I could at least blackmail Preston.

> Sherlock Holmes, Sam Spade, got nothin', chile, on me—
> Sergeant Friday, Charlie Chan, and Boston Blackie.
> No matter where she's hidin' she's gonna hear me comin'.
> Gonna walk right down that street like Bulldog Drummond.
> 'Cause I been searchin' . . .

PRESTON WAS happily sitting in the kitchen of the Morrows' house watching the chicken cook and listening to Jeanne Morrow, Cassie's mama, dispense advice to anybody that came near the stove. She still looked real young to Preston, who thought her looks exotic, but then, he had learned that her family originally came from the islands somewhere. She was a deep reddish brown, somewhat plump but shapely, with absolutely glowing skin. Unlike many of the women, she always wore makeup and some earrings. She always held her head straight and looked directly at you with a twinge of coquettish vanity. He sat in her kitchen quietly, secretly, happy as could be.

"Boy, I hope you're hungry. These girls around here have to diet but you don't 'cause you're skinny, and I don't 'cause I'm old, so you and me gon' do some eatin'. Left the house without eating, didn't you? How'd you get out of your house anyway?"

"Well, Mrs. Morrow, I just walked out."

"You always callin' me Mrs. Morrow. Sounds strange. I guess 'cause you the only kid I know who don't call me ma'm. Your parents tell you not to say it or something?"

"Well . . . not exactly."

"You don't have to get embarrassed about it. This boy is shy, I tell you. So what's the reason?"

"For what?"

"For not saying ma'm."

"I don't know, really. Don't like the sound of it, I guess. They just told me to call people by their names." Preston was starting to fidget. Whenever people got real curious about him or his folks it made him feel as if he had on white socks or his pants were too short or something.

"Thought your old man had you working around there today."

"Yeah, but we finished and he went around to have drinks with somebody."

"What about your dinner? Who's gonna cook? Willie cookin' yet?"

"Willie?" He laughed. "I know how to cook more than she

does. Anyway, on Saturday Dad usually fries some fish or something, especially if he's been fishing."

"He's gon' be wonderin' where you are."

"That's okay. He's used to not knowing where I am."

"Well, we all have to be worrying more about where you-all are ever since Jack got shot. Maybe you ought to give him a call in a bit." .

"Well, it's okay, I don't think I have to."

"It coulda been any one of y'all—you know it, don't you? These crackers see a young colored man somewhere in the dark and they get crazy. Cassie still wakes up screaming some nights. I don't know how this baby is making out."

"Really? Yeah, I guess she would."

"I take it she didn't tell you. You should try talking to her, she likes you. You're not like the other boys at school, she tells me. And it's been nice of you to come around to try to help, telling us about the lawyer and all. I told Mrs. Dempsey, but she's just given up, couldn't hear a word I was saying about it. Told me that's what white folks might oughta do, but for colored folks it don't make no difference. I don't know, though, I think it's worth a try. Hi, baby."

Jeanne Morrow hugged Cassie, who then eased into one of the chairs at the kitchen table and smiled at Preston, embarrassed at her newly discovered awkwardness. Pregnancy was just beginning to catch up with her. Preston usually thought he was coming to see how Cassie was doing, but he really came to visit her mother. Cassie was the most beautiful girl he'd ever seen—deep golden colored with brown wavy hair and startling deep-set black-brown eyes. She was round everywhere he liked girls to be round and taller than any of the rest, almost his height. She looked sweet, in fact, much too sweet to have gotten five months pregnant and bulging. Still, she had never been the girl for Preston.

58

Jeanne, on the other hand, was one of Preston's favorite people on the planet. She never failed to have time to hear him out on whatever small subjects he felt like talking about. And she would tell him what was what in the plainest way. "Cassie, set the table, would you? This is about done." Cassie got up to get the dishes and Preston helped. Taking no notice, Jeanne went on inquiring about folks with Preston. She didn't know them that well but had a keen interest in what they were up to all the same.

"That hincty bitch Maddie." She laughed. Preston laughed too, and rolled his eyes knowing what was coming. "Excuse me. Tell everybody to sit down, would you? I mean my Cassie's been Maddie's sitter for years. Her husband, Bill, he's not so bad. But that Maddie, she comes to all the PTA meetings, and does half the damn talking and none of the damn work. Not like your mother, you know. She was not one to mouth off, and she wasn't one of those do-nothin' bitches. She helped with everything, the kids' shows, making food at Thanksgiving."

"Yeah, I remember that. She was forever sewing costumes or something."

"Made 'em for Cassie. I can't sew a lick." Cassie's younger sisters Patricia and Chookie came in, testing the food at the stove before they sat down.

"Get your hands out of the food and say good evening to Preston."

I TRIED to call Marian to tell her about the new boy who had moved into the neighborhood. His mama brought him around past the back hedges where the irises still had to be watered after dinner. I knew Marian wouldn't believe it, because nobody ever moved into her neighborhood or mine, and she'd want to come over tomorrow and stroll past his house just in case we could get a look. He looked like Little Anthony and the Imperials, and that was just fine.

Dixon saw Mrs. Parker coming down the street while we were hauling the hose out to the far end of the garden. When I saw there was a boy with her I knew I should have checked myself before I came outside. All around the waist my shirt was soaking wet from doing the dishes. I could've died. I couldn't tell the old man I'd be right back and reappear in another set of clothes.

"Cleo, whadaya know?" The old man sounded real delighted. "Haven't seen you all summer!"

Cleo had a lot of pizzazz. She was the one teacher at the high school that Preston commented on all the time—just about the most modern-looking colored woman in Turner since Cousin Maddie put on weight when she quit smoking for a while. She was slim, chocolaty smooth, and wore her hair swept up. Her clothes were always at least snug, and she had big bright eyes that she flashed at you when she dropped her black movie-star sunglasses—the kind that cost ten dollars instead of two-fifty.

"Well, Dixon, I came by to tell you we're on your side of the creek. We're taking the old Livingston house. It got too cramped in that apartment on Union. So we're going to be neighbors."

Dixon was clearly delighted with that. "I guess your son will be in school with Willie, then?"

"Yes. Julian will be in Mrs. Taliaferro's class." Cleo Parker told her Julian to say hi. The new boy muttered a hello. As they walked on down the street, the old man looked at me distractedly.

"You know how things slip your mind? I can't remember if she got divorced or if they were *thinking* about getting divorced."

"Why don't you ask Preston? He might know."

"Oh, no," he demurred. "It's not important. That thought just crossed my mind."

It was a busy evening. After Cleo left and Dixon put up the hose, Charlesetta Roberts, Tonda's mother, came by. Dixon was sitting down on the porch. Charlesetta was a real business-looking type, almost always wearing suits and never at home when I visited Tonda. I didn't really know what she did to be so busy all the time. Guess I never asked. I knew she didn't pay much mind to what Tonda was doing. At least that seemed to be the reason Tonda was always having these interesting experiences going around on her own. And they weren't from Virginia, either, and that seemed as good an explanation as any for why Charlesetta looked as if she were trying to be older than she was, and like a business executive or something. Tonda was not so mysterious, she was just fast, and there was nothing special or foreign about that. When I heard Charlesetta wanted to find out about meetings of the Douglass Literary Society I decided to vacate. It was a subject that was sure to be over quick with the old man.

"I promised to help work on the schedule, Mr. Tarrant, but I don't really know how you plan things."

"Oh, there's not much to it. We meet every month at somebody's house, people make presentations of about fifteen or twenty minutes. They keep a little office in Ralph Johnson's house. You know him, the barber in town?"

"Yes. And I got some of the old programs. People talking about *The Hamlet, The Negro in Virginia*, your cousin Bill discussing *Native Son*."

"You really saw some old ones then."

"Well, actually, that's why I'm here—to come up with some subjects. There are some new writers here I wanted to mention to you for the programs this winter, like James Baldwin. Do you know his work?"

"No, I don't really. I've only seen his name in the magazines."

"Well, last year he put out this book called *Notes of a Native Son,* and it caused quite a sensation, what he had to say about Richard Wright and all."

"Is that so? Well, I'm sure the English teachers like Coleman Boteler will be anxious to discuss something like that. I'm just a chemistry teacher and I do what they tell me to do. I read what they tell me I should read, and I try not to talk at those things so they'll be over quicker." He laughed. "My wife wanted me to keep up with things, so she roped me into the club. I'm sure whatever you pick will be just fine. Anything you think I should do, just let me know. I'm not really one for novels, you know. Coleman would be much more help to you. If I may make one suggestion, though, I think we'd better do more on the integration question."

"Yes, sir, that's a good suggestion."

"I'm afraid that's going to be the only topic around here for a while."

"You think so, Mr. Tarrant?"

"Yes, I think so."

When she finally departed he fixed himself a scotch and sat out staring at the trees and sky for another hour or so. He only belonged to something like the Douglass Literary Society because his wife had liked that sort of stuff. Actually, he loved a good novel, he just didn't care to hear his friends and colleagues pontificating on their meaning. But his wife had preferred to sit around talking about books rather than talking to some of the women about the gossip in town, so he put up with it. And as with many other things she'd gotten him into, he kept them up

after she died, like it or not, just to hold on to ways they'd
shared. He was still married to her—she just wasn't there the
way she used to be.

COLEMAN BOTELER'S breakfast was served to him by his wife,
as always in the dining room with linen, silver, and total quiet.
Through the long white curtains sunlight streamed in from the
river, falling in soft angles as if it were orchestrated for him,
beams of brass arranged by Gil Evans—Coleman's solo, morning. Miles Davis was playing *Porgy and Bess* and Coleman
Boteler in a crisp white shirt, collar open, was eating a soft-
boiled egg in a white eggcup and sipping black coffee. Slim,
ebony, his aristocratic nose like a long note on his well-sculpted
head, Coleman at this time of day knew he was a creature of
beauty, music no one had hummed. He crossed his legs and sat
back with his arms on the chair. They were all out of sight,
thank God for that. The son, the wife, the fishing boats, all
quiet and out of sight. The water barely moved. Miles was
right, you could not let them have as much as they wanted. You
couldn't let them have more than just what it took. A man's
song was solitary. He admired the cunning of the music. No
one should know how he felt—they should only know what he
knew, what he let them know. What he thought, that is. How
he felt was something apart from articulation. How he felt was
really none of their business.

Coleman was convinced he couldn't think when people were
around, so he got up very early. He routinely rose at five-thirty
and went into a little corner room downstairs to write until his
wife got up and fixed breakfast. If necessary he could fix himself
coffee, but he preferred not to because it took away from his
thoughts. Many mornings he simply forced himself through

pages because he had to go to his job and he couldn't know how many days it might take for some good pages to come. Maybe the day would come when he couldn't write, couldn't do anything but think. He couldn't let things all pile up. It was painful either way. A man was a pained, solitary creature grappling for relief.

Everyone else, it seemed to him, wanted things they could see or touch, children especially. They wanted everything without knowing they couldn't even breathe because there was no space allotted for them to be free. A Negro child stood outside the world and watched and wanted and didn't know. Nina Simone could open her angry mouth and find it. A Negro man stood and watched and knew he was just there to stand and watch, and someone might want to kill him for doing that. There was nothing to want but the possibility of another arrangement, and that was like saying there was nothing to want but another God. Little Cole's problem was simply that he didn't know a damn thing. That was it. So far as Coleman was concerned, his son was going looking for a place where there would at least be a reason for somebody to shoot him. No standing, no watching.

Coleman Boteler had always felt he had something to say, something he could say, but it was ridiculous to say it. Still, every morning he got up and wrote something down, every morning except Sunday. On Sunday morning, alone in his dining room, taking sly glances at the high or low tide outside his windows, he conducted the orchestra with long-fingered hands and hummed something Miles would play. In his crisp white shirt, he drifted.

Lillian Boteler came in to clear the table. As she did so, she offered to make the trip into town to get his *New York Times* and *Herald Tribune* because Mrs. Roberts had asked to come by to talk to him about the literary society. Coleman lifted his head to the heavens and almost yelled out his complaint. "Oh, Lil-lian, you didn't tell her she could come by, did you? It's Sunday. You know I want to read the papers and watch a game. And it is the last day—"

"There was no other time, Cole, and she promised me it wouldn't be long."

"Christ." He removed his napkin, crumpled it on the table, and rose. She retrieved it, folded it, rolled it into a cylinder, and put it in a napkin ring. He went upstairs to exchange his slippers for shoes. Lillian thought no more about it and re-stored the dining room to perfect order, setting out the dishes for dinner on the sideboard while she was at it. Soon Coleman hollered down, asking where his son was. Lillian went to the staircase, climbed halfway up, and said she had no idea, she was in the bath when he left. Lillian never shouted. She would rather travel the distance to be heard than sound coarse. She walked down a step, and he asked where Little Cole might have gone. She stepped back up and said once again that she had no idea and she wasn't going to worry about it. Coleman emerged from the bedroom in loafers.

"I see you've decided not to let any of the rest of us concern you today," he said.

"That's not exactly it. You're damn close though."

"Well, I'm no fool," he said, teasing her. "I know when to leave well enough alone. When is this pain-in-the-ass woman coming by?"

"Any minute now. She's very nice."

"I'm sure she is. I just hope she's nice enough to keep it short. Didn't you tell her that today it might be awkward to have a guest over?" He stood at the top of the stairs, his hands in his pockets.

"No, because it isn't going to be any different from any other Sunday. Was there something you were planning to tell the boy that you haven't already said?"

"Well, no. Not necessarily. No."

"Well, then. I'll be back in a little bit."

Lillian continued down the steps, got her purse, and headed out for the store. Coleman came down to the living room and put on an LP. He took a Camel from the cigarette box on the cocktail table, lit it with the silver-plate lighter that Lillian always kept filled and working. Exhaling a plume of smoke, he waved his hand in time to the music, turned round once, and took a seat where he could see the water. He resumed his reverie, content to wait for his papers, his son, or Mrs. Roberts, whichever came first.

The doorbell meant that it would be Mrs. Roberts. Not a bad-looking woman, he thought when he saw her, a bit over-dressed. Apparently she either thought a Sunday call to an unsung local writer required gloves and hat, or she'd just escaped from church. Coleman only went to weddings and funerals himself, and he tried to stay away from weddings if he could.

"Mrs. Roberts? How do you do? Won't you come in?" She thanked him and stepped in. He offered to take her hat and gloves and then had to think where to put them. Once in the living room he started to sit but thought he'd better offer her coffee or something. When she said yes to coffee he walked into the kitchen, panic near at hand, and discovered Lillian was ahead of him. She'd left the electric percolator making a fresh pot. He fetched the cups and saucers and returned triumphant with coffee, sugar, and cream. He was already cheered. That wasn't so bad, and the new lady seemed nice enough indeed.

Charlesetta queried him about new writers the Douglass group might read, and he became more enthusiastic as he listened to himself talk about the young Negroes being published. Charlesetta seemed bright, especially to have already learned of some of the barely known authors. He didn't know anyone in Turner who kept up with such, *really* kept up. They bubbled along. She seemed preoccupied with James Baldwin. Coleman felt himself withdraw slightly. "Oh, the man is a masterful writer," he granted her, but he didn't continue. In fact Baldwin made him quite angry, made him feel quite helpless as a writer. With Baldwin already doing everything God gave a man talent for—what were the rest supposed to do? He couldn't feel generous when he faced down one of the man's books. Just couldn't.

"Yes, the man writes a masterful essay. Of course we should read him." He began to think about her stockings and to wonder if you could tell a woman's age by her legs. Lillian said it was the neck that told the years. It was nice that there might be *someplace* that didn't tell it. Age didn't make him like a woman less, it kept him from looking. Charlesetta continued chatting and Coleman simply fitted her into his reverie and looked as if he were musing over her ideas.

"Are you optimistic concerning the future of the Negro writer, Mr. Boteler?"

"Coleman."

"Coleman. Are you?"

"Of course. You know, Coleman is very different from my last name, Boteler. Don't you think? I mean it's so English, and depending on how you say it, so colored. Boteler is Haitian— Bo-te-lay—well, not *Haitian,* of course, some corrupted French. Anyway, altogether, first and last, the name is one of those laughable proofs of slavery. The point is, in Haiti, where my people were slaves, we began producing literature from the moment L'Ouverture and his houngans threw those bastards over. No one pays it any mind, but Negro writers have been at it for a while now, you understand." He paused and ended dryly, "So, of course, I'm optimistic. Although, of course, it is absurd."

"Absurd?" Charlesetta looked puzzled. "What is?" she asked.

"Writing, the Negro writer having a future, whatever that was you asked." She was too earnest, he thought. Not wishing to appear rude, she tried to push him a little more.

"What do you mean, it's absurd?" she asked.

"I don't mean much. It's just that it seems to me one must end up angry in the end."

"Why angry?"

Coleman Boteler thought of Miles Davis as he reached for another cigarette.

"Is your coffee alright?"

THE DEACONS were on their knees moaning. Their backs were to the congregation yet the women sitting in the front rows were right with them, just a hair behind with the high notes. Preston and Little Coleman got seats right in the middle, where they were sure to be too hot but that's where the usher put them and that's where they'd be. They had left pretty early to take the bus out to New Jerusalem Church, a peeling white wood structure standing up on blocks at the edge of town.

New Jerusalem was one of the old-fashioned Baptist churches, which seemed to be losing out to Daddy Grace's House of Prayer for All People. One whole section of Turner, poor black cottages on the bay side of town, had been taken over by Daddy Grace fever. Every house had a white cross marked in chalk across the front screen door. To Preston it was like a mystic cult, more mysterious than the Daughters of the Order of the Eastern Star, or the Daughters of Isis, who re-vealed themselves only once a year, and only in white except for their ribbons of rank. Preston could not fathom Bishop Daddy Grace, with his robes and beard and red, white, and blue fingernails. And what about the people in Harlem who had let him baptize them with a fire hose a couple of years ago? It was easier to understand the sanctified folk who didn't like music and wouldn't let their kids go to parties. Negroes could be every kind of religious, no question about that. And in his way so was Preston who, in spite of his Episcopalian family, wanted to "lay down a Baptist and get up a Baptist still."

The low tones turned to loud "ahs" and a few words came forward, but Preston couldn't be sure what they said. It was still English, but all the same he couldn't make it out. He thought if he kept coming to church there, one day he would understand the words they were saying as well as the moans.

Preston told Cole he wanted to get inside the language till he could slip there into the belly of it without even knowing. He told him it was a place he had to go back to—a place he'd been when he was a boy. Once he was with Mama at a church somewhere in North Carolina, way out in cornfield country, where he never understood a word that was said the whole time. It got hotter and hotter and folks jumped up possessed and talking in tongues. That time lived inside him, and he could sweat just remembering the wood plank walls and pointed beams of that church. A middle-aged woman next to him had bolted up, then rocked back and forth on her thick square heels. Her flowered hat slid off her just-pressed hair, and her arms flopped back like a dead body's limbs. Preston threw up and went into convulsions. Mama put three fingers down on his tongue and swooped him up in the air over people's heads. He thought he was dying and being offered up, but then she hugged him close to her body and walked out of the church with him.

He had sweated up his starched white shirt when the women

outside loosened his little necktie and stretched him out in the cool grass under a tree. He lay there sweating and jumping till every witness had witnessed and they sang "This Li'l Light o' Mine." When the crowd poured out to spread the food on tables under the tree, he was still lying there cooling.

"Oh Lord, oh Jesus." Preston, a stranger even to himself, eased into the communion knowing it was there, but feeling apart. How did the followers know what the leaders were trying to get out? They breathed the next breath of every word as if it passed through the deacons' backs to their tongues. Someone said, "Oh Lord, ha' mercy," very slowly, painfully, and then it became a tune. "Oh Lord, ha' mercy," slowly, painfully, but a song. A deacon's voice rang out from the front of the church. He was off to one side on his knees, his head and hands buried in the seat of an ancient caned chair in front of him.

". . . Hear each and every one, hear the sick and the lame this morning, Sweet Jesus. We sometime up and sometime down. Oh Lord, oh Jesus, remember those who didn't have shelter this morning. Oh Lord, I know You're water in dry places. Oh Lord, oh Jesus, remember those that call Thy name this morning. Oh Lord, oh Jesus, remember those that have children awful hungry this morning. Oh Lord, oh Jesus, we need You this morning. Oh Lord, oh my Father, we know You got all the power in Your hands. Oh Lord, oh Jesus, Sweet Jesus, take me in Your hands, let me lay my head in Your bosom . . ."

People were still filing in, dressed in nylon and frills, straw hats with ribbons, stockings, heavy, shiny textured suits of maroon or gray green or reddish brown. They were not like suits the men wore at the Tarrants' church, and they didn't even always match top and bottom. Some were decades old. The men had the heavy weathered skin of all fishermen, hands that were dry and parched from the salt water. After years on the bay their deep brown skin had become a deeper black than the skin of any other men you saw in town. The mothers were heavy and one after another had scars on her hands from picking the meat out of crabs all day long. They had to work at top speed or lose their place, and the creatures had left their marks on all the women who worked crab. The children came in fancy clothes, mostly slim and straight as rods. They sat without making a sound. New Jerusalem was solemn, and calm, and easy to be in. The clapping started and the rock became irresistible. Preston and Little Cole rocked too. A single rhythm was pounded out on the floor by hundreds of feet. "Down through the years, the Lord has been good to me." It rocked like the blues to Preston. The groove just took him in and he sang out. "Down through the years, oh, the Lord has been good to me."

"Let the church say amen," started the preacher. "Amen again. We want to thank God for being here, for truly down *through* the years He's been good to us," he continued, winding up. "The Lord has sho'nuff been *good*. When the choir say, 'He's been good to me,' I can say He's been good to *me*. Can you say that? Has He been good to you? He's a good Lord, idn't He? Oh yeah, oh yeah. We didn't have no assurance that we were gon' be here this morning, but the good Lord just looked and saw that some mercy needed to be spared, and some of us were able to go on just a little while longer.

"We been having our hard times now. Just the other week they killed one of our young, Jack Dempsey, down by the river, the same river that boy was baptized in. A boy that rose to be a scholar and a football star, who had a bright future ahead. It's very hard to understand when we have to bury our young. Very hard." Amens came from heads nodding around the room. "And those that live on need some of God's mercy, to understand His ways, to understand the ways of folk around us, to ease our suffering. 'Cause it ain't easy, the road can be rough, am I right?"

"*Yes*, Jesus." The crowded church was stirring. Just the mention of the murder made people shake their heads and mutter.

Preston and Little Cole looked at each other. For weeks adults had been reminding them that their lives could be cut off with no notice. If they had thought about it at all they would have wished for a sermon on almost anything else—some word that might answer any one of the many questions they were holding private. But not that one. Even though they went most places together and spent hours listening to jazz and r&b in their rooms, the two boys rarely confided in each other for more than a few minutes. New Jerusalem took the place of intimate conversations. They simply went there together and shared their need for something else. They were quiet during the sermon, and sang when the church sang.

"It's good to be here. So we gon' go on, and we gon' ask the ushers to come down, and we gon' make this offering. Only you and the Lord know how blessed you are. I can't look in your pocket and see what you have, but you know what you have, and you know who's in need."

Little Cole had enlistment papers in his pocket. Coming to New Jerusalem was his last search for a blessing. He was leaving home without the blessing of anybody he knew, so he hoped to get at least a calm response when he told Preston. Only after telling his folks that he absolutely would not go to college, even if they didn't sign the papers, and then letting his mother believe she'd be saving herself from a possible pregnancy scandal, did his father put his signature on the government's papers.

New Jerusalem, with its singing and river baptizing, was just about the warmest thing he'd ever found in the town of Turner, and he was happy not to have to come back summers. While he and Preston weren't quite in agreement on that, they shared discomfort with their parents' pushing and striving and driving. Where would it go but where they had already been? They thought the younger ones would go higher and farther, but where was that? Into an all-white world somewhere? A white college, a white office, a white neighborhood somewhere up north? Where was up? Out would do for Cole, just out in the world. Little Cole had signed up for the Army Airborne. Since there was no war going on he thought it would be fun, and the pay was better than infantry or any of the other stuff. He would learn to jump, go someplace he'd never been, then get out and get a job, be on his own. Or he could go to college, but he'd go for himself if he did. He'd do whatever he was gonna do in his own good time.

"I have a home, / a room in Glory," a woman's voice sang out. "Waiting, waiting for me there. / For this old world / is not my home, / it has nothing to offer me." Little Cole closed his eyes and rocked hard. "I have a home, / a room in Glory . . . I know my Jesus, / Jesus is Glory. / I know He promised me just—promised me just—everlasting life." He pounded his fist on his thigh and thanked Jesus or whoever was there, he wasn't sure, his head shaking out the beat. He had one foot out the plane and after one jolt from the chute, his pack would thump against his back and he'd be falling free, his eyes on his toes. "I want to go there. / I want to go there / beyond the sky." In unison everyone began to whisper, "Don't / you want / to go there?"

All Preston could say was, "I don't believe you did that." Cole nodded and said, "Tomorrow I'm gone." He felt clean and happy. The bus was hot, especially where they were sitting, back by the engine. All the windows were open, but there was no air moving. Preston stared out the window while Cole tried to reconstruct the whole scene with his parents. Coleman

Boteler, Sr., had been so affronted by his son's turning his back on him that he'd said only a few words. He told his son he was too young to understand what it meant to have lost a whole generation to war and running off to join the army was some kind of peacetime romance, a lark. Coleman junior couldn't understand how serious it was to throw away an education to play soldier. He was an adolescent, a child. Preston thought about his own father. He was no doubt still asleep, where he always was while other folks were in church. He knew Dixon would say something like, "He could do a lot worse than the army," or "Not such a bad thing, it'll make a man out of him." That was only because it was not *his* son.

THE BACK-DOOR screen slammed shut and Lillian could be heard bustling around the kitchen. Charlesetta turned her head in that direction and Coleman studied her profile and the back of her neck. Lillian burst in cheerfully with a stack of newspapers. After ascertaining that all was well, she disappeared again. She knew someone seeking Coleman's opinions would brighten him right up. In fact, she was so sure of it that she had taken her time getting the papers, browsed the magazines, and gone by the grocery store to give him some time. When Little Cole breezed in a half-hour later and headed straight for his room, Lillian wondered if maybe she hadn't at least been wrong about her son. He'd been hiding out for days.

"Don't be rude, go in and say hello."

"Ma, this my last day here."

"That's no reason to be rude."

Little Cole went in to say hello and got trapped into sitting down. He could see his father had turned into some sort of blithe young prince.

"Charlesetta and I were just talking about some of the Negro writers out now. Little Cole's read quite a few of them."

"Have you now? Isn't that wonderful, a young person who likes to read." Charlesetta looked to the young man like a homecoming queen trying to dress like Kitty Carlisle or one of the contestants on *What's My Line?*

"It's required around here, like doing the dishes. I'm more into music." He sounded bored. He knew he sounded bored, probably looked bored too.

"Very nice," she chimed. He was bored. But he still felt good from church, so he sat up straight and tried to look like a book reader. His father was hoping to make a good impression, it was obvious.

"Little Cole thinks more of Thelonious Monk than any novelist."

"Who?"

"A jazz pianist," the father answered.

"Oh!" Charlesetta made a chime sound again.

"Writers are square," Little Cole said flatly. "They have never known what was happening. If you look at it, in every decade they have been *behind* the musicians. Only the cats who play music really know where it's at."

"And where is it *at,* Son?"

"Out of here." Little Cole rolled his eyes skyward. "Out of Sphere." He started laughing. "Look, excuse me, I gotta go pack. Nice to meet you." He ran. Coleman Boteler, Jr., shut the door to his room and flopped down on the bed. He lay there thinking it was going to be a long day since he'd been packed for two days.

WITHIN DAYS of Charlesetta Roberts's visit Coleman Boteler had decided he wanted to help her to fulfill her secret dream to be a writer. By the Labor Day picnic he had quietly arranged for Charlesetta and her husband, Tom, to get invited. One morning that week he had told Lillian that the woman had sent him quite a nice note thanking him for his help and asking if he would be kind enough to read a story she had been trying to write. He boasted how delighted he would be to take on a protégé of sorts. Lillian smelled a rat. She didn't say a word. As far as she was concerned, her son was in boot camp and her husband had gone stupid. He mentioned this business of being a mentor several times as if seeking her permission, or worse, as if she might *insist* that he must help the woman. Lillian hadn't been that dumb for some time.

Actually, when he read the story Coleman had burst out laughing at how awful it was. With few exceptions, he thought, Negro women probably didn't have the clarity of mind to be good writers, not sufficiently tough-minded. However, the note from Charlesetta left thoughts in his mind about how he could spend time with her, coach her. He had sat and read and reread the note, undressing the woman all the while, looking for hints that he could start with the gloves, finger by finger. But he only got as far as the gloves when something checked his daydream, as he folded and unfolded the paper. He thought he'd tell Lillian the plot to see if he'd overreacted.

Charlesetta's story concerned an eccentric spinster, a Negro lady of some refinement, who'd lived alone in a small southern city for many years. Her only friend was her pet dog, Minxie, who'd suddenly died, leaving the woman bereft beyond any explanation to her friends. In the phone book, she found an ad under "Pets" for a pet cemetery, which seemed a wonderful thing indeed. She immediately called them to find out what kind of arrangements could be made for a fitting interment for Minxie.

"Wait. What in God's name is a pet cemetery?" Lillian asked.

"Lillian, I presume it is exactly what it sounds like," Coleman answered, trying to keep very serious about the matter. "I think they have them in Hollywood."

"Good God," she muttered. "Well, you can tell Mrs. Roberts they don't have such novelties in the South."

Coleman continued on, explaining that however it came about that there was a pet cemetery in this southern town— perhaps she could make it Orlando or Miami or some town full of old folks—the lady wanted to have the interment described to her on the phone. When she persisted with the pet mortician about burying Minxie, she forgot herself and made the arrangements although she knew somewhere in her mind that the cemetery was probably whites only.

"Whites only?!" Lillian shrieked. She started laughing.

"Segregated. Well, no, I guess 'segregated' is not the right word. For white pet lovers."

"White pet lovers?!" Lillian wouldn't stop giggling long enough for him to go on. "Lovers of white pets? *White* lovers of pets?"

"Owners."

"Maybe it's a private-membership cemetery, Cole, for whites with dead pets. I know you can't be serious about any of this." She kept chuckling and he kept on explaining. He was starting to get annoyed with Lillian. He hadn't thought it was the story for *him*, but the young woman was so sincere, so breathlessly enthused, excited. When he was alone he could see her mouth open in his mind and imagine her aroused, but not with Lillian laughing.

The woman gave the mortician her preferences as to a plot and a little bronze plaque to be laid flat in the ground, reading, IN LOVING MEMORY . . . MINXIE. He asked if a vehicle could come pick up the body. She told them she could get Minxie ready very quickly. When she gave her address the man abruptly cut her off and said that the pet mortuary did not have colored clientele. The woman hung up deeply disappointed. She racked her brain as to what she could do. Could she pay the Negro mortician some amount of money to quietly give Minxie a proper burial at the Negro cemetery? No, it would be the talk of the town. She finally remembered her white school-mate from summer classes up north, a woman from the same town with whom she had struck up a friendship that they maintained by phone.

"No, Coleman," Lillian interrupted, "you are not going to go on."

He assured her the ending was interesting. After talking her friend into pretending to be the dog's owner and carrying Minxie across town herself to the woman's house, the burial at the pet cemetery was accomplished. The sad woman went to the rites posing as the white woman's maid. Her satisfaction with the arrangements quickly faded, however, when she real-ized she could never go to visit Minxie in the cemetery, where she knew, amongst all the white people's pets and the visiting white pet owners, Minxie rested uneasily and alone.

"She should have put it in the backyard."

"Perhaps," Coleman granted. "But she had something she wanted for the dog."

"Greener grass," Lillian quipped.

"Why shouldn't she want a little plaque and ceremony?"

"Oh, Coleman. Charlesetta must have made quite an impres-sion on you," she teased.

To bring it to a quick close before Lillian got to the point, he explained that the white woman didn't want to hear anything about returning to visit a buried dog and the woman pined over her loss until a fortuitous event—the end of segregation. Segregation was outlawed, taken off the books.

"Ha! What brings that on?"

"Well, I don't know, I'll have to ask her to flesh that out."

"Flesh indeed. So, in the end she can visit her pet. If she can get rid of segregation for a dog, I guess she might make miracles if she wrote about people. You know, that's a bad story, but the worst thing about the story is there's no story without the kindness of the white woman who doesn't really want to help. Such *brief* kindness. There's gotta be a better way to tell the story. Is everybody happy after integration?"

"Maybe. I don't know, Lil. Maybe other colored folks' dogs can be there and her dog won't be stranded by the kindness of the one woman. Maybe that's the point."

"Oh, God. It's a dreary story."

"It's kind of touching, personal. And the white woman is just a device to let you see—"

"A device! Since when was a white woman ever just a device! Honey, a white woman is a white woman. Once you put her in there it's no longer about the Negro, it's about the race question, the ways of white folks and all that. So much for the damned dog." Lillian dismissed him. "It's like *Imitation of Life* for pet lovers, as you call them, except integration breaks out after the funeral. What's that hateful girl's name, the daughter?"

"For Christ's sake, Lillian. I don't remember stuff like that." Cole was getting depressed.

"Maybe she meant the story to be funny," he wondered aloud.

"It's funny alright." Lillian laughed and laughed.

Lillian knew Coleman was going to help Charlesetta with her story and ask her serious questions about how they passed a law to integrate everything including cemeteries. She also knew the Roberts family had somehow been invited to the Labor Day picnic even though the same seven families had been going for years and years. The men had their little group that they liked, and the women would never be permitted to change who could come and who couldn't. Different women might even appear if somebody changed up, but not different men. The women would just have to deal with the new wife and be civilized. That's the way it had always been. It simply would not have occurred to any of them to change the routine, unless Coleman had made a plea to open the doors. Lillian would be dishing out Charlesetta's potato salad as sure as she would be breathing.

THE SATURDAY before Labor Day, when I came down to breakfast I found Dixon suffering through cereal with Bobby from down the street. I had heard his voice when I hit the back stair and gritted my teeth. Bobby was the only nice-looking boy I knew that I did not like at all. He acted crazy sometimes and he liked to brag about the "women" he knew, all the while making his adventures sound like anything but fun. In fact, by my lights, most of what he said was unbelievable. Bobby Robinson got on Dixon's nerves worse than any kid he knew, partly because he showed up for breakfast a lot, but more because he never stopped talking.

"Where's your father this morning?" Dixon would inevitably ask.

"Dunno. Went out early," Bobby would say, usually his euphemism for "Didn't come home last night."

"How about your mother?"

"Same." Bobby's father always left him with money, which he used to buy Twinkies and Coke at Lucas's store if no one answered at our back door. No one cooked him meals at home, or even seemed to see him much. This vexed Dixon beyond belief, but his normal politeness made the situation awkward. Should he wait up late for the parents to get home and go knock on the door and say, "Your son comes to my door every other morning for food and some attention?" What was the etiquette for dealing with a child whose folks were lousy parents? He fed him breakfast or told one of us to do it, and left hoping Bobby would be gone by the time he came back for lunch. Sometimes if Bobby showed up I would pretend I had to go with Dixon over to the campus, just to put an end to it. I would say I had to walk over to the campus post office or something and scoot out, even though God knows as hot as it was I didn't want to walk the four blocks with Dixon to his office or trek across the grassy fields of the college to the hot hundred-year-old post office building just to get rid of Bobby. Dixon's usual tactic was just to get up after the meal and say, "Boy, don't you have something you need to be doing instead of sitting around all day?" Until that moment, Bobby knew he had his time and the old man would let him do all the talking.

"Whew! That smells bad, whatever that is you're cooking. What is it?" Dixon was parboiling some mackerel.

"Well, Bobby, you don't have to eat any, you know. It's mackerel. Willie will make you some bacon. She doesn't like mackerel either. You kids don't know what's good."

"Oh, that would be nice, Mr. Tarrant, real nice." Bobby had his fake, supernice voice on. Feeling uncomfortable was the thing he hated most. He generally felt okay around Dixon, as if he were kind of liked, but then he was usually so nervous that he almost never got it when Dixon cracked on him.

"I just got back from New York, Mr. Tarrant. I had a really good time there. I went out on my own, went to movies, clubs, the Palisades Amusement Park, whatever I wanted to do."

"Sounds like fun."

"It was, man. I went out with older girls and they showed me around, you know what I mean?" Dixon looked over his bifocals at the boy. No kid called Dixon "man." He let his face mellow into a little smile, which Bobby took for friendliness. Dixon reminded himself that he had to feel sorry for this poor boy who'd probably end up behind bars one day or, worse, cause some poor mad soul to choke him to death to shut him up. I slunk into my bacon cooking hoping not to make any sound that would give Dixon the chance to give me the evil eye. Having any kind of boy, lonely or otherwise, showing up for breakfast, Dixon would tell his friends, was one of the many curses of having daughters. The world was full of hardheads, he would say, trying to seem just right for somebody's daddy. Bobby had a knack for hitting every wrong note, like bragging about the five-inch-long scar running down the left half of his face.

"I got in a little tiff with this Puerto Rican cat in New York. He didn't want to let me into a pay party. I knew some people in there and they were waiting for me. Mainly it was this girl— or *woman*, I should say."

Dixon didn't flinch. He looked at him very calmly, as if he had a gun cocked and was trying to decide whether or not to shoot. "Do you go to a lot of pay parties up there?"

"Well, sometimes. I mean, usually I don't have to." Bobby was trying to sound impressive, not knowing that actually Dixon was gathering ammunition; he would stack up all the details and toss them back as warnings to his children when Bobby left. The incriminating words piled up as Bobby rattled on: "tiff," "women," "Puerto Rican," "pay party." Dixon had been to Harlem rent parties when he was young, but Bobby conjured up something he knew was quite different.

"So what did the guy cut you with?"

"Just a knife, one of the regular switchblades. It was a punk knife actually. I woulda got it from him but some guys grabbed me and held me and he cut me. But it wasn't nothing, just looked bad."

82

"You know, Bobby, some boys would have been very scared by that, and maybe think twice about spending time running around places in Harlem where they don't know the folks."

"Yes, sir." Bobby sat up straight, feeling good. I put the eggs and bacon in front of him. His mouth made his crooked little half-cut smile. To Bobby, he was getting a nod of respect. Even I could see though that Bobby Robinson probably had cried like a baby when he first saw that his classically handsome face would always be dug in by a shiny wide keloid from his cheekbone to his mouth.

"Eat up, boy, I gave Willie plenty of chores to take care of today and you and I need to get out of her way." Bobby was chomping on his toast. He looked up, eyes bright, and mumbled "Yes, sir" with the toast in his mouth.

3

THE MORNING of the Labor Day picnic we couldn't hear a
thing in the house for the birds outside squawking like crazy. It
was as if something had set them off. Looking out the bedroom
window, I thought maybe they organized like this for the first
wave south. I wondered if they had been signaling each other at
the end of every summer and I'd just never noticed. Preston
and I spent the morning making deviled eggs in a kitchen
raucous with birdcalls coming through the screen door and all
the windows. After the food for the picnic was packed in its
ancient basket, I put my swimsuit and a change of clothes in my
ballet case. The bag was very chic, I thought, round, black
patent leather with a single loop handle. It looked sophisticated, like something Audrey Hepburn might carry. I could see
myself working in a bookstore in Greenwich Village, wearing
black from neck to toe. Even though it was a little too big to
carry gracefully, and it sometimes banged against my calves as I
walked, in my mind the black ballet case looked very New

York. Preston and I threw a bunch of towels in a pile to load up and he tossed in some fins and a snorkel mask.

"You know the river up there is going to be just as brown and murky as down here," I complained. "What are you planning to find?"

"I'm not *planning* to find anything, Willie. Why don't you mind your own business. Besides, I see stuff all the time."

"What? Eels? That's all I see, and when I see them, I go the other way."

"You haven't seen any eels."

"Shut up, both of you," the old man said as he came in.

"Besides, Willie, you don't swim—you float," Preston whispered.

It was obvious that he thought he looked cool. I didn't point that out to him, though I would make a mental note to save that observation for the next time he got on my nerves. ("Plus you think you look cool with fins on.") Boys were like that— they had to have their *equipment* with them: fins, goggles, Geiger counters, binocs, transistor radios. They liked to look as if they were doing something serious, not just sitting around at a picnic. The old man was yelling from down the hall. "And turn down this crap you have blasting all over the house!"

Saturday was dedication day on WRAP—Rrrap Radio— and we had put the radios on in the living room and our bedrooms. The colored station was nonstop, rapid-fire jokes, plus a lot of commentary from the DJs on why they were great. On Sundays, though, we listened to the white stations because WRAP did church from can-do to can't. That involved a lot of dial flipping because the other stations only played r&b every tenth song. Every Sunday I counted to see if they would ever play more than two an hour, or even two an hour twice in a row.

Fat Freddie was running his mouth and reading out the plays. All the Busters and Judys and Cookies and Marvins were on the waves in love. Preston and I could never understand how come we never knew any of them. Of course, Preston maintained he was too cool to call in to a radio show. All the same, with all the Negro kids going to three schools, it seemed as though we should at least have *heard* of anybody calling in. Just how many colored kids were out there anyway? We made the old man keep it on in the car. If we did hear some familiar names, it would be something to talk about.

The old man preferred to drive in silence or tell stories. On Sundays he liked to get in the car and drive in whatever direction struck him at the moment, and tell what he knew about the places he passed. Usually he told anecdotes about people he grew up with or family members. One day it was the old house that was once a bordello by the white folks' country club, and the gal he knew who worked there. Nearly covered with kudzu vine, the whorehouse had become a bus stop where you sat on the front porch to wait for the Grey-hound. The only integrated institution in town had died or moved on to better real estate.

Another day there was the one about cousin so-and-so who used to meet her man in the cemetery by the Baptist church. She couldn't be seen with him because she was married, and besides that, to a man dying of TB who had already gone to jail for killing somebody. When World War I came along they had to stop meeting there because the gravediggers started leaving lots of empty pits to be filled the next day.

Even the tumbledown shotgun cottages expiring among overgrown weeds and barely tarred roads had a place in his local movies. He called the roads by names no longer used, associated somewhere back in time with some person who had once lived in Turner. As one learned his world one learned a second language, knowing when he said to go out the old Ketchum Road that it meant to take what we knew as East

Shore. He used old names for places that were too far for me to have seen, places running north all the way up the Chesapeake Bay to Kiptopeke and south to a place called Cape Fear: Accomac, Nansemond, names from way back in the Indian past. The names were like second nature to him though they were often no longer on the maps. Times in his life mixed with times before his life. Often Preston and I could only tell that it was long, long ago because the circumstance was inconceivable in our lifetime, like the fact that a black man was sheriff when Dixon was a child. The past often defied the present.

The radio station was lost after a half hour on the road. Once we came off the highway, the trip up-country to Plum Landing was wonderfully winding. Plum Landing was not a town, but a place where maybe ten vaguely related Negro families lived. We went through Yorktown, which sat like a formal garden on its high bluffs, across the silver York River, past signs for a place called Ordinary. We snaked our way through shacks and small family farms down from the broad York cliffs toward the intricate lowlands running into the Chesapeake. In less than a minute we were in and out of the ancient village of Gloucester, which was round in the center and looked to have been abandoned after hitching posts went out. Small historical markers appeared every few yards between the staggered rhymes of Burma Shave ads and four-corner junctions announcing towns like Little Chance. The car trundled across tiny wooden bridges over creeks and brooks and a piece of the Piankatank, now more a riverbed than a river. I knew I would never be able to find my way there even if I could drive, because once we turned off the two-lane highway there were no signs at any crook in the road. Small, crudely fenced yards encircled weary shanties, chicken hutches, and wells. Scrubby grasses greeted the road while lush gardens hid behind the houses, bursting with tall corn plants and rambling, unharvested tomato vines. Odd bits of whimsy appeared—a milk can standing guard at the gate, painted like the American flag, or an elegant oak vanity sitting proudly on the front porch, its huge round mirror reflecting all who passed by. Patches of tobacco turned up here and there near an ancient stone farmhouse with three chimneys rising above the rooftree.

As we neared the belly of the bay the houses got grander here and there, and yet somehow they moved further from view, obscured by trees, vineyards, and tall hedges. Any sight of them was also made hazy by the thick, almost visible humidity stretched out across the fields of high grass. On the shoreline sat several old plantation homesteads, hidden from each other by the curves in the land and large stands of trees. From the road one could see only the rear entrances and outbuildings. Near Plum Landing there was a rutted sand driveway up to the back door of the old Barnwell place. Dixon pointed it out as we passed, forgetting we'd seen it half a dozen times. Though I'd never been in the house, it was a spot known to anybody who'd been up in these parts.

No Barnwells had ever lived there in my lifetime. The backyard grass hadn't been cut in at least a month. The hedges had begun to grow out of their neat, flat-topped shapes. Dixon said there were no Barnwells in the state anymore and hired help maintained the place. Joshua Giddings Barnwell had been born in slavery and became an educator and Negro leader before the turn of the century. He was famous for telling the story of his name: that a Congressman Joshua Giddings was sent home from the capital for defending some slaves who had revolted on a ship leaving the waters off Fort Monroe around the time Barnwell was born. Some said he'd bought the old plantation house for revenge, that he once was a slave there. Some said he'd bought it out of sentiment, though of course he wouldn't admit it. Some said it was for the irony. And then some said

Barnwell bought it because he thought he was massa, and furthermore, that he'd named himself Joshua Giddings Barnwell because he liked the sound of it.

"If you knew what Barnwell was like," the old man said, "it could have been for all those reasons. Slave turns massa, or for revenge, or because he's important and where he was a slave must be important too. He might have thought it was going to be a historical monument like Thomas Jefferson's birthplace or something. You can never tell what's really important to a person." Now that he'd found something he wanted to talk about, the old man got on a roll. "Take a man I know. If you listen to the guy, he's a man who wants revenge, but then too, he could be master to slaves as easy as he is tyrant to his wife and children. He'd have his shirts laid out for him every morning by one slave, and have another to put them on his back. It wouldn't bother him a bit, believe me. Some days he can go on about the sweet days in school up north when the white folks, especially the white women, were so nice to him, and then again he talks about the slave ghosts watching over him from the creek and swamps outside his house. Negroes are not so easy to figure. When it comes to how they feel about being Negroes, they can get really complicated on you." By the old man's reckoning, anyway you sliced it Barnwell had a yearning for the plantation house that he felt was worth paying for. So be it. "That's one problem I'll never have."

"What's that?" I asked.

"Whether I should buy a plantation."

Plum Landing the town, if you could call it that, was where three roads intersected at a gas pump and general store of sorts. On the square sat two houses and an old wagon shed that served as a car repair shop. The heat of the day was already up in Plum Landing and no one was out. The landing itself was on a small lagoon down the paved road if you kept straight past the store and the soda machines just beyond. Where the other roads went I never learned, for we always kept straight on to the Murfrees' place, a vagabond of a farmhouse straggling all over its waterfront acres. Dusky and unpainted, the house's rooms seemed to crawl on top of each other and up toward the sunny spots between the trees in the yard. The desultory structure was like the free-spirited Negroes who lived in it, unruly and unmovable. The Murfrees would have been troublemakers if they'd lived somewhere big enough to have trouble. Plum Landing was so small it was nearly all kinfolk who basically didn't give a damn how crazy the Murfrees wanted to be.

Familiar cars were jammed all over the grass around the dirt drive. The river air was different—sweet and a little cool. The honeysuckle was blowing ever so slightly and along the fence mixed its light scent with the mint that had gone wild in the grass. The "front" porch, which wrapped around three sides of the house, was empty except for a half-dozen tall, slat-backed rocking chairs with cushions tied to them. It didn't really look like a picnic even though picnic tables were standing around under the trees; everyone except the kids was indoors. We cut around the overgrown bushes to the back door, where we were greeted by their two yapping, jumping dogs, Ebony and Jet.

The enormous kitchen was crowded with women putting together all the contents of various baskets, coolers, and plates wrapped in aluminum foil. They had opened the cavernous pantries and covered the huge sinks and drainboards with coconut cakes, potato salads, mounds of fried chicken, pound cakes, heads of lettuce, and tomatoes. And gossip was bursting out of the pots and paper plates. The women made sure I just put down the basket and kept moving.

Mrs. Murfree yelled out hello to us, causing everyone to look up. All the Murfrees were red. She was round and red, with red hair and freckles. They were all pretty loud. And they liked to party. They let the kids run around wrestling, playing, and being loud, a fact the women would be talking about when they got home. Preston had looked in the door and gone around to the front to avoid the crush. Dixon greeted everyone effusively and took the first opportunity to scoot through the mayhem to the living room. Before directing me upstairs to a bedroom to deposit my attractive black dance case, towels, and "nosiness," Maddie gave me a rundown of all the children I should go outside and look for, namely Marian, all the red-haired Murfrees, Charlesetta's daughter Tonda, who was "new to the picnic and would be looking for a familiar face," Dallas of the first kiss, and Ronnie Brown of the great body.

The very mention of the boy of the first kiss and Ronnie of the body made me feel a little nervous about what I had worn. Even though I knew they'd be there, I didn't know thigh-wrapper Tonda was coming and I just had to reevaluate. My outfit might have been a little too nice, not sophisticated enough. She probably had on short-shorts. I tried to linger in the kitchen by admiring each cake and pie. The women picked up on whatever it was they had dropped when we came in.

"So what did the woman do to you?" Alice Murfree was asking.

"She was trying to get elected president of the PTA," Maddie answered. "Can you imagine?" Obviously Mrs. Murfree didn't even know whoever it was because she didn't live in Turner, but she was pumping Maddie for a story.

"What was wrong with that? That's good if a woman wants to get involved. These kids need it."

"Oh, it wasn't that, girl," Mrs. Ernestine Johnson said. "You should have seen how she looked."

"Well, what was she looking like?" Mrs. Murfree instigated. She could tell just by looking at the prissy, mature Mrs. Johnson that she viewed herself as a woman of achievement.

Ernestine was a librarian at the high school, though she often reminded people they hardly needed one since the school board thought Negroes didn't want any books and the town wouldn't think of building a Negro library.

"She was wearing the wrong dress," Maddie spoke firmly. Even the women who hadn't been there cackled at the offense Maddie had taken.

Red Mrs. Murfree got loud. She was truly amused. "Was she showing her boobs or something?"

"Shush, now!" said Mrs. Johnson.

"Hell, girl." Mrs. Murfree was warming up. "That woulda sure got her elected at my PTA. When our fool president got chicken shit about fighting for integration, I thought about showing mine to get him out of office!" Everybody fell out till they remembered I was standing there. They stopped long enough for Maddie to put me out of the room, and then Mrs. Johnson tried to take the floor from Mrs. Murfree, who was by now demonstrating her election strut. As I climbed the stairs I could hear her carrying on.

"Honey, these men don't know anything too much at all when a woman gets into her civic-mindedness. I told 'em, 'Lock me in a room with the crackers who closed the school on my kids, I'll give 'em a little what-for.' "

Through the window on the landing I could see Preston was cornering a very tall Murfree girl who was setting a table under one of the trees. With his buddy Cole gone, he probably had lost some of his enthusiasm for going up the river as they usually did. Down on the dock I could see Dallas and Ronnie in a haze of white-on-white clothes against the bleached boards of the pier where they sat talking. Marian and Tonda must have been down in the water. I debated if I should put my suit on at all. Would I have the nerve to take off my shorts and top and get in the water? Really? I put it on anyway and decided to worry about it later.

Downstairs, the men gathered in the living room were comfortably in the midst of an argument. They were seated around the room as if for a portrait, smoking, drinking, and looking serious, as if they'd been meeting there every Thursday night for cordials or a game of snooker. Barrel-chested Murfree, with his ruddy, sunburnt farmer's skin and couldn't-be-bothered tee shirt and jeans, was surrounded by the men from town, dressed mostly in their casual best. They were hardworking men too, but it had been a long time since they'd worked with their hands. Most of them, young and old, had gone off to school to become their families' first educated men. And most of them had found that if they weren't going to preach or bury folks it would be hard indeed to make a penny with their degrees. All the same, they'd made it. They had respect, and comfortable homes, and to a man, they believed they had made something to pass on to the children they thought would do better.

"You can't expect anything from these white folks," Mr. Murfree was insisting. "We learned that here. We tried to integrate and they just shut it all down. 'Let your kids rot,' is what they said."

"Damnit, man, they can't shut every school in the state," yelled Coleman Boteler, who was pacing up and down. His temper was always close to the surface. Coleman cut an elegant figure as he turned round the room. He was wearing a jacket, despite the heat. He was proper that way, and always wore a jacket.

"They will," said Calvin Murfree. "And I say, make 'em do it. Make 'em shut every goddamn school in the state and get these white folks mad and then we'll do some talking." Dixon saw me standing in the door and looked away. "Didn't they just shoot a black boy down there? I heard they ain't doin' nothin' about it."

"Nothing so far, Cal," said Emmett Brown. Brown was a small, gray-haired man who dressed in old-fashioned clothes, beautifully made clothes, but clothes from another era. "They're saying they don't know who did it—that the witnesses didn't see the license plate on the car or anything." The oldest man in the room, he expected very little from southern justice, or even police work, when it came to a young black man. He had been a teacher for thirty years before becoming the first and only Negro on the Board of Education.

Ralph Johnson was getting agitated in the corner. Ralph didn't have much patience on the race question. "They're not going to do anything about it, like Murfree said," Ralph said. "Let's not fool ourselves about that. I've been living in this town all my life except for going to school. Last time they had some change was when they burned the place down. We got to be ready to put something on the line if we really want anything to happen."

"Well, we seem to have a consensus on that," said Murfree.

"Ralph's a bitter man," said Coleman. "He's worse than I am. I don't see him wanting to do anything except to raise a ruckus for the hell of it."

"I'm only almost bitter," laughed Ralph. "You, sir, are the genuine article."

"Let's not try to settle that one," said Dixon. The old man knew the two could trade lost-expectations stories all afternoon. Ralph was a schoolmate from elementary school days and had gone away to college with Dixon and then to engineering school. He'd never been able to get a job in the state of Virginia with that degree and he thought he'd make a lousy teacher because he had a permanent short fuse. But when it came to that he was eyeball to eyeball with Coleman. Having them together at a poker game always meant it might stop being fun. Bill Alexander, Maddie's husband, who was looking depressed by the whole discussion, decided to get in it.

"Look, man, I know these people, I deal with them every day," said Bill. Slight, fair-skinned Bill took his glasses off and put them back on. He wasn't that comfortable having everyone's attention. "I don't suppose anything will happen about that shooting but this other thing is different." He got up to get a cigar from his jacket on the back of the chair. "If we just go along with meeting with them, they'll let some kids integrate one school, and we'll get this thing started."

"You may be talking to them every day, Bill," Coleman interrupted, "but you aren't really doing business with them. Why should they even care what you think? It isn't much different how they deal with a murder and how they deal with the lawsuit. You think because you put on a suit and go to a business, it's different." Coleman swaggered a bit and closed in on Bill. "You act like you're in the Chamber of Commerce or something. When do you talk to them, passing on the street? You don't think they take you *seriously,* do you?" Coleman was getting out his daggers as he shook a cigarette out of his pack. "Man, I'm telling you, we just play along and we play into their hands. Come now, this whole business is a scheme of theirs. They want to appear to be cooperating to head off a suit. It's one big lie, a fiction. And you all know it."

"It's true," said Ralph. "They don't mean a word of it."

"You know our problem?" asked Murfree. "We always expect a moral response to an immoral situation. If they were moral, it wouldn't be like this in the first goddamn place. They have set up an immoral, unjust system and we're telling them to change it, and they're going to come back with an immoral and unjust answer. And all de quiet bull de butcher kill."

"What are we talking about here?" asked Ralph. "This is our

home. We been here long as they have. We can lay claim to it same way as they can. They are irrelevant—"

"Irrelevant!" Bill jumped in. "They only run the damn state."

"Irrelevant." Ralph stood his ground. "Just how much do they have to do with your life, really? They matter if they get you in a corner and have a chance to blow your brains out. But otherwise? Most of the time, what does it have to do with white folks? Nothing. It's time for us to figure out what we want and to hell with white folks. Like the man said, they set the shit up dirty—if we want it clean, we gonna have to clean it."

"You saying stay with the segregated schools?" asked Dr. Roberts, the newcomer to the group, who looked genuinely puzzled. Ralph looked at him as if to size him up, and continued.

"No, I'm saying don't be following their lead, responding to their moves. These are our lives we're talking about, not theirs. It's our dance." He spoke very slowly. "It's *not about* white people."

"Well," Bill said, calming down. "They don't want us to get anywhere but they will obey the law if the law changes. I believe that. If the suit goes through, they will go along."

"My question is, what if they *do*?" said Carter Charles. Someone laughed and then the laughter caught on in the room. Mr. Charles, always a thoughtful man, with no pretensions, was serious. The tall, handsome, brown-skinned man with high cheekbones and close-cut hair like the boys wore stood up and smiled his gorgeous wide smile. "Yes, I know we don't have to worry much about the possibility that they might do it, yet and all, I thought about what if they did? Do I want my kids going to school with those little bastards in the white school?"

"That's it, amen," said my old man.

"Watch it, Dix, we know you ain't religious!" teased Bill. Everyone laughed because it was true.

"Carter, I'm surprised to hear you say that," said Roberts. The slim, stylishly dressed young doctor seemed to be testing. "You're one of the few people here who works with whites. Aren't you some kind of supervisor up there at the shipyard?"

"Low-level supervisor, yeah. I supervise Negroes."

"But don't you work with whites hand in hand too?"

"Yeah, sure."

"Doc, you haven't been around here long enough." Ralph was trying to keep things congenial. "You just don't know Charles very well."

"What he doesn't know is how I had to pass by every redneck in the yard from the bottom up to supervise other colored men. You all been hearing me talk about the guys that tried to break my back right on the assembly line, or get me crushed up under the riggings where they put those big mothers together. All I'm saying, Roberts, is I know what mean men those children's daddies are, what kind of homes they come from—go to church on Sunday, kill a black motherfucker on Monday."

"Well, it's true," said Bill. "Ain't nobody said it wouldn't be rough on the kids. We're not fool enough to say that."

"What choice do you have, man?" Coleman whined. He was getting impatient again. "They're not teaching 'em shit in the Negro schools. My boy never did get math straight—some of these Negro teachers don't half know what they're doing. You all know it's true!"

"That's enough, Cole!" Dixon stood up. "First of all, you're talking to Negro teachers. Second, you're really talking about one teacher you didn't like. In fact, you're just talking to hear yourself talk, man. You're not going to be there when we need you. When it's all said and done you will say *we're* not good enough to be bothered with either. Nobody's looking for you to really help. So just sit down and be quiet. And stop pacing the goddamn floor."

"Take it easy, Dix," said Ralph.

"Man, you know, you don't have any kids going into this situation either." He sat down again. "I'm like Charles, I'm not so damn sure I want to send a kid of mine to Patrick Henry School."

"Sure you do," said Dr. Roberts. The group looked startled by the new man's patronizing tone—Dixon was at least fifteen years his senior. Bill gave Coleman a look that said this is what we get for having somebody new in our midst. Roberts, who must have been showing the old boys he had a mind of his own and didn't have to act grateful, took the floor. "You've got to let them go. It's the only way. And they'll be the better for it, even if it's rough. When they go on out there in the world and compete with the whites, it'll be the same way. Might as well get straight about it now. Sometimes I think it's pretty cozy for them, not ever dealing with those people until they are grown. Then one day they go into the bank and try to get a loan to buy a car or get a house and find out all their hard work doesn't count for anything."

Dixon interrupted. "When I go into the bank—or the drugstore, anywhere on Raleigh, it doesn't matter—the man behind the counter, whichever one is back there, calls me Dixon. Not one of them calls me Mister. I deal with the little scrapes here and there with those people who are still willing to take my money, but the school is another matter. They don't see any reason for her to be there at all. Why does Willie need to go straight into the hornet's nest?" He looked at me and looked away. The other eyes followed. He had never made me leave a room where adults were talking, not since my mother died and I'd found him crying in the kitchen. He decided to go on.

"She's only twelve. My God, does she have to have grown people throw rocks and eggs at her, spit on her, to learn about the real world, as you call it, to find out about the man in the cage at the bank who thinks I'm a boy, to find out that she's supposed to be dirt? I'm not going to do it. You may think it's the wrong attitude, or that I'm not for change, or rocking the boat, but I'm not tough enough to send my kid to take the kind of shit we took from these crackers in Turner. If they want to integrate, then that's it, integrate the whole system. We'll wait. I have a kid who's at risk of being picked for this mess. She's always at the top of her class, she tests well, never been in trouble—she's likely to get caught in their net. So I have to ask myself about this very seriously. Am I going to tell her some soldiers are going to take her to school? And do you think Eisenhower's even going to keep sending soldiers to take colored children to school? Plus, you socially conscious Negroes will be telling me I can't take my gun with me to get her to school."

"Well, I, for one, am not going to say *that!*" said Murfree, breaking the stillness. The men chuckled. "I got kids down there too now. I'll come bring my rifle and all my boys!"

Bill Alexander got up from his seat. "Sorry, just a minute, Dixon." He moved toward me sternly and said, "Willie, go on outside, this is not a discussion for you." Turning me round by the shoulder, he showed me the direction out. He shut the doors to the living room. I kept standing there. Bill chastised my dad. "I never will understand why you insist on letting her sit around when adults are talking adult business, Dix. It just isn't right."

"It's her life we're talking about, Bill. Better she should know we're dealing with it the best way we can. She's going to have the last word on this anyway, you know. If I said she could go, it's still up to her, because she's the one who's got to go back day after day. I can't make that decision, none of us can."

"But you're not helping her to find the courage," said Bill.

"Can't," said Dixon.

"We're all getting too excited over this." Coleman's voice came near the door. He had taken the floor again. "This whole idea of white folks integrating is bullshit. It's just a scenario, a fictional circumstance, I tell you."

I stepped on out to the porch and let the screen door slam to so Bill wouldn't come looking for me. For a minute I sat down on the porch steps. If the old man was scared about my having to go be a guinea pig, there was definitely something to worry about. I had just wanted to have a good time at the picnic, and it was obvious things were going to get worse than this. It was gleaming hot outside. The little kids seemed unaware of it, practically rolling around in the grass after a dog. When I got up to walk down to the water I made a quick decision not to tell the kids down at the dock about the big argument going on up in the house. It would just ruin what fun was left for us to have. The little ones caught up with me as I reached the pier.

"You going crabbing? They're crabbing down there. We can show you if you don't know how to do it. We catch crabs all the time."

"We'll see," I said. I didn't even know exactly who they were, except for the Murfree boy, who was easy enough to pick out. Maybe the others were neighbors. Sure enough, Marian and Tonda were hanging over the edge of the Murfree pier in their wet swimsuits, holding out big nets on poles. They had a bucket with a couple of their victims scraping around inside. On the dock sat a pair of pink short-shorts—undoubtedly Tonda's. Ronnie and Dallas, who were watching the proceedings, greeted me as I walked up: Dallas with an obvious strain to suppress any uncool enthusiasm, and Ronnie with a body-length appraisal and a hand sliding down my arm.

"Hey, girl," said Marian, "want to help us catch crabs? We're gonna cook 'em up and everything." I thought about how I would smell of crabs and river.

"No, thanks. You're not going to catch anything too much longer," I said. "The tide is going out." I took off my sandals and climbed down to the sand where the water had receded. The silvery river looked greener and browner as I stepped into its soft muddy underbelly along the tiny shore. The water was cool and the bottom slippery. A rowboat was bobbing slightly against the dock. Soon it would be sitting in the mud. Wading in up to my knees, I climbed inside it to sit and watch the crabbers. The boat rocked. The day was not so bad. If I could just sit there it wouldn't be particularly hot and I could listen to the kids jabbering or kind of put them in the background and watch the water.

The sight of the old man up in the house had made me feel strange. It seemed as if ever since my mother died four years ago he couldn't be tough with me and Preston. He treated us as people that he shouldn't push around just because he was the old man. He said he was trying to take her point of view some of the time. But it meant we had to be grown too. I wondered if I could have talked to her about what I was scared of, things I had nightmares about. I never told the old man anything like that. For him you had to be brave. I wondered if she was the kind of person you could really talk to.

"You wanna go see the Barnwell place?" one of the Murfree kids yelled out. "The boys wanna see it."

"Yeah, come on," Dallas said. "We hear there's a pool table in there." Just the idea of walking with them was good enough for me.

"Hey, you guys should wait for us," said Marian.

I laughed. "No, you should finish getting dinner."

The kid showed us how we could walk around the shoreline to it, so, shoes in hand, the boys and I followed. Out in the river I could see my brother heading downstream where some tiny homemade sailfish were bobbing along. Dallas and Ronnie went on with their conversation about who would be pitching some ball game, and I walked between them thinking this was just like a moment from the life of Nancy La Haute Couture, the pretty private eye.

Nancy La Haute Couture was my answer to Nancy Drew. She was a Creole colored woman detective. She hadn't started out as a detective—she started out as a curious teen who got trapped in a wardrobe case when she was sneaking around backstage at a Negro revue on Broadway. It was a long story how she got there. She was from Louisiana but had turned up in Harlem during the twenties, where she went to a lot of rent parties and heard a lot of Negro poets talking a lot of poetic mumbo jumbo. Anyway, at this show she got caught in a situation, *et voilà*! That is to say she found herself in Paris with a show starring the fabulous Josephine Baker, who was not happy to find Nancy in her dressing room in the Gay One. Ever since then Nancy had learned always to carry a toothbrush, hairbrush, and a change of clothes. She carried them in a chic black case, round with a loop handle. Nancy was able to help out Josephine with some dubious princes and a purloined leopard because she already spoke French since she was from New Orleans.

Nancy La Haute Couture stopped being a teenager very quickly and became a slightly older young adult because the adventures in France and elsewhere involved quite a few handsome men. She had to be of a certain age to hang out on the scene. (After that, Nancy La Haute Couture never aged.) The counts and dark, crooning stage-door Johnnys had instant admiration for Nancy's stunning beauty, as well as for her smart detecting mind. No one knew it, of course, but when she got real stumped Nancy consulted the gris-gris. That was her secret. She got it from a hairdresser in New Orleans. And now it was off to the ghostly, uninhabited plantation home of the famous Negro who may have made up his name, a new life for himself, perhaps to hide a mystery from slavery days.

As she made her way up the murky beach, on her left walked the sincere and handsome sweetheart of her childhood, now a successful banker, no, doctor—she may need a doctor. On her right was the nightclub singer and sometime movie actor with unbuttoned shirts, who just happened to, just happened to have a flat tire on his Lincoln Continental—Jaguar—near this spot. The two men, previously strangers to one another, and both very attracted to Nancy La Haute Couture, were talking ball games to pass the time as they walked the Creole detective to the Barnwell homestead.

From the shore they could see the house had six tall columns rising two stories to the roof. The windows of the first and second floors, with their black shutters, looked out between the columns onto the narrow river and beyond. Leaded glass windows shaped like diamonds were set on either side of the front door.

The Murfree kid told us to wait and ran around the back. Soon he emerged at the front door and let us in.

Nancy La Haute Couture's knees felt a little shaky, but she thought of how she must continue to look composed. She patted her hair and braced herself. Setting foot in the gleaming front hall was jarring as it was meticulously preserved from some other time, some unknown family.

It became instantly clear that one knew nothing of the oriental rugs, the mahogany tables with glasslike veneers, and the glistening chandeliers, except that the original owners were in the slavery business. The first floor had, in the common fashion, only two rooms—a parlor with a black marble fireplace on one side of the hall, and a dining room on the other. The severely formal living room had high wood walls and dark red overstuffed chairs, sort of Victorian, like a copy of an English library. Giant crystal ashtrays sat on the end tables. It gave the impression more of a boardroom than a family room. A kitchen had been added behind the dining room at the back of the house, and the front hall opened onto a rear door that was no longer used. The only sign of Barnwell himself was in the hallway, which housed a collection of Barnwell memorabilia: plaques, photographs of Barnwell's triumphs—meeting President Theodore Roosevelt, opening the first Negro bank in the state, naming a Negro school.

The house had a forbidding kind of luxury, not exactly comfortable. It probably soothed the inner princeliness the man had felt— the kind of princeliness that could make you think you're massa. In the photographs, he seemed to have been trying to look extremely cheerful. His long black suits with the superwide lapels looked like they must have been very hot. The brown man with a deeply furrowed brow had eyes that were eerily light—maybe eyes from a slavemaster father. They looked like they were gold or gray. Actually, he looked like a Negro leader from another planet.

Nancy began to think this might be a science-fiction story: invading aliens who had accidentally landed in the wrong place at the wrong time—Virginia, 1840s. Of course, if this alien being had had any superpowers he would have freed everybody; that is, unless he had been very perverse, or—dah, dah—a master himself. He had adapted to his surroundings but he could not disguise the glow from his eyes, which used to be bright yellow on his other planet, the planet known as—

"What are you doing?" Dallas asked. "Come on, we're going to look around some more." He took my hand and led me upstairs behind the others, who were running up. The stairs were so worn they dipped, but the wood banister with its carved white posts was sparkling like in a house in a magazine. The second-floor hallway was lined with louvered doors. When we opened one, there was a regular door with a brass latch handle instead of a doorknob. Dallas guessed that at night the people there would open their windows and the solid door and use the shutter door to draw the breeze. In the master bedroom there was a huge bathroom with a tub big enough for three or four people. In most of the bedrooms there were slim trundle beds that came out from under the beds.

"Where slaves slept," said one of the boys.

"I wouldn't want no slave in *my* bedroom," quipped Ronnie. Dallas laughed.

"You wouldn'ta had nothin' *but* slaves in your bedroom!" answered Dallas. "They just wouldn't have been working for *you*."

"Awright, awright, man. You know what I meant. Or maybe you don't. Let's go, this place gives me the creeps. Let's see if there's a pool table around."

"I like it, it's nice up here. A nice house," Dallas said. He was comfortable and would have stayed. Maybe he had a princely streak too. The house was so spacious, he had remarked. If the windows were open it would be full of river air. Dallas had lived in the projects at the far end of town, where they had once planned to modernize the black neighborhood. Instead, the town threw up these airless little garden apartments with dirt yards in the middle of nowhere and decided to modernize elsewhere. The parents had built a sandbox or two and chipped in on some swings. Dallas's father worked two jobs and finally he moved them back into town into an old wood house white folks had abandoned when Negroes moved into the vicinity.

We walked to the end of the hall to look out at the view. There was a small door there that opened onto a walk-in closet with a tiny bed in it. It was more like a coffin than a bedroom, and I couldn't imagine who would have slept there, let alone closed the door. Out the window was the river. Whoever had to stay in there must have dreamed of creeping out of the house and swimming away wherever the river went. Dallas thought we should stop and sit there for a minute. He put his arm around me. When he tried to shut the door something snapped in me and I leapt up and ran out. The room was not a room; it was too small, and I lost my cool.

"There's probably a ghost in there. I could feel it, I'm serious," I said as I stood outside the room. I realized I wasn't really afraid of Dallas and just stood there.

"Willie, I'm, uh—"

"I better get back." He followed me down the steps. "I'm sure they'll be looking for me to help soon as they hear I'm over here with you-all." Embarrassed, I dashed out the back door, leaving Dallas and Ronnie and the boys, and went back by the road to the Murfree house. As I got near the house Marian and Tonda were coming up the road, no doubt sent to get us.

"Coming back already?" Tonda asked.

"It's probably a good thing," Marian said. I was sweating from moving fast in the heat but I had got ahold of myself.

"Yeah, I figured somebody would be looking for me by now."

"Yup, there's women's work waiting for you. And they're all cussing and fussing about school integration."

"Oh. Yeah. So how many crabs did you catch?" I asked. I was glad to see them.

"Well, we got about six or eight. Not enough to feed too many people!" Marian laughed.

"You cook 'em?"

"Yup. Well, they're doin' it now. So what were you doing up there?" Marian asked.

"Just looking around the place. It's pretty interesting. They kept it just like it was when Barnwell was alive." Tonda's eyes got kind of big.

"Do they have all his old clothes in there and stuff?" she asked.

"I don't know, I didn't really look in the closets!" Tonda looked up the road to see if the others were coming. We were just standing in the road. No one was eager to go back to the picnic. "What did you look at?" She wasn't really asking how interesting it was. "Did you go in the bedroom?"

"Bedrooms."

"Oh, I see," she said with a snide tone. "I know I would've known what to look at. Up there with two cute boys, roaming around the bedrooms in a mansion. Hmph."

"Oooh! You know you are disgusting, Tonda." Marian was trying to shut her up. Even if I had seen something interesting on those boys, she wouldn't want Tonda knowing anything about it or it would be all over the place. As it was, there was no telling, in Marian's mind, what this would sound like by the time Tonda finished with it at school. I actually admired Tonda, though. She could handle situations that I knew I couldn't handle.

"Besides, Tonda," Marian went on, "you're nothing but a little hussy."

"So what? Marian, you wish you *could* be a hussy. You're *never* gonna find out what it's all about."

"Let's head back," I said. We turned around and walked down. The sun had gotten a little lower in the sky, and the heat was letting up. Two cats were stretched out asleep in the yard of the first house we passed. One was in the grass, one on the shaded concrete driveway. Not far from them a girl was asleep on a chaise lounge with a radio blaring. Two little girls were sweeping the driveway and singing out loud to the music. Their voices couldn't get on key. One ran to get a jump rope and the other came over and stood in front of the radio and sang at the top of her lungs. She rocked from side to side as she sang.

"You know, I learned a lot this summer already," Tonda said. "Me and this little fella next door—you know him: Nicky—

we've been practicing when our parents go to work. We've been having *some fun*."

"Practicing?" I said.

"Doing it."

"You did it?" I asked, incredulous.

"Yep. The *good thang,* honey."

"With Nicky?" Marian was grossed out. She started to lower her voice as if people were nearby. "But he's only eleven! Ewwh." She scrunched up her face.

"I don't care. He knows what to do. He's only a year younger, anyway." I was starting to hope the boys back at Barnwell's had decided to play pool and would not come bopping down this road.

"You're only twelve, Tonda," Marian said.

"So? You sound like somebody's mother," she answered. She was not bothered about our sounding horrified. She figured she had found out what everybody wanted to find out. "He's cute too, don't you think, Willie? You seen him."

"Yeah, he's cute. But he is *younger*. So how did that happen?"

"Well, he came over and we put some records on and we were slow dragging. He's a fast boy. He reached up my dress and put his hand in my panties and I let him. Then he started rubbing on me still grinding to the music. Umph. It felt good. So he said, 'If you go all the way it feels *real* good.' So I said okay. I didn't know if he even knew what he was talking about, but he did. So now after the old lady leaves—Dad goes out early—he comes over and we take all our clothes off, and get in my parents' bed, and we do it, girl."

"You did it?" I asked again.

"I just told you I did it."

"What do you do, *exactly?*" asked Marian, frowning. Tonda looked at her with a mix of contempt and utter satisfaction. She stopped and grabbed Marian by the shoulders and sat her down on the ground on the side of the road. Tonda stretched out on the road like a cat lazing in the grass. She leaned back on her arms.

"I get naked and let him put his hand in my hole. First one finger, then a couple more. And he plays with it and he sucks on my titties and licks on 'em like. It makes them act funny—"

"Like what?" I asked, even though something inside me was scared of getting any more information. Tonda rolled her eyes, enjoying the torture.

"Just funny. And then I open my legs and let him stick his thing in. And we just play around in the house like that all day." She sat up and looked us both square in the eye. Marian just shook her head. I could feel the hair stand up on my arms and legs.

"Don't look so disgusted. It feels good." She eyeballed us again. "When he puts his hand in my pussy it makes me squirm. I get shivers all over. Anyway, I not only did it, I've done it about, let's see, since I got out of summer school, I've done it about thirty times." Tonda smiled.

"Oh my God," Marian muttered. I had to laugh, I didn't know why. Even Marian knew it was stupid to ask her didn't she think it was immoral, or she would burn in hell or something. But what about getting pregnant like Cassie? I wanted to ask her didn't she think about ending up like Cassie. I stared at the little girls dancing around their yard. They were singing and twirling. Ronnie and Dallas came into view and we all jumped up. I told them I was going on and headed for the house. I would not have been able to look at them without thinking about eleven-year-old Nicky and his thing. The tables were set up outside the house and Cal Murfree was holding court.

"No, I tell you, man, we are thinking about starting a voter registration drive around here. We're gonna have to get niggas to vote if we're going to do anything. You got one or two colored folk who can vote down your way. We don't have one in the county that's ever voted."

"Willie, what happened to you?" Maddie called out. "Did the girls find you?"

"Yeah, they're coming right behind me."

"Man, you really biting off more than you can chew, Murfree," one of the men said.

"Yeah, probably so. We'll just start small, see, send three or four folks down there every month to take the test. They might not notice anything."

"Well, come on and get something to eat," Maddie said to me. "Get a plate, and see if your father's got some food yet." She addressed the group. "I take it we've agreed to form an integration committee, since you-all have gone on to voter registration. What should we call it?" I went over to the food table and tried to pile everything on without looking as if I were piling everything on. There were ribs, hot dogs, hamburgers, grilled fish, salads of all kinds, beans, grilled corn on the cob, and five lonely crabs that everyone politely left for someone else. I went and sat at the table with the other kids. Preston, I noticed, had insinuated himself at an adult table next to the tall Murfree girl.

"How about the Turner Integration Committee?" ventured Ernestine Johnson.

"Lord, no," blurted out Alice Murfree.

"Turner Advancement Association," tried Emmett Brown.

"That's worse," Alice reacted. The group started to laugh. The dogs started yapping and jumping at all the noise. "See, y'all even upsetting Ebony and Jet," Alice crowed.

"United Turner—" No one said a word, everyone smiled, the kids giggled.

"We're not going to get anywhere in this mood," said Bill. "We can think of a name later."

"Hell, let's not call it anything," said Ralph. "We're not going to hang out no sign. The less the white folks know about it the better off we'll be, if you ask me."

"I like that idea," said Charlesetta. "We'll just organize ourselves without calling it anything. When the time comes to get people out, we'll just appear."

"What do we say when we call people on the phone to get them out?" asked Ernestine.

"Just tell them who it is organizing," said Charlesetta. "You're going to have to tell them anyway if you call and say 'United Turner' is having a meeting, right?" Ernestine nodded.

"Alright, everybody. Mrs. Roberts likes the idea, I say we defer to our guest," laughed Bill. He didn't care either way, knowing his role would be to gather intelligence, not to go around as a spokesman. "And may our newcomers return for many years to come. How about a toast, folks?" Marian eyed me and we started laughing.

"Hear! Hear!" We all picked up something to toast with and lifted our drinks for the Roberts family.

"And here's to Nicky's thing," whispered Marian. We clinked our Dixie cups.

"Dixon, you're gonna have to be in it, you know," chided Maddie. "No matter what you think."

"I know with my relatives here I'm gonna be in it whether I want to or not. You just put me in it, didn't you?" Dixon answered. Folks chuckled.

"That's right. Willie is a good tester; we're probably going to need her," Maddie said, unaware of the earlier conversation among the men.

"That's right," chimed Helena Brown, Emmett's delicate, white-haired wife. "It's the good testers you're going to have to put up. Emmett, weren't you saying that that's what they'll be looking for first?" He nodded and kept eating. Helena went on,

"They think they'll get rid of us right off the bat with those standardized tests."

No one said anything to me about it, and no one would. Good testers, or good athletes, or good debaters belonged to the teachers, the whole school, were community property. If they wanted me to sit down and take tests like a school representative at a testing tournament, I would be doing it. As Helena Brown ran it down, there would be an equal number of boys and girls, the right grades, the right test scores, proper attire if they all had to sew it, and proper attitude, provided by parental muscle. I had ended up in at least one school play that way, and one or two spelling bees. If a kid had a talent, they identified it and put it to use. There was no choice in the matter. If you wanted to be left alone, you had to be a bum or pretty crazy.

"Who should be in charge of this group?" asked Bill.

"How about you, Bill?" asked Carter Charles.

"Naw, we need somebody crazier than Bill," Ralph said. He was in his cups now and no longer concerned himself with how things sounded.

"Then you sound like the man," Murfree shot out.

"How about Coleman?" asked Charlesetta.

"Coleman!" Lillian squealed. She started giggling uncontrollably.

"Thanks, Charlesetta," he said, pretending not to notice Lillian's uncomfortable humor. "No, that's not for me. As you said, Dixon, I don't even know if I'm with you-all. I mean, theoretically I'm with you—"

"You're going to write whatever we need written, Cole," Maddie informed him.

"As you can see, Maddie's going to tell all of us what to do, and we're going to do it. Like I said, I don't know if I'm with you. I know one thing, I'm not following anybody here into anything. I suggest you do yourselves a favor: don't have a president, or whatever you're getting ready to do."

"Someone's got to be in charge to keep us moving," objected Helena Brown. Ernestine Johnson followed with a little, "Yes, yes."

"Bullshit. Whites folks gonna keep you moving," said Coleman. "You know what you're doing. Don't have a leader, I say, just go on and do what you have to do."

"Well, what about Maddie?" asked Dorothy Charles.

"Absolutely not," said Bill. "No one will stand for a woman leading. They'll think it's a bridge club and stay away in droves. It's got to be someone who would ordinarily be too busy— unless it was very important. You know, to give the group more credibility."

"Credibility? I like that!" said Murfree.

"We could get one of the ministers, perhaps," said Helena.

"Like who?" Bill snarled. He wasn't much for men of the cloth. No one said a word.

"No leader has emerged, that's obvious," said Maddie, who was just as happy with the arrangement. As she saw it, she'd have to keep tabs on whichever one of the men they chose.

"That's it then," shouted Ralph. "Let's have a toast: The no-name group citizens' group is called to order. And we got no one minding the store!" He laughed and raised his glass.

"Ralph, we're all minding the store, honey," said Alice Murfree. "I'll drink to that."

When we headed home the old man was real quiet. The roads were incredibly dark. Pickup trucks occasionally zipping by with their brights on seemed to be flying like bats out of hell. We couldn't pick up anything on the radio. Preston fell asleep in the back and I watched the lights flickering where farm-houses were hiding in the distance.

LILLIAN SAID nothing as she drove Coleman toward home. He'd had quite a few drinks and she hoped he would fall off to sleep. She wanted to think. She felt drained and full, raging and empty. As she stared forward at the white line and the pitch-black road, she kept seeing Coleman taking his plate over to sit with Charlesetta and, as the evening wore on, pressing against her. It must have been obvious to everybody. Actually, her jealousy was not over his affection, but any affection. She missed that feeling of being courted by a man, even when it wasn't entirely sincere. Why did women need that? Hell, men certainly needed it. Why were women supposed to give up being cared for? Men didn't have to do that their whole lives long, not at all.

Back in the thirties the men, she thought, used to sit around talking about socialism instead of failing students. She'd been converted. She'd wanted to make some suggestions, though, like socializing hotels and giving all women a key to a room where nobody could find them for two weeks a year. Well, none of them were socialists anymore. And she had the con-stant problem of wondering how she could get a job that paid more than two thousand dollars a year so she could set some-thing aside. Over the years she hadn't had much solitary plea-sure in what was her life. A few hours in Leigh Tarrant's kitchen had been her due. If the two of them had a bit of time alone on Sunday to discuss ways to keep from getting pregnant time and again, that kept them going more than two hours of church, or an occasional movie. Then, of course, Leigh had died suddenly without telling anyone that for days she'd been noticing the light fade too quickly from the trees outside her window. Apparently she'd told Dixon to find a nice woman to marry but without much explanation. It had been four years, Lillian thought, since she'd had a decent conversation.

"I'm glad those people didn't decide to ask some puffed-up Negro in town to run the group. That would be all we'd need, another Negro leader who's out there to promote himself."

"What do you mean 'we'?" she asked. "I don't really see why you even care what 'we' do with that group."

"Don't you start too. Dixon already called me out in front of the men and said I wouldn't want to have anything to do with them."

"Well, he called a spade a spade."

"I just don't want to be bothered with any foolishness. If they're serious, I'd like to be involved."

"How will we ever know if they're serious enough for you?"

"Oh, Lillian, stop it. What's eating you?"

"Quite a few things, really. Too much to go into now."

"You're just upset that Cole's gone. You'll feel better in a couple of days."

It was true they had never been to the picnic without the boy. Still, she thought it was as if her son's anger about everything recently had kept her from noticing anything else. Like the fact that Coleman was not the least bit concerned with her, except so as to maneuver around her. It was interesting to stand back and look at it, then to recognize all the patterns, the lies he had told a thousand times. She found it deadening, too. That perhaps was the chief insult. He thought no more of her than to use the same old transparent bullshit year after year. Coleman wasn't going to help the group; he'd bail out after a while, bored with the disagreements and bored with the labor. He would be at the meetings, though, at least until he got a hand under Charlesetta's dress. If the woman put a stop to it there, he'd be back in his corner room writing something. And he'd write in the evenings as well as the mornings until he passed through it.

"Did you have a good time, dear, talking with the other women?" he asked.

"I wish they had boot camp for middle-aged men."

MADDIE ALEXANDER pretended to listen to Bill pontificating on the integration question as they drove to Turner. She encouraged Marian to ask him all about it and get his views. She was excited and making plans in her head. There were a few things they could do, such as meet with the churches and other groups who could support the issue. It would be better if they didn't seem to be merely a small group of parents active at the school. It was odd but she felt gay, like when she and Bill used to go dancing. Like when she walked into the dance in a new dress and surveyed the room and decided there was no one looking any cuter than she.

She knew she could get people organized, and she would be calling them and "suggesting" things they could do. She would do it well, too. She took a cigarette out of the case and felt in the dark for her lighter. She lighted it and tapped the lighter shut against the edge of the window. Some snappy Sarah Vaughan song came into her head. Annoyed, Bill asked her, "Why are you tapping the window like that?!"

"I was thinking, Bill, it might be a good idea to give a dance or a party, you know, to raise money."

WHEN SCHOOL opened that week we moved into our new building, Wells Junior High, but since it was next door to Carver Elementary that was the least exciting part of returning to school. Tonda Roberts was the talk of the school. She was wearing a bra, which was just about all she needed. Now she was walking around with her shoulders pulled back and her chest sticking out. She wasn't that tall but she looked down at all the boys by way of her suddenly larger breasts, as if to let them know they were no longer in her league. She was looking for a boy who knew what to do with a bra. The boys smirked but they stayed away from her. They'd seen her grinding with the ninth graders. But Tonda didn't get quite as much attention as she must have thought she would with her straight skirts and newly snug blouses. There was also the new boy, Julian Parker, who turned out to be attractive to just about every girl in the class. It seemed as though he was also supposed to be smart. However, the new boy and the new body quickly lost their novelty. By the third day of school there were two white people sitting in the seventh-grade classroom taking notes.

The confusion about the white people didn't worry me too much. I was glad to have Mrs. Taliaferro as a teacher because everyone said she was great, and I figured she could handle them too. She was not, however, answering any questions.

Wednesday morning before the white men appeared she told the class that several members of the Board of Education would be sitting in to observe the class. She said there would be different people from time to time because the board was fairly large and they all wanted to see the class. It was very strange that so many people from the other side of town wanted to see the Ida B. Wells School.

"It has to do with integration, and that's all I'm going to say about it for now," said Mrs. T. "I hope you all know what the word means. And we're going to show them our stuff. We're going to show them we're as good as any class anywhere."

At recess, playing games was suspended and some of the class crossed the huge green field to a bench at the edge of a neighboring yard. A few of the boys hung back to play softball while the talkative bunch tried to figure out what was going on. It seemed that only Mrs. Taliaferro's class had the white visitors. Kelly Jean Johnson and "Fatboy" Simpson speculated that maybe if the Board of Education people saw how terrible our books were they might order us some new ones, but the idea of showing someone we were as good as somebody was weird. Suenona said they were taking notes the whole time.

"I got nervous. I didn't want to raise my hand. What are they looking at?" she asked.

"Tonda's bra," snapped Fatboy.

"Be serious," said Kelly Jean. "Mrs. Taliaferro said something about proving we were as good as anybody. Who are they trying to see if we're as good as?" I mentioned the integration suit I'd heard about.

"You think they're trying to figure out if we're as good as other colored kids or white kids?" Marian asked. Everybody shrugged.

"Like those no-'count little peckerwoods at Patrick Henry?" Fatboy shouted. Kelly Jean screwed up her face.

"I guess so," she said. None of us had ever even seen the kids at Patrick Henry up close.

"I've seen them downtown. They look pretty dry to me," Marian said.

"Yup, pret-ty dry," said Fatboy. "And they ain't gonna be too friendly."

"Nope," said Kelly Jean. It got very quiet. We knew the kids across town went to a nicer school, but we'd never thought about who they were, or what they did. We thought what we learned was what everybody learned. No one had ever said anything about being as good as the other people. The teachers always said we weren't being all we could be, living up to our "potential." They all said it over and over.

"If the tests said we could read like ninth graders, or even

118

seventh graders, then that was any seventh graders," said Kelly Jean.

"*All* the seventh graders," Fatboy said.

"How did you do on those tests last year, Suenona?" Kelly Jean asked.

"Ninth or tenth grade, something like that. My dad said I was doing really good."

"Really well," said Kelly Jean.

"Shut up, you're as bad as he is. What difference does it make? White people just think we're stupid."

"I thought white people were supposed to be stupid," said Fatboy.

"Me too," said Marian.

"They've sure been wrong every time they thought a Negro couldn't do something," Fatboy summed up.

"Yup," someone said. Everyone agreed.

When the bell rang we ran back in and behaved like model students. No notes were passed, and Fatboy didn't say anything dumb to be funny. Mrs. Taliaferro said we would be reviewing how to diagram sentences just to make sure everyone knew it. She wrote a sentence on the board and started drawing lines around it, dividing it into parts.

"If you want to use the language well, it helps to know how to break it down, take it apart. It's the same as when a young man goes into the army and learns how to use a weapon. First he must learn how to take it apart and put it back together. He has to break it down, clean all the parts, and put it back together, even blindfolded, because he must depend on it every minute. Language is the same way. First we identify the parts of speech."

She started with a simple sentence with a little modifier hanging down from the direct object. Then she made more complex pictures of indirect objects and compound subjects.

Words started going at angles all over the board and dotted lines began making triangular shapes as the sentence went up or down and finally across the board. She made funny sentences about language and weapons and soldiers and students, mixing up the subject of one sentence with the predicate of another. We laughed at the nonsensical meanings she created. "The soldier cleaned and oiled his ideas and put them back together." Like many other things she said, the crazy sentences stayed with us like posthypnotic suggestions.

And so we sealed a silent pact, teacher and students. Without another word being said we knew we were going to be better than any other seventh graders that the white men had ever seen. The new situation had an ugly edge to it. The watchers never smiled. Everything we did now was driven by an enemy. We were on some scary red alert all day, as if the watchers might call in an air raid. Before that week no one had ever expected us to be dumb, or fail, or waited for us to act like savages. No one had waited for us to mess up—they waited for us to do it right, whatever it was. What place did these other people come from that was so different, so right, so smart and sparkling, so beyond us, that they had to see us to know if we were normal? I looked at the class, and I looked at the teacher, and I couldn't see them any differently than I had ever seen them.

Mrs. Taliaferro also assigned five of us to lead a part of the class every day, and my section was the first thing in the morning. It made me very nervous. I could not be late to school. I had to be able to answer any question anyone had about the social studies homework. The only saving grace was that I got it over with early in the day. When I got up from my seat I went through the lesson slowly, measuring my words, trying to make sure I didn't make any poor sentences. Was I speaking English, or did I mess something up? Did I make sure "pen" didn't come out sounding like "pin"? There was an invisible minefield in the room, always exploding in my head with the question "Is that all you know?" I imagined the white people asking, "Is that all she knows?"

In the back of my mind a dizzying reel of fearful thoughts played on and on. Maybe, I thought, we were the victims of some horrible plan. Our textbooks all came late. They came weeks, sometimes months late every year. Because the books came from wherever the watchers came from, they *knew* they'd left us shorthanded, sharing old books, and playing catch-up with a schedule from that same other place. Maybe the clock we raced against sped ahead faster than time really moved. My palms got sweaty underneath the heavy textbook. I called on the kids who eyeballed me that they were ready.

When at last I could sit down, I stared straight ahead, as if paying strict attention, and went over the performance, hunting for missteps, listening for the bombs until I assured myself it had been okay.

The old man didn't have much to say when I told him that I no longer liked going to school. "If you liked school before, you were lucky. You're not going to get to like everything, you know." At first he didn't understand what my problem was, and finally I told him it was the white people sitting in the room taking notes. "There are two things about the white people trying to evaluate you. One (and this will be true now and for everywhere you go): Whatever you set out to do, you're going to have to do it twice as well as the white person doing it. And you can do it. The second thing is: It still isn't very important, and nothing to worry about. You can't take it to heart. If you take it to heart, they've got you. Just do what Mrs. Taliaferro says and forget those people. They don't even know what they're looking for. They don't want to integrate the schools, and they're going to look for any excuse *not* to integrate the schools. They just diggin' a hole to fill a hole."

"What's that mean?"

"It means when they get done messing around with you and your school, the same hole's going to be there, just in a different place. My dear, the garden still needs watering out there, white people or no white people."

Once out in the muggy heat that evening he started to talk about when he jumped on a train to go to Chicago to go to college and what happened when he got there. He said when he sat down for his first French class the teacher asked him why was he there. He didn't understand her question. He said he was there to learn French, he needed to master two languages. "For what?" she had asked. He explained he was in the sciences and she laughed. "Mr. Tarrant," she called him, "I am very sorry but Negroes cannot learn French. Your race is not suited to it because, you see, your lips are too big to pronounce it." The old man said he felt he could not let her put him out because he did need the two languages to get a degree. So in the midst of the laughter in the class he had to stand and tell the teacher that he would like her to allow him to stay and flunk out. She could not resist the opportunity to prove herself right.

"What happened?" I asked him, knowing he'd never flunked anything.

"I made sure she could never give me even a B on any test."

"What did she give you in the end?"

"An A-minus." He started laughing. "She said I had an irreparable southern accent."

"But you don't," I said. He kept laughing.

"Of course not. She had to give me A's for three more years because I was in her classes several more times."

It was the kind of story he told a lot, a story about perseverance, and unacknowledged victory, like the one about how the college gave his Phi Beta Kappa key to a football player rather than have it known that a Negro earned such an honor, and how it took him two years to have them forced to award him his key. "Of course, that was 1919, that wouldn't happen now." But I began to see what he was really saying, that the pressure was there. It was not in the work, it was coming from the other people's minds, unyielding minds that did not give in to reason.

He asked if he'd ever told the story about Fannie joining the Episcopalians. He couldn't remember for sure if the family was already Episcopalian or not at the time, but the point was that Fannie was trying to run off to join the Red Cross during World War I and she got caught up with these Episcopalians. Actually, Fannie got caught up with one Episcopalian white lady who came around to the colored Episcopalian church looking for a helper. The old man could only remember her as Mrs. Lady because that's what the family called her. They liked to rib Fannie about the white lady who was going to help her join the war effort. It seems Mrs. Lady needed extra help because her husband—Major Mister Man, they called him—had been called to Washington to assist with enlistment once the Americans got in the war. To Fannie's ear this was a train ticket to a government hospital, or the Red Cross, or something, if she could impress Mrs. Lady with her skills. Mrs. Lady was delighted that this young colored woman was so informed on the war effort and so interested in her husband's work. She took to Fannie instantly. And a schoolteacher—even if she was a colored schoolteacher—would be just right for her children.

Fannie went to Mrs. Lady's home over by the mouth of the river in a little court behind a stone gate. It was the most beautiful home she'd ever seen, though clearly it was the most modest house in the court. It had probably all been one plantation estate in the old days. Mrs. Lady's house was very small, and Fannie puzzled over who might have lived in it before the major. It had a hallway through the middle with a parlor on each side, but the second floor was short like an attic and seemed to have once been one huge room. Dixon still remembered the most astounding feature of the house in Fannie's story, two back-to-back grand pianos in the lavishly draped and carpeted living room. Fannie arranged to come in the afternoons to take care of the children, and Mrs. Lady warmed up to the idea of telling her all about what she would need to do to qualify to work in one of the Washington hospitals.

Fannie had a persistent little cough, which she hid as best she could. Her mother had made Dixon and one of the other boys take over the garden so Fannie wouldn't have to be outside in the dampness when it was cool. But Mrs. Lady thought her children must be taken out for air every day, and soon Fannie found herself trying to show Mrs. Lady what must be done about her garden as well. When Mrs. Lady asked about the cough Fannie said that the doctor had described it as some kind of nervous tic, and Mrs. Lady was satisfied. At the same time she set Fannie on a course of studying medical books and told her she must familiarize herself with many procedures before setting out for any hospital work. Fannie gave up her beloved adventure books and convinced the woman to make one or two trips to the library for her to acquire the necessary books. After a while Mrs. Lady managed to convince Fannie that a note from her to the librarian would be all Fannie would need to go herself to get the books.

Two of Fannie's brothers had gone off to Washington already to join one of the Negro units, and Luke was considering leaving his railroad job to go. On Wednesdays, Louisa always cooked beans, ham hocks, and yams for her mother and several old ladies living on the block who had been in slavery with Louisa's mother. Normally they sat around talking about the plantation and telling ghost stories and everybody would leave them to it. Nobody wanted to hear about the haints. The old women paid no mind to the young people and laughed till they cried. The war talk, though, had gotten them frightened. All they could imagine was that the war was soon to be nearby, tearing up the fragile fibers of unfettered life. The young men would disappear, they predicted, just like before. Why, the colored folk hadn't had but a generation, they said, to put back together what had been broken up and scattered to the sea and winds for years by the hundreds. The war would take the children, they said, and force them to relive the horrors of another time. After so much killing men were never the same, and would the women have kept the life for them to come back to? No one listened to them talking on with the near-wailing sounds of mourners. The old encampment was now a town and a way of life to young ones like Fannie, hardly changeable enough.

Each time word came from the major, Fannie would ask Mrs. Lady if she wouldn't mind asking him for his advice about a hospital she might write to for a job, or if he knew if there were something she could do with the Red Cross. Mrs. Lady would assure her that she would press him to look into it.

Fannie stayed on with Mrs. Lady from summer to spring, when Vernon appeared, rich from being overworked on understaffed trains, and gloomy to be losing friends to the Negro regiments. He was thinking maybe he also should go. Fannie's old man, who was all for the boys' signing up, told Vernon that with his eye for a dollar he could probably keep getting rich in the army. Fannie was too lost in her own dreams to worry that something might happen to him, and so excited about it all that she could barely sit through her father's comments on the subject.

She had Vernon walk her to Mrs. Lady's gate one afternoon so she could tell him her plans. He tried to tell her that her father had out-and-out suggested that he marry her. She stopped and looked at him as if he were crazy and went on as if he hadn't said a word, explaining that she had been studying and practicing how to dress wounds in her room at night. He didn't really understand why she was doing all that. Well, she continued, Mrs. Lady had told her she must be well trained. Vernon didn't believe a word of it, didn't believe the Red Cross would take a Negro if *she* were a *surgeon*. He told her Mrs. Lady just had a maid who was reading a lot of medical books. Vernon told her unless she wanted to do laundry at an army hospital she had to find some colored folks up north to help. He suggested she write a woman he knew at the freedmen's hospital in Washington. She jumped at the idea but she still didn't really believe she'd been deceived.

Fannie asked him to wait outside for ten minutes and then, if she hadn't returned, to go on. She wanted to put the question to the woman for once and for all. Fannie ran into Mrs. Lady's quite beside herself, rushing into the living room without even taking off her wrap. She asked the woman directly if she knew whether a colored woman could get work with any of the people she had talked about, if she had even inquired. The woman hemmed and hawed and finally told her she ought to have known that to get a job of the kind she wanted would be nearly impossible. Fannie ran out of her house crazy with anger, mostly at herself for being a fool. Dixon said she lost her good sense for several years.

In the old man's way of telling the story, the Mrs. Lady madness drove Fannie to commit a rash act. Actually there were two, but the old man only knew one. Fannie's act of recklessness, according to the old man, was to run away from home after she got a letter back from the woman at the colored hospital in Washington. No doubt, the woman said, Fannie was probably plenty skilled for any of the work women were doing at the hospital. The war had left the colored hospital quite shorthanded, and besides that, it was a training hospital and she might learn as much as she pleased. I asked him why he told that story.

"I think there was something about today I was trying to tell you, but this story seemed just as good a way to get it said." He paused, trying to think back himself. "You know why the fastest runners on earth are Negroes? First off, you have to beat all the whites that ever ran before they let you on the team. And then you can't fail. There's an extra dose of electricity pumping through your body just because you know most of the people sitting out there watching think you can't do it. You're never really running against the clock—you're running against what you think you can do. The clock is just there. You can't give in. And then no matter how fast you get you still have to have an extra little muscle near the heart that keeps it from breaking and making you crazy. That's why the fastest people on earth are colored; most of us grow that extra layer of muscle."

Fannie's extra layer was her willfulness. And that is where the old man and I parted on the story. The rest of her seemed not to make sense to him. Then again, the old man never could figure out why what he called "a slightly different chemical makeup" made women inscrutable. In his world everything living was chemically similar to some other living thing, so it had to be understandable. His list of mysteries was pretty short, but women were on it. No matter what he thought, though, he certainly would never have said that Fannie probably enjoyed her reckless adventures more than anything else she ever did.

It was 1917, and at twenty-one, Fannie could have stayed home and been an old maid.

4

Dear Preston,

After four weeks in this miserable Georgia shit hole, I envy you, man, going into senior year, BMOC, or should I say HNIC, all the babes to yourself. Yeah, I don't know what this is I got myself into. I'm an E-1, which is below zero, nobody, here to get stepped on. I thought it was going to be a few weeks of push-ups, some classes on parachutes and jumping and shit, and whoosh! But I've been a sorry motherfucker since I last saw you.

First of all, you would not believe the redneck motherfuckers down here—they look funny, they sound funny, they act funny, and they run the place. They really get in my ass every chance they get 'cause I'm "different" and they think I'm snotty (I am) and think I know more than them (I do). Some of the other splibs look out for me, try to keep them out of my way 'cause I went berserk on one of them and tried to kill him. I didn't have the faintest idea *how* I was going to kill him—I'd only had a week

128

of basic—but I was going to kill this motherfucker anyway. They act like niggers can't talk, can't read, can't cut the shit.

Mikey, this blood from Florida, told me I was wound up too tight. I'd have to roll with the shit. I don't know, man. He told me my problem was I've never been around rednecks and I told him yeah, that's right. He couldn't understand it. He thought only the northern spooks got bothered about peckerwoods. He's a good man, tries to hip me to what's happening and how to get through the shit. He says it won't be so bad in Airborne because the stupid ones and the hotheads wash out. Brother, that might be me! And you wouldn't know me if you saw me. I sent my mother a picture—ask her to show you. I look like somebody blew me up with air, but it's all solid muscle. 155 pounds of Airborne steel, baby! Once I get in uniform and get all the gear strapped on I feel like a big tank trying to get up a hill. They feed you shit and potatoes and potatoes and shit.

I thought I had run away from all that American Dream bull, but these people are pushing that crap too. They say you can stay in here, be a "lifer" and get ahead like you can't out in the world. But I don't see niggers doing so goddamn swell in here. They tell me the niggers get washed out of OCS (officer candidate school), Airborne, all the high-paying stuff, and it's hard to find a blood who's made better than sergeant. But you know who all the volunteers are for the dangerous shit. Yep. Splibs.

Everybody's hoping to get shipped to Europe but the spooks say things are kind of nasty in Germany if you're colored. They're hoping to go to Asia—Japan, Manila. Korea sounds like a dog. Rumors are that the Airborne guys get dropped in strange shit— the COs don't even necessarily tell you where you're dropping into—special operations, they say. We were trying to figure out where the hell that would be. Russia? I don't know, man, sounds like crap to me. If I survive all this crawling in the mud and goddamn heat, I'll be a happy nigger. Drop me out there and let me go! Still don't see myself doing "freshman week" at college, going out to be all-American what? So I'm taking my chances.

Don't hurt all those females I left in your hands.

See ya on the other side,
Cole Man

P.S. Been hearing some mean sounds—Johnny Griffin, and Clifford Brown. Check 'em out.

"Do you always read other people's mail, or just mine?" Preston had me cold, reading the letter on the couch.

"You shouldn't sneak up on a person!"

"Yeah, especially when they're going through your private business! You got Ray Charles on so loud you couldn't hear a Mack truck come in." He turned it way down.

"*What'd I Say* is the greatest album ever made. It has to be played loud."

"You don't have to play it so they can hear it a block away. You must be driving people crazy playing it over and over like that. Give me my letter."

"Here, I've finished it anyway. He sure curses a lot."

"You'd curse a lot too if you were in the army."

"I wouldn't be that stupid."

"He has his reasons. You don't know anything about it." He put the letter in his back pocket.

"What did he mean he was running away from that American Dream shit?" I asked. He looked at me sharply when I said "shit." The record finished playing and he took it off.

"He doesn't believe all the stuff the folks say about getting ahead, you know, going to college, all that. Cole thinks there's no point to going around chasing somebody else's idea, you know."

"What do you mean somebody else's idea? What idea?"

"You know, like they teach you in school how the immigrants come to the great melting pot and they all become Americans and they can go from rags to riches—that stuff."

"Oh." I had no way of even knowing if any of that was true. I can't say that I thought that stuff had anything to do with me. I guess I thought it didn't. And that was ancient history anyway.

"It's white folks' stuff," Preston said. "Cole says it's like a big trap, if you believe in it you're going to get suckered. He was trying to tell his parents that when people talk about having the American Dream, they don't mean colored folks, and we ain't gonna get them to mean colored folks by going to college. He thinks his parents want him to go to college and be like white people and then everything would be okay."

"Is that true, or isn't it?"

"I don't know."

"Well, they all sure act like if we go off to some northern school then we've got it made—Dixon, the teachers, all of them." Preston looked a little troubled himself, as if maybe he'd been wondering too. He sat down in the old man's chair.

"Yeah, well, they figure it's the best shot we've got. It does seem like if you believe that being like white people is the answer then you're going to end up being weird. I mean, you've seen those friends of Dixon's who come back here and it's like they've been in one of those makeover hospitals in the Twilight Zone."

"Yeah, like the white woman who thought she was ugly and wanted plastic surgery and you can't see the doctor's and nurse's faces till the very end when they take the gauze off her face and she still looks like a white woman and they're all ugly 'cause they're on another planet, and she wants to look like them."

"Yeah, but her surgery didn't work," Preston said. "I'm talking about the people who look the same but think the surgery worked."

"What do you mean, like that poet who came here with the English accent?"

"Yeah, like that guy. Let's put it this way, Willie. You still have to decide who you're gonna be."

I was confused because I'd heard Reverend King talk about the American Dream, and I thought what it meant was that we should have a chance as we were. Since I didn't really know any white people, it was kind of a mystery to me why Preston and Cole thought somebody wanted them to be like white people.

We'd heard the preacher in the summer, when he came from Alabama to speak to a conference of ministers at the college. In fact I halfway thought that speech was the reason the folks had gotten so indignant all of a sudden about the schools. For me it had been a shock.

On that day, he was the minister I'd been assigned to as a guide, as part of my job that summer working for the chaplain. I had to take him to his room and then to the church, where he would speak. I didn't think anything of it since I didn't know anything about him. Rather dapper in his gray suit and wide-brim hat, the minister looked much younger than most of the other men there. He seemed to be a real gentleman, almost pliant—he seemed just to go along so. There was a sweetness about him. As we walked across the campus, he stopped every few feet to greet people who seemed anxious to talk to him. After a while I began to realize he must be famous, at least among colored folks. People kept saying, "Reverend King, we've been reading about you, and praying for you." The old man finally pulled my coat, told me his full name was the Reverend Martin Luther King, Jr., and that Reverend King had led the Montgomery bus boycott, that he was a new leader among our people. Turner didn't really have any leaders, and those that I knew about from school were people you didn't hear about anyplace else. Of course there were Booker T. and W.E.B. in the old days. Dixon had been a pullman porter for four years, so he used to mention A. Philip Randolph, who led the Brotherhood of Sleeping Car Porters. There was Roy Wilkins in the Negro papers, and *Jet* often had stories about the congressman from Harlem, Adam Clayton Powell, Jr., the flamboyant one. Still I couldn't say that I ever felt as if they were leading us down in Turner, Virginia. Leaders seemed remote. I had heard about the bus boycott, though, and the very idea of it had made the buses in Turner look so different, so dirty. And the boycott was shaming too because it meant we had been just putting up with something that other people had managed to stop.

It was one of those gruesome hot afternoons when you had to have a fan and a hankie for the heat. The church was packed with dressed-up Negroes, and the windows only opened at the bottom. In fact I'd never seen the place so full. People from all across town had showed up. The church was crowded with other ministers—city preachers gussied up in the latest styles and men from country towns, all in black suits, black suspenders, plain white shirts, and straw hats. Some of them wore shiny summer wing tips that looked as if they had air vents; others wore high-top old-man comforts with lace hooks. There were stout, prosperous men who wore diamond stickpins and monogrammed shirts, and there were gaunt backwater exhorters who seemed to have the third eye. They were serious men of God's word who looked at no one, but straight into infinity. Though most knew who Reverend King was, the electricity in the air sparked more from the conviction of his cadences than his fame, for they knew a mere stump speaker from a man who could preach. They knew if a man had the spirit or if he was a scholar of religion. Reverend King was a scholar who could preach the spirit.

I knew he was a scholar because my old man seemed so

pleased. I knew he was a preacher because he made me feel joyful instead of ashamed as he talked about segregation. He took away the shame I had even though I was a child and hadn't been anywhere. He took away the shame that I had inside me but never thought about—the shame that enveloped me when I had to think about how I couldn't go in the parks or playgrounds, the library, or the drive-ins, the churchyard now owned by white folks where my great-grandfather was buried. William Walker Tarrant must have been tapping his feet in my bones as I listened. King's speech had rhythm the way the blues has rhythm. For that matter, the speech had melody as well.

He told the story of Montgomery. And it *was* a story, too, full of heroes and heroines, and he called their names. He told about jail, and what he thought in jail, and how it brought out the spirit, and he took away the fearfulness of that too. He talked about Negro children like me going to the same schools as white children, not having the dilapidated buildings, torn-up books. I had never even realized that our stuff was so old because somebody else had what was new: the desks, the books, maps, and charts. I couldn't move.

It seemed as if we were there for hours, drenched in gratefulness, sweating and not feeling the sweat, and feeling more and more full till the whole church seemed ready to burst. The exhorters moaned amens, patted their thighs, and rocked. We all rocked. People witnessed and clapped, sang out and got to their feet trying to hear the words deep down. The house rocked and rocked.

I could still remember when I didn't know what the word "segregation" meant, when I hadn't noticed the white side of town and its seats at the front of the bus. It seemed as though I had just gotten big enough to go out on my own and see the town when it began to look blighted. I knew what "nigger" meant when white teenagers yelled it at me on the street. I knew what it meant when someone Greek or Italian who'd landed at the nearby port and didn't yet speak English came to the door of a shop and shoved me back to the sidewalk. I had never even wondered why a foreigner would come to Virginia and hate Negroes, it was just the way things were. If I had never before noticed COLORED signs because most places didn't have any accommodations for Negroes, I couldn't miss the many places I had never set foot in because I was colored, and never would.

I knew everything downtown or where white people were was named after heroes of the Confederacy, and what it meant when rebel flags were hung outside motels, or school bus windows. Before I'd gotten thrown out of the Girl Scouts for being "insubordinate" with Anne Taliaferro, I found out Girl Scout events did not mean little brown scouts in their sparkling green uniforms. On the one hand, adults seemed to be saying that all we needed was to get enough money to have Girl Scout troops and uniforms and Little Leagues, yet we'd gotten thrown out of a Girl Scout jamboree we tried to attend. We were invited to pay to go to a Girl Scout camp, but only when there were no white girls there, and also no horses, no archery, no balls, nets, or official Girl Scout activities. I knew I was only a Girl Scout in the mail, where they couldn't see me. But everybody kept joining and participating and hoping for the best.

Reverend King kept saying that things could change, *we* could change them, because it was right to change things. He said everyone who ever came to this country came to take part in the American Dream, and Negroes too must be able to have those chances. He said race was the greatest "moral question" facing the nation. As I got it, he was saying that what was happening with us, the American Negroes—and what was happening with us I didn't really know—what was happening with the American Negroes, he said, was the most important issue in the country because it meant either the country was something or it was nothing. If we were wrong, the Constitution was wrong, America was wrong. I felt as if I had never known who I was or where I was living. And I felt good. And I felt full of power. I closed my eyes and soaked in a feast of spirit. When he finished, the chapel exploded in joy, touchable joy.

Reverend King had made me angry and happy to be angry, really more happy than angry. He also made me feel that day that Negroes felt the same way about things, that the same kind of fire was in all of us. Preston and Cole made me feel it was temporary. They were more angry than happy, they were always talking about jazz and what beat poets said and how it was all *illusion*, man, *illusion*. The white boy should be more like the Negro, and it was all clear in the music, no illusion. I couldn't understand them at all. Martin Luther King was talking to me about where I went to school and how Turner was and I could understand it. For Preston and Cole, reality was a place they'd never been called the Five-Spot. Preston's last word on going off to college to get his "chance" was that he was going north to hear the music, and he wouldn't be hanging with anybody who couldn't get to that.

"You gotta go to Grandma's," he said. "Dad will pick you up later."

"Where are you going?"

"Out, Willie, *out*. Come on, I'll take you over there."

"What a drag. She doesn't even have a TV."

"That's the breaks."

I got Preston to stop and let me run into Woolworth's for comic books. Inside the store, colored women who got off work at four were filling the aisles, looking over the glass cases at the hair pomades and dark lipsticks. Racks of plaid and flowered oilcloth stood six feet tall in the aisle next to bolts of wallpaper. As I came past the women in their hairnets and plastic caps I could smell the pungent odor of the crabs they picked all day, the brine and dock smells of the factory. After making my selections I took a place in line behind several white women and waited for them to finish paying for their goods. I slipped out the back door with some women who were merely walking through the store as a shortcut to the colored neighborhood behind Raleigh Street.

"Aren't you getting too old for those things?" Preston asked when I got back in the car. I didn't know the answer to that. Everybody read them. I tucked the *True Romance* and *True Hearts* in my notebook and kept the Marvel comic out.

"Everybody reads them. They keep bringing out new characters."

"Like what?"

"Supergirl's the new one." I looked into the notebook at the covers of the romance comics—white people embracing. They were hardly Tonda and Nicky, but then Tonda and Nicky weren't having a romance, they were just being nasty. If they'd had comics about Tonda and Nicky, though, I would have got those too. The faces on the cover didn't look like real people, but I pretended I was the girl and that the boys were boys I knew.

The thing about *True Romance* stories was that they showed what the boys and girls were thinking, and when the girl was thinking that she liked the boy and that maybe he liked her too, he did. Sometimes she liked him and would think he didn't even notice her, and then it turned out that he was thinking about her. The boys were secretly in tune. This meant that other boys, real boys, could be thinking what you hoped they were thinking. Even if they weren't, when you read the comic you could make the real boy who was symbolized by the white, dark-haired boy in the book think things you wanted him to think. *True Romances* were great because they didn't waste time with all the other stuff boys might be thinking about other than you. *True Romances* were in tune with your secret thoughts, like alien beings and God. The only drawback was that you had to buy a lot of them because the stories in previous issues did not materialize. There was always the chance that the stories in the next issue would actually turn up as your own.

"What you got in the notebook?"

"Homework."

Preston snatched the notebook and shook it.

"Don't!" I screamed. *True Romance* and *True Hearts* flopped out. "You're going to mash them up!" He cracked up.

"What is this shit anyway?"

"Watch where you're going—you're going to run into somebody." I smoothed out my books.

"I can't believe you're spending money on those things." I stared out the window. "You're going to get warped reading that stuff."

"Nobody asks you what you do with your money. How about all those dumb peckerwood Elvis Presley 45s you've got?"

"If you don't want me looking in your little comics, don't be reading my letters, you hear?" I kept staring out the window, watching the tired workers walking by—heavyset women, some still in their aprons and light-colored uniform dresses. They were loaded down with shopping bags and packages tied up with string. It was stupid, I knew it was stupid. Stupid to be reading high school romances comic books. They came from a stupid world where there was no style, where white kids were named Dick and Jane, had dogs named Spot, lived on streets with names like Pleasant Street, and never said anything cool that you had to know about to understand. I didn't look at Preston anymore.

"Kelly Jean has the first *Supergirl,*" I said. "She has the biggest collection I ever saw. She only collects superheroes, though. She doesn't collect romances 'cause she doesn't like boys."

"What do you mean, she doesn't like boys?" Preston asked.

"Just doesn't like them."

"You trying to say she's funny or something?"

"I don't know. I mean, no. I'm not sure. She doesn't act funny. You know, I mean, she acts like a tomboy but she doesn't do anything funny. Do women who're funny do something weird to you or something?"

"What would I know about that?"

"Miss Morgan never acted funny around me till Daddy told her to stop coming to visit me. She's really nice. What was she going to do to me?"

"I don't know. Nothing."

"I liked her. I didn't know she was funny."

"Yeah, well, you don't need to be thinking about that stuff all the time—romance comics, Bea Morgan."

"That's all you and *your* friends think about, girls, sex. You think I don't know anything, but I know a lot."

"Oh yeah?"

"Yeah. I got a friend who's done it lots of times. She told me all about it."

"She probably lied. Who is it?"

"Forget it, man. Don't bug me."

GRANDMA LOUISA'S house was exceedingly dark. She never came downstairs that I knew. The story was that she'd gotten tired after all those children and when Charles Walker Tarrant died in the middle of the Depression she went to bed to rest for a few years. It turned out to be twenty-five years and she was now ninety-two. The house was still full of heavy Victorian furnishings: an old velvet-covered sofa and chairs with doilies hung on back and arms; a huge eating table and sideboard took up the middle parlor. Up in her back bedroom, Louisa sat propped up on three or four pillows from which she usually pulled her change purse and rewarded my visits with a nickel. I knew better than to ask her anything because she was almost always curt.

As I saw it, my function was to let her look at me once in a while. She would remark on how I looked like my father and that would be that. Louisa was not interested in children and her grandchildren were like visiting phantoms to her, phantoms with faces that changed slightly when one left and another came by. If we said too many nice things she started laughing and asked us in so many words to cut the crap. She had never convinced me she knew exactly which child I was, and she never touched me. Dutifully I greeted her and asked if I could get her anything.

"Tea would be fine," she responded. "Dixon teach you how to manage in the kitchen yet?"

"I guess so," I answered, knowing that getting her iron stove lit without burning myself would be a job in itself.

"Don't say you *guess* so, young lady. Either you do, or you don't, and at your age, Lord help you if you don't. The tea is in a tin over the stove."

The dark house gave me the creeps. The old pictures on the wall were faded almost beyond recognition except for a photo of all of Louisa's sons at Fannie's funeral nearly forty years before. I didn't really know which face belonged to which uncle: none of those living looked at all like the faces there. I put the water on and snuck back up the steps to look around.

Fannie's room looked like a cell in *The Nun's Story*. Louisa had moved everything out decades ago. Only a slim bed, a rocking chair with tired old pillows, and a few books were left. A handmade afghan was folded on the end of the bed. There was a photo of a family picnic with Fannie decked out in a brim hat and lace collar, and a portrait of her father sitting cross-legged in a high-backed chair. On her dresser sat an odd little wooden contraption. On one side it had a faded picture showing how to operate it: two hands holding the wooden sides between the palms. Once I held it like that the sides slid back and forth making a loud clacking noise. On the other side was a picture of a pickaninny stealing a watermelon. I couldn't imagine why. Louisa heard the noise and yelled for me to get out of there.

"Girl, I think I need a fire," Louisa crowed.

"It's not even October yet, Grandma. You burning fires already?"

"Don't be smart, girl. I've got a chill and I want a fire. There's logs but I don't have kindling." The fireplace in her room was clogged with last year's ashes. I swept them to the side and headed downstairs.

"I'll find something. I'm gonna get your tea." Making a fire was positively loony. Outside the back door it was still warm. Grandma Louisa's deserted yard had peaked mums trying to bud. In the years of neglect since Fannie or Louisa had tended the plot in the yard, the chrysanthemums had overbred and overtaken everything else. The vegetables that needed to be started fresh every year had long gone, and even the tireless strawberries that annually sprang up with a few quickly perished fruit had been trampled by the mums' tenacious, expanding offshoots. The flowers were pale and too fragile to do much more than provide a swatch of color where they were: there was no use clipping any to take in.

I looked round where the garden had been and found some branches scattered about, all green. I brought the tea and a stack of papers up to the room. I put the logs on the grate, paper under them, and paper under the grate and lit it. She watched every move.

"It'll probably burn hot for a minute but it will settle down."

"Yes, ma'm."

"Don't say ma'm, it's an awful habit. How old are you now?"

"Twelve."

"You're a handsome girl. I hope you haven't gotten stupid over boys."

"No."

"Boys'll make you stupid." She thought for a minute. "Then, so will a lot of things. I remember girls who were stupid over blues music—they'd go round and listen to that low-down stuff, sooner or later they'd run off and wind up whores. World War I made my daughter stupid. You seem to be alright— scared of your shadow, but you'll be alright. I didn't have very high hopes for you. Frankly, I thought you might turn out wild without a mother. I told Dixon maybe he ought to let some childless couple raise you." A flush of anger heated up my face.

"Let somebody raise me?!" Scared, I tried to sound surprised instead of indignant. It didn't work.

"Girl, don't you cut your eyes at me like that. Dixon said you had a temper. I see it in your face. That's that wildness I told him about. I told him to give you to somebody for your own good, and he almost did. I expect you didn't know about that. Dixon's too soft to have told you. He didn't know what to do with a little girl to raise. Didn't have the faintest idea what to do next. He asked that little social worker lady Mrs. Winston to take you. She's a kind woman, and her husband makes a good living—I think he works for one of those whatchacall'em, showrooms, for automobiles, doesn't he? You were so young

142

and he didn't know what to do about getting you dressed, combing your hair, and all that. Dixon doesn't know two things about managing a house. You were having nightmares, wetting the bed, and wouldn't talk to nobody. That lady didn't have any children, so he talked to her.

"What did she say?" The heat was making me sweat. I pulled off my sweater and hung it on the chair.

"Oh, I don't remember all that. I 'spect she talked to her mister about it. Don't you remember going over there to spend weekends?" I did remember. I loved Mrs. Winston. She had the face of a tropical angel, deep burnished brown with her black hair pressed in shining rolls framing her face.

"It just didn't work out. I think they were afraid people would talk. She didn't even want him to tell anybody he asked her to take you." My eyes filled with water. I started to blink, still watching Louisa's secretive old face for a sign of softness.

"It wouldn't have been the worst thing. You children are softer than we were, you don't understand about life. Many things are taken from you. My mother had most of her children taken off from her, except for my half sister, whose father was a white man. They didn't want to sell her and they didn't want to keep her, so they let Mama raise her and put her to work round the place. My mama was very hardened. Her children that come back and found her after the war, couple of my brothers—I didn't know them at all—they lived around nearby. The family never got back together really, even though we were all around. Their children livin' right around the corner on the lane right now." I'd never met her family, nor heard tell of them. I just assumed they were someplace else.

"The Tarrants didn't want no parts of their poor relations, so to speak. That's what they were, my nieces and nephews. And what all didn't happen to them! Everything happened to them. My mother she just couldn't put it back together. She stopped trying, just stayed in her house with my half sister till she died. Toward the end, one of her nephews used to make a little money selling bootleg, he'd bring her some money, but then he went to jail. You see, she used to tell me children don't belong to you anyway. That's some white folks' notion about white folks' children."

"How come you didn't bring your mama over here?"

"Oh, God. Your grandpa would never have stood by for that! My family was just poor folks and he would never have stood for his children's little poor cousins to be around all the time to see Mama or ask for anything. I used to feed them sometimes when he was out. Everything was for his children to be raised up better than us. If they came by asking for some work I would give them some change to do something for me, but not when he was around. He would just send them on. Half-pint thieves, he used to call them. Never come to no good. I wanted to try to make my mother comfortable in her last years but I couldn't do much. Women get wore out so, sometimes they can't even take care of each other. My half sister used to try to get stuff for her from the white man who was her father, and she worked cleaning houses to keep them going, but it was never enough.

"I tried to make Fannie see her life wasn't going to be no different from mine and the other women around, but she bolted and ran like a horse out the barn. That's how she got the TB. First it was the children, going to all the children's homes out there in Slabtown where they didn't have no clean water. Then, it was the war. She had to find a hospital to work at changing bed linens all day. The only good that came out of that was a doctor took notice of her cough and sent her back home to me. She didn't know what she had, and she didn't care.

"That was before the Prohibition, so Charles Walker hadn't stopped drinking yet. He didn't profess to have no deep interest in Fannie's foolishness. It broke him up, though, her laying in the house dying. Then Luke died over there in Europe from the mustard gas. Theodore was still over there. Dixon had to go get Charles out the saloon.

"He claimed he had a system for getting home no matter what kind of shape he was in. He would just come down the back road there and turn right and count seven houses till he was here. Of course it didn't work. One night he turned left and counted seven houses and passed out in Reverend Downing's flower bed. Dixon and Robert had to fetch him in the wheelbarrow after Mrs. Downing found him. Robert was still a boy; he cried all the way back here. Dixon never said a word, acted like he didn't even remember it. The poor man just didn't know what to do with himself during the war. He had plenty of work, especially from Burleigh and his sons, who were building everywhere. Still he got drunk a couple of nights a week.

"Watching her die was the last thing I let God ask of me. After that, I told him, I'm finished. When He wants to take me, that's His problem. I'm not bothered about living and I ain't worried about dying. He left me alone just like He forgot I'm sitting up in this house. And I've forgotten Him too. When my time comes, He'll probably forget to send the angels or sighing voices, probably just send Undertaker Murphy and his truck, if *he's* still alive. He's old as me." I was looking at the floor, the wide boards Charles Walker Tarrant had put in himself. She had been staring out across the room, talking to no one in particular anymore, it seemed.

"What's wrong with you, girl?"

"Nothing."

"Somebody's got to talk to you straight sometime, you know. Don't be frightened. You sure don't need to be scared of me. I'm an old lady laying up in the bed. There ain't nobody sitting in that chair but you. That girl sitting in that chair is all you got to count on, but that's enough. You have to appreciate that. When you get down on your knees praying for help, God's gonna look at you and keep doing what He was doing. He's gonna whistle the breeze in the trees, bring the sun up and down. The worst thing in the world can happen and the trees gonna look the same and the grass gonna keep growing under your feet. You have to get up and do like them, let the breeze rustle your leaves, let the rainwater quench your thirst. The sweetness of it is the sweetness of it. The roughness ain't nothing but the roughness. The trees got what they need. God didn't set them up so that they had to pray once a week for relief from being trees. Sometimes they get the rain they need, sometimes they don't. You don't need to cry over shoulda-beens."

"Why didn't Dixon try to give Preston to somebody?"

"He's a boy. Then too, he's older. I'm gonna take a nap now. You get your homework done." I rose from my seat by her night table, grateful to be leaving the oppressive heat.

"Oh. I have something for you." Reaching under her mound of pillows she found her red change purse and took out a nickel and handed it to me. I thanked her and turned to go. "And I have a couple of books for you. You're the last girl, you might as well have them. Somebody like your father or Undertaker Murphy might find them under the pillow and throw them out. Put 'em up somewhere."

One was a white leather Episcopal prayer book. The other was a small, beat-up leather account book with THE CHESA-PEAKE & OHIO RAILWAY COMPANY lettered across the front. Inside was the handwritten name of Vernon Talbert Taylor. Below was a note written in another ink: "Beautiful, now you have all of my love and the last piece of my life on the rails. Use it to keep notes of everything you want to remember to tell me when I come back—*to you*. Get better and pray the Kaiser doesn't get your boy! Love, Vernon. June 1917." The pages were filled with Fannie's handwriting. I put it in my schoolbag, went downstairs, and opened up *True Hearts*.

"Love in Doubt"

When Victoria came to the first day of school she saw her old friend Stewart had brought a new boy with him to school. She didn't want to stare at the startlingly handsome boy, so she just smiled and looked away. Her best friend Pattie rushed up. "Isn't that new guy really cute?" Thought bubble: *The nicest-looking boy I've ever seen.* "Yes," Victoria said. "Let's go introduce ourselves," said Pattie. "No, you go ahead, Pattie." Thought bubble: *I feel too shy, and I'm sure I'm not his type. Sigh.*

"Hi,, Stewart," said Pattie. "Who's your new friend?" Thought bubble: *I wish I could be outgoing like Pattie. I'm just too shy to introduce myself. Sigh.* "Pattie, meet Bob. His family just moved to town. Pattie's a cheerleader, and a member of the Glee Club." "I can show you around the school, Bob," said Pattie. Thought bubble: *Oh, they're going in together. I'm sure he didn't notice me."* Thought bubble: *Pattie's a nice girl but I wonder who her girlfriend is standing there. Maybe I'll have a chance to meet her later.*

The nightmare hadn't been around in a long time. When the sweat on my neck woke me up I realized it was the same as always. The old tar road, hedges in their winter skeletons, the house a smoldering charred gray frame. Child, cold, in a nightgown on the worn road.

"WILLIE?" SAID Mrs. Taliaferro. "Who fought the Civil War?"

"Excuse me?"

"Who fought in the Civil War?"

"Poor whites, mostly."

"Did Negroes fight?"

"Yes, ma'm. Some from the North, and slaves fought."

"Does anybody know what the so-called 'twenty-nigger law' was? Yes?"

"That was a law passed by slaveholders that said if you owned more than twenty slaves you didn't have to go fight in the war," said Suenona Murphy.

"Very good. Can you think of a modern-day situation that would be comparable? Let's say there was a war on, and people who owned giant farms passed a law saying they couldn't leave their farms. Give me another example."

"Businessmen."

"Okay, well, then who is going to go fight the war?"

"Their children?"

"Maybe. If they want to. But if the man who owns a giant farm needs help managing it, he might say he can't spare his sons, at least not all of them. And if the businessman doesn't go, who's going to go? Julian?"

"The people who don't own anything."

"Who's that?"

"Well, like the people who work for him, or who have small farms?" Smart *and* fine. He was tall and coppery, with long limbs and big, deep black eyes. He seemed very serious. He never looked around the room at the rest of us. I wondered if he'd noticed me yet. I looked to see if Dallas saw me looking.

"Good. So, this law is very interesting. After all, weren't these the people who were trying to protect slavery? If the war was fought over slavery and the people who owned large numbers of slaves weren't willing to fight for it, they forced those who did not have slaves to fight it for them. Doesn't seem quite fair, does it?" A hand went up.

"Yes, Timothy?"

"Mrs. Taliaferro, didn't all the white people have slaves?"

"Oh, no, Tim. Most of the slaves were owned by a small number of families."

"Why did they do it then, the people who didn't own slaves?"

"That's a good question, Tim. And we'll get to that. Barry, who was allowed to vote back then?"

"Slaveholders," answered Dootsie Burleigh, whose real name was Barry.

"How about their wives?" asked Mrs. Taliaferro.

"No, ma'm."

"How about Negroes?"

"No, ma'm."

"How about the poor whites that Willie says were fighting the war?"

"No, ma'm."

"Well, who voted to go to war?"

Dootsie was silent for a minute. "I guess those same guys that had the twenty, uh, Negroes." Everybody laughed.

"It's hardly a laughing matter, class. Lots of people have gone to fight for this country who never voted for any of its laws. You need to think about that. Julian, how did Negroes get in the war if they were slaves?"

"President Lincoln made a law saying that slaves who escaped to the Union troops could have their freedom."

"Good. Okay, class, you need to pick some current events topics for tomorrow's reports. Take a few minutes to look over the papers we've got here and figure out what you'd like to do."

The white men whispered to each other and stood up to leave. One of them, quite flushed in the face, asked Mrs. Taliaferro to step outside the room with them. Everyone stopped to watch them leave and the room became deadly silent. It was as if we could all feel the tension in Mrs. T's neck and see something steeling up in her face. She smiled stiffly at us and nodded for us to keep doing our work. No one uttered a word.

"You go to the bathroom, Kelly Jean," Suenona said. "Go and come back quick and then Fatboy or Tim can go."

"It'll look funny, she'll kill us," said Kelly. Kelly rose and left the room.

"THAT'S JUST not how it's done, Mae. I've never heard such ridiculous, unpatriotic talk in a classroom in my life. Insinuating that if a man is a businessman he might not serve his country like everybody else. My God! We're all Americans here! And what does all that have to do with the Civil War? Nothing! We don't teach the War Between the States like Russians. You sound like a goddamn Russian!"

"Pipe down, Herman," said Nathaniel Burleigh. "What he's trying to say, Mae—" Kelly passed the group, rounded the corner, and stood out of sight against the wall. "Just where did you get that material about the so-called 'twenty-nigger law'? That's not in our texts."

"I do some studying on my own. I have to supplement the books provided by the state because they simply are not adequate, and in the case of my children, the books are often biased."

"That material has not been authorized by anyone," said Burleigh.

"It doesn't have to be!" said Mrs. T. "If I had to get everything authorized that I give those children, they'd be months behind!"

"I'm sorry, Nate," Herman Shaw blurted out, "this woman should not be teaching in our schools—making up her own teaching materials!—she's not qualified to teach in public schools." He turned his back to Mae Taliaferro and spoke directly to Burleigh. "We just can't have this sort of thing. I'm surprised some of the good Negro parents haven't demanded her job. We have plenty of colored citizens who fought for this country who wouldn't appreciate this kind of talk."

Mrs. Taliaferro finally could not contain herself. "If they were from Turner, Mr. Shaw, they went without being able to vote in their own hometown. Do you seriously think Negroes never think about that fact?" Kelly moved to the girls' room door, opened it, and let it swing shut again.

"Well, they're not all hotdamn upset about it like you. You've gone crazy over this integration thing. Besides, if they go down to City Hall and pay the poll tax, which we *all* pay, and take the test like the rest of us, there's nothing to prevent them from voting."

Mrs. T started laughing. "You can't be serious."

"I'm deadly serious. How dare you laugh in my face! You're really stepping over the line. You know that this is not going to go well for you. You've been pretty damn daring, insinuating all kinds of dangerous notions right in our faces. Did poor whites vote for the Secession indeed! We give you state-approved textbooks that *plainly* outline that the war was fought over states' rights, and you ignore them, tell the children the whole thing was about keeping Negroes as slaves and this other red talk! You better start going by the book right now, Mae, right now!" Kelly opened the door again and let it shut, and moved slowly back to the corner.

"Let's go, Kelly Jean Johnson," said Mrs. T. "Get a move on. If I went by those books, Mr. Shaw, they'd be dead long before they came to work in your hardware store." Kelly passed the group.

"That's unnecessary, young woman," said Shaw. "I can see you're just going to be defiant. And I'll tell you one thing, anybody who works for me gets a decent job and is a good

American. You're not training children to be Americans. You're not going to be training *anybody* too long. And don't think you haven't hurt this effort we're making to accommodate you Negroes on this integration. It's not going to go down well for your side." Kelly went in the classroom. "We're through here." Mr. Shaw stomped off. Fatboy came out of the door and found Mrs. Taliaferro leaning against the wall looking up at the ceiling. He started moving fast.

"Everybody's got to go at once, huh, Donald?"

"Yes, ma'm," he said, practically running. She didn't move.

"That old man was calling her a Russian," Kelly reported. "Said he was going to do something about her job. She stood right up to them."

"A Russian?!"

"A *goddamn* Russian."

After school Dallas said he had to go to Walters' department store with his brother. Maddie had picked up Marian early for a doctor's appointment. On the way home I walked slowly behind Julian and Timothy. I pretended not to even notice them. The trees had begun to turn to brilliant golds. I gathered one or two leaves and several acorns, which popped apart in my hand, all the while making sure not to let the boys get too far ahead. And as I saw them turn for the corner store I decided to get a Hostess cupcake if I had a dime left. Otherwise, I was certain I had a nickel and I could get a Coke. Mr. Lucas's store had a funny smell that was always a shock coming from school. Maybe it was all the giant jars of dill pickles and pickled pigs' feet. The pigs' feet he put in wax paper and bagged for workmen during lunch hour. The counter was loaded with jars of pork rinds, and giant shortening and sugar cookies that must have been made three states away, from the look of them. Behind the counter down from the candy he had bins of cornmeal and slabs of salt pork.

While Tim and Julian got their nickel bags of Wise potato chips and some sodas out of the cooler, I tried looking around so that the boy wouldn't feel the intensity of my staring on the back of his neck. They went out and I found a dime for my Hostess. Since they were still outside as I came out, I sat down on Lucas's bench hoping they might stop, but they kept going, still carrying on their conversation.

It was as if they hadn't seen me. I got a miserable, aching feeling, and a tiny loneliness crept into me that I had never felt even though I was almost always alone. Being alone was me. Alone playing in the house, alone in my room just in my head, even when I was little just after my mother died, alone curled up in the bottom of the closet smothered by dress hems and crinolines. Sometimes then I would dress up in my sandals and my red Mexican jacket, all the special things my mom had bought me, and be alone in my room sitting thinking, and yet the feeling was more empty than hurting. It didn't matter if I sat outside Lucas's store all afternoon or went across the street and in the back door of the empty house and threw down my books and flopped on the couch.

June 18, 1917

I guess all those times I thought about being one of those blues women singing strange songs I never really thought I would feel like that. Desperate and all. I feel that aching feeling now, my body shifting from hot to a shiver. I brought it on myself I suppose that day with Vernon when I broke our rules. We were supposed to keep things at a distance, so to speak. And yet I don't regret a moment of it, not a moment of knowing I'm a ruined woman, not a moment with him but the sadness, I never knew I'd feel this sadness. I guess it was wrong. I was just so mad, that day my so-called employer told me there was no hope for me to get work in Washington. I just ran out of her house breathless. I wanted to kill her. I just wanted to kill her. I begged

Vernon to take me somewhere where we could be alone. I hugged him and threw my arms around his neck, quite embarrassing him, right there on the street. And I took his face in my hands and stared straight into his eyes. He took my hands away because then I think he knew what was in my mind. We walked to our place behind the marina.

We walked through the town where everyone was coming out onto Raleigh Street from work. Negroes coming out of all those white folks' places, the shops, the docks, off the daywork wagons. The plantation folk are paying wages but it would be "very difficult" for any of the bosses to see their way to letting their colored "help" have a decent job. Very difficult. And it would be very difficult for any of the Negroes to get out of the trap they are in, the back rent owing on shacks, the debt at the grocer's. We passed the grocery store where Father pays his men at the end of the day and stays to get drunk with them. I couldn't talk. I thought about our family, the house, assorted unrelated things like how the beams are awry under the first floor and how it would take the old man paying eight men to help him fix it. How Mama will cut up the boys' suits to make suits for the smaller boys till they all grow up and leave. We crossed the bridge and strolled along the stone wall till it rounded a bend. I asked Vernon if he knew how the Underground Railroad had worked around Turner, anything to break the silence, let him talk.

He told me they used the creeks at night. Coming out in little boats, moving silently past the docks into the bay. They rowed around to the bay side of the land, where the steamboat docks are, then they would meet up with someone with a bigger boat, a sailboat. Then they headed straight up around the Eastern Shore like the steamboats do. I told him how thrilling it sounded to me and he laughed and said I didn't ever think anything about what it might have been like for them after that. It's true. I think of them escaping and that's enough.

We were there kissing in our spot under the trees, in the last of the daylight on the river, when I simply looked at him and told

154

him what I was feeling. I told him I no longer wanted to be this kind of child-woman I had been, with a lot of hand-embroidered layers covering a body hardened by lifting children and carrying water, cleaning house, and working the garden. I wanted to be a woman-woman. The way my body felt I cannot explain. First I knew some kind of strong and muscular creature had been set loose from inside me. And I felt a hot vapor coiling its way through my chest and up my thighs. I pulled him to the ground and told him to put his hand under my blouse, to feel my body. I unbuttoned my chemise and, like a brazen cat in desperation, rubbed myself. I took one of his hands and flattened the palm against my underclothes, pressing it hard to my warm flesh, and told him he could not refuse me. I know you know, I told him, when a woman wants you, and I, right now, am that woman. Taking care that every part of me would be anxious and glad, he ruined me.

ONCE OR twice a week the old man headed out right after dinner to one of the citizens' group meetings. He said they had decided to ask some other folk to come, to get more people involved. The integration suit had changed his life in a way that Dixon didn't care for at all. He was a solitary man who already hated the endless meetings and the reports from the lawyers, and he said there were going to be months more. He didn't like leaving the house after dinner, much preferring to sit on the porch as long as the weather lasted. It was still unreal to me. I hadn't talked to him about Mrs. Taliaferro fighting with the Board of Ed men because I was no longer sure why he even cared if I was going to integrate the school or not. He was no doubt sorry that his daughter had to be involved. My problem was finding a current events project to keep Mrs. T from going off on me.

"That was a pretty good one you did on that Buddhist monk running out of Tibet."

"Dad, that was months and months ago!" The twenty-four-year-old god-king of Tibet and his escape from Chinese troops taking over his country had been a real find. I came home and gave the report again for the old man. The class was so fascinated with the story of all these monks escaping from their thousand-room palace that they didn't even ask me one question about Buddhism, which was good, because I didn't know one thing about it.

"So nothing interesting's going on in the world?" Not to me: Khrushchev and Vice-President Nixon meeting, totally boring, or Khrushchev's visit to the U.S., almost as boring; Hawaii becoming a state—ugh. The rest was totally grim: arms agreements, some military guys going to the Antarctic, the Taft-Hartley Act, whatever that was. The old man couldn't make a case for any of it. He left more irritated than before. He didn't want to hear any more about it but it was a real problem because the school suit was sending Mrs. T around the bend, and she was sending the class around the bend.

Kelly had discovered in an issue of *Life* a Negro woman writer who had a play on Broadway. Tonda had asked to do the new movies out but Mrs. T said no—she said entertainment wasn't news. It was pretty silly anyway since we couldn't go in any of the big movie houses to see them. Taliaferro suggested she write instead a profile of the Catholic senator who might run for president. Tonda made a face. Timothy said he would write about the vice-president. Tonda got huffy and asked Mrs. T why Kelly could do a play and she couldn't do movies, which seemed like a fair question. Taliaferro said Lorraine Hansberry's play, *Raisin in the Sun,* was "art," which was different, she said.

"Furthermore, children," she went on, "it is by a Negro, and about Negroes, which is real different from Hollywood movies." She seemed on the verge of giving a speech about how serious Negro art is when she seemed to realize that she was looking at twenty children who rarely saw plays or movies. She looked all shook up, as if she wanted to cry, and changed the subject. We figured the Board of Education people had gotten on her nerves. Someone mentioned that all the schools in Little Rock were being integrated now, but she said to leave that one alone for the time being.

When I called Marian to find out what she was doing for her project she said she couldn't talk because the parents' meeting was just getting started and already they were getting loud about the scene with Mrs. Taliaferro and the Board of Ed people. They were mad as hornets, she said, and Mrs. Taliaferro was calling the whites all kinds of sons of bitches and stuff. Marian was in her mother's bedroom, she said, reading a juicy book she'd found under Maddie's mattress, not working on her report. She said it was about slavery times, and it had slaves in scanty clothes on the cover and anywhere you opened it something violent was going on.

"Where do you suppose the Tarrants were slaves?" I asked. "You have any idea?"

"Oh, God, no. You ever heard any of 'em talk about their people being slaves? Old Louisa won't even say she's a Negro, she's just colored." She was right. The old man told the slavery stories that were funny. He never mentioned any real details. I asked who was at the meeting, and she said all the people from the picnic plus Reverend Hardy from True Vine Church, Mrs. Taliaferro and her husband, George, and her sister-in-law, the dreaded Anne Taliaferro.

It was hard to believe Maddie had even let George or Anne Taliaferro in her house. The Tarrants had never gotten on with the Taliaferros since anybody could remember, and no one carried the torch of that feud more steadily than Maddie. She didn't even remember what the origins of the enmity were; she said she just couldn't "take" George or Anne. Whatever it was, though, Maddie took it so seriously she drove us to the next town to another beauty parlor rather than let us get our hair done at Anne Taliaferro's shop, Chez Anne—"We make your beauty our business." Bill Alexander always said the only beauty in it was that Anne could make money getting into other people's business. Maddie was nothing if not particular about whom she gave her trade to. If she didn't like their ways, she didn't give them her money. George ran a four-booth sandwich place next door, and if we got desperate and snuck in there for a chili dog or barbecue sandwich and somebody saw us, we would have to say we'd been looking for somebody.

The Taliaferro clan had been in Turner for a hundred years, like the Tarrants. If you heard the Tarrants talk, it was easy to see they felt that that fact alone was a problem. None of them were really convinced the Taliaferros had been there quite as long as the Taliaferros *said*. Sure the Leighs and Spencers had been there. Dr. Blalock was himself about a hundred years old and he was known to have been there at least eighty years, but the Taliaferros had never lived in the old neighborhood, so maybe they had never really been in Turner back then. Maybe they were still on some plantation. Truth was, no one could remember hearing about when they came, or remembered when they weren't there. More likely it had to do with William Walker Tarrant's political ambitions.

During Reconstruction the old boy got caught up in the Negro convention movement when Negroes thought they would be changing the destiny of the state by voting. Tarrant supported a white radical who ran for state office promising to put colored men in office. One of the Taliaferros' ancestors, who was supporting a go-slow white man, saw to it that Tarrant and his boys were shut out of the convention, literally locked outside the doors. Tarrant never forgot the humiliation and never forgave. The bitterest pill of all he never mentioned to anyone but his wife, which was the fact that Taliaferro's candidate was a Burleigh, though that wasn't his last name. The Turner Burleighs had owned William Walker, his wife, and all but the last of his children. William Walker had sworn never to utter the name after the Emancipation and he never did. Old Massa Burleigh had fathered William Walker's oldest child, his wife's firstborn, whom Walker had raised as his own. Then Burleigh's son made some black Burleighs too. No Negroes were appointed to office when the Burleigh man turned out to be a Jim Crow man. Tarrant was eventually barred from the saloon he drank in, and from the church he attended downtown. He sold some land to the Episcopal church behind his house on condition they let him be buried in what used to be part of his lot. After the sale he discovered the pastor had agreed to abide by the new laws and barred him from setting foot on the property. When he died they sold his wife the land long enough for her to bury him and then bought it back. William Walker Tarrant said that Taliaferro had made a nigger out of him.

THE MEETING was packed. People were even on the floor of Maddie's living room and dining room. Aside from the Alexanders, the Johnsons, Browns, Botelers, Cleo Parker, Carter Charles, Tom Roberts, and three Taliaferros, there were two young teachers from the college—Bob Mollette and Danny Cobb—Bobby Robinson's father, Bernard, Reverend Hardy, and a friend of Maddie's from out of town. Mollette and Cobb were real excited about getting involved with an integration move, and Bernard had most likely been dragged there by the old man, probably hoping to turn the guy into a good parent by making him civic-minded. Reverend Hardy was apparently going to try to organize some ministers.

The folks in the new citizens' group harangued for a while about confronting the Board of Education on behalf of Mae Taliaferro. Most of the group wanted to wait until the board tried to take action against her, if it did. Bernard Robinson wanted to know which board members were at the school.

"Herman Shaw, Nate Burleigh, and another man, whose name I did not catch, somebody from the state," said Mae. "I only talked to those two."

"We can count on Shaw to make trouble," said Bill. Reverend Hardy thought it best to "lay low" till something else happened. Skinny, disheveled, and bearded Bob Mollette, wanted to know why the group had even agreed to have the men in the classroom for an indeterminate number of weeks. "You should have put a time limit on this observation business," he said. "They're likely to do this all year."

"That's probably right, Bob," said Mae. "We just didn't know how tough to be in the beginning."

"Do you have the group of kids picked out?"

"Just about. We're trying to get six, and in general we've agreed on four with the board. But we've got trouble with them about one and trouble amongst ourselves about another," she said.

"Who's that?" he asked.

"Well, I don't know if we should air all that here. It's a pretty sensitive matter. And all the parents still have to agree about their own kids—it's a matter of personal concern with them to think on it alone."

"Well, where else is it going to get aired, Mae?" asked Danny

Cobb. Danny, who grew up in Turner, had been a prized student of several of the people in the room. To him, most of the teachers were like family and he was uneasily becoming a peer. Like his friend Bob, he was slim, and most of the time wore sneakers, blue jeans, and tee shirts, signs of bohemianism, and to the older women, prolonged bachelorhood.

Mae hesitated to answer him. "I don't know, Cobb. I don't think it's my place to go into it."

"Let's have it all out there, Mae. These folks are going to help us, they might as well get involved in the whole business."

"Any parents here have objections?" Mae asked. No one spoke up. "Okay then, let's see. Ralph and Ernestine's daughter Kelly Jean has been agreed upon, and she and her parents have made a commitment to go through with it. Timothy Wilson has been agreed upon and the Wilsons are thinking it over, the same with Dixon Tarrant's daughter, Willie. Even though Julian is new to our school, we've asked Cleo to let him participate since he's obviously such a fine student, and she's said okay. That's right, isn't it, Cleo?" Though listening only distractedly, Cleo nodded. "Dallas Charles was an obvious choice from the point of view of his grades and temperament—we're trying to make sure we have kids we think can handle themselves without flying off at anybody—but we are very concerned about jeopardizing his father's situation at the shipyard."

"What does that mean?" Reverend Hardy asked.

Ralph Johnson responded. "It means without him getting lynched up in that yard, Reverend."

"It's a consideration," Mae said. "Any of us that they can get fired, they probably will, and Carter's the first one of us there to move off the line. We submitted Barry Burleigh's name in his place, but we've run against a blanket resistance from the whites on him. They've never said why, just no."

"You know what that's about, Mae," said Bill Alexander. "I told you what that's about."

"Bill's theory—and it's the only theory we have—is that they don't want the name Burleigh turning up in the papers." Everyone laughed.

"And in particular, Nate Burleigh don't want it turning up," someone said.

"I'm sure they don't want any confusion, or questions being asked," said Bill. The laughter continued.

"Bill, I think you've got a point there," said Reverend Hardy. "I guess the white folks in town don't rightly know there's any colored folks named Burleigh."

"Probably nobody but the old ones," said Bill.

"So what was the other problem?" asked Mollette.

"Well, we have not agreed on a sixth child," said Mae. "I recommended Amelia Morrow, but we have not even submitted her name because some of the other parents in the group thought it was inappropriate."

"Amelia Morrow—you mean Patricia?" asked Bob. "Isn't she older, or are you talking about Chookie?"

"Chookie," answered Maddie. "Patricia's the middle one, this one's the baby."

"Anyway, the main objection to Chookie," Mae continued, "was that her older sister Cassie is expecting a child out of wedlock."

"Oh my," someone said.

"The other objections I wouldn't care to characterize except to say that I thought they were unhealthy for the group."

"Uh-oh," said Cobb, "sounds like a little middle-class bullshit has crept in here. What's the problem? She's poor like I was? I know you all, now." Maddie, Bill, and Ernestine Johnson were starting to look uncomfortable.

"In some respects the answer is yes," said Helena Brown.

"First of all, we think the situation of the older sister brings the wrong kind of impression, the wrong kind of attention, to our little group. These children have got to withstand the closest kind of scrutiny. Their backgrounds will be all over the papers and it will just bring down the worst kind of mess on us. You know what they'll say. Secondly, her mother's got no husband, single woman raising three girls, and one of them pregnant. Need I say more?"

"And another thing too," said Maddie. "It's an advantage in a way that these children are all friends already. They're going to have to see each other through a lot. She might be isolated. The others have been playmates since nursery school and they'll stick together real tight, we don't have to worry about that."

"That's the part that worries me," said Mae. "I suggested Chookie for several reasons—first of all, because she fits all the criteria everybody thought were important: she makes good grades; speaks well in front of the class; quiet, well behaved; dresses beautifully, neat and tidy every day; good manners and not afraid of anybody, especially the snotty children who've been told she's not good company for them." She eyeballed the other women. "She's got her own mind.

"And let me say one other thing about all these children. They've come through with flying colors the whole ordeal of having these crackers snooping around them these couple of months. I had to look at that, too. The question is, who's *tough*? Some of them are just arrogant enough not to be bothered by the whites; some of them just won't care who's in their classroom, they'll go on and do what they've got to do. *All* of them have done what they had to do without coming to me when they were nervous or bothered. But they've been put into little groups already, groups they'll be in for the rest of their lives. It's important that this group represent everybody, as much for them as for the white people to understand: change is coming for all the Negro children. They're only handpicking them for *now*. They're not going to have that choice down the road. The kids, though, they have to understand too what the process means. If I'm telling them and you're telling them that it's for the race, we've got to mean it."

"That's all well and good, Mae," said Helena. "But what about the pregnant sister?" Before Mae could answer Danny Cobb jumped in.

"What about her? These things happen nowadays. We can't condemn the girl for her sister's problem. I think Mae has said it all here." The mood of the room had not swung with him. No one said anything for a moment.

Danny became animated. "I've been there. It meant more to all the people on my street that I went to college than it does to any of your families when your kids go. You've all taken that for granted because you went. The people on Chookie's street are expecting you to pick your own children, of course."

"Oh, come on now, Danny," Maddie blurted out. "Nobody gave you a hard time coming up; everybody knew what an exceptional kid you were!"

"Exceptional. That's the point. You have to be exceptional. Are you all willing to go on the line for an ordinary kid? I understand you want good students so they won't get frightened into flunking anything over there at Patrick Henry, but let me tell you, this is really about ordinary kids."

"This is why I didn't want to air this," Mae answered, "and I didn't want to be the one to bring these issues up. Nobody here is going to say we're wrong, Danny, but they aren't going to support the idea, either. I think we have to let people go home and discuss and think about it and come back. We've got one more week to get the parents to agree anyway, and if need be, we'll go with five. I just want people to search themselves a little more about it. Whatever we decide to do, it's a problem we're going to have to wrestle with down the road. I just happen to think that little girl will be a fine representative of our community."

"Do they have an adviser, somebody who's going to see them through every day of this and work with the parents?" asked Mollette.

"That would be me, Bob," said Mae. "They're all in my class. They may try to get rid of me for that very reason, you know, to throw us off track."

"Yeah. I would say that's pretty likely."

"Doesn't matter. I'll be there with them."

"I know you will," said Danny. "Good enough, then. Whatever I can do, let me know."

Maddie was flushed in the face. She felt as though she were running over with mixed emotions. She wondered why she had even let the thing get under her skin so much. Her little girl wasn't going to have to integrate the school on this round, and she had nothing against Chookie, really. She was a sweet little girl. Still, something bothered her about having folks tell her she was a snob. She went on and made a pitch to the group for money for the lawyer's fees and explained the committees she had drawn up.

Cleo was watching a woman she didn't know sitting next to Carter Charles. At first she had been sitting at a business distance from him. Then Cleo saw her scoot her chair closer to his and begin to chuckle quietly with him. The man was so handsome, women who met him sooner or later would drift to his corner of the room. Sometimes he flashed them his seductive smile, sometimes he didn't. He usually did not encourage them, which made them all the more persistent. The new woman reached out for his arm each time she whispered some other amusing remark. Her fingernails were long and curved and deep red. Cleo knew she wasn't from Turner. She would have heard. The woman would have to have bought her clothes out of town too—much too vivid for Turner, and highly styled. Her hair was long and waved and turned up at the ends where it met her shoulders. Cleo always kept her fingers slightly curled and her fingernails out of sight; she felt it was a real shortcoming that she couldn't keep decent nails. She watched them with an intense dismay. Finally she pulled out her checkbook to write Maddie a check, and turned to her to ask how to make it out.

"Just 'Turner Citizens,' Cleo. Can I put you down for a committee?"

"Sure, put me down to work with the kids, whatever you need." She asked Maddie who the woman was.

"Oh, that's Alice, she's an old girlfriend of mine from school. She's in town to visit the college. She's thinking about sending her daughter down here."

"Down here from where?"

"Oh. Washington. She's from Washington."

Cleo looked at her own hands as she signed her name. Thick and humble. Studying them made her feel as if she'd shown up at a dance in an overhauled, out-of-style dress. No, it was not a good evening for her. Maddie kept looking at her as if to see what was wrong but didn't say anything. Cleo could feel depression creeping up like sweat creeping into a hairdo. When Carter finally moved to the back of the room and spoke to Cleo she relaxed. He kissed her cheek, ran his hand down her back, and coaxed her out of the room into the hall.

"You look wonderful," he said.

She lowered her eyelids, tried to sound like a movie star rather than an English teacher. "So do you."

As they stepped into the kitchen, he mentioned Maddie's friend Alice. Cleo's head started to whirl. The meeting had worn on longer than the installation of a cardinal. Only etiquette and rum and Cokes had kept Cleo from jumping up and running out. If she acted funny, she'd figured, people might think something funny was going on. Still, Maddie had kept looking at her. Since they had been talking about plans to integrate the schools, she really couldn't leave no matter how she felt. You just can't walk out on a sudden rise in race pride, she'd decided, even if it might fade in a few weeks for most of the folks. They would know something. She called Carter Charles the C.C. Rider. The only person she'd told that to was Maddie. Maddie had looked at her then like, "Girl, don't even tell me about it, I do not want to know." But she had to tell somebody something. So she just said, "Maddie, I'm tellin' you he's the C.C. Rider. I hate to even run into him; he makes me go into a stupor like Georgia on Ray's mind. You know one night I ran into him after a dance and he sidled up to me and said, 'Do you play around?' I was so dumbfounded, and so mesmerized by that deep voice of his, I said, 'I don't know.' " Maddie had laughed and said that was a good answer. "Why?" she had asked her. "I don't know, it's like saying give me a reason," Maddie had said.

He would call sometimes when she hadn't talked to him for months, and say, "Hello, Mrs. Parker," real slow into the phone, and she could feel her garters tug. She would rework his words. What was it he said first? How did he sound? If he sounded on edge, it went through her. She cajoled, she coaxed, she dared him to warm up. She couldn't bear for him to sound like it was business, because they didn't have any business. No business at all. And if he was blue about business, why should she be blue about business? This wasn't love, after all. His wife could get depressed. Cleo didn't have no nickel in that dime. She had told him earlier that she would be at the meeting. She had tried to sound like a movie star. On the radio Ray Charles sang, "I got fifty cents more than I'm gonna keep."

But then the other shoe dropped. Alice suddenly appeared at the kitchen door and said to Carter with an annoying cheeriness, "Let's not forget that dinner you suggested."

"Oh, okay, I'll have to make my excuses," he said. "Why don't you say that you have to go back to the college, and I'm going to take you." Clearly he knew he was dead in the water. He looked at Cleo with a kind of twinkle in his eye, as if to repress a laugh, or to say, "Guess you've got me." Alice disappeared, oblivious to the dissonant clanging her voice left bouncing around Cleo. Carter suddenly became nonchalant.

"I hope you understand that I've got to do this. I kind of promised Maddie I'd help to show her around, and she just can't bear to go find a restaurant and eat by herself, so I told her I would."

"A restaurant? Isn't she staying with Maddie?"

"No, the college gave her a room in the guesthouse, and she decided to take it. So that's how it is."

"Yes, I understand exactly how it is." She smiled.

He spoke very softly, looking at her as if they were discussing taxes, arms crossed. "When can we get together, maybe you'll have another night free?" She wanted to laugh and cry at the same time.

"Yes, maybe I will." She smiled her most beautiful smile. She wanted him to have regret, to figure it would be a cold day in hell. "Look, I've got to go."

"Oh. You should stay," he said. She thought it sounded patronizing. "They haven't finished the meeting yet."

"Not tonight." Cleo headed back to the living room and fetched her bag, started digging for her car keys. She whispered to Maddie, who was looking at her, knowing that some disaster had struck.

"Look, I've got to get going—so many reports to grade, you understand."

"Sure, sure," said Maddie. "I'll call you later, girl, when I can talk."

"Okay, fine. I'll be up."

She got in the car, shut the door, and sighed out loud. On the radio Little Egypt was showing her ass.

> She did a triple somersault
> And when she hit the ground,
> She winked at the audience
> And then she turned around.
> She had a picture of a cowboy
> Tatooed on her spine,
> Saying, "Phoenix, Arizona, 1949."

RALPH JOHNSON was still playing *The Chase*, a side from 1952, every Saturday at noon, when the shop got wild with men lined up shooting the shit so loud he couldn't remember what kind of cut to give the head in front of him. But he knew Dexter Gordon would get respect. It cooled them down. The tenor man traded runs and licks with Wardell Gray, Dexter honking his entrances and exits, punctuating Wardell's smoothness, reminding him, as Ralph heard it, "You may be a tall, lean nigger but I'm the tallest, leanest, meanest mother you've ever heard." Wardell had to take it to a scream. The crowd roared.

"I play Parker in the morning 'cause he's so sweet, but when the rabble gets to roaring in here, man, I give them something to shout about—listen to it, man." The record skipped. "Hey! man!—who stomped in here? You wreckin' my side! I get a scratch on there, man, and it's your ass." He left the head in the chair and went to the hi-fi set up near the back of the shop, took

169

the record off, and inspected it. He replaced it with another and came back shaking his head in little moves from side to side. He was keeping time with Art Blakey. The mood turned easy. "All the Things You Are" flowed breezily past the now-quiet customers.

"Nice sound, Ralph, who's that?" someone asked. Ralph didn't look at the man but closed his eyes and bopped a little to the music.

"Hank Mobley, Johnny Griffin, Paul Chambers, Art Blakey, Wynton Kelly—*Blowin' Session,* 1957."

He stood over his customer. Blakey slipped into a whimsical meringue on the drums, slapping the rims with his sticks, and Johnny Griffin snatched the melody into a jaunty bop. The lithesome head of Jerome Kern and Oscar Hammerstein's tune became a filigree moving forward at faster and faster speeds. Griffin handed off to a young tenor player named John Coltrane, whose runs were wider, and more plaintive. To Ralph the sound was fat but agile, and a little rough around the edges. Ralph swooned back a little and rocked in place, eyes closed, his hand poised for his shelf full of shears and pomades, waiting for the sax to give it up so he could get his razor, but he couldn't move.

" 'All the Things You Are,' baby!" Ralph shouted. "They never sang it like that!" Everyone laughed. They were used to Ralph's bouts of showmanship on Saturday morning. It was part of the beauty of stopping in to get a shave or cut, even though they didn't have any choice in the matter 'cause there was nowhere else to get a cut.

"Blee-do, blee da—," he sang, imitating the trumpet's first notes. "That boy is only twenty years old, man. Lee Morgan. You b'lieve that?" Dexter Gordon was Ralph's man. Amid the endless LPs issuing out of the broken-up and reassembled bebop units of the early fifties, the guys who'd gone churchy or blues or cool, he'd found a man who was keeping the faith, the edge. Of course Griffin was keeping it too, but long, tall Dexter was Ralph Johnson's own discovery—a voice that spoke to him across the miles of whites-only country that separated him from the live sounds of jazz.

"Are you gon' cut my hair, nigger, or you just plannin' to dance over it?" the client said. Ralph daubed the man's neck with a little talcum powder and turned the electric razor on. He approached the man's head, grabbing him under the chin.

"Your head will look like all the other heads walking out of here—clean, glistening, impeccable."

"Yeah, impeccable, *that's* what I came in here for."

"Well, shut your mouth then."

Dexter helped Ralph to keep his edge too, there in the soft easy belly of his hometown where life seemed so complete, rolling along on slow hums and simple chords. Turner was the kind of place where you could go on forever, so long as you didn't try to force your ways on anybody else. You could even be different—all that was required was that you remember the etiquette people lived by.

He and Dixon had been pulled away from the town by some missionary teachers who'd come through during World War I. They were in high school, thinking about learning a trade, although Ralph's mother had given him a handiness with barber's shears from times when she used to trim folks' hair on the porch, after his father died. His pop would never have stood for it, having some of the old African ways of his parents—women should never cut a man's hair, he would say. Dixon already had a trade really, building, which he'd learned from his father, but old man Tarrant was very stuck on school and kept telling him to go on and learn something else. When the missionaries got hold of them they couldn't believe two Negroes could be so "smart, and well spoken." They went on about it till it got insulting, yet they had the idea to write to some northern colleges about giving these young men a chance. Dixon found out from his brother that they could work summers on the railroad and the adventure was too much to turn down.

Since coming home in the twenties, and giving up on finding work in engineering, he'd gotten all smoothed out. He put aside the anger of waiting on the white folks at college to cool down, put aside the anger of being mauled in locker rooms, having teachers laugh when he tried to enroll in their classes, being told he was too brutish to learn literature, how it went against his "nature" to concentrate too much on scholarly pursuits, how it was best not to try to turn a sow's ear into a silk purse.

Anger, he decided, grew in proportion to how often you had to see white folks. And once he decided to open up his little wood frame shop, he realized he would almost never have to see them at all. He could get through his days like a human being—get up, have a good cup of coffee, put on a fresh, starched shirt, stop in old man Brown's paper stand and soda shop on the corner, get some cigarettes, a *Jet* and an *Afro* for the shop, and go in peace to his work. Everything was right there at the south end of Raleigh: Dr. Wells, and now Dr. Roberts; Dentist Cheney; the insurance office; shoeshine; two churches; two funeral parlors; a taxi business; the Chez Anne beauty parlor; George Taliaferro's barbecue shop; and old lady Moore's dress and millinery. One of the boys he grew up with had a gas station on the corner opposite Brown.

Negroes had taken over that end of the street where the first one or two Jewish merchants used to have shops. In the lane across from Ralph's shop were a couple of joints where the men drank before the state went dry, and the only haberdashery left—owned by a Negro—after the last two Jewish tailors moved up the street toward the banks. Ralph could step in the lane and play his number in one of the joints and stroll round to the Knights of Pythias to put money in his account there. It was the closest thing they had to a colored bank, originally being a place where folks set aside burial money, ten cents a week. White people only came down their way if there was a fire or an election going on—not even once a year.

Yet and still, the more the white folks became just those tired faces down the street, the fuzzier his edge got. And he knew he shouldn't let it slip 'cause all the mean shit of life was still there, and he didn't want it for his kids, nobody's kids. If he didn't keep some of his hard edge he wouldn't know what to tell them, wouldn't know how to warn them not to be too trusting, not to let anybody talk down to them, how to tell them where to draw the line, whatever the line was for them. Or even why they should go out there and deal with the shit. That's where Dexter came in. He could listen to the horns and be filled with himself and know why Negroes deserved whatever chance they wanted. They could tell you the meaning of a moment in a sound like nobody ever made. The power of it made him feel they should all be acknowledged, celebrated, and left to live their lives the way they wanted to. The music was his own specialness in the whole wide world, his personal victory over the meanness of life, even though he had never played a note.

"Hey, Ralph man, ain't you gonna tell us 'bout the time you met your good friend Dexter Gordon?" one of the men asked in mischief.

"No way. Y'all done scratched my record. Ain't that enough damage for one day? Now you want to tease me 'bout the man." He'd talked so much about the time he *almost* met Dexter Gordon that it was a joke.

"I met the man in a club in New York. You know that, I told you that. You ain't ever been in a club in New York, so shut your mouth."

The thing was, though, that Dexter Gordon had spoken to him that night and Ralph was thrilled because he had never actually been that close to any jazz musician in his life. He'd literally bumped into him one night when he was in New York, standing hypnotized in front of Max Roach in a club. Ralph wouldn't sit down. He just stood to the side of the bandstand and, like a man possessed, watched Max play. He stepped to the side and almost threw his head in Dexter Gordon's chest. He looked up in the horn player's icy gray eyes and a tiny sharp fear sliced down his body like a stiletto.

Dexter smiled, almost innocently, his eyes saying, "Watch it, fool," but Ralph couldn't say a word. Dexter smiled again, flashed a big ring on his right hand as he reached for a cigarette, and said in a deep, gravelly, and impenetrably hip voice, "It's cool, man, relax." The horn player turned his head and lit the cigarette. He looked as if he weren't listening to the music at all, as if he was waiting for a bus. From then on Ralph Johnson knew that Dexter Gordon was one of the reasons God had put black people on the planet. To those who worshiped the fast-running hipness of Charlie Parker, he would always say Dexter Gordon made Charlie Parker look like a child of God—sweet, chubby, and honestly crazy.

Before Ralph let the client up, he splashed him with bay rum. For the man who didn't want to be *that* impeccable, Ralph had everything from Aqua Velva (for the young ones) to limewater (for the old boys). He had rows of exotic essences in clear, long-necked bottles with flowered labels brought around on an irregular basis by the traveling distributors from Washington, Baltimore, or Harlem. These days the men wanted to be splashed with scents from Puerto Rico or the Virgin Islands and carry out to the ladies an unadmitted hint of Harry Belafonte or of high rollers from Cuban open-air floor shows, where an after-shave had to be strong. To Ralph it was as if

Negro men were trying to leave his shop with the strut of Negroes from someplace else. Cigars, panamas in summer, open shirts, a little brazenness where they used to look so buttoned down for the job.

The young ones were stranger still, dressed like prep school boys with penny loafers and Arrow shirts. They kept their hair short and waved like the rhythm and blues singers. Ralph didn't like the look, too pretty-boy, too shiny headed. And the ones who came in with suspenders and their pants three inches too short on purpose—they just looked bad to Ralph.

"Oh, man, what is *that*?" one of the young men in the shop was asking. Ralph's assistant had put on Thelonius Monk playing "Body and Soul." The young man was not happy. "Mr. Johnson, I thought you was just kind of old-timey with the jazz, but that sounds downright weird. Sounds like that guy can't play at all." Ralph looked at him and the song went on for a minute.

"Boy, why don't you get your Julius Caesar haircut down the street?"

"Down the street where?" Everybody laughed.

"Anywhere down the street. Maybe old man Maxwell might give you that cut."

"You talking 'bout the white barber?"

"Yeah, you won't have to hear any weird music in his shop. I can guarantee you that." The boy became embarrassed as everyone laughed some more.

"I just don't get it, Mr. Johnson. The other stuff was cool, but this guy, he's goin' plinka plinka plink. The piano even sounds funny."

"You sit here long enough you'll get an education, young man. This next one here's 'Ruby, My Dear.'" Ralph sang along. The boy looked in amazement. "It's pretty, it's heartbreaking. I know you understand that. Nothin' strange about it."

"I'm more for heartbreak like the Flamingos. That stuff's too serious."

"That's only 'cause your heartbreak ain't that serious," quipped Ralph. With "Ruby, My Dear" striking its lonely crying notes, one of the men began to talk.

"Man, speaking of strange, I saw the strangest movie the other week. It was about the end of the world. You know, like if they dropped the bomb. These people were in Australia, the last place the radiation would reach if the bomb went off. And like, all the rest of us are dead, and they're just waiting for it to get to them. Everybody has to do what they're gonna do, you know. And Gregory Peck is in the navy, and he has to take a submarine to California to see if there's any life left. One of the guys jumps out in San Francisco, which is like a ghost town, and he goes and looks for his family, but they're dead. When they leave him he's sitting on a dock fishing and waiting to die. I mean fishing for what?"

"Fishing for his past," said a voice up by the window.

"Fishing for nothing," another said. "I mean, why not? What would you do if the world was ending and you were still alive?"

"That's what I was asking myself."

"Where'd you see that?" Ralph asked.

"Down to the Robert E. Lee."

"You see there, man? You go down to the white folks' theater and you come home with white folks' problems." Ralph laughed.

"I'd get it over with quick," said another man.

"I'd get me some pussy and get it over quick."

"Watch your mouth, there's a young lady in the room," said Ralph.

I was looking at the book Grandma Louisa gave me, but I could feel everybody look my way. The old man had told me to wait there while he went to the hardware store before he got his haircut. The men went on talking about what they would do if it was the end of the world and how they had been scuffling for all their lives and white folks were just going to blow the shit up anyway. Actually it was pretty funny because nobody could think of too much they could do except "get some pussy" because they figured out there wouldn't be electricity for long, or anywhere to go have a last blast, except the beach, if it was warm. And maybe the water would be too hot. Then they went into how they can't even vote for which "motherfucker that's gon' blow up the shit." Voting was definitely the new subject folks were on to—it was strange, I'd never heard people mention voting so much before in my life. Every time I looked up now somebody was saying, "Well, we didn't even vote for these no-good crackers," or something like it.

"White folks don't think nothin' about wipin' some folks out!"

"You ain't said nothin' there, Jim. They was just testing it out on the Japanese. Now they figure they can just blow the whole shit."

"The whole shit."

"Makes you wonder what we been here for."

"Yep, we been scraping all our lives. They been calling us stupid coons and stepping on by, taking all the money, all the land, hanging us up in a tree after we come back from the war, man. What it's all been for? Every time you look up now they talking about what if somebody push the button."

"Yeah, somebody come down from outer space and take a look, they probably say, 'Yeah, man, push the button. You-all done wasted the place anyway, we can't use it.'"

"We just been here to clean the shit up. That's all."

"What you wanna do?" Ralph asked. "You wanna run the shit?"

"Damn right I do."

"You gon' do a better job?"

"Damn sight better."

"Man, you'd probably start thinking you white and do like they've done. Black folks turned into white folks—that would probably be worse than white folks."

"Black folks? Wait a minute. Where you come from calling us black? We're Negroes, if you don't mind."

"You're black folks too."

"I don't like the sound of it."

"You like 'colored folks' better?" Ralph asked.

"Yeah, I like 'colored folks' better," the man said.

"Somebody colored you?"

"Naw, but if they did, they didn't color me black."

"That's the problem, man. Somebody let you run the shit and you'd probably get rid of all the shit with color in it. All the *blackness*. And you wond'rin' what you're here for. You're here to deal with *that*, for one thing."

"What you mean, man? I'm living it every day. What I'm doing *besides* 'dealing with it'?"

"Naw, man," Ralph insisted. "You don't really accept it. 'Colored folks'—sounds like you trying to get away from the point." He leered at the man. "*Africa*," he said, glaring, and then laughed. "The *jungle,* the *black* continent. You jungle bunnies be trying to pretend it never happened."

"Well, Ralph, man, let me tell you. Long as I can remember they done told me I come out the jungle. I never seen it, I don't know 'bout it. The part that troubles me is I don't know nothing that come out of the jungle. Rubber is all they ever tol' me, rubber and woogies."

"That's 'cause you don't know."

"You know somethin' come out the jungle?"

"The point is don't none of us know what mighta been

happening where *we* come from. There were great civilizations over there, I hear."

"You hear? You went to college. Did you hear 'bout them civilizations in college?"

"Naw, man, but I didn't hear 'bout you in college either, and you sitting here in my chair big as day. Most of what I know about life they weren't teaching in college. Get real for a minute, my friend—if Negroes had done something, do you think they'd tell us about it, or just leave us alone so we can keep doing this work for these folks? The times we've been here for, there won't be no record of them, just like there ain't no record of the times your folks remember. Man, you hear that music? You been in a church full of Negroes when the spirit come down?" asked Ralph.

"Yeah, man, so what?"

" 'Yeah, man, so what?' You been at a dance when they played 'Take the A Train' and everybody poured onto the floor? You seen these young kids running in the backyard when they should hardly be able to walk? You heard that Reverend King preach that time he was here? You ever just been in a room where ten black people sat together and hummed, talked, moaned, or laughed? You been here for the feast, man. If you ever put your feet under our table, you have been at a feast for the eyes, the ears, and the soul! You have shivered and cried when some sister got up and sang over your mama's passing on, or the fishermen threw you in the boat and showed you how to haul in a net. Man, you go somewhere else and see what *that* shit is about, you'll be glad you were here for the feast. The feast. You been here for the feast when one nigger stood up in a white man's hotel and asked to buy a newspaper and got arrested. You have been at the feast every time one nigger took a bullet for the rest of you, or 'cause he looked like you. You have seen the best a human being can be, old and smart with years or young, dead, and floating in a Mississippi swamp after some woman give him a piece of bread to keep running with. You been here to see Satchel Paige stand up and look like his slave ancestors into the distance before throwing the fastest ball that was ever thrown. You been here to see your woman walk down the front stair in the finest yellow dress you ever saw and look you in the eye and say, 'Come on, honey, we gonna be late if you keep staring.' "

"Or take you upstairs and take off the prettiest yellow dress you ever saw," one of the men butted in.

"Ralph, shut up, man, you ranting." Everybody laughed. "This end-of-the-world crap has made you too serious."

"Nothin' serious about it, really," Ralph said. "It's everyday stuff, man. That's what you missing, man. The feast is everyday stuff. You sound like this boy talking about the music sounds funny. You got to be a man to live this everyday shit, and you got to stay a little bit crazy. I don't like this punk shit—'It's all been a waste'; 'What are we here for?'—you're here for nothing and everything." He had not really let go of his mood. But he returned to the hi-fi and turned the music up so the talk would quiet down. The strange tones of the piano sounded lonelier than before, heartbreak—just like Ralph said, serious heartbreak.

As if he'd heard my mind say "heartbreak," a man in the shop started talking. "You can have heartbreak for yourself, but then you can have heartbreak for more than just yourself, too. Ralph got the general heartbreak," he said, chuckling a little under his words. "Me, I got the *specific* heartbreak—the kind you get when you got a good woman and you meet a woman that ain't *the* woman, but is *one* of *the* women and what can you do? You can't leave your happy home for a woman that's only one of the

180

ones, but you still have that feelin' like you'd like to leave for just a little while."

"That's the sometime woman you talking about," said another.

"Naw, it's the in-between-time woman."

"In between what?" the young boy asked.

"Everything," the man said, "what Ralph's talking about, everything. It's the in-between heartbreak."

"The lonely spaces."

"Yeah. The lonely spaces when that gal sits across from you at a table and smiles like she never seen a man like you in her life. Yeah."

"Well, what do you do?" the young boy asked. "When you meet the in-between woman?" The conversation had moved around to a topic he was obviously interested in.

"You order another cup of coffee and talk to her," said one of the men. Laughter again.

"Then what?" the boy asked.

"Then you in trouble," another answered. My old man walked in and the men greeted him warmly, calling him Professor, or Doc, to tease him. He told them he hoped they hadn't been exposing me to any of the crude side of men's talk, and they assured him they'd been discussing "philosophy."

The old man laughed. "That's what I mean," he said. I wondered if he'd have anything to say on the subject of in-between women, but then, I knew he wouldn't talk about it in front of me. Besides, I was trying not to pay too much attention to anything he said. I had still not quite done with what Grandma Louisa had said to me about his deciding to give me away to somebody after my mother died. I was still chewing on it. Every time I looked at him I got angry, and I had made up my mind to wait till the exact right moment to tell him what I thought about it. I couldn't understand it—I would never understand it. That was like a vow—I would never understand it.

The talk turned to the integration business and how the Board of Education had decided for the time being to leave my teacher alone after all the parents signed a letter saying they would take some kind of action if she was removed from the classroom. They felt a victory had been won, but it never seemed like a big deal to me. She hadn't said one thing that wasn't completely ordinary for Mrs. Taliaferro. Everybody knew Mrs. T took no tea for the fever. The men who'd been in my classroom hadn't seen her when somebody got her goat. Since I'd heard most of it before, I returned to my book.

The volume Grandma Louisa had given me was Aunt Fannie's diary, kept from the spring of 1917 until she died. It was stuffed full of clippings from ladies' magazines—advertisements for "Mr. Edison's wonderful phonograph—$1 after free trial"; housedresses for forty-seven cents; Jap Rose soap; Vapo Cresolene to help whooping cough, spasmodic croup, bronchitis, etc. Evidently Fannie liked to order all kinds of things in the mail. The clippings themselves were peculiar, forever harping on being ladylike, and having skin like Mary Pickford. At least the stuff was cheap.

There were several ads with the same words at the top— BECOME A NURSE—that promised, "We have trained thousands of women in their own homes to earn $10 to $25 a week—send for *How I Became a Nurse.* . . ." She had clipped fashion articles and drawings of the latest styles—"the barrel skirt," which ballooned above the knees and then narrowed down to the ankle, "to vary the monotony of the straight silhouette." It looked pretty awful but most of the other clothes were worse, big in the waist like maternity clothes, straight up and down, frumpy.

Fannie's account of her days was largely uneventful. She stayed in bed, read many books, waited for letters from Vernon. He sent wonderfully cheerful letters anyone would wait to receive and items from papers everywhere he went. One of these seemed real strange: an article from a paper in England about some man named Jan Christian Smuts giving a speech on how white people should deal with the African natives in South Africa. I couldn't imagine why he'd sent it to Fannie. Smuts—what a name—had talked about how they—whoever "they" were: the British, the South Africans?—were going to conquer central Africa and the "enormously valuable military material" that lay in the "Black Continent." Mostly, though, the story said the man had talked about how the black and white races had to be kept separate. Vernon had marked a quotation on the second page and written on the side, "Sound familiar?":

> Natives have the simplest minds, understand only the simplest ideas or ideals, and are almost animal-like in the simplicity of their minds and ways. . . . We have realised that political ideas which apply to our white civilisation largely do not apply to the administration of native affairs.

Vernon had been in England only a few weeks and was shipped to France. His letters sounded eager for their arrival at wherever it was to be that they would see the fighting. I wondered what Fannie wrote back to him, if she wrote him. What clippings would she send? Maybe she would mention things in her diary like the fact that the minstrel shows stopped coming around and people were caught up in a new dance craze. She was very disappointed that there was nowhere to hear some of the new music people had told her about that was supposed to be real sinner's music. The old man signaled me to follow him out the door and silently we headed to the co-op grocery store.

"Your brother told me that since you didn't get to read his mail today I should tell you that Little Cole wrote and said he finished basic training and was shipped to Fort Bragg to airborne school."

"What's that, pilot training?"

"No. What they call jump school. They teach them to jump out of planes. I don't know why he wanted to do that instead of going to college, but I guess it can't hurt."

"Yeah."

When we got to the store I told him I had a headache and I didn't want to go in and help him do the shopping. I knew he hated doing it and liked to have the company. That was too bad, though, because I wasn't going to help.

September 25, 1917

Today I had my first outing in weeks. I rode with Alabama Burleigh to take some washing back to some of her customers. It was very warm and I was glad to get some air. She just had three stops to make and her brother had offered to take her in his wagon. At one of the old farm places I had the most astonishing experience. The maid there, a girl from round in the lane, said the family was in an uproar and had gone off to the train station or somewhere because one of their daughters had eloped. The maid said she'd snuck out during the night through an old secret passage in the house that went to a door hardly anyone knew was there. We were so intrigued we asked her to show us where it was.

She told us we couldn't get there from the ground floor, that first we would have to go upstairs. She said she'd been cleaning the gal's room right along and never knew a thing about it. Someone told her they used to hide slaves through the passage.

We climbed the front stairs of the ancient farmhouse and came into the narrow hall where the bedrooms were. Alabama asked her why they would hide slaves. The girl said, "I don't rightly know. One of the workmen told me that wasn't even true. That they used to hide them*selves* from the Indians way back." I thought this was very funny even though she said the Indians did come around killing folk in the old days.

She lifted the latch on a back bedroom door and we were in the prettiest room I ever saw. Little white curtains in the windows under the eaves, a grand four-poster, colorful hooked rugs on the floor. Everything else white. White dotted swiss coverlets, curtains, draping round the bottom of the bed, lace on the dressing table, lace pillows thrown around in the armchair. Then the girl went into the young lady's closet! We were astonished and asked her what she was doing. She said that was the way. She pushed back the clothes (handsome linen dresses, silk waists and such, lace and more lace) and knocked at the back wall of the closet. On the sides she found some tiny latches and turned them and then banged again and out popped the whole back wall of the closet!

Beyond the wall was a beautiful little stairway, perfectly polished. We climbed down what seemed to be two flights instead of one but when we got to the bottom we were clearly only at ground level, for there was a door and the bushes outside! The maid told us evidently they had taken away the stoop and the ledge over the door and disguised it as a window, planting bushes in front of it, etc. The girl said she'd been dying to look down there ever since a workman swore to her there was a hideout in the middle of the house but you couldn't get to it. Behind us we found a tiny hatch door in the wall. Showing no shame at all, we pried it open and peered in. At first it looked like a tiny scrubby little hole, and then Alabama got down on her haunches and put her head in there. She said, "Oh, my God, it's a tiny little smokehouse or something," and disappeared inside. All we could see of the floor was soot and what looked to be a few ancient eaten corncobs. A good place for rats, I thought. Then I leaned in further and I could see her feet—she was standing up inside.

Then I could no longer resist and started to crawl inside. Alabama shrieked for me not to exert myself and said furthermore that the air in there was foul (and it was), but in I climbed. Inside the space was like the inside of a chimney or something, a brick teepee. The bricks were laid in tiny leaning steps upward, virtually resulting in walls that leaned as they went upward to the sky and narrowed. The walls were black with soot and the ground covered with those molding corncobs. While I could stand up in the chimney, I would not have been able to stretch out in the cramped space. Above my head hung a sturdy plank of wood with fearsome hooks hanging from it. "Hams, they must have hung hams in here," Alabama said. We couldn't make sense of that since they have a smokehouse. After a minute I felt I couldn't breathe at all and crawled out. Never could I have stayed in such a space even a few hours, much less any number of days. I couldn't believe slaves would have hid there for any time, but then of course I know they would have. It was like being at the bottom of a well with only the smallest hole winking at the sky way above your head, a hole one could never squeeze through. Two arms might be able to wave round in that opening, no more. And deep inside the center of the house like that, how would you know anything of what might be going on? One could not hear through those bricks, only lean against the little hatch to the abandoned stair. When I crawled out my skirts were covered with soot and I couldn't imagine how to explain it to Mama without bringing an end to any hope of further outings and some kind of banishment upon Alabama. We tried to shake out our skirts into the hatch and then replaced the wood paneling. Then, fleeing back up the steps and through that eloped bride's closet, I had time to wonder why she did not take those clothes with her.

By the time we got home I could not breathe at all. I had told

Alabama and her brother to go on, and I had to crawl up the steps—that is till Mama came running and found me. I felt so exhausted I thought I'd never stand on my own feet again. She was so frightened she was speechless and of course it was the end of my outings, not because she said so, but because I no longer have the strength even if I had the will. Often if I try to get up quickly or move too much it's as if something had sucked all the air out of the room and I find myself standing in a closed-up box, something like that chimney space. Some days the whole world becomes such an airless space as that. I know the lid will shut down on me before the coffin. The air will just close off and leave me.

IT WAS dreary and gray in the parking lot and getting chilly. People hauled brown bags into their cars and went. Other cars came. It was boring, humdrum, nothing more going on beyond the Saturday chores everyone had to do. White women and their children stared in the window of the Buster Brown shoe store, lined up in front of the gray movie house with the chrome arches above the marquee. Cartoons and an adventure movie were playing. There was no sign out front but everyone knew only whites went in there. And only whites went to the bank across the road, the dentist's office, even the drugstore. It was tidy, neat, complete. The co-op was located in a white area of town, where blacks came only to get their groceries, which the white teens never hauled to their cars. There were lots of neatly kept garden apartment buildings around the shopping plaza, all fairly new. Even though Fannie's Episcopalian lady lived out this way, there were no signs left of Fannie's stories—not even in her room over at Louisa's house. The town she talked about was in another world, a place of other names. The stores and plantations, wagons, even the white women's clothes and bed linens were unimaginable. Fannie's wonderings were too far away, fairy tales where a girl could live on her dreams because everything else was laid out before her. Something turned over in me like the day I'd turned around in my room and let my eyes rest upon my favorite doll and discovered it was dying like something that had lived.

It was a doll someone had made of Josephine Baker, with a peacock-feather headdress, a fabulous stole of golden orange feathers strung from a necklace of little glass stones, a velvet dress. That day as my eyes fell on her I felt a shock of horror as I realized the golden feathers around her neck and shoulders had been stripped down to their spines, as if they had been gnawed by some small beast with sharp teeth. Nearing her, I saw a yellowish powder all over, like pollen encrusted in drips all over her dress. I felt sick. In a panic I went and got scissors and cut away the feathers, letting them fall into the trash. The pollen was still encrusted underneath the stones.

I forced the scissors into the stitches and snapped off the band of stones. As I pulled it free I found tiny white wormlike things clinging to her cotton neck, maggots maybe? I didn't know what maggots looked like. I dropped the doll in the trash. I wanted to throw up. What had infested the doll's clothes? It was as if the feathers had been alive all along and eaten themselves, leaving only the bones. I was afraid to wipe them off. Frantically I picked up the other dolls, swiped their skirts clean, almost beating them clean of the yucky stuff.

Even so I hadn't been able to bear the idea of throwing her away. I picked her out of the trash can by one foot and yanked the velvet dress off. Her face was still a bright jewel, tiny shells for round eyes, blue feathery lashes, a button mouth. I took the scissors to her fancy headpiece and cut it away. Underneath, the dollmaker had left one little braid of cotton across the crown of her head. My favorite doll was gone, the fabulous Josephine with jeweled wrists and rainbow crown. Now only an absolutely plain, black cotton rag doll with sparkling eyes, she looked beautiful in another, simpler way: long skinny legs, straight arms, rounded hands, and perfectly round head. And when I looked at her face, I could still see all the rest the way it was. Only now it was just in my head, my eyes studying a black rag doll that used to be dressed like a living legend.

The old man came back from the grocery shopping somewhat disgruntled and announced that we had to talk about whether or not I was going to be one of the kids in the integration group. I told him I didn't care and he didn't say anything else. At home after we unloaded the bags he started again with the same subject.

"I don't care. If you want me to do it, I'll do it. I just don't care anymore."

"I'm afraid this is one thing you're going to have to care about, one way or the other."

"I think it's going to be horrible but it seems like I don't have any choice. I have to do it, don't I, Daddy?"

"No, you don't have to do it, Willie. But it is the right thing to do. That's probably what bothered me all along. If it wasn't the right thing to do, we wouldn't have had to think about it too long, would we?"

"I don't know."

"It's like this, your gut tells you right away when a thing is wrong. My gut told me this was trouble, that was all. Not that it was wrong. It has to be right for us go after our due, what is given us by the laws of the land. That's the easy part. I just didn't know if it was the right thing for me to let my *child* do it, instead of finding another way. I still don't know if it's right to let you be exposed to danger. But these are also the cards being dealt to you. Your life is not going to be what I may want or imagine or dream. Your life is what comes to you. That's one thing I learned when your mother died. I would never have imagined we would lose her, and certainly not so young, when you were such a little girl. When your mother died I realized my expectations were foolish and I could not shape your life. Your life shapes itself. I have good intentions, but so what? I can't make them all happen." My chest felt tight with anger, my neck tight enough to pop. Who was he kidding? Of course I still had to do what he thought I should. Now and forever maybe. What did he mean, he didn't shape my life?

"It's what the old folks used to call having your trouble early rather than late. You're having yours early. You're gonna have trouble anyway, they say; some have it young. That's the way it's been for you, Willie." He smiled. "Maybe if you're lucky, you'll skate through the rest of it. Of course, trouble is a resilient thing, bounces back and it's generally no use to think you're going to get rid of it. But then, what do we know?"

Obviously he'd thought about all this for some time. Some of it was skating past my ears like the wind. I wanted to hit him hard and stop him. I looked at him hard. "Grandma told me you tried to give me away. Why didn't you keep trying?"

"Oh, Willie," he groaned, obviously unhappy that Louisa had blabbed. He looked pained. "It would've been wrong, that's why, even if I could've done it, and I have no idea if I could. I felt pretty desperate." I was feeling something turning over in me again. I knew he was telling me something true, but I didn't really want to hear it. It dug too deep. "I couldn't accept her dying. Couldn't. And I couldn't accept my own situation either."

I couldn't help myself. "You mean having me to raise?"

"Yep." He was so matter-of-fact. "But those were the cards, weren't they?" Too matter-of-fact. He wasn't going to back down. "The cards dealt me and the cards dealt you. You had to scuffle by with me and I had to get used to having a full-time child." His good humor returned. "We haven't done so bad, have we?"

"Nah."

"I may even get you to speak English instead of making noises."

"Yeah."

He was honest but it didn't make me happy. I didn't know how to feel. I went to my room, shut the door, and lay down to have good cry. I guess I let him hear me cry.

I have learned to travel in my head now. I travel with Vernon sometimes on freezing cargo ships loaded with frightened men. Sometimes I travel on my own, simply sitting in parlor cars coursing along his old rail routes. Sometimes I walk with a knapsack from Virginia to Washington, into Maryland, sometimes on to Pennsylvania. It has been several months now that I have been confined to wandering about the house (when I am able) and resting in this bed. I believe that I have conquered the anger I felt upon being returned like a wasted runaway to my mother's arms. She has indulged me beyond her means for softness and gentleness, and yet at first I was so overwhelmed by disappointment that I performed mercilessly. I grieved at what seemed the loss of my very self. I behaved horribly toward her. She became for a time the center of my raging heartbreak.

The disease wore me down, though, and I soon became grateful for her scalding baths, warm towels, her plates of baked fish, plain vegetables, and spoonbread, and the regularity with which she would have some of the boys come move me to whatever sunny spot she found near her in the house. She keeps a daybed for me in the kitchen, pillows on the sofa, which she had relocated by the front windows so I can look out upon the street. Mother behaves as though I'll be going out any day, that it is only for want of a new dress. She fills the day with little pleasantries, dreaming up the marvelous dresses we could make

if Mr. Woodson will order some yards of cotton in the new
China blue.

FANNIE'S BOOK got on my nerves. I should've just told the old
man I was scared as hell. I didn't want people throwing rocks at
me, or to be around soldiers with guns, or screaming rednecks.
I liked my school, my friends. I didn't know what to do. I didn't
know where *my* mother had gone with all the little pleasantries
of a day alone with her. I didn't know where the big hugs and
embraces had gone or why. It hadn't been enough for her just
to say she wasn't feeling well. One day she couldn't lift her left
leg. One side of her face slowly fell. One day she couldn't see.
Another day she couldn't move out of the bed. And one day she
didn't know where she was. She never gave me any clues, never
told me it would be okay. Or if she did, I couldn't remember.
She never said how not to be scared when you're scared. And
she must have been scared too, but she never said anything. If I
couldn't sleep, she'd stroke my head.

I didn't know why I had never cried about it or told anyone
why it was so awful. What if I couldn't do all this stuff everybody wanted me to do? I had never just gone to the old man
and given up. I'd never clung to him and cried. I tried to stand
up from my bed, but the sobs escaped like shouts and my body
seemed to be shaking out of control, falling. I crawled into the
closet, mashing my knees and elbows on the shoes and stray
books on the floor of the closet. What if I couldn't do it? I was
alone. There was no coming home to die or even to be sick.
There was not much left of my mother in my head. It made me
feel really guilty. Nothing there except the shadowy figure of a
warm smiling being I ran to every day as she came up the street
from work. Not the sound of her voice. That was gone. No
little pleasantries, not a conversation, not a word, only "mama"

was left where all that had been, and a coldness around the arms and shoulders, exposed skin never held. I pushed the shoes aside and dug for the bare and pitiful rag doll I'd ditched there after cutting off her rancid feathers. She was lying there somewhere in the dark.

LOUISA TURNED over and watched the day going in what seemed the middle of the afternoon. "That's the trouble with winter," she told herself. "By the time you have to be fetching water for dinner the light's going." Then she remembered she didn't fetch water anymore. The town outside her window was in silhouette. Only Anna Parker had a light on. It looked the same as it always did, except they had finally paved some of the streets with the same stuff they used on white folks' streets, and colored folks had cars all over the place. The tallest thing she could see was the American flag flying on its pole down by the post office. That was only in the corner of her view. Most of what lay quiet among the leafless bones of trees were the little bungalows and two-story houses of the colored part of town. She told Charles Walker he should be grateful. "I kept my peace and now it's all going with me. Everything you wanted to bury is going right into a hole in the ground with me." She laughed 'cause what she did remember now—which wasn't much compared to what-all she'd learned from her mama and once knew so good, and what-all he done told her, and everything she saw for herself—she didn't care about anymore much at all. She wondered if they would tear down the house after she was gone. It was like her—once handsome and sturdy and useful, and now of no use to anyone.

"They might oughta rip you down. My sons will just leave you standing here. Either way, house, you gonna be here longer than I am, if it's only a month or two. House, I'm gonna tell you, nobody wants to know what you been through, only where did you end up. I'm gonna tell you, house, 'cause I been here longer than I been anywhere, spent my life here cleaning you, polishing, dusting and sweeping, put all my muscle and sweat in your floors and walls and rugs and all the things in here. I put the oil from my hands in the wood, and all the things I never said to anybody I beat into crisp sheets, tucked and folded and pressed tight. I'm telling you, house built by Charles Walker Tarrant, even though nobody ever asked, that I was the first child born to my mama who was not a slave, would never be a slave, that she gave me the second name Hope because I was all the hope of all her line—most that she didn't even know—that we would never no more be slaves to nobody. She didn't know who had birthed her, only that the woman died of work. She told me over and over, 'You are free, chile, and being born free you will never know what it means.'" Louisa's voice got louder and louder. "And she let me do as I please with my life because of it, 'cause my life was a free life to her. And she stayed away when I married and had children 'cause she said they was new people like me and they didn't need to know the old way of folks who couldn't change." Louisa put her head back against the pillow and sobbed.

"And I'm telling you, house, that it was never hard to keep my peace about what they wanted kept quiet 'cause *nobody,* nobody wanted to know nothing. What they thought they wanted was some little old lady up here being grandma to the children. My supplies ran low long ago." She started to shout. "The last family what owned my mama was named Griffin, near Kinston in North Carolina, where the land usedta be called by the name of the Indians there and the Indians there called themselves Tuscarora and Secotan. I was born just after the Emancipation and was brought here by my mama, who came here where she had been one time and lost her children. But we couldn't never keep it together. And the last family and the only one they knowed about that owned Charles Walker's folk was named Burleigh, which Charles Walker remembered 'cause he remembered the man Burleigh himself. And he said he was never to say the name round his old man and then when the old man died he never told about it out of deference. His father's name was William and his father's mother was Eva. I birthed ten children: the first girl died a sickly baby, my eight boys lived, one of them I buried a hero and one I buried who lived a full life. My only girl, who I named after my sister, died at twenty-six of tuberculosis, and I had two who never saw the light of the sun, or breathed the air. I am the only one who knew their names because I am the one who gave them their names and I am the one who took their lives. I put their remains in the back of Charles's land here. I named one Tuscarora and one Secotan because they have gone back to the only place I knew of as a place near my ancestors."

LOUISA DIED at Christmas and her house was opened up and shaken out like a carpet on the clothesline. Old ladies I'd thought I'd never seen in my life appeared at the door, knowing me, knowing my dad, all of us, as if they'd changed our diapers. They threw the curtains open and cleaned the windows, beat the furniture with feather dusters and filled the house with the smell of linseed oil. The women unearthed all of Louisa's china from the sideboards and pantry, and still other women showed up with huge containers of divine-smelling ham sliced thin as wafers, yams swimming in sugary juices, soft, sweet yeast rolls folded in gentle curves and baked just brown enough for reheating. Death brought out banquets as if the mourners were starved by their loss, and yet the grievers never ate, didn't sleep, and among the Tarrants, usually never let out their grief.

Maddie told jokes about Louisa's house rules, and how she scared all the children. The women paid tribute to how much work she'd done. Then Maddie got preoccupied with trying to find out from all of the Tarrants present if anyone had ever asked Louisa if she knew about the family in slavery. Maddie wanted to know if Louisa had ever been told who owned the Tarrants and where their farm was. Maybe Charles Walker had told her. When she asked what were they going to do with the house, no one said a word. They all looked as if they were getting old to me. I took a last look at the bed piled with pillows in white cases, white linen on white linen, a nubby, white woven spread. I felt cut off at the limbs.

5

WHEN EIGHT students went into our local Woolworth's that Monday morning, February 8, 1960, and sat down at the counter, I didn't know anything about it. No one did. It was a short walk from the college into town, and likely no one paid attention as they passed. The eight boys, whose names never made the newspaper, wore suits and ties and fresh haircuts, all their "Sunday best." When they got there only a handful of mothers with young children were shopping in the store. Several elderly white men were having coffee at the counter. It may have been that they had coffee there every morning. There were many faces any of us might not normally notice in Woolworth's, faces belonging to people we were not supposed to know, or even look at too carefully. As a result, people could be poor witnesses for sudden events—they were likely to report there was simply a white person, or just a Negro. How dressed? I couldn't say, I just saw a Negro standing there. Men in suits. White. Colored. A tie, pens in his pocket. Eyeglasses. Unless they were in your face they weren't supposed to be anybody in particular. Black folks probably never took a good look at the faces at that lunch counter because we all knew not to stop there. It was as if that part of the store did not exist.

The young Negro men looked at each face very carefully, though, as they sat on the red vinyl and chrome seats and gently rested their arms on the chipped edges of the deep red counter. Once they were seated, time slowed down to a creep and each sound pounded around the counter. The old men stared in disbelief, their faces flushed as if they'd been pinched. In moments the room was full of fear like a dryness in the mouth, first in the students, then the waitresses and everyone who could see what had happened. The young men were made speechless by their own presence—shocked at how simple, almost meaningless it was to sit at this worn-out little lunch counter. Yet, at the same time, it was as if they had smashed all the windows and stood by to watch the glass fly.

I WAS sitting in class just beyond the bridge they'd crossed, marveling that there was snow sticking to the ground, indeed there seemed nothing more incredible than snow on a winter day in the town of Turner. It had been only six months since the fever to agitate white folks had overtaken the adults I knew. Maddie kept referring to this fever as an "opportunity" that had "arisen" when the suit against the segregated schools got the Board of Education nervous. From then on I had been in basic training to integrate a school that would probably never integrate. Maddie's "opportunity" had made it necessary for the first time for me to imagine myself as a lot of other people— all the kids in my school, all the colored kids my age in the state. I still didn't know why it came to them at that moment to want things to change. No one ever said—not my old man, not

Maddie, or the teachers—but their desire got right up in everybody's face. I was a twelve-year-old black girl in a small southern town who thought the world was out somewhere beyond the last houses. You went out there to see how it was, and how it was reinvented you. How it was, though, was getting used to the idea that white people couldn't decide if my friends and I were good enough to sit next to their kids. After six months of watching them watch me, I was tired of white folks I didn't even know and had lost my curiosity about who they were. I had incorporated the white school across town into my imaginary life side by side with my comic books, TV shows, a new boy who had visited church, the need to have a pair of red flats, and the snow that too rarely fell on Turner.

TWO OF the old men paid for their coffee and got up from the counter. They didn't want to leave the store, they just wanted to get a little distance from the situation. Women finishing at the checkout counters stood by the front doors and watched.

"Can you imagine that?" one woman said. "Imagine that!"

"Somebody should get the police. It's against the law, ain't it?" The voice sounded unsure. "Yeah, sure it is."

One of the old men got in it. "Those niggers must be from out of town. Maybe it's a mistake."

"Ain't no mistake," his partner said. "I saw they done it in Carolina on TV. Ain't no mistake." He turned to the cashier. "Mae, call the police."

"I can't, Mr. Riley, got to get the manager," she answered. "Get Mr. Anderson," she yelled to one of the salesgirls in the back.

The boys listened and made silent, acknowledging nods to one another. The waitresses cleared out from behind the counter and stood behind them, waiting for the manager. As he rushed up he was met by his employees. In the confusion all they could hear was his repeated question, "What's going on here?"

One of the young men muttered to the boy next to him, "Okay, we're in it now, stay polite. Ronnie, you talk to 'em."

"Let's see if we can get this settled peaceable." The manager was taking charge. "Exactly what's going on, fellas?"

"We'd like to be served some coffee," Ronnie, the spokesman, said.

"I see, well, I'm afraid you're going to have to go down to Brown's place at the other end of the street, if you want a cup of coffee. Colored people have never gotten coffee here at Woolworth's. Maybe you boys are from out of town. The place is Brown's, right down Raleigh Street here 'bout two blocks." Mr. Anderson thought his meaning was clear.

"Well, sir, we'd like to have our coffee right here in your establishment."

"I see. I'm afraid that will be impossible. You do understand that, don't you?" Mr. Anderson took a breath. He was a man on his way up with the Woolworth people. He didn't want to let loose with anything too sudden or rash. He just wanted them to go away.

"We understand *exactly,* sir, and we'd still like to be served here at Woolworth's, right at this counter, sir," Ronnie said with a little exaggerated friendliness. He wanted to laugh at himself. To Mr. Anderson, though, they looked a stern bunch. He wanted no truck with them, none at all. They couldn't be just kids, yet it was obvious they were kids, fool kids at that.

"If you don't leave, I'll have to call the police. You know this is just no good. It'll cause trouble."

"We did not come here for any trouble. We would just like to order some coffee."

"It's against the law, boys. I don't mind the idea so much of giving you some coffee in a container or something if you would leave, but it's against the law for you to be sitting here at my counter, and you know it." Mr. Anderson was becoming intensely aware of his audience. "I can tell you're southern boys, even though I don't b'lieve you're from around here. I know you know."

"Oh, yes sir, we know."

"Well, hot damn, there it is," said one of the old men. "They know what they're doing! They came here on purpose to break the law!" Mr. Anderson walked away and quietly instructed one of the girls to go call the sheriff's office and tell him what was going on.

"Tell him he's going to have to take eight of 'em outta here, but I don't want no ruckus in this damn store!"

Pretty soon nearly everyone on Raleigh was trying to get in the store. Anderson locked the rear doors, and people trying to come in the back parking lot got annoyed about having to walk around the block to the front. Very few of these people were black. One or two stepped hesitantly from the bank on the corner to the display windows of Woolworth's when they saw a crowd gather. From that perspective they could only see that there were some neatly dressed black boys sitting at the counter without being able to make out who they were. The boys were just sitting there while the whites in the store whirled around, whispering and going from huddle to huddle, all the while watching the eight. Of course it was obvious what they were doing, but how long would they just sit there after being told no? No one was behind the counter. The boys just stared ahead as if they didn't notice the panic all around them.

Sheriff Wilson took a while to get there because he had to stop by the mayor's office. The sheriff was two blocks from Woolworth's and the mayor was one block away. The sheriff thought he'd better go in his car, though, just to put everybody on notice that it was a serious matter. He had several other cars to follow him. When he stopped at City Hall he found an agitated Mayor Ellis standing outside waiting, gesturing for him to get out of the car. The mayor and the sheriff were not from the same side of the tracks and the sheriff had been in his job a lot longer than Mayor Ellis. They were friendly but rarely had any reason to talk to each other too much.

"Whatcha got all this shit for?" the mayor wanted to know.

"What? Anderson told me to come get eight colored boys outta his store."

"Look, Wilson, it's gotta be *quiet,* you understand?"

"What's the big deal? He said he's got eight colored boys in there in suits sitting all nice-like purposely breaking the law, sitting there like they're going to get some coffee. Ain't going to be no problem."

"I don't want any problem and I don't want too many people hearing about this. We don't want anybody else getting any ideas. I hear this happened down in Greensboro for a week or so. We want to go in there and get those boys very quietly."

"If you don't want anybody to hear about it, you better go gag all those people standing out front of the store then. Look, I'll go in the back and take 'em out quiet as I can, okay?"

"Okay, Sheriff. Thanks. I'm just going to walk down there to the back door and see how it goes. Don't say anything about it, though."

"No problem, sir." On that morning the sheriff wondered for the first time whom the mayor talked to. Someone had made him nervous, the sheriff thought, some of those lawyers in the City Hall.

At the store he banged on the back door until one of the girls came and let him and his men in. People still inside scattered as the officers came forward to the lunch counter. A tall, thin, reserved man, the sheriff had put on his cap and his full-dress jacket with his badge on the outside. As they wound through the aisles of makeup and notions, hairnets and pipes and cases of ready-made reading glasses, the crowd inside pushed toward the front door and those outside had to strain to see what was going on. As they neared the students, who by now were watching their approach, the officers behind the sheriff dropped back to give him some distance and to clear the folks from around the counter.

"Well, well, well, you boys look pretty nice. All dressed up, aren't you? What exactly are you trying to prove here?" Sheriff Wilson asked. The boys looked at one another and Ronnie spoke up.

"What we're trying to prove here is that we ought to be able to be served at this counter."

"And you're trying to prove this today, right?"

"Yes, sir, you could put it that way."

"I hate to tell you this, boys, but this is neither the time nor the place," Wilson said. "You are not going to prove a thing at this lunch counter today because you-all are going to have to go to jail for breaking the law and that's going to be the *end* of it. Now you-all ain't going to give me and my men any trouble here, are you?"

"No, sir," Ronnie answered blandly. He looked at the others as if to give them courage, but did not move. Wilson took out his own cuffs and handcuffed the student. He gestured for the other officers to follow suit.

"You better let those kids in Greensboro, or wherever it is, make your point," said Wilson. He pulled Ronnie upward till he stood up from the seat. "We never had no kinda stuff like this around here, and you're going to go nice and easy with me today and we're not going to have *anymore* stuff around here." This time he laughed lightly as he lectured. "You from the college?"

"Yes, sir."

"Somebody know you boys are here?"

"No, sir."

"I hope you know somebody's phone number." He had them in hand now and the mayor could watch him pass out the back door. Nothing more he could do for the man.

THE WAY I heard the story over dinner, acted out minute by minute, one of them was my dad's friend's student, one of them was the brother of a boy in my school. He didn't know who the others were, except that the Turner College dean said they were all good boys. That pretty much took care of my father's central issues—they were in school and somebody knew them. Before dinner he'd been fussing and wouldn't let it rest. He was pretending he was upset because the kids would get themselves thrown out of college. I knew he just didn't like the whole idea. My old man did not like a fight. Sitting next to white people wasn't any big deal to him. He was inclined to take life as he found it. But that had become a question too. The whole school integration suit had turned him around; now, as he'd told everyone on the phone that night, here were these kids turning everything upside down.

"I don't like it one bit," he told Maddie. "We've got everybody we know organized for this thing and it's barely holding together as it is. . . . Well, I know you know. . . . Yes, Maddie, I know you know better than I know how fragile it is. But you understand my point. We've got enough trouble with these white folks; now we got students getting themselves arrested." Maddie must have been chuckling. She'd dragged the old man into the citizens' group and ignored him when he'd complained about sacrificing his last born for their ambitions and a few choice words about some of the folks involved. She probably ignored him that night. When the dean called, he shifted gears, started telling the man he didn't think there was anything to it. "They just wanted to try the thing out for themselves. Nothing to worry about, man."

When he was on the phone in the hall I listened as long as I could while wiping dishes near the pantry door. He finally went into the living room and turned on the TV news, discovered there was nothing about the eight kids, and started muttering to himself. I went up the back stairs so he wouldn't notice me. I knew if he saw me he would think of integration, remind me that I was representing the race, and ask me about my homework. Every time he saw me it was as if I were wearing a sign on my forehead that said PROGRESS or FORWARD THE RACE. He had started acting as if the integration might happen and wondering aloud was I going to be able to kick butt when they sent me over there, because everybody was sure going to be trying to kick mine. Homework was no longer homework, it was the race struggle, the French teacher who once told him "Negras'" lips were too big. Homework was his old man, who'd said Negroes had to be *better*. Dixon could go on till the race had its teeth on your last nerve. This was one night there would be no talking to him, no watching TV, and no talking on the phone.

THE DAY after the sit-in, it was still not clear from what I heard who the boys were and how they got out of jail. At Ida B. Wells it was as if martial law had been declared. The teachers weren't having any loose conversation anywhere, not in class, not in the halls. I stared at the snow, longing to get out of the classroom and go down to the Woolworth's just to look at the lunch counter. Mrs. Taliaferro was wearing one of her plain brown suits that made her look especially severe. She seldom chose bright colors and wore her clothes so loose that I could never tell if she was really skinny or merely thin. She was actually pretty but she didn't show that off. It was as if she didn't want to draw attention to herself in any way so you'd just have to concentrate on what she was saying. She began reminding us that we should not believe everything we read. In fact, she went on, sometimes getting the truth can be like pulling a rabbit out of a hat. She pulled out the town newspaper and went over the stories.

"On page two are the arrests, all Negroes—criminal mischief, driving under the influence. But there is a story missing. There were some *other* Negroes arrested yesterday. Still, I don't see anything about it." She asked how many of us had heard anything about eight Negroes being arrested all at once the day before. Everyone's hand went up.

"Isn't that odd? All of you children heard about some arrests yesterday but there's nothing here in our town newspaper about it," she said. Mrs. Taliaferro went on in a singsong that was usually reserved for leading a wary student down the garden path to admitting she hadn't done her homework. Even though I trusted Mrs. Taliaferro with my life, it never occurred to me that she was a courageous woman as she sat there carrying on about a story that was not in the paper. I'd forgotten about the three white men sitting in the back of the classroom. In fact, by that February in 1960 all of us in her class had become so accustomed to the men who sat in the room and watched that we failed to observe anymore when they took notes and when they did not.

In the beginning they'd asked questions, sometimes ordered tests, all kinds of tests. There were six of us who were being prepared to be the first to go to the other school: Kelly Jean, Timothy, Julian, Dallas, Chookie, and me. Chookie had become one of "us" even though some of the parents weren't crazy about it. And we still got up every day and showed off. The men just went on sitting there in the same corner, September, October, November, December. Sometimes the faces changed; occasionally a woman sat in one of the seats.

Mrs. Taliaferro's lesson in critical reading that day was really aimed at those men, who already knew that our history books were lengthy defenses of slavery—if they didn't know it when they came in there, they had certainly heard it from Mrs. T. And they also probably knew about a little event that had occurred in town the previous morning. If Mrs. Taliaferro had asked us all to write down our versions of what had happened the day before so we could discuss it in class, the one thing we would all have written was that we hadn't known it was going on. The very unrealness of the event gave it a special meaning. In fact, as we did discuss it, the eight boys walked into town again and once more found eight places at the lunch counter. This time they had one teacher outside who was prepared to pay the bail. And this time, two white women moved over to make room.

At the end of the school day the old man appeared, standing outside my classroom. Since he never showed up there unless I was sick, seldom left his job for any of those daytime duties like polio shots or science fairs, I was alarmed. Mrs. Taliaferro looked a bit surprised too.

"Dixon! I can't imagine what brings you here. Hope nothing's wrong," she said.

"No, no. I came to take Willie to town. I hear the kids are down there again."

"But I heard they got arrested early this morning. Somebody called the school and told the principal," she said.

"Yup. Those kids went back and got arrested again and then some others up and went a couple of hours ago. I don't know what's happened yet."

"Oh, my," she sighed, and sat down on her desk. "This is

more than we bargained for, isn't it? Who would have thought the college kids would suddenly get concerned about segregation? Most of them don't live around here."

"Right. One day they're running around doing all the fraternity mess, the next they decide they're upset they can't get any service in Woolworth's. The thing that worries me is that it's probably some passing fancy and next week they'll be worried about winning the football game. Meanwhile somebody's liable to get hurt. You know these crackers don't have it in 'em to be nice for too long."

"No. No, they don't. More kids, you say?"

"Uh-huh. I don't know what we can do, but we can't let them all start running down to get put in the jail."

"You thinking of trying to get them to stop it?"

"If I could I would, or if I knew somebody who could talk them out of it—"

"We should think about it first, shouldn't we, Dixon?"

"What do you mean, Mae? This thing can blow up in our faces, and after a lot of hard work we're all organized."

"That's just it, Dix. Think about it. *We're* all organized. The students aren't."

"Oh, God. Mae, the further this thing goes, the crazier you get."

"You're right about that, Dixon. I'm getting crazier every day." He motioned for me to go and said good-bye.

When we got in the car he said, "We're just going down there and take a look." He asked me if I knew why the students had staged this thing called a sit-in.

"They wanted to sit at the counter and be served because white people can sit there and we can't."

"That's right, Willie," he said to me. "It's a protest. I don't see how it could work just by itself, but it's very clever. It's like

208

a metaphor that anyone can see. Just sitting there at that counter."

"A metaphor, Dad?"·

The old man reacted to life as if it were literature, as if it had to be retold. To him, this scene he had not seen was an image that explained everything that took too long to explain. "It's like a picture of you sitting in class across town when you can't go over there and see it for yourself. What it means. Just by sitting there they let you see with your eyes a picture of something that is supposed to be impossible. They let you see how stupid the law is. A law that doesn't make any sense. As long as nobody really looks at the law, we go along. Those fool kids didn't bother about going to court and arguing the law and all that, they just went over there and sat down and everybody could see it."

"But we didn't see it, and it wasn't on TV," I said, somewhat dejected to have missed this picture that had gotten him so excited.

"That's not really that important."

When we got downtown the Woolworth's was closed. A few people were milling around outside talking and Anderson was pacing back and forth waving people away. The old man turned the next corner and announced that we were going to the jail.

"You see the people out there? Those people saw it. The people who can't imagine it. And you saw it in your head when somebody told you about it, didn't you? And it said, 'Willie should be able to do what she wants to do, go where she wants to go. Not just the lunch counter.'"

"I certainly don't want to go to eat at that lunch counter."

"You probably won't. If this keeps up we don't have to worry about anybody eating there." He laughed.

"You think they'll go there again?"

"It seems like they have to. I guess they plan to keep going long as they can." He thought about it for a second and turned serious. "That's no good though. They can't keep getting arrested. Their folks don't have money to be getting them out of jail. None of us do. To tell you the truth, Willie, it's gonna be a mess, that's what it's gonna be." He pulled into the jail parking lot.

"Come on, let's see if they're still here."

"What are we going to do?" I asked.

"I don't have the faintest idea. It'll be a miracle if they don't try to throw those boys out of school for this."

The front office of the jail looked pretty grim. Behind a low wooden wall extended across the room were a couple of old desks, piled high with papers. Under the glare of the fluorescent lights hanging from the ceiling, faces posted on the bulletin boards seemed to menace the deputies. Police radios blared off and on. The deputy sheriffs were obviously having trouble answering the phones. They looked up at my father quickly and went on about their business. He asked if the sheriff was there and one of them said he was busy.

"You here to pick up one of these colored boys in the back?"

"No, I'm here to find out what their situation is."

"We don't have any time to answer questions unless you're here to see about getting 'em out. You from the college?"

"Yes."

"They said somebody from the college was coming." We sat down to wait and soon the sheriff came out of his office.

He looked at Dixon for a second. "Tarrant, isn't it?" he asked.

"Yes, sir."

"Which one are you—I know there's quite a few of you— Liberty Street, right?"

"Dixon Tarrant. We used to be on Liberty, yes."

"Yep, I knew it. I grew up over on Walham, few blocks over."

"Oh yes, sure. I remember your father."

"You here 'bout those boys? I've been waiting on somebody."

"I came to see what the situation is. Some of them are my students," Dixon lied. "If you want to release them into my care, I'll take them off your hands."

"Nope, Tarrant, no can do. I would normally, you know. I know you and all. The mayor's got his foot on my neck, though. This is some kind of bad business. Y'all got to talk to them, tell 'em this shit's gotta stop. The mayor's all worked up about keeping it quiet one minute and going rough on 'em the next. No telling what'll happen."

"I understand, but—"

"But nothing, I'm tellin' you. It's bad business. It's gotta stop right here. We're thinking about keeping 'em just to discourage them."

"You can't do that—"

"We can't, and then again, if the mayor *really wants* to, we *can*. You understand?"

A reporter from the Negro paper came in and tried to get into the conversation and the sheriff turned and walked back into his office. The dean soon came through the door, obviously in a state of agitation.

"Tarrant, what are you doing here for God's sake?"

"Came down to see what was happening with our boys, Dean. That's about all."

"We've got it well in hand, Tarrant. I hope you're not one of the ones helping them, because not only are they in a world of trouble, but any of the staff getting in this mess will have to answer to the president about this."

"I just thought somebody ought to make sure they were not staying here any longer than necessary." Dixon looked the dean in the eyes.

"This was their stupid idea. Maybe they need to stay down here awhile."

"Dean, I can see you're angry, but we don't want to leave any Negro boys in this jail."

"Don't be so sure, Tarrant. Might do them some good, see what they're messing with. I know one thing: next time these little idiots come down here to get arrested, we're going to call their parents and tell them to come get them. I'm washing my hands of them after this afternoon." He brushed the old man off and asked for the sheriff. I got the signal to move it and we left.

"I got half a mind to go down there myself tomorrow," he muttered. "Suffering white people is one thing; suffering these fools is another. They want to leave these black boys in a cracker jail. Don't they know where the hell they are?"

The next morning right at nine o'clock he did go downtown, just to have a look. He put on one of his business suits, his gray winter overcoat, and a black fedora. His preference for Italian-style fedoras was the only clue that Dixon had any interest in being stylish. This time he found there were lots of whites who'd come to watch, and at the door, about twenty kids with picket signs. Six boys were lined up ready to go in when the doors opened. Bob Mollette and Ralph Johnson were with them, and Jeanne Morrow, with her daughter Patricia. Though he usually smoked cigars, he took a cigarette from Ralph. The store was late opening. The students all said hello and warily watched to see if Dixon had been sent to tell them to go back to school.

"Bob, are you with these kids?"

"Yes, Dixon, I'm with them. Danny Cobb and I decided somebody needed to be with them."

"They shouldn't be down here, but I guess if they're not going to listen to anybody, somebody should be here with them. The dean still threatening to leave them in the jail?"

"Oh yes. I expect he'll keep his word on that."

"Damn shame."

"Dixon—," Ralph interrupted. "They send you down here?" Dixon put his arm around Johnson's shoulder for a second.

"Naw, man. I went down to the jail to see what happened to them and they threatened to put *me* out of school too!" Everybody laughed. The two men walked a few feet away from the group to smoke.

"Dix, I think this is a great thing, you know."

"You do? This could get real bad, man, you know that."

"Yes, well, it could. But I don't care. We've been fighting with these folks the nice way for months and where has it gotten us? Look around, I've been up here three mornings now and I just stand here and look and I can't believe it. You and I grew up here, you know how it's been. Nothing's ever changed. We'd have to come down Friday evenings afraid to look straight at these rednecks, and pull our fathers, your pop and mine, out of the back room at Brown's and take them home. Hope to God they wouldn't pick a fight or say the wrong thing to one of these crackers, 'cause we'd have to do the fighting with them that drunk. Remember how they'd collar us on the street, say, 'Here, boy, here's a penny. Watch this buggy for me while my wife goes in the store'? Just like we had nothing to do but wait on white folks to shop."

"Yeah, yeah, Ralph, I remember. What you want to get into all that for?" Ralph put his arm around him.

"You see me, Dix. Went to college, thought I was going to make it—"

"You did make it, Ralph. What're you talking about?"

"You were here. You know, Dix. You *know* I couldn't get a

job in the state, not a job for an engineering degree or any other kind of degree. You *know* if I wasn't gonna teach school I had to come back here and cut hair for a living. There's nothing wrong with it, mind you. But you know why I'm down there cutting hair!"

"Yeah, Ralph. I know. So that's why you're down here encouraging these kids to mess up their lives getting arrested?"

"Hell, man. They started something we need to finish! Yeah, I'm gonna help 'em. I'm going to give them as much bail money as I can give 'em. I thought maybe you'd come to help too."

"I just came down here to see what's going on. Let's go back, we can talk about this later."

"This is a chance to wake the whole town up, Dix. We got everything we need already. We could really get some picket signs down here. These kids can't last long, and it's our fight anyway."

At the store Mr. Anderson was looking out and fumbling with his keys, trying to decide if he was ready. When he did open up he immediately started shouting that the counter was closed. The waitresses stood behind the counter with their arms crossed. Signs saying CLOSED were placed all along the counter. The boys went in and sat down. One woman outside watching started yelling.

"Didn't you hear the man? He said it's closed! Go home, niggers, go home!"

"Ain't that nothin'!" another said. "Now they think they gonna picket too!"

"The police'll be here in a minute. Put 'em in the jail, that's where they belong."

When Dixon looked at the counter, he thought it looked kind of funny really. The boys sitting there with the CLOSED signs in front of them. Jeanne was standing at the door with

Patricia, the girl primly dressed in school clothes and her hair freshly curled. Jeanne was giving her a tough-minded look. It was sort of strange to Dixon because, as he saw her, there was nothing stern about Jeanne Morrow, not in her warm face and round looks, not in her self-conscious beauty. Jeanne and the girl started to walk into the store. Dixon stopped her.

"Jeanne, what are you doing?"

"I'm here with my girl. She told me she was skipping school and coming down here whether I liked it or not. So I came. I couldn't let her come down here alone to God knows what."

"Take her home, Jeanne. She's just a baby. How old is she, fourteen?"

"She's fifteen now. Tenth grade. What am I going to tell her, Dixon? Am I going to tell her it's wrong?"

"No. But it's dangerous. It's something for adults to do."

"Well, as she put it to me, 'Ain't no adults doing it.' " The girl stood and waited and when they paused she quietly said she was going in. Her mother nodded and promised to be right behind her.

"She's been real angry ever since the Dempsey boy got killed. You know, my daughter Cassie's boyfriend." Dixon nodded. "It's better for me to let her do something like this than let the anger eat her up. Hard as it is, the anger is harder."

"Cassie have the baby yet, Jeanne?"

"Yep, in December. Beautiful little boy. You ought to see him."

"Yes, I should," he said. He laughed. "Yes, I should. You know, they tell me it was almost one of mine. I'm not old enough to be no grandfather!"

"Ha! It would have been my good luck if it had been your grandchild. But, Lord knows, the Tarrants would never have lived with that!" She whispered into his ear, "Y'all too fancy to have a bastard child on Ulysses Grant Street."

"Ah, Jeanne, you don't know me." He smiled and took her arm. "I'm going to wait and see that you're alright."

"Suit yourself, Dixon Tarrant." Jeanne Morrow strolled into the Woolworth's store in her worn old overcoat with her head held high, her purse hung on one arm and clutched to her waist. She walked like a woman who'd been admired all her life for her looks. Dixon wondered that he'd never noticed that before. She looked back at Dixon and asked if he could get her a newspaper. He nodded and she turned and took a seat at the far end with her daughter. Dixon stepped back outside the door and walked past the hecklers and onlookers to find Jeanne a paper. He was glad to have that little mission because he knew he didn't want to stand there and just watch. He wasn't a lawyer and he couldn't just write a check to get them out of jail. And he couldn't leave them and go back to work. He got the paper and a cigar from the little tobacco store across from the bank. As he headed back across the street he heard the sirens coming up Raleigh behind him and he hurried into the store.

"Come on now, Jeanne, you and your daughter come with me. The police are here and you don't need to go down to the jail."

"No, Dixon. We're sitting right here. Is that my paper? I'll be needing something to read." He handed her the paper. Nearly a dozen men came in behind the sheriff. This time Sheriff Wilson didn't say a word. He moved his head in the direction of the counter and stood back. The officers grabbed each of the kids by the collar and jerked them upwards then down to the floor. A pair of eyeglasses flew to the floor. The boys did not make a sound. One of the men had trouble getting one boy to the floor.

"You resisting arrest, boy?"

The student grunted out a "No, sir." The officer pulled his wrists back and cuffed him and jerked him up again. They next grabbed Jeanne's daughter and knocked Dixon back into the post behind him. Another man grabbed him and shoved him back down the aisle till he fell. Two took hold of Mrs. Morrow. Dixon yelled out at them to stop. Jeanne turned her head from the hold the man had on her and yelled back at Dixon.

"Don't, Dixon. We're not fighting them. Meet us at the jail."

Dixon Tarrant hadn't been knocked on his ass since he was a kid in the town of Turner. He got up and dusted himself off almost by instinct, and picked up his broken cigar and his hat. He also hadn't given one thought to this idea of nonviolent protest. Ralph Johnson ran in and helped him.

"I'm alright, Ralph."

"I know you are, man. I saw you about to get yourself shot in here. Come on, let's go out the back here. I got my car."

As they walked Dixon asked, "What's going on, Ralph?"

"We're going to get them out of jail and get this thing organized. If people are going to be coming down here, they got to come together." They went out the back door to the lot.

"This is crazy, Ralph."

"Doing it like this is—come on, get in. When we get there we're going to call everybody and get them to put up some money."

By LATE afternoon Dixon dropped Jeanne Morrow and Patricia off at their house and asked if she wouldn't come to a meeting at College Hall in the evening.

"Who's having a meeting?"

"Well, there's the small group of us who've been trying to follow through on this school integration, mostly parents of the kids the Board of Ed chose to go Patrick Henry School— haven't they been calling you to come to our meetings? You've got a daughter involved."

"Oh yeah, but they don't really want my Chookie. I figure they don't want me coming up there telling them what I think of them. No, I'm not coming to meet with them till they decide to get behind my kid a hundred percent."

"It's not my business, but that ain't the way to get it done if you want to get it done."

"It's my way."

"Look, just come on anyway. We'll deal with that later. It's gonna be those folks and one or two teachers. We're going to meet with the college students, Bob Mollette, and whoever else shows up."

"Those people don't have anything to do with people like me."

"Maybe it's time we did."

"Who's the leader of the group, Ralph or somebody else?"

"Don't have one."

"*That* must be something!"

"We manage."

"I don't think they'll want me joining their little group."

"Don't worry about that. Most of them aren't even going to want to be in the group when they hear what the students have to say."

"What's that?"

"They want somebody to go down there every day till they put the store out of business or the store changes its policy." Jeanne laughed. "They're pretty nervy, aren't they?"

"Yes, sir. And just what are you-all going to do?" she asked.

"Don't know. The sheriff's saying that he's heard white kids are planning to come down there tomorrow, so we've gotta do *something*."

"White kids?"

"All he said was, 'Don't be surprised if you meet a couple

218

hundred kids from the high school tomorrow. *It might be outta my hands.*' Jeanne, it's not a kids' fight."

"Can you-all get a lot of people out?"

"If you help."

"Well, okay . . . I guess you were waiting for something like this."

"Waiting to see you walk into Woolworth's and sit at the counter that they've closed so they can't serve you? No." They both laughed. Dixon didn't know what he'd been waiting for. At the moment it was almost a relief to know maybe he was waiting for a crowd of angry white kids to be out front of Woolworth's.

When Dixon and Jeanne Morrow walked into College Hall that evening several hundred people had cut their dinners short and showed up. People from all over town were sitting and standing in the cramped little meeting hall wanting to know what was going on, wanting to know if they could go downtown with the students. The students looked as stunned as the citizens' group, all of whom Mae Taliaferro had called to get out the troops. The Burleighs, Charleses, and Browns, Cleo Parker, Bernard Robinson, and all the rest were there, and Reverend Hardy had brought out most of his flock. Mollette and Cobb were up on the stage beaming. It seemed as if word had spread through every crack in every board in town. Even ministers from far-flung churches like New Jerusalem showed up to see what was going on.

One of the frat boys from the college came up to the old man and said, "Big Brother Tarrant, we called every Que in town; for that matter, every Greek organization called all their people. Quite a turnout, isn't it?"

"Well, that's good, young man, but this sure isn't just Greek organizations. This is half the folks in town."

"Yeah, man, I never seen any of these people before. Anyway, I know you're down with us, big brother," he said, giving him the Omega Psi Phi handshake.

The old man was never much of a frat man, but he returned the shake and said, "Yeah, I'm down with you, whatever *down* is."

"Big Brother Tarrant, man, I believe you are square on purpose. You like to make people think you're not hip. But I know—" Jeanne started laughing. The old man stared at the student in his Que sweater and glasses.

"What's your name, brother?"

"Wallace, sir."

"And how old are you?"

"Twenty, sir."

"Brother Wallace, I hope you'll understand and won't be offended, but I lost interest in being hip ten years before you were born."

"Yes, sir."

Danny Cobb was calling the meeting to order.

"To put it the simplest way possible, folks, we don't know how all of y'all got out here, but we are happy as hell to see you!" The crowd laughed. "As you probably know, these students have started going down to Woolworth's to sit in, and they are determined to keep it going until the store ends its policy of refusing to serve Negroes at the counter. Now, we don't know if it can work, but we know it *can't* work if we don't keep it going." A hand went up.

"How can you keep it up if you keep getting arrested?" a voice asked.

"We don't know," one of the students answered. "We're basically going to need a lot of bail money if we keep getting arrested."

"That'll be the first thing we're going to ask you to do," said Cobb. "We're going to collect money for a bail fund."

"Even if we want to help," said one woman, "we can't afford to keep bailing them out indefinitely."

"And are they going to get thrown out of school for this?" asked someone else.

"We're working on that," said Cobb, eyeing the college dean seated on the first row. "Perhaps you all can put in some calls to the president's office to prevail on him not to persecute these students."

Ronnie, the student spokesman, got up. "We don't really see any reason for the college to toss us out just for trying to exercise our rights as citizens. This is simply a civil disobedience action, a civics lesson."

A man yelled out, "Some civics lesson. Boy, you've never seen a lynching. Those white folks going to be downtown tomorrow to lynch your butts. I heard it when I was down there today."

"That's why I'm here," another said.

Cobb tried to call the group back to order. Ronnie spoke up again. "One thing I must remind everybody of, and that is that we see this as a nonviolent protest. We haven't been formally trained in nonviolent techniques like some of the students in other places. We know that some organizers from the Congress of Racial Equality have been down at Greensboro. And Reverend Martin Luther King was there too to help students. But we do know that the main thing is that everybody must keep their cool. And we would like this to remain a student-led action. So we are asking you all to help, but only if you are willing to follow our lead and use passive resistance. There's a lot at stake here." The crowd murmured its assent. "Good. Then I think we can turn this town around."

Ralph Johnson was calling out Danny's name. Ralph finally strode up to the front and onto the stage, waving his hands for everybody to be quiet.

"Now y'all look here. You can see we got some smart kids here with a lot of heart. We're going to get behind them and their program the whole way! We got to have some money for these kids' bail, and we need some men to form a security committee to be ready to be down there *tomorrow morning* if some business has got to be taken care of. Now I got two hundred dollars I'm putting up for the bail, and I'm going to give it to Danny. Everybody in this room needs to give something, if it's only a dollar. Danny, you in charge of the bail, and that's gon' be that! Now, you all heard Reverend King when he was here. I don't have to tell you how we were all talking then about how we ought to do something to make life better for ourselves, stop taking all this mess from these white folks. I don't have to tell you how full we were of such a strong feeling for ourselves and how we could do something like those folks in Alabama did. And I don't have to tell y'all we didn't do a thing—"

"That's right," a voice rang out.

"Well, we gon' do something now. This is it," said Ralph.

"What about the school integration?" someone yelled out. Ralph had just taken over. He paced back and forth across the stage as people talked to him from the crowd.

"The school integration suit is well and good," he continued. "But it ain't happening and you know it. They might be ready to take a big step like that after y'all start to force them to take a step and break down this segregation downtown. But even if you had your way, even if you won, what good is it, I ask you, if you send your kids over there to be guinea pigs for the school integration and they come out into a town where they can't hold their heads up, can't sit down and get a cup of coffee, if they still go on being second-class nobodies for the rest of their lives as long as they have to live around white folk? What are we talking about here? It's all the same thing, you *know that!*"

People started muttering, "Yeah."

"Now, y'all come on and help us get this thing together. What the young people start, we gonna have to finish, 'cause we the ones who're living here. Yeah, Jeanne, what is it?" Jeanne Morrow stood up. At first her voice shook as she spoke.

"I never thought about this till my girls practically made me ashamed of myself for living with this situation so long. If children are going down there, *I'm* going down there. And I think every person in this building, and everyone you got at home who can afford to bail themselves out even just one time, needs to get on a list to go down there one day and take whatever these children take, whatever comes. I don't *want* to get arrested or get hurt neither, but I'll take whatever it's gonna take to see it through if that's what these children are going to do. And one thing's for sure, if we win it, I'll be damn prouder to live in the town and be going downtown there giving those white folks my money."

The students cheered, and then the crowd joined in. Another woman shouted, "If the children can go, we can go." Mollette offered to make up a sign-up sheet and make up a mixed group of students and adults for each day.

Some folks complained that they didn't know if they wouldn't lose their jobs if they got arrested. A man from the packing factory said that most likely fishery workers would get fired, because they got fired for missing a day for any reason as it was. Mollette offered to meet with them to see what they could figure out for people who would surely be at risk. Maddie raised her hand.

"I think Jeanne has raised another issue too. She made me think. We shouldn't be spending our money down there while this is going on. We need to stay out of that place. Boycott it."

"Great idea!" yelled Ralph. And so it was agreed as the hours wore on that a group of women would show up in the morning with signs to alert Negroes to stay away unless they wanted to participate, and a security group would go with the students to protect them at least until they got in the store. They could not protect them from the mob or police once the cops showed up, but if the sheriff was going to keep his men away, there might be trouble.

Dixon decided he would go along with them because he didn't know what else to do. He certainly didn't have any better ideas if the kids were going to keep going downtown to sit in. All they could really do was try to make it worth the misery, he thought. He spotted his friend Coleman across the room smiling down on Charlesetta Roberts, who was smiling back. He crossed the room, entirely out of curiosity, and came up behind them. From this vantage point he could see Cole's hand fingering the belt at the back of Charlesetta's dress. Coleman was pontificating as if he were watching the scene from an aerial view. "A nigger mess, my dear, that's all this is going to be."

"Oh, do you really think so?" Charlesetta sounded disappointed.

"Honey, you don't even know. I know these niggers."

"And this nigger knows you too," Dixon said, grinning.

"My dear man." Cole straightened up and took his hand away. "What a surprise. And I suppose you'll be down there with the ragtag band tomorrow?" Dixon nodded. "Good luck to you then. Call me if you need me to bail you out."

"I will," Dixon said bluntly.

Cole said he had to get Mrs. Roberts home. Dr. Roberts was on duty at the hospital, he added needlessly. "And I did give some money to the bail fund."

"Good."

Dixon found Jeanne at the door with Mae Taliaferro, who was organizing a meeting of the school integration parents for later in the week. Jeanne said she'd rather not come.

"After that speech you gave in there, I think it's time you came and fought for your child with these Negroes," said Mae. "It's not just white folks we got to deal with, you know." Jeanne said maybe and she and Dixon left the hall and walked to the car.

"I don't know what's happening anymore," Dixon said.

"Well, they tell us in church every week that we don't ever know what's happening 'cause the Lord works in mysterious ways, so I guess this is one of those days."

"Yes, I guess so. You leave your house one morning, just like always to go to work, and next thing you know the whole world is standing on its head and you're stopped still with your briefcase in your hand."

"Yep."

"Let me pick you up in the morning," he said.

"Why? I'm closer to the store than you are. You'd have to come past downtown to get me and then go back."

"I've never known such an opinionated woman before. Are you always like this?" Jeanne Morrow laughed.

"I'm on my *good* behavior. That's why I'm going to say okay and let you pick me up at eight. Then you'll be able to meet up with the men by eight-thirty. And my friends usually call me Jeannie." Dixon just nodded and smiled.

When he got back to the house he was still laughing to himself. When I asked him how the meeting was, he said everybody was shouting each other down but he thought it was a lot of fun.

"Fun?"

"Yeah, fun. Your old man has probably lost his marbles. I

think I'm even going to enjoy getting my ass kicked tomorrow morning. Where's Preston? I left him at the meeting."

"Not back yet. So, you sweet on Mrs. Morrow?"

"Mrs. Morrow? Where'd you get that?"

"I heard you planning to pick her up for the meeting."

"Girl, this is serious business. Ain't nobody got time to be being sweet on somebody. That just shows where your mind is."

"Yeah, well, that's good. 'Cause if Preston's *s'posed* to have done something he wasn't *s'posed* to be doing, it would be pretty weird for you to be over there dating your grandchild's grandmother."

"Where'd you get that?! You been minding everybody's business but your own. Besides, I doubt if your brother is anybody's daddy yet."

"How do you know?"

"He doesn't swagger. He goes out the back door to smoke cigarettes so I won't smell it in the house. And he still hasn't gotten up in my face to tell me to go to hell yet."

"Does that mean you're grown?"

"Yep. When you get up in my face and tell me to go to hell, I'll know something made you a grown woman."

"I'm probably going to do that before I'm Preston's age. I got more reason."

"You *have* more reason. And if that's the case, you're going to have to stand on a box to do it; you're still pretty short. Isn't it time for you to go to bed?" I didn't think he was funny.

"Well, you didn't try to give Preston away. He's a boy." Dixon stepped out of his good humor and asked me what I was talking about. I didn't answer.

"You still on that one, Willie?"

"I told you."

"That story's not like you think it is."

"That's a lie," I said. Dixon boiled over and slapped me across the face. The slap stung and I burst into tears.

"You don't ever talk to me like that. I don't care what it's about. I told you that wasn't true. Louisa told you that story her way and some of it she probably made up." His voice backed away. "She was after me to do something like that, but that was all."

"What about the Winstons?" I said, still angry enough to corner him. He looked on the brink of tears himself.

"I can't speak about what happened to me when your mother died. It was the most crushing thing that ever happened in my life."

"You talked to Preston about it. He told me."

"Oh, Willie, you were such a little girl, such a baby."

"And I had a hard time too. And I never talked to anyone. I watched you sitting in your chair every night staring into a drink, so sad nobody could say a word. Christmas after Christmas nothing we did could keep you from sinking away into the walls somewhere. You wouldn't get up, you wouldn't fix the house up, you didn't want to get a tree, you didn't even want to get presents. Just like this year, we put on your favorite music, baked things for you, tried everything to get you to be here with us and you'd just go get a scotch and sit in a corner till you fell asleep. I felt bad for even being around. You wake up one day and you're okay again, but what about me?" He grabbed my arm but then his tears did come, and he let me go. I shouted.

"I've been alone, Dad." I had wanted to hurt him but I couldn't watch. I ran upstairs and slammed the door to my room. He was just standing there.

After a while Dixon got up and went into the kitchen to fix a drink. He put the glass down and went to the phone.

"Hello, hi again. Sorry for calling you so late but I wondered if I could impose on you for a minute. No, no. It's not about that. Everything's okay."

WHEN PRESTON came in he found Dixon in the kitchen slumped over the table. He panicked.

"Dad, what's wrong?" Dixon slowly sat up, looking sleepy, and looked at Preston.

"Son, nothing's wrong. Everything's fine. I'm just tired. I've just been thinking. Your sister's made me realize what I've been doing."

"What's that?"

Dixon smiled. "Nothing. Just going along so. I can't do anything about what she's talking about. I can't do anything about the past, but I don't have to live in the past, either. I went to the meeting tonight and I was kind of frightened because it seemed like everything was about to go out of control, but you know, I also had the time of my life. It felt good. I haven't felt that good in a long time."

"Oh," said Preston. "I'm not sure I understand all that, Dad."

"I know. Look, it doesn't matter. I'll work it out. Come on, boy, let's get some rest. And why are you getting home so late? Walk some girl home?"

"Yep. Well, I couldn't *drive* anybody home 'cause somebody else was seeing a woman home besides me!"

The old man smiled. "Well, who was the girl?"

"Never mind, Dad."

"Aw, man, you ruin all my fun. Next thing I know somebody else will be coming to visit me and accuse you of being some baby's father." Preston laughed.

"Dad, I got babies all 'round this state. You just don't know about it."

"I'm glad I don't, buddy, 'cause I'm a poor man and you ain't got no job. I need to put your ass out to work!"

"That's okay, Dad."

UNOBSERVED, TWO people left the meeting that night, as they left all the meetings, saying good night as if they knew each other quite casually, quietly heading for a car, or separate cars. Sometimes people could feel their desire fill a room for a second like a sigh, but no one knew what the sensation was that passed through and left. They might be sitting side by side or across the room from one another, seemingly indifferent to each other, and yet their own impatience gave the air an edge of anxiety.

It was a funny thing about these two that after so much impatience, when they met they never talked. Well, not about themselves, not about what they were doing, never a word. Sometimes they talked about their jobs for a minute or two, but usually they did not talk at all. She could never remember anything he'd said later when she returned to her life. He always wondered why he hadn't asked her something. It was never anything important yet he still wished he'd asked. He wanted to know all about her, everything that had happened up until he met her. It was just that he never wanted to know right then. She would ask how he was and he would kiss her, and keep kissing.

The room was stuffy; snow or rain was coming. She had cracked a window. Fearing the rain would come in, he closed it. She wanted to make love to him with the cold wind blowing in, even the rain. The air on her body would chill her just a bit and he would warm her. Cool and hot would get all mixed up. He did not want to be disturbed by night wind, curtains flapping against the windowsill. And he didn't want anyone to hear her if she wanted to scream or talk in tongues or something. That was for him. He didn't bother to sit or lounge or pull the covers back. He held her and tugged at her clothes without getting buttons unbuttoned or a belt undone. He kissed her mouth and face all over.

He was always intense like that, whether he was tired or happy, fast or slow. His eyes were open, looking at her, and yet they were not. It was as if he were staring into the nothingness, infinity, the countryside he saw when he first saw anything. As soon as he brought his face to hers, he could feel all his other faces fall away. He was no longer himself from any one particular moment, barely himself at all. There were no buildings, no trees, no shore, perhaps only the sea lapping in at sundown. Soon just breathing was where he was.

He kissed her neck and kept kissing. His face searched for each patch of exposed skin, nudged her buttons and straps out of his way. He kissed and tugged until she was out of her clothes still standing in the middle of the room. She pulled at his clothes and he laughed. He didn't care about his clothes or if she was making some kind of ritual of undressing him. He wanted to smell the skin of her neck and between her breasts. She was so excited she wasn't excited. She was trying to be calm to keep from acting desperate or grateful. She was both. She was losing it.

Her body felt damp and chilled in small places all over as the clothes fell away. Her skin became her only sense of existence. Her breath stopped as each finger touched. She was a spiny sea creature shivering all over at each touch, each small current passing. She squirmed and shrieked and remembered this feeling of being taken by surprise. He put his hand between her legs and the hairs on her neck stood up and blood rushed to all the soft places. Her whole body seemed to swell and open its pores. She wanted to reach for him, grab his perfect body and push, roll him down on the floor maybe, but she could not move from his hand.

Falling back toward the bed, hoping she would land, she pulled him down, groaning, and went blank. All she could feel was the deep inside of the center of herself. A man could not see from the inside out like that. Could she reach in there where his inside was? He shook a little and then shuddered again. Haplessly thrown upon the beach she could feel the dampness, like seawater, as it dried on her skin, and each wave that swept up and jogged her this way and then that way.

She saw his eyes looking at her but not seeing. Deep in there somewhere was the light, her light, in them. Her own eyes sank back into the sound of her breathing. "Now let the weeping cease." She wanted to scream really really loud just to let the world know there was one mother's daughter out there completely out of control and as glad as hell. Even with the curtains closed she could tell the moon was more yellow than silver. Its light would last only long enough for her to drift.

"I'm frightened about tomorrow."

"I am too. But we'll be okay."

"What will we do?"

"This."

"I'm serious."

"I'm serious too."

IN THE morning Preston, Dad, and I piled into the cold car. They dropped me off at school and Preston drove the old man downtown. At breakfast Preston had refused to go to school after he saw that the old boy had put on his fishing sweater and some old pants and was planning to go see some "friends downtown." They parked behind the five-and-dime, stopped at the bank and took out enough money for bail, and walked around to the front of the store. Preston went to join some high school friends who were carrying placards.

When Dixon Tarrant took his place with the security committee in the morning he had dread written all over his face. Ralph Johnson kept asking about the gloom and telling him not to worry about the white folks. Dixon got annoyed.

"I ain't worried about no white folks, Ralph. White folks are just white folks. We have to change things because we have kids, not because we have white folks. And after we deal with white folks we have to deal with the next problem. What's been left wrong too long covers more than white folks, I'm afraid."

"I hear ya', brother, but let's just start with this, okay?" Ralph laughed. "You know your college president sent his spies down to the meeting last night, and look, he's got one down here this morning." Dixon spied a young man from the president's office.

"Well, if he throws these kids out we'll just have to do what was done for us. I thought about it last night. You know what we'll do, we'll get on the phone and get them in another college. I was so worried about that before but it really isn't anything to worry about. If he throws them out, we will call those distinguished white folks who taught us, or those distinguished Negroes we know here and there, and tell them, 'If you really mean any of that crap you say, you'll take these kids *and* give them scholarships if they need it.' I mean, shit man, I gotta tell you, I'm tired of worrying about what might happen."

"Dixon, I don't know what happened to you these past days, but I'm glad of it."

"Nothing happened to me except I realized most of life can't be fixed, prevented, stopped, or started. People try because they're afraid to roll with it. This right here this morning is life. I didn't start it and it ain't gonna be stopped. Not here, not by these people. If it stops it'll be because we all stop, because the

232

old fear comes back. I've lived with it, I gave it to my kids. I regret that."

"You gave them the rest too."

"I don't know, man."

"Man, I'm gonna get you down to the shop and turn you on to some jazz!" Sensing the chance to pounce on his old friend, Dixon snapped out of it.

"Jazz, Ralph, man, I hate to tell you this but I was dancing to Fletcher Henderson when you were still singing in old man Taliaferro's church choir."

"Man, you lying and you know it. First of all, you can't dance. I never seen you dance in your life except once or twice your wife would get your lazy butt out the seat at a dance. You were dancing to Fletcher Henderson, man, you are full of shit—"

"I'm telling you, Ralph, when my brother Teddy came back from the war, every chance he got he dragged me to dance halls and gambling spots. Took me on the steamer to New York once to his place in Harlem. Bessie Smith lived in the building next door to my brother Teddy." They spotted Coleman Boteler standing across the street. Ralph yelled out to him.

"You better come on over here, man." Cole crossed the street.

"What you come out here for, Cole? Taking notes for your novel or something?"

"I don't know what I came down here for, to tell the truth. I don't really believe in this kind of in-the-street bullshit. What can it accomplish? Something symbolic? You look like a bunch of nicely dressed Christian colored men going into the lion's den."

"Don't start, man. Can you carry a sign?" asked Ralph.

"What kind of sign?"

"Don't ask me what kind of sign, man. Here, we'll just give

you one, you get in with us. We're gonna be the barrier between these white folks and the kids, and if some mess starts,
use the stick." Ralph handed Cole a sign.

"You must be kidding, man."

Ralph grabbed his arm. "You know, you a good-for-nothing
elitist Negro. I'm tired of your shit. Just get in here, we need
another body in this group. And shut up. Are you with us,
Negro, or not?"

"Take your hands off me."

Dixon took hold of Ralph's arms and pulled him away. "He's
okay, man, he just wants us to talk him into it. He wants us to
convince him with some logic, but we don't have time for that
now."

"That's alright, Dixon," said Cole, straightening his jacket.
"It's worse having to listen to you try to explain me to somebody. I'm as tired of the shit as the next man. What do you want
me to do?" Dixon tried to keep from looking surprised and
sounding too cheerful.

"Just get in here with us." They got the signal to move down
to the door of the store. Ralph patted Dixon hard on the
shoulders.

"Brother mine," said Ralph, "let's give the white people
some blues."

As it neared nine A.M., white people had stopped on their
way to work and assembled on the opposite side of the street.
When the eight students walked up they were dressed formally
as before—suits, ties, trench coats, hats, polished shoes. One
young man wore his ROTC uniform. And for the first time
there were several coeds in the group. The young people were
accompanied by eight adults. Both groups would enter the
store. One group would sit while the other pretended to shop.
Once the first group was arrested the second group would take
their seats. In the window of Woolworth's was a large sign that

234

read, WE RESERVE THE RIGHT TO SERVE THE PUBLIC AS WE SEE FIT, and there was Mr. Anderson, obviously so nervous he'd become stiff as a board, warily unlocking the front doors. Ralph, Dixon, and the other men lined up on either side of the protesters and slowly started to walk toward the Woolworth's doors.

Whites started screaming until they settled into something close to a chant: "Niggers go home." A woman stepped across the street and threw her paper coffee cup at the marchers, spit at them, and walked on. At first the protest group looked shocked by the noise, but then, as if in silent agreement, they looked forward and the procession moved on. A white kid broke loose, ran up, and lurched into one of the men before being yanked away by an adult. The eight boys and girls followed by eight men and women filed into the store, followed by the security committee. None of the sheriff's men were anywhere to be seen. The second group of protesters dispersed into the aisles, while the security men stood behind the students seated at the counter. The waitresses put up their CLOSED signs and at about that moment a thunderous roar was heard outside.

From Dixon's vantage point he could only see the white crowd across the street moving back up the street almost out of sight. Some looked terrified, some started to cheer. The picketers backed up too as screaming became audible from outside. One of the boys on line stuck his head in the door and yelled, "A gang of rednecks comin'. They've blocked off the whole street. You want us to come inside with you?"

"No," Ralph yelled, "you get the women and kids the hell out the way. Go on now." The boy disappeared and started moving their people back away from the store windows. The glass doors of Woolworth's were slammed back and one shattered as a gang of white teens stormed in all at once. They stopped dead in their tracks when they saw the students at the counter. The young white men, their hair slicked back into ducktails or hanging long in the front and pressed neat around the sides like rock 'n' roll singers, wore only jeans and tee shirts or sweatshirts, some had on sunglasses, some looked like farm boys. Some had pencils or cigarettes sitting over their ears, or cleat shoes hanging around their necks as if they'd just run out of football practice, and some carried baseball bats. The waitresses in pink nylon uniforms with white aprons and white paper folding hats ran to the rear of the store. One of the girls dropped the plates she was loading onto a shelf.

"Looka there, looka there!" the leader shouted, raising his hand to slow the mob down as more and more boys rushed in. He sauntered toward the counter. Mr. Anderson ran up, waving them off. "Don't y'all come in here starting no trouble. The sheriff is on his way. Y'all just go on home, now."

"What's the sheriff gonna do, arrest alla us?" He started laughing and pushed Anderson aside. "Get out my way; we're gonna do what you didn't have the guts to do. We're gonna protect white people from this kind of slime. Look at this, niggers sitting at the counter waiting for some food." The security committee stepped closer to the counter seats.

"Where in the hell is the sheriff?" Cole muttered to Dixon.

"Likely he's on a sick-out today. These are *their* boys."

"These no-good bastards," said Cole. "They don't change from one decade to the next. You're staring down the same rednecks when you're a man as you did when you were a child."

"Where's the damn sheriff? Fuck, man!" said Ralph.

The ringleader of the mob stepped closer and watched them and then said, "I need my linebackers here." He motioned and about forty boys rushed the men, grabbing their necks and pushing them back. Mr. Anderson started screaming at them to stop. Punching and shoving started as the security committee struggled to maintain their positions. The boys pushed one of the men to the floor and began stomping him till he moaned and everything stopped.

"So you niggers want some food?" he jeered. The boys laughed. The leader grabbed a sugar jar from in front of one of the students and began dumping the contents on the students' heads. Two others reached for the lemonade cooler slowly stirring and sweating further down the counter, ripped it from its moorings, and threw it onto the floor behind the counter. "Lick it up, niggers." The mob roared with laughter and began trashing the students with ketchup, mustard, salt, pepper, anything in sight. The students sat stoically still, metamorphosing into grotesquely disfigured, forlorn human sculptures with whitened hair and ketchup-bloodied clothes. The teens lit up cigarettes, flicking the ashes on the floor or at the students, and admired their handiwork. Some wrote words on the backs of their victims; some just convulsed in fits of laughter. Slowly they realized there wasn't going to be any reaction, and angered by the protesters' silence, they began to jeer. One flicked his cigarette ashes on Cole's tweed jacket and blew the smoke at his face.

"You're getting sooty, nigger." He grinned. Cole flinched at the smoke and stared back at the boy without speaking. One of the other bullies began to hold forth.

"Did you cut your balls off before they sent you down to sit at the five-and-dime? Are we integrating here with a bunch of ball-less little black pussies?" One of the girls was grabbed from behind, and she jumped.

"Hey man, this one's alive, get a feel." Ralph Johnson lunged free from a choke hold and knocked down one of the whites. Dixon yelled out as he struggled with two others, "Anderson, where's your goddamn sheriff?" The teens near the girl kept talking as if they'd taken no notice.

"Can we date if we integrate?"

"Man, I don't touch no nigger trash."

"Let's see how you sit through this, Mahatma Gandhi" said one of the boys who was smoking. He put the cigarette out in a young boy's back. The boy flinched as he realized what was happening, and one tear popped free from his eye.

"We're wasting time here, boys," one of them yelled. "Let's just get the niggers out of this place."

"Right." Then the melee began in earnest. Some of the young blacks outside the store tried to force their way in. The white teens yanked and pulled at the students, who held on to the counter. They beat them, ganging up three to one, and jumped the security committee members. The students, who had sworn not to fight, struggled only to get back to their seats, or covered their heads and crumpled up on the floor. The older men like Dixon and Ralph assaulted the mob with no restraint. A black man from the town got hold of one of the baseball bats and began to cut a swath through the mob. He smashed rows of jars, hair ointments, and shampoos off the shelves beside him as he moved on the whites. In relative safety behind him, Ralph, Dixon, and one or two other grabbed anything that might be useful as a weapon—broken jars, broom handles, hoses torn from the counter water faucets. Cole backed up as if to get out of the way, trying at the same time to rip the placard off its stick. He was grabbed from behind by a teen who had snuck into the aisle behind him. Dropping the stick, Coleman grabbed the hands locked around his neck and snapped forward so hard and fast that the boy flipped over his head. Cole fell on him viciously, choking him till the boy started coughing and trying to yell for help.

The white crowd surged again and everybody started swinging. Finally sirens were heard somewhere up the street. Two whites grabbed Dixon and shoved him into a now-bare shelf, slicing his head open at the crown. Seconds later the teenagers ran like a cloud of locusts swarming away from fire. All thirty-four Negroes present in Woolworth's were arrested. When they emerged from the jail the crowd of two hundred Negroes waiting to take them to the hospital cheered.

By noon parents and car pools started showing up at my school to pick up kids to keep them from walking home through downtown. Preston appeared, looking as if he'd tangled with the creature from the black lagoon.

"What happened? We heard some people got hurt down at the store."

"Yeah, some people including your dad. A mob of white kids came down there and attacked everybody. It was horrible. And no police, no police around anywhere. He's okay, though. Had to get his head sewn up. He's home resting. He's so riled up, it'll probably take two weeks for him to calm down." I was so scared I couldn't talk. Preston went on. "I mean it's weird, he's mad as hell that the police just let the mob come in, but aside from that, he seems happy as shit."

The old man was not resting at all. He was on the phone talking about he had a headache and he wanted a drink, and didn't the people need to have a meeting with the mayor? His face lit up when we came in. I was scared out of my mind.

"There's my baby," he hollered after getting off the phone. He hugged me and I broke down. "What's all this?" he kept saying. But he knew.

We turned on the news at six o'clock and there was no mention of anything happening in downtown Turner.

"It's a conspiracy," the old man started hollering. "They're going to let Negroes go down there and get their heads beat in and try to sweep it under the rug." He tried to get up, wanting to pace up and down the way he did when he was excited, but he was too dizzy. He had to stay home that evening while the protesters met again, which seemed like a good thing not just because we were scared as hell he might drop dead or something but also because he was in one of those moods that he probably would have been moved to get up and subject the people to a speech.

Preston took me with him across the campus to College Hall, which was overflowing a half hour before the meeting. People were screaming and hollering with each other about what had happened that day, but the protests were going to continue. Reverend Hardy had called the mayor and asked for a meeting about the mob and the police disappearing for the morning hours. He said the mayor told him on the phone that he'd spoken to the sheriff and the sheriff said he and his deputies had been overwhelmed with other duties that morning and just didn't get there soon enough.

"Overwhelmed doing what, writing parking tickets?" an old man snorted.

The mayor refused to have a meeting with anybody, Reverend Hardy said, and he blamed the college for causing trouble.

"Anybody else who goes down there," said Reverend Hardy, "will be charged with trespass, resisting arrest, riot, and anything else they can think of. He seems to have lost any sense of decency, or Christian moral values. I don't need to tell you they tried Jesus just this way. It seems to have fallen to the Negro this time to teach the Christian lessons of brotherly love."

"Reverend Hardy, sir, it has not fallen to me to teach brotherly love here," said a leader from the fishery, a short, stout man with a graying beard coming in on his face. I knew his face from the docks. When I went with the old man to get fish he was the boss you saw first to get a man who would pick you the fish from his barrels and get them cleaned if you wanted them cleaned. Inside the dock where the fish were on ice in barrels all down the pier, you saw only Negroes working. They wore huge rubber boots and plastic aprons and were usually covered to the ears in fish scales and blood. "Now, if they're going to sic hoodlums on Negroes right there on Raleigh Street, me and my people will be there with them tomorrow, but we are not here to teach rednecks what they're not going to learn. We'll go with it either way it goes. We need many kinds of changes around here; integration is only one of them. Some of us don't care much about sitting next to white folks at a lunch counter, but we're with you 'cause we're for changes. But let this only be the beginning. We've been trying to get a union in the factory since the forties; other peoples wants the vote. The point is to you students, who'll be leaving here when you're done with your schooling, and to you integration folk, who I hear was trying to get your kids into the white folks' school—we're here, you got the whole town behind you, *but* you got to be for us too." Cheers rang out. "When they start firing folk at the factory, we want you college people with your suits down at *our* door!" More cheers. Everybody who'd ever bought a fish knew what he was talking about. If you went into the packing house where they put the crab up in cans, dozens of black women sat before huge piles of steamed crabs and mounds of the refuse from taking them apart and sorting out the meat. They sat talking in aprons and shower caps, their arms, massive or spindly, in a blur of motion. Everybody knew they had to get through bushels of the stuff for a few cents every day.

Ralph was beside himself, bandaged up and sitting in the front. He shouted back, "Y'all heard the man now!" Folks sitting next to him laughed and patted him on the back. Ronnie gave some notes on procedure for the next day. He mentioned that in a town in North Carolina people had thrown ammonia into the store where a sit-in was going on, and suggested everybody bring something cloth to put over their faces. And he asked for more bail money.

"The situation got out of hand today. We have prevailed on

everyone to remember that this is nonviolent. We're not fault-
ing anyone for what happened today. We had some courageous
people who kept those of us at the counter from getting hurt
worse. I'm ashamed to say I don't even know all their names. I
know I saw some professors who've been giving me some
rough grades down there"—people broke in with laughter—
"folks that I didn't expect to see, and I'm grateful." People
cheered and slapped anyone near them who had been among
the arrested. Coleman Boteler looked downright stunned by
the arms reaching out for him as he stood against one of the
side walls. "And my mama's grateful. So I just want to say, for
all of us, thanks."

Electricity crackled through the crowd. And despite the cold
outside, the packed room was starting to get overheated.
Danny Cobb said he knew everybody wanted to get home but
he had agreed that two more people could speak. The college
dean got up and put a damper on everything as best he could.
He was nearly shouted down as he tried to threaten the crowd
that their actions were "wrongheaded." Then Emmett Brown
got up. He was an older man, severe, formal, and, I'd always
thought, really stuffy. I figured my feet, which were getting
weary, wouldn't last through much of his speech. Brown
started slowly.

"I've always been a man of caution." I knew I was right. I
started looking for somewhere I could sit down. "I'm an old
man now, and there's really no reason for me to change. But I
was born in this town and I've lived here all my life, and I feel
time is due for an accounting. Negroes built this town, built it
from the scraps of slavery. Some of our folks ran here from
hellish places during the Civil War. Some came later to work in
tobacco or on the boats." Here he began to sound almost
angry. "It doesn't matter how we came here, we had it hard. I
don't know how many of you in here know it, but we were the

majority in this town from the time paterollers were riding curfew patrol through the slave quarters on these plantations till the 1880s. We had built this place and were running it, *running it.* I hope you hear what I'm saying. Our people had more to say about their lives then than we do now. Couldn't nobody call out no mob to clear us out of no store on Raleigh, it was all ours. We *voted,* we elected political leaders, we put the sheriff in office. Now, what that man from the fishery was talking about, we need to think about that. When they built the shipyards we went in there working. We had our churches standing way back then.

"What I'm trying to say is that the white people think we are asking for something they have, to join them or be part of their town. It's not so. At least that is not what I am doing. I want to take back what has been mine. It was my daddy's. It's been paid for. I'm going to do whatever I can do. If you want to sue to integrate the schools, alright. If you want to go down there and worry Mr. Woolworth, alright. But we need to have our own too. What's going to happen when you-all *can* sit down in Woolworth's? You gonna stop eating in Brown's place, that's what. My mother used to always say, ask for something too much and you might get it. Let's keep that in mind and try to look out for Negroes first, whatever that takes." The whole crowd was quiet and then somebody started clapping, and then everyone joined in. Maddie said she had only one note to add for the next day's work.

"Mr. Brown's got a point for us here. I just want to plead with everyone, don't go in any of the stores downtown and give those people any of your money. The mayor won't even talk with us, so let's show them something. We are the backbone of this town and the bulk of their business. Give your money to the Negro merchants. And tell your neighbors. Don't shop down there. If anybody wants to spread the word on this, see me after we're done here." A cheer went up. Maddie beamed. She had found her natural work, organizing folks. She stepped down regally to get her people together.

Cobb nodded to a gentleman in the back and suddenly Preston looked startled as the minister from New Jerusalem came forward. He walked up on the stage and bowed his head and everyone else followed suit. The man's voice started off in a prayer but began to sing and soon folks started humming. He asked God to bring us all together in his sight, stronger in his spirit. And he rocked a little. Slowly his hum became familiar and people began to rock with him. His voice started out high and lonely. "This li'l light o' mine . . ." We all came in behind him in a swell. "I'm gonna let it shine . . ."

"So, THEY all going down there?" Dixon asked. He was lying on the couch watching the TV.

"Yep. They raised more bail money," Preston said.

"Good. Was Cole there?"

"Yeah, man, you didn't tell me he was in there getting down!"

"My name ain't man, Son. I didn't know if that mess would send him back home or what."

"Well, he was there."

"What did the dean have to say for himself?"

"He made a speech. Said that now that the teachers were also getting arrested the college's reputation is being 'dee-*stroyed*.' But he did decide to suspend disciplinary action for the time being. People said that it was really because the mayor's acting like the white mob didn't exist, but he doesn't want to admit it," Preston reported.

"Maddie made a speech about not going in the stores," I

added. "They told everybody definitely do not go near Woolworth's to *buy* nothing."

Dixon laughed. "Willie! You've made your last lipstick-
shopping trip to Woolworth's."

"I don't buy lipstick in there. I don't wear lipstick, remember?"

"Willie, I don't believe it." He started laughing so hard he
had to grab his head. "Lying right to my face. You tell me
you're going in there to get bobby pins and go straight for the
makeup. You think you been fooling me!" I tried to keep
looking indignant. He was ridiculously happy again. Preston
and I looked at each other and shook our heads.

"I've never seen him so happy about stuff he disapproves of,"
said Preston. Dixon heard him and laughed again.

"You-all talk about me like I died twenty years ago." He kept
laughing. Finally the phone rang and we were saved from the
mysterious laughing black Buddha. It was Jeanne Morrow.
Preston and I eyed each other. Maddie called. Mr. Murfree
called to say he was coming, count on him. And Little Cole
called. His mother had called him to tell him his father got
roughed up at Woolworth's. He said he just had to check if
everybody had lost their minds. Little Cole was now in some
kind of special training at Fort Benning, Georgia. He was sort
of strange about it and said he couldn't say what he was training in. "Nobody at Fort Benning says what they're doing at
Fort Benning," he said. We all thought that was weird. He told
Preston he'd had a leave after finishing jump school but he
figured his parents didn't want to see him so he didn't come
home. Went to Atlanta instead. "Met some babes." Preston let
me listen for a minute. "The Deep South is real fucked up, man,
it's funky, let me tell ya. I saw a real live Ku Klux Klan march in
Atlanta, man. Eerie shit, man." Cole sounded four years older.

"Yeah, I oughta write a book about what's happened to me in 'this man's army' and I haven't even gotten out of training yet. It's good, though, I guess. Anyway, gotta go. I'll write when they ship me out, if I can."

Lillian and Cole called, elated over talking to their son. Coleman didn't even mention the incident at Woolworth's. Mrs. T called, and when it was late, Ralph called. They all sounded just as crazy as Dixon—that is, except for Dixon's sister-in-law, Aunt Joyce, in Washington, D.C., who was appalled and threatened to come down to Turner to have every member of the family committed, along with all our closest friends.

But Aunt Joyce wasn't there and we couldn't explain to her that it felt important. Each one of us had become precious to many; the many had become precious to each one. Dixon was the hero in our household, but that night there were heroes in dozens of households. Each one was the inspiration of five more that would be there the next day.

AT SCHOOL the next day, Friday, Mae Taliaferro told us how we fit into it. How we'd better *not* go near Woolworth's anytime soon and it would suit her fine if we didn't go in any of the white stores for a while. And then she took out the newspaper once again. This time she just said, "I suppose you know what's in here today." No one said anything because we'd all seen disgusted faces at home in the morning. "That's right, nothing." This time, though, there were no strange faces in the back of the room to get enraged over Mrs. Taliaferro's reading lesson. For the first day in nearly six months there were no white observers in the classroom.

"Today," she said, "I think our friends have left us Negroes to tend to ourselves." She smiled. "I thought we'd talk about an idea called 'civil disobedience.' "

When the orderly troops of protesters and sign carriers arrived on Raleigh Street that morning the sheriff's cars were visible at the intersections. A handful of teenagers were scattered about the street, this time accompanied by a few adults like Herman Shaw, one of the classroom visitors who'd tried to get Mae Taliaferro fired. He called the Negroes "dirty Communists" as they filed past. The Woolworth's was locked up tight with a sign taped to the front door that read, CLOSED FOR REPAIRS. Neighboring stores were closed too, with emptied display windows and signs saying CLOSED FOR REASONS OF PUBLIC SAFETY. The protesters contented themselves with forming a picket line and chanting, "Integration now!" Occasionally they would improvise a song to an old spiritual, refrains like, "It was good enough for Greensboro, it's good enough for me!" or whatever came to mind. Inside the store Mr. Anderson climbed on a ladder to take down a sign splattered with condiments that used to advertise HAMBURGER 10 CENTS. A gang of carpenters and handymen were ripping out the seats from the floor in front of the lunch counter.

When the air raid drill sounded at school after lunch all of us got the giggles. It seemed like a kind of funny time to review all the duck-and-cover procedures. As we lined up in the halls, stood against the walls, and waited for the janitor to unlock the basement door, everyone snickered. We had been taught to imagine that in an emergency we might have to live down there for weeks with the bags of canned string beans and yams we had brought to stock the "fallout shelter." Were they worried about the atom bomb coming down or the white people? Kids were muttering on the line.

"If they come we can throw these cans of old food at them rednecks, boy! Ain't nobody gonna *eat* that shit." One of the kids started singing a gospel song that played on the radio: "Everybody's worried 'bout the atom bomb, / but nobody's thinkin' 'bout when my Jesus come. . . ." The whole line started laughing. "Everybody's worried it'll be like Japan, / but nobody's thinkin' 'bout when my Jesus come—"

"Shhh!"

After the bomb run-through the school again let us out early, this time an hour early so that we would get across town or wherever we had to go before the white schools got out. At the last minute when I was wondering if anyone would be outside to pick me up, Julian Parker walked up to me.

"Uh, I forgot to tell you you're supposed to come over to my house today. Everybody's at some meeting with the lawyers."

When Victoria left school that day the startlingly handsome new boy smiled at her, and she smiled and looked away. Thought bubble: Hmm. He's still the cutest boy I've ever seen. "Hi," he said. "Since your pop got his head busted in the sit-in yesterday, my ole lady told me I better look out for you today. So, if you don't mind, you are in my hands." Smiling again. Thought bubble: I'm too shy, and I'm sure I'm not his type. Sigh. What will we do? Will we do our homework together, or slow dance to his 45s while his mom's not home?

"Oh. Okay, sure. I'll be ready in a minute." When we came out of the side door Dallas was standing at the door as usual to say good-bye.

"Hi, Dallas. My dad told me I have to go over to Julian's till he can get me later." He looked in Julian's direction, raised one eyebrow, and decided to be cool.

"Oh. Well, okay. I'll call you later. Or maybe you could call me 'cause the last couple of times your dad said he was using the phone for business and you couldn't talk."

"Yeah? Okay, I'll call you. He's probably got to go to a

meeting anyway. See ya." As we stepped out of anyone's ear-shot Julian spoke without looking at me.

"You feel like taking a detour the back way to town to see what's going on?"

NANCY LA Haute Couture found the unseasonably warm winter afternoon quite glorious as she strolled the streets of the handsome little country town to which she had been summoned by fate—?—by an urgent phone call from her old friend Della in Virginia. Who the hell is Della? And she was grateful for she had just escaped the cold, long-nailed clutches of Doctor Doom in New Mexico—no, Hart-ford?—Nome, in Nome, Alaska. But now the problem was what to say to—what to say to this boy. She looked at the creature out of the side of her eye. He was still such a boy. She said nothing and tried to keep up with his strides down the side streets, out of the watchful sight of their own street and over the stone bridge. He seemed happy to lead, which is to say he walked to downtown as if he had planned to whether she was there or not.

How odd, how very charmingly odd, thought Nancy as they entered the rear screen door of the A&P and were pitched into the dark of the loading area with its smelly boxes piled around.

What the hell were we doing? I wondered as we strode through the fresh-produce section nearly empty of shoppers, sauntered past the giant red coffee-grinding machines, past two white cashiers, and out the front door back into the blazing light. We crossed the parking lot opposite the A&P and strode again rather determinedly into the even darker back door of Pierce's hardware store, bobbing around the garbage cans full of up-ended rakes, shovels, and hoes, past the musty smell of endless boxes of nails, right under the face peering across the hundred-year-old cash register, and out the front door. We stood hugging the corner of the display window and peered on the scene only a couple of doors away.

We could hear black people singing down the street but couldn't see the front of the dime store half a block down because right in front of us a clump of white folks stood gathered around someone talking. Even though I mostly saw the people's backs, the few I saw from the side were looking pinched up and mean in their faces. I could see the nervous feet of the man who was ranting in the center of the group.

"What is it?" I asked Julian, who was taller.

"One of those men from school."

"From school?"

"You know," he whispered, "one of those white men who've been at school." Oh, God, I thought. We were gonna catch hell. Still, I started inching forward into the coats.

"What are you doing?" Julian said, still whispering.

"I'm just going to look for a second." I pushed my face in between two of the people. It was Herman Shaw, the man who had hollered at Mrs. T.

"You-all have become complacent. You've gone slack and let down your guard. You've forgotten where your klavern is, home watching TV every night while these niggers are planning to run you out of your stores, run you off Raleigh Street. You just stand by and let Sheriff Wilson and his boys wrastle with 'em. You gonna let these coons take over this town and tell you what you do?"

"Shaw, you don't need to be talking this stuff right here on Raleigh Street."

"Where the hell else should I talk it? This is my street, a white man's street. This is the white man's town. White men built it, and defended it, defended it in the Civil War, the world wars."

"Shaw, Shaw, come on now, you gettin' carried away listenin' to yaself talk. Those planters left this place and let it burn."

"Hell, we built the ramparts here. And we poor working *rednecks* ain't never run nowhere. We been here and had our klavern, kept things like they should be. We been here right along while these bankers and such was comin' and goin'."

"Shaw, you ain't authorized." Shaw took a breath and was silent for a minute. The man who spoke to him walked away.

"Do you know why the coloreds are among us?" Shaw shouted. I jerked my head back. "They are here to serve the purpose of being the scourge of God."

Julian yanked me by the back of my coat. He jerked his head in the direction of Pierce's front door. I followed. Inside Pierce's they were talking. "He thinks he's Exalted Cyclops; he's not supposed to be out there talking his head— You kids in here again? This ain't no thoroughfare!" The back door slammed as we hit the parking lot.

I stopped still, a tear trying to come up in my eye. Julian was walking on. I took in the full stride of him, tall, books packed sensibly in a Boy Scout khaki bag, so neatly dressed, vain.

Nancy La Haute had never walked behind anyone, not even in—
She could feel herself losing interest already.

When you got down to it, it was boring to walk behind some boy skulking around town. He turned and spoke from the distance.

"We can go down and just look in the back door of Wool-worth's, but then we better go back." That said, he turned and walked ahead toward the Woolworth building.

"He said we were put here to be the scourge of God," I said.

"Yeah, I heard him," Julian said, walking. "I saw rednecks

getting heated up like that when we were in North Carolina one time," Julian said. "And some people got killed."

"Shit. What's a klavern?"

"That's Klan talk."

"Oh, shit."

He stopped and looked at me shocked. "Do you say that a lot?"

"What?"

" 'Shit.' "

"Everybody says 'shit.' "

"You trying to sound like everybody? You're supposed to be Miss Thing, the last little Tarrant girl, head of her class, Jack 'n' Jill, debutante balls—look at you."

"You don't know what you're talking about." I felt stupid, searching for something to say. Miss Thing! "Miss Thing! Debutante balls! What's wrong with you? Besides, there's *never* been any Tarrant debutante." I was almost furious enough to tell him Tarrants were too snotty to be in cotillions, but I didn't. Self-preservation took hold. "What are you trying to say, anyway, that if you think I'm supposed to be Miss Thing, miss Jack 'n' Jill and debutante balls, that I can't say 'shit'?"

"Somebody who looks like you seems stupid trying to sound filthy-mouthed."

"Somebody who looks like me? That's the stupidest *shit* I ever heard in my life." I knew I was blowing it but I just kept on blowing. "What do you mean, somebody who looks like me?"

"Look at you. In your little ponytail. Look at your clothes. Your white blouse and navy blue skirt. You got on the coat they got in the store window downtown." His voice turned whiny and mocking. My eyes started to water. "Saddle oxfords like the kids on TV. You look like a girl who doesn't know anything." He turned and headed for Woolworth's. I didn't want to step another foot anywhere with this horrible boy. Bobby

Robinson who lived down the street and had a scar on his face and came around being creepy and talking about he was waiting for me to grow up was better than being around this horrible boy. But I had come all this way, risking getting into deep shit to see what there was to see in Woolworth's, so I was going at least that far. I could hear the singing getting louder.

There was nothing to see, though. The back door to the dime store was locked and only two lights were on inside. The shelves around the lunch counter were empty and black tar circles marred the floor where the stools had once stood. All the way through the store and the front windows I could see the picketers and people standing around jeering at them. The protesters sang and smiled at each other. A cop parking his car behind us slammed the door and barked at us.

"You little niggers get away from that door, y'hear?" We both turned and looked at him. "Didn't you hear me?"

"We heard you." Julian slowly turned back and strode away, never looking back to see where I was. As he crossed from the parking lot back to the A&P he suddenly turned right and headed for Raleigh Street. I followed. After taking a minute to study the length of Raleigh, he turned left and in long steps walked toward the bridge. When I got to the foot of the bridge I didn't see him anymore. Once at the top I could see him way up the street, pounding his way toward our street. At the foot of the bridge I ducked off the sidewalk and ran down to the waterfront. The tide was out and the smell was rank.

A rowboat sat beached down from the Botelers' yard. I put my books on the concrete beach wall and stepped in the half-dried mud, right away getting mud on the sides of my black and whites. I pulled at the rowboat's line tied to a post stuck in the mud. It wouldn't budge. Underfoot the mud gave way and then swelled again like a dampened sponge. The exhausted cove, which was slowly filling with little islands and turning to marsh at the farthest corners, was breathing and sighing as a coming tide began its pull on the earth. The tiny holes scattered about where clams lay hidden exhaled and weeped as my feet packed the mud. I went out farther and grabbed the boat on one side and shook and shook and shook. I began to pound the boat and rock it till the back end finally gave way. A sliver of water crept underneath the hull. I kept pushing. The boat dislodged from its helpless rest and gently rose. Soon it pulled at its line and eased back, riding the surface of the lapping water. I sat on the wall and watched it float, moving toward freedom and back, straining again and again for the river. The tide seeped in, easing the other boats into motion. I could tell by the sun that it was getting near five o'clock, so I cut back over to the road, sure that by now Julian was long gone. He was a totally horrible person. I hoped nobody saw me following that fool down the street. Hey, I could say we weren't together—we sure didn't look like we were roaming around together. Of course, if anybody saw me my ass was grass anyway. I figured he'd lie and say I'd gone home early, even though he wouldn't know what I had done. I would tell the same story.

I was acting natural when the old man came in. Actually, I was trying to get my shoes back to normal. He didn't even notice, just flopped down on the couch and said, "I swear this has been the longest week of my life!"

After a few minutes he turned his head toward me and asked, "Why are you polishing your shoes in the living room?"

"I was watching the TV. I got newspaper."

"Get that stuff out of here. On the double."

"You still having your headaches?" I asked, trying to change the subject.

"The only headache I have is trying to decide if my daughter gets into more trouble with some boy or by herself. You interested in hearing about my headache?"

"That's okay."

"Then best you leave it where Jesus flung it."

THERE WAS no sign of scourgin' Herman on the six o'clock news. No mention of the dead Woolworth's, even though it used to be the busiest store in town. The main news was about this huge thing they called a "shopping center" that was being built several miles out at the edge of town. They showed a model of the monstrous parking lot and all the glassy stores built in a horseshoe around the lot with its towerlike lights. "Buena Vista" would be the biggest boon to the local economy ever, they said. It was out where the white folks now had huge flat tracts of tiny houses that the old man said were called "matchbox" houses. There were hundreds of them out there, street after street of them all just alike. They had new roads, no trees, and lawns that hadn't started growing in yet. It was as if men from outer space had just blinked and manufactured this fake place for alien humanoids to live, complete with street names that were made up from magazines: Sunset Street, Poplar, Elm, Maple. The mayor was out at Buena Vista overseeing the progress. A reporter asked him about his plans to meet with Negro citizens.

"I have no plans to meet with the school integration group," he said. Dixon jumped up and stood over the TV.

"School integration? It's not the school integration group trying to meet with him!"

"But Mayor Ellis? What about the other Negro group?"

"The only recognized Negro group here is the one that has seen fit to pursue their goals lawfully by filing petition of suit in the courts. However, I can't say that I think the court will find any merit in their suit, and I might as well take this moment to say that the city has made a firm decision, after due consideration, not to rush into any experimental plan on school integration. We want to comply with the law of the land, and we will be in compliance when Turner has reached a state of readiness for compliance."

The old man yelled, "What?!" Ellis was a tight little man enjoying a moment of vengeance.

"So you will fight if they win in court."

"I doubt seriously if we will have to fight anything."

"Mayor Ellis, was this decision reached in reaction to recent events in the town?" The mayor laughed.

"This, sir"—he waved his arms at Buena Vista—"is the most exciting recent event for Turner. We have some troublemakers in town, and they have greatly chagrined the good people of this town. Let me tell you, sir, the white community of Turner has been wounded by your 'recent events.' We're all victims here."

THERE WERE no more visits to the stores on Raleigh Street. No more browsing pretty hats in Idell's millinery. No more sunglass fitting at Woolworth's. No more lipstick. No more comic books. Or hooks, nails, bamboo rakes, and liniments for sore muscles. No hair rollers or hairnets. No more teen apparel for spring at Walters' department store. No more yard goods to have the same outfits made by Lillian Boteler when I'd picked one I liked for Easter. No buttons, no zippers, no more sewing experiments on Ma's old machine. No stops at the Girl Scout equipment counter to look at what I could have had on my uniform if I hadn't felt like a fool being one. No more window shopping at Berman's shoe store, even though he always let Negroes try on the shoes before buying and even let us have an account.

That Saturday morning after Friday night's inevitable meeting, Dixon laid down the new laws of life over breakfast. I was told I was not ever to set foot in the white folks' record store, where they let you go into a booth and spin the 45 one time before you decided to buy. If I wanted to waste my money on records, the old man said, I would walk, not take the bus, over to Dootsie Burleigh's daddy's shop by the Baptist church. Don't let him ever catch me or hear about me stopping at the white man's food stand at the foot of the bridge for a barbecue sandwich, not even a french fry. Don't buy a Coke out of the white gas station's soda machine. Nothing. And there would be no more movies, period.

"Willie Katherine Tarrant," the old man said. "You are off that hook you didn't want to be on. The man has officially told you now he doesn't want you coming across town to go to school with his children. And before you get too happy about that, I hope you understand that it's a setback for us. I expect you to be an adult about what we're going to do now, and be responsible in how you handle yourself. If the church group asks you to participate or contribute something, I want you to tell them you will be happy to do it. Or if Maddie asks, you help her. Even though you're a girl and you won't ever be asked to serve your country like your brother, I'm going to tell you what I'm going to tell him. You don't just stand up to serve the country when it calls, you have to stand up for yourself, stand up for the people in the country. And those two things will sometimes not seem to go together, but they do. So we're all going to do what we have to do here." Preston asked how long he thought all the boycotting would be going on. "I don't have the faintest idea, but it doesn't matter." It was like the old man's Gettysburg Address, short and, in the end, his final words to us on the subject of "recent events."

By the next Saturday we had passed through a frantic week of meetings and organizing that made the old Saturday chores look inviting. Maddie Alexander had more than got her way. After a week of sit-ins and the mayor's sudden recollection that white people voted for him, the Negro citizens' group had swelled till they had to have their meetings at First Baptist, the biggest church in town, and war had been declared. The churches had joined in and the college students would send bodies for the picket lines. Murfree and his boys were camped out with friends and "on call" in case the Klan folks wanted to threaten anyone. The black radio station announced an endless stream of special events at every black business establishment in town. "Rock 'n' roll with the barbecue at Robert's Roller Rink." "Walk, don't take the bus, to Taliaferro's Chili Joint."

We had to ask questions to find out particulars, like was Coleman Boteler at the meeting. "No, we haven't seen Cole since the night after his moment of glory downtown. I don't know, I should call him, it almost seems like that might have shook him more than I thought. I guess I'd started to assume he would hang in there with us."

"Especially with Mrs. Roberts coming to the meetings," Preston threw in.

"Watch your mouth. You don't know what you're talking about. I have the most smart-mouthed kids in Virginia."

"Yeah, Preston, what are you talking about?"

"Well, Dad, *you* know what I'm talking about."

"You're out of order, boy." The old man changed the subject. "Apparently, one of the facts puzzling the mayor and other whites who are so greatly disturbed by the town's uprising is that they don't know who's in charge." Dixon laughed.

Word was, the frightened Negroes the sheriff hauled into the side door of City Hall to appoint as spies told them, "They just doin' it, is all." The equally frightened Negroes who volunteered to see what they could see told them the same thing. The old man said it was so obvious who would be telling them anything that they would just have a church usher put them in the worst spot for hearing the meetings, or ask them to man the door, just for the fun of it. Parking lot duty, they would call it. "You check outside every ten minutes or so, 'cause we don't want anybody's tires slashed if we can help it. You know how white folks are."

Bobby Robinson knocked at the screen door and asked if anybody was home, knowing full well that the bacon he smelled was not being cooked by ghosts. He came in grinning and the old man told him to have a seat at the table. "I take it you'd like to skip cereal, Bobby, and go straight to the eggs and bacon?" The old man smiled. Bobby burst out laughing.

"Man, you are too funny, Mr. Tarrant. I like you."

"I know," said the old man.

"My dad went to get the car fixed or something, left early."

I got up to serve him a plate and hand him silverware. Preston passed him the comic pages from the paper and got up to put his plate in the sink. Dixon eyed Preston carefully and said, "Don't plan on running too far, I got work for you to do. Bobby, what are you planning to do today?"

"Nothing. There's nothing to do. It's going to be kind of boring around here with this boycott thing going on. From what I hear it sounds like we can't go nowhere."

"Anywhere."

"Anywhere. I'll be glad when school's out 'cause maybe my parents will let me go to New York like last year. This place is usually dead, but it's gonna be really dead if you can't hang out downtown. I mean I wanted to go down there and join in the protests but my parents wouldn't let me. I'd like some young white punk to get up in my *face* and say something."

"Toast, Bobby?" I asked.

"Yeah, thanks. I'd be time enough for 'em, Mr. Tarrant. You know you older folks"—I coughed—"shouldn't be down there getting your heads busted. I know you can't be trying to handle those high school punks. You need to let some of us young-bloods deal with 'em."

"Bobby, your face has already been in trouble." Bobby laughed, his keloid cracking his smile. "But thanks for offering. I think that's over for the time being. I don't know, the picket lines could get a little rough, but I think we can handle it the way we're handling it, young man."

"Yeah, right. Well, like I said, I'm blowin' this joint soon's I can."

"Cool, man," the old man joked. "But in the meantime I think I'm going to put you to work. I got more work around here than the three of us can do. Think you can handle that?"

"Well, yes, yes sir."

"Good. I think you could start by washing the car. Preston will bring it round to the side of the house. He and I have some painting we have to do and after you finish with the car, you can help us. Willie will get the hose for you, a bucket, sponge, whatever else you need. Then she's gotta get out of here and get over to her cousin's house," he said, looking at me.

While Bobby was eating I had to get the old man out of the kitchen and tell him that we had to get rid of Bobby by dinner-time because I had some plans. He just looked at me.

"My friend Dallas is coming over and I don't want Bobby sitting around visiting when he comes because he always acts so stupid and—"

"Young Dallas will think he's visiting you?"

"I kind of have enough problems with that. It didn't help that you told some of the parents that me and Julian were downtown listening to the Klan."

"Well, you shouldn't have been down there."

"Yeah, I know, but that's not the point. I mean, the point is he thought I lied to him."

"You probably did. You weren't doing what you were supposed to be doing."

"Well, yeah, but I didn't *know* I was lying to him at the time, and that stupid Julian tricked me."

"This gets more and more complicated. How could that poor boy trick you, the master schemer? I hope you don't expect me to believe that Katherine the Great was tricked by some mere boy." He started laughing.

"Look, Dad. The main thing is I just don't want Bobby sitting here later."

"The boy is just coming over to visit? What do you have planned?"

"Nothing, Dad. There's nothing to do, remember?"

"The college is showing a movie over in the auditorium for the students since nobody can go to the movie house. I don't know what it is but I thought I'd go over there." A movie with Dallas and my dad. Oh boy.

"WHAT'S THE dress? Informal. Any old silk dress you have." Maddie was on the phone trying to turn one of her club parties into a fund-raiser without sacrificing her principles.

"Sequins? Oh God, no. Just velvet or silk, honey, and don't you dare come in there in something new or I personally will wring your neck. I'm sure you've got something in there to wear. Just look at it as giving up shopping for Lent. I've decided I'm giving up white folks for Lent."

Maddie's kitchen table was covered with mimeographed flyers that said, "Resurrect Your Old Rags for Easter, Don't Shop Downtown, Let Your Feet Walk and Your Money Talk. If you have clothes you can donate for the poor, bring them to your church at least a week before Easter. —Turner Citizens and Combined Churches of Turner." Marian and I were "assigned" to do the Saturday morning dishes, bundle the flyers, and be ready to roll when Maddie gave the signal. It was even worth doing dishes twice in one morning to get out of my house before the old man could make me listen to Bobby Robinson's mouth anymore. He'd convinced Bobby that he needed to work with the church youth group and told me I should take him there for the meetings. I knew they'd make me work with him, but I had gotten out of it at least for a week. Saturday was Maddie's big day to hit the stores as a boycott monitor. During the week she worked the picket lines but on the Saturdays leading up to Easter she had to go in and roust any colored folks who were not honoring the boycott. After she finished telling several more women what to wear to her dance, she hoisted her purse, which was the sign to pile the stuff in the backseat of the Oldsmobile.

In the parking lot of Walters' department store Marian and I unloaded a couple of stacks for the picket group and took them around to the front door, then returned to the back door, which was unmanned, to leaflet anybody coming in from the lot. Maddie bounded into the store and scoped out the first floor: yard goods, notions, men's wear, casual wear, women's accessories, and cosmetics. Coming upon some poor, unsuspecting Negro in any department, she'd walk up and stand very close to them, pretending to look over some item, and say very quietly, "I know you're not intending to shop in here today with your neighbors outside walking the picket line." Usually they'd say they forgot. If anyone was hardy enough to venture an attitude, she'd just eyeball them and say, "We all have to stick together in this thing. Why don't we just put these things down and stroll back to the door? We could talk about it outside." They always said thank you and left. In twenty minutes she'd scoured the three floors of the store, including the women's dressing rooms, and returned to the car.

Marian and I talked as we stopped and waited outside every store on Raleigh, meeting and greeting on the sidewalks jammed with neatly dressed Negroes with signs and leaflets, and the scowling whites passing by. By late afternoon we headed out to the new shopping center, where only four or five shops were open for business, and then drove back to town to drop leaflets at some of the supermarkets. On days when Dixon couldn't get out I had his food list and would have to go in the Negro butcher shop and down to Mr. McArthur's farm near our house for fresh produce. If we wanted ice cream, we went to the college dairy as the last stop before heading in.

That night Dallas appeared right after dinner and we played records and talked for an hour while the old man sat on the porch. Preston went off to meet up with some girl, and he said he'd see us later, which meant he was probably going to the movie too, since there was nothing else happening. When it came time for the movie, I pretended I had to fix my hair again and told the old man to walk on down and we'd see him there. It was barely dark when we left, but Dallas and I walked slowly down to the auditorium. Hundreds of people showed up for the movie, which turned out to be *Elephant Walk* with Elizabeth Taylor. Once we had let the old man see we were there we snuck up to the balcony.

Set in a lush tea plantation in Ceylon, the movie was about these white people who lived in a lavish mansion built across the pathway always taken by the local elephant herd as it moved from watering hole to burial ground, or wherever they went, round and round every year. First of all, I was trying to figure out where Ceylon was because the whole setup looked like India to me. The white people, who looked really good, suffered terribly from the heat and mugginess and they were surrounded by murmuring Indian—Ceylonese?—servants who understood the gods and had problems of their own. Hundreds of sweating Indian-looking folks picked the tea leaves and were cruelly disregarded by the white planters because they were consumed with their problems with boredom, marriage, the heat. The surly owner used fences and walls to force the elephants to go around his land as they went on their predestined way. I realized there were lots of movies like this one. The white people were very nervous in these places they took over. And even though they thought it eerie and scary, they had natives dancing on the patio. The old native woman knew everything but said nothing. Dallas and I kissed till the monsoons came and everything went into disaster. When the elephants came barreling through the yard and crashed down all the marble balconies and columns and cracked the floors, the Negroes all cheered. And Liz Taylor got the other guy, who wasn't surly like the troubled white man. Next week they would show *The Bridge on the River Kwai*. Surly, scheming Japs take honest, undaunted Brits as prisoners in Burma. The famous theme song played. Everyone clapped.

ON SUNDAY mornings leafleters made the rounds of churches. In every church in town the sermon, with varying degrees of passion and oratorical flourish, was the same. Although the ultimate accounting comes for all of us at Judgment, some earthly debts now had to be paid. Everyone brought to the prayer bench the miseries never assuaged, from Jack Dempsey being shot in the back to the abuse heaped on the kids in Woolworth's. Old folks brought the long-kept hells of survival back to the forty acres and a mule. Teenagers were still reeling from the shock of facing down bottles of urine tossed at them on the street by roving bands of white thugs. The song of crowded churches became all the stronger serving as a balm for so much anger and so many privately held, privately known moments of living as shifting shadows on the sidewalks of a southern town.

Coleman Boteler, who had stopped coming to any mass meetings, started to come to church, not every week but maybe every other week. He was always quiet, no longer as gregarious and social as he had always been among folks. In church he appeared to study the interior of the room, staring without expression at the beams over the altar, or at people in the church, and then sometimes he just gazed outside the clear windows of our church that was too poor to have stained glass. Sometimes he looked annoyed.

Coleman was most annoyed with himself for having a fixed opinion only on what he did not want to do. He could not get a handle on what he should do. Since he had had his fight with the white bullies, and one night of exhilaration, he hadn't written a word. Without even being able to articulate the futility of trying to write, he had just come up against the stupidity of it all. But why was it stupid? Round and round. Finally he tired of facing the same blinding, invisible wall on Sunday mornings and offered to accompany Lillian to church. She had not the vaguest idea what was wrong with him but she knew something was wrong. He dressed without all the usual preening and fuss; he just dressed. When she slid close to him in the bed one night he turned and looked at her and simply said, "I think I'm not interested in sex anymore. I don't feel anything about anything, except those crackers." And he didn't even glance toward Charlesetta, that she noticed. Charlesetta noticed too. Lillian could see at church that, in spite of having looked more and more beautiful as the fall and winter went by, now Charlesetta always looked puzzled and panicked. She wanted to walk up to her and just tell her not to be hurt, something unaccountable had happened to the man. She wouldn't have minded doing it at all but she thought

Charlesetta couldn't stand the embarrassment of having her questions answered by a wife who'd become friendly.

One night Coleman got drunk and went into his office and started ripping things up. When Lillian spotted him going out the back door with a trash can loaded with typed pages, she knew it was the manuscript he'd nearly finished. He hadn't let her read it yet. As she looked through the kitchen window she could see him bend down, flip open his lighter, and set the papers on fire. When he'd passed out on the couch she got her phone book and went up to the bedroom and called Mrs. Roberts.

"Charlesetta, this is Lillian Boteler. I wanted you to know that Coleman is in a bad way. I have no way to help him. If it wouldn't be a problem to you to speak with him, maybe you could be of some help. I'd be grateful." Then she hung up the phone.

THE WEEK before Easter the city fathers brought out their dogs. Maybe they had just acquired the dogs, because no one had ever heard tell of the sheriff's office having to use dogs for anything. If they'd ever had a manhunt with dogs running somebody down in the woods, it hadn't gotten in the papers like that. And there is no question that after they got the dogs they began to use them real regularly, showing up at black folks' apartment courtyards and opening the backs of the caged-in station wagons to let German shepherds out when neighbors reported a party was too loud. But when they opened up the wagons out front of Walters' department store and held them on long leads in front of Maddie Alexander, Cleo Parker, Jeanne Morrow, Helena Brown, and Martha Ruth, and Dootsie Burleigh's mom, the women were frightened out of their minds. That first afternoon the cops just stood there as the dogs lunged and growled at the women circling Walters's front door. Helena yelled for the children who were out there to get back up against the front door of the store, where white patrons inside were pressing their faces against the glass in panic. The women stopped and lined up in front of the children.

"I hope you don't think you're going to block the doorway there," said Sheriff Wilson. Cleo ventured forward. The dogs barked. The youngest children began to scream. She shouted over their noise.

"You have no call to bring these animals out here to terrorize us. We are within our rights of lawful assembly and demonstration."

"It ain't lawful anymore," the sheriff shouted back. "Y'all need to clear on out of here right now."

"We're not going anywhere," she yelled, without so much as a glance at the other women. "You better get a court order or a judge or somebody to declare we ain't citizens anymore if you think you're going to stop a legal demonstration."

"I don't have to go get anything. I am the law. Besides, I'm out here to maintain order on my streets. If one of these dogs should get away from me or my men, that's just too bad."

"We got to send the children away from here," Maddie said. Mrs. Burleigh agreed and called her daughter Martha, who was the oldest child there.

"Martha, honey, you take the children and you-all hold hands and walk very slowly away from the door and go down the street here to Mr. Johnson's barbershop. Tell him what's happening. Then you just sit in there and wait till we can get you. Now if he tells you he's going to take you home or call your father, you just do what he says, okay?" Martha agreed and took everybody on down the street, all of them looking back over their shoulder as they went. The owner of Walters' came out, looking sheepishly at the scene as he stepped across the street away from his own front door to watch. Nathaniel Burleigh and Ivalou Ellis, the mayor's wife, joined him.

"Well, either they're gonna do something or they're not," said Maddie. "Let's just go on and see what it's gonna be." The women reassembled in a line and began to circle again in front of the door. Excited by the movement, the barking dogs began to jump wildly. Cleo started the chant and the women began to shout.

"Segregation has got to go! Mayor Ellis says go slow, but segregation has got to go. Mr. Walters says go slow, but segregation has got to go. Eisenhower says go slow, but segregation has got to go. Sheriff Wilson says . . ."

Ralph Johnson appeared, followed by several black women who joined the line. Ralph asked if they were alright. Helena Brown, suddenly emboldened to her own surprise, said, "So far, so good, Ralph."

The sheriff kept shouting, "This has gone far enough," but his words were hard to make out over all the noise. Herman Shaw strode up, excited and grinning, and took a position behind the deputies with the dogs.

"You niggers better get on outta here or you deserve what happens to you!" Shaw yelled. Nathaniel Burleigh came over and tried to pull him away. Ruth Burleigh, tiny, brown-skinned, broke from the line and rushed in the white Burleigh's direction.

"Why you pulling him away, Nate? He's your boy, you got him out here doing your dirty work for you. Him and all his Klan buddies are out here every day calling for blood, itching to get us all killed if they can. Don't think you fooling anybody. You're in it too. You and Miss Priss over there, Ivalou Ellis, acting like you don't have nothing to do with it. You-all think you still own us. You gonna sic dogs on your own kin, Burleigh?" Nate Burleigh backed away. Turning even more fierce, Ruth went after him, a German shepherd now snarling and leaping for her arm.

"That's right, back away. You chicken-shit cracker. Let your

268

cops and dogs take care of the niggers for ya. Don't nobody have to know your grandpappy was still making black Burleighs while you was growing up to be a high-and-mighty round here!" Ruth started laughing demonically. The dog snatched her arm in his teeth and she howled and fell toward the dog as everyone began to scream. Ruth laughed and screamed and the other women bolted in her direction. Burleigh, Shaw, and the other bystanders backed away in horror as the deputies slackened their leads and the dogs tore into the women's legs, purses, skirts, arms. A siren pealed. Maddie pulled Cleo back from the dogs. Helena ran toward the store window. Suddenly the dogs were swept back to the wagons, raging as the deputies' grips dug the leashes into their necks. Two of the sheriff's men had Ruth in a choke hold on the ground. They hoisted her to her feet as the other women screamed. They handcuffed her behind her back. Her left arm was ripped open where the dog held on until called off. Tears streamed down her face. She locked her eyes on Nate Burleigh's face. Before she could speak again one of the deputies muzzled her mouth with his hand and, slapping his other hand onto her head, pushed her down and into the backseat of a sheriff's car.

"I'll get over to meet them at the jail," Ralph shouted. "Your kids are safe at my place." He ran down the street to his car.

The rest of the sheriff's men pulled out. White onlookers began to disappear. Maddie, Cleo, and the others inspected each other for cuts and bruises, shaking their heads, hugging, crying. Helena Brown said, "C'mon, let's not do that here. We can do that at home. Let's get our stuff and get out of here." They gathered up all the scattered signs and flyers, purses and hats, and those who had children at Ralph's headed down to pick them up.

"Be here tomorrow?" one of the women asked.

"Yes, ma'm!" answered Maddie, "I've never been so mad in

my goddamn life. But I tell you one thing, I'll be in some damn blue jeans and tennis shoes."

"You think we ought to get some of the men out?" asked Helena.

"If you want to, but I don't see what good it will do," said Cleo. "They've already proved they would sic the dogs on women and children out here in front of everybody on Raleigh Street, you know damn well they'll do it with the men here. Besides, who's going in this place spending all the money?"

"We are."

"Yeah, well, hell will freeze over before you'll ever catch my black ass in Walters' again," Cleo said. "I don't care if they integrate every dressing room, shoe department, toilet, water fountain, and the whole damn staff of the store."

"Amen, honey, amen. I'll probably be ordering from Sears Roebuck the rest of my days," said Maddie. Everybody laughed.

"They're just as bad."

"Don't start, honey, don't even start."

AT NINE the next day about fifty Negro women and about a hundred students from the college showed up outside Walters'. The other picket lines down the street were manned by one person at each store, just as advertisement that the boycotts were still on. The sheriff showed up at nine-fifteen with his station wagons and more dogs. The picketers sang and chanted and ignored them. "Woke up this morning with my mind . . . stayed on freedom." Some cracked jokes about the kennels being emptied out. The buds were peeping out from the branches in the churchyard across the street. Just above the trees there Louisa Tarrant's bedroom looked out on the scene, empty and dark. I looked over at her old view of Charles Walker Tarrant's grave, unmarked somewhere inside the church wall, a spot her eyes alone could find among the gravestones of two hundred years of town fathers. Drapes were going up over the church door for Easter. The old man let me out of the car with three thousand warnings and said he'd be back after he parked. Business was real bad. No one had been in the store much: Negroes had stayed away for weeks and whites had started going out to the shopping center where a clothes retailer had hurriedly opened. Walters' three floors of Easter stock was still on the racks. He agreed to go on with the business of using dogs out of revenge because even an end to the boycott now wouldn't save him a nickel. He put up a sign at the front door asking customers to use the rear entrance.

Sheriff Wilson had his men pace up and down the sidewalk alongside the demonstrators. All of us on the line had been told not to look at them but to look straight ahead and keep the singing going. The old man had given in and decided to let me come because he reasoned that the incident the day before had only happened because Ruth Burleigh broke the line and got in Nate Burleigh's face. He and some of the other men gathered at the edges of the picket line to keep an eye out for troublemakers or to jump in if things got hairy. Maddie had on her jeans and sneakers and was trying to look as if she weren't concerned about the dog at her heels. And so we walked up and down Walters' sidewalk for two hours. I felt frightened and yet I didn't care.

I had the funny sensation that if the dogs attacked perhaps it would hurt and still not hurt, as if the feeling of fullness in my chest would protect my arms and legs against the dogs' teeth. I felt faceless in the crowd of feet stepping to our chanted rhythm and yet I could feel every muscle in my face moving with the song that came out of me. At the same time, I could feel every muscle in my face being watched by hostile faces I'd never seen in my life before, looking to see why we would be doing this thing we were doing that no one had ever done. In spite of the utter fullness of feeling—as if I couldn't feel anything more—I could still feel their fear come out from their bodies like heat waving off a car engine in summer and feel it move near to my body and try to touch me, but of course it could not. Occasionally I shifted my sign from one hand to the other and looked at my hands, which no longer even seemed a part of my body. I could see they were red from gripping the wooden stick as if it were a bar by which I hung from the air. After an hour I barely had any sensation left in my arms from holding them up so long. But as we sang I would forget, and my mind would drift into a place I went often in church, or whenever the people had one of the mass meetings.

If we were in a big church I could feel myself float into the center of the room, into the center of a field of energy in the room. My heart would pound against my whole body and sometimes sadness, sometimes pity, anger, or relief would sweep me against the very walls of the place like a tide slapping me toward the shore, and then letting me glide in, only to draw me back out. On the street there, or when we marched from the college into town, I drifted to the free place. I didn't think about my life. All the particulars of my life would fall away and I could not keep them in my mind, sometimes not even enough to remember which shoes I'd grabbed that morning to put on. The songs would come out as if I'd sung them every day of my life, full of meaning and beauty, not like my voice, which couldn't produce a song at all, but beautiful and whole and there was no past, no next moment. And all the insurmountables shattered and fell around in soft pieces quietly around us. Defeat was small like a pebble, and even though I too was tiny and harmless, like another pebble, I would wash past the stones that looked large only if you didn't approach. The free place was a place I hadn't known was there.

My father brought me a Coke at the end of my shift, and

walked me over to a bench in front of Johnson's barbershop. He looked just then once again like my dad, the man I had always recognized as my dad, worried, tender, embarrassed to feel so helpless being a parent. He looked like the nice stout copper man who came home tired from work every day, or picked me up from dance class, or occasionally let me go on the fishing boat with him. Not the man I tried to prove things to or show off for, or the man who must've tried to give me away, according to Grandma Louisa, but the man whose chest I'd cried on when the white boy down the way kicked me in my mouth with his brown Buster Browns and knocked out my front tooth. He looked like the dad who went to the white boy's house and did something, because I never saw the white boy again and for all I knew the boy had disappeared forever. The dad who took me to the dentist and told him not to hurt me when he took out the rest of the tooth because I was hurt enough already. The dad who held my hand while they put the needles in the roof of my mouth.

When the second shift of protesters started up the deputies shouted and riled up the dogs. Before we knew it they were urging them on till people began to jump back, which upset the animals even more. People screamed and the deputies all at once let them jump the protesters. Dixon jumped up, told me to stay where I was, and ran toward the crowd. The deputies were grabbing hold of whomever the dogs attacked and tossing them back to others for arrest. When they had about a dozen demonstrators in hand they chased the others in all directions up the street. I ran inside Ralph Johnson's barbershop and watched at the door. It was all over in an instant. The sheriff's car doors were slamming, the sirens crying. The street looked as if a tornado had hit. People were scattered about, yelling, picking themselves up. One deputy remained, shouting over a bullhorn for everyone to get off the street.

* * *

EASTER MORNING came and the old man got me up early, saying that he had to take me to Lillian's before going to church. He and Preston had on their good suits for church. He told me to be sure and put on my good shoes. I put on the best dress I had. At the Botelers', Lillian took me up to her bedroom and pulled out a little navy blue suit with pearl gray buttons. Underneath the jacket was a little white blouse with pearly buttons.

"I hope this fits," Lillian said. "I didn't really have a chance to get a fitting on you, but your father brought me something you had in your closet." Then she pulled out a straw hat with a ribbon and flowers. "This I had my sister get in Philadelphia. Isn't it pretty? Do you like it?" The hat reminded me of the Madeline books I'd read when I was little, but the suit was beautiful. I hadn't really thought about having any Easter outfit. "I just thought you might like to have something new, white people or no white people."

Everyone at church looked more splendid than they'd ever looked before, decked out in a mixture of old and new clothes and the pride of having driven everyone out of the stores for almost two months. People hugged and kissed and spread the news of troubled businesses all around town. On the way to a dinner of roast pork, a pig Coleman had acquired at a farm up in the country, I asked the old man if he felt anything special at the mass meetings sometime, or on a march.

"Well, yes. I don't know if I can explain it, though. Sometimes it's like when I hear spirituals I heard when I was a child. Kind of a consoling feeling. And sometimes, like the other day with the dogs, it's like standing in the middle of a storm, but it's not blowing around you, it's like it's coming from inside. Power, it's a feeling of power."

6

THE SUMMER heat rolled in right after Easter and started to cook the town from the ground up. In the mornings that summer I'd put on something very neat and walk down a half mile to the church. There I usually met up with Marian, who was my partner for voter registration. Reverend Hardy personally took charge of the youth group from Anne Taliaferro, and set us on a career of visiting every Negro home in town. One week he loaded us into the church van and took us to the state's oldest church so we could worship blatantly as equals with the stuffiest Christians in the state. They were too stuffy to make a redneck scene and throw us out right there before God and in their Sunday clothes. On another outing he decided we should integrate one of the national historical sites, which technically wasn't supposed to be segregated but somehow managed to discourage Negroes from roaming out over the grass.

Marian and I would head out to the far end of Union, or

Lafayette, or Raleigh. We went to all the far ends. Going out Raleigh we would cruise past Lafayette, past the hardware store where the men used to get paid after daywork, and start stopping at every door. The first few houses had pretty gardens and freshly painted shutters. Women answered the door in the midst of washing or ironing, patting their hands on their aprons and smiling at how young we were to be coming round to tell them to vote. Down past the new barbecue joint the yards got a little scrubbier and more practical. Although the ladies with nice yards had neat rows of vegetables in the back along the fences along with the showy flowers, the smaller houses kept only the vegetables well watered and left the rest to fend for themselves. Fruit trees appeared randomly as good fortune in one yard or another.

At Bolden's Corner out-of-work sentries always stood, slightly inebriated, by the turn-of-the-century lampposts. A Coke machine stood along with them, too large to fit inside the tiny grocery, the only storefront left in business on this other-wise abandoned corner that was a dicey place to be on Saturday night. There were card games somewhere there behind a door that had two centuries of untended soot on the windows. The place wasn't meant to look open at all. We asked the men on the street if they voted and they smiled and just said, "Naw, honey, I try not to go to the courthouse." I'd never been in there either. We kept on down Raleigh till it ran out and doubled back down Ulysses Grant. Sometimes we ran into kids from school, sometimes their brothers, sisters, or just the family dog on guard. Usually, though, there was an older woman home, washing or fixing food. They talked the nicest and were the toughest to persuade. "It's so nice of you girls to come round here," they would say, and right away you knew they were not interested. Sometimes one would just stare off through the torn screen on the porch, rocking in her housedress with her ankles wrapped up in Ace bandages, and say, "To tell you the truth, I don't go anywhere too much," or "I got to watch the children, I can't be goin' downtown." Sometimes it would turn out that the woman didn't want to say she couldn't sign her name, so she would just say she didn't want to go. If we pushed her, she might just say that was enough, but most of the people we met signed. They all had their reasons, stories about how they lived.

I had my worst days when I went out with Bobby Robinson. We worked Beach Street together and right in the middle of our pitch one day, right in the middle of some woman's living room, he pulled a gun out of his pants pocket. I nearly fainted on the spot. Bobby began running on about how the gun was the only way to deal with the white man. The woman was very calm, told him to put the gun away, and heard him out. She said she'd think about registering, that was all. When we got out of there I started screaming what was wrong with him anyway, and was it loaded, and he was likely to accidentally shoot somebody, maybe me. He alternated between laughing and being mad. He told me all the voting stuff was crap. Negroes in the North could vote and what difference did it make? The gun was the way. I asked him if he'd been carrying it and telling people that every time he went out to organize, and he said, "Yeah." I told him to forget it.

At the next house he didn't take the gun out but he gave the rap. It seemed to me he was probably really worried about some white person shooting him for being out there canvassing the neighborhoods. Everything with Bobby was personal. He got thrown out of school all the time for carrying knives or fighting somebody although most of the time he was getting his ass kicked. He was a very jittery boy. I parted company with him at the third house. He hated heat and I figured he'd give up pretty quick without somebody to write down the names.

The town gave up its stories one by one, on the front porch or in the backyard feeding the chickens. People drifted out as if they'd been waiting for somebody to come by and ask the family name and how long they'd been there and what was the problem with getting indoor plumbing, especially in Burleigh's Fields.

One day Marian and I got way out Lafayette Street and were nearly lost looking for three streets we were supposed to cover. We crossed the broad avenue and headed across a field of high, dry, brown grass for a clump of shacks by the railroad tracks.

"Is that where the train didn't stop and killed Junie's brother?" Marian asked.

"I think so. But why would he have come this way? The tracks are closer to the road down there." I said pointing to one of the cross-county roads.

"They lived out here someplace," she said.

"You think there's streets over there?"

"No, but it's the only place left for these streets to be."

"Well, half the streets we've been on don't have signs. We just knew what streets they were. There ain't going to be no signs."

"Nope."

Finally there was a dirt road, deeply rutted and dusty in the heat. There were a few crippled cars sitting on blocks in yards down the road. At the first shack we spoke to the elderly woman sitting on the screened-in porch but she didn't answer. We walked up the steps and spoke to her again, but she still didn't answer. I opened the screen door just a little and stuck my face in.

"Ma'm, you mind if we speak to you for a minute?"

"That's alright, girl." I didn't know whether that was yes or thank you no. But I stepped on in, Marian behind me. She looked us up and down but didn't seem bothered.

"My name is Katherine Tarrant, ma'm, and this is Marian Alexander. We're here from our church." She nodded. "Have you ever voted, ma'm?" I asked. She looked surprised and spit a tar black fluid into an old paint can sitting by her foot.

"I tried oncet. That was a way long time ago. The forties maybe. Went down to the cou'thouse and saw them white folks. But they wouldn't let us vote."

"We're trying again, ma'm, and there's lots and lots of people who're going to go down there and register. We figure it's time."

"Won't do no good. Whatchu votin' for? You too young to vote anyway. Nothin' gon' change."

"If we Negroes vote, some things might change." She spit again. It was then as I watched her cough and spit that I saw she had a black tumor sitting on one side of her neck. She was very frail and her hands were battered as if she'd spent her days up to her elbows in some corrosive. Her age I could not guess.

"Look right there, girl, at that road. That's why I tried to vote."

"You wanted to get the road fixed." She glared at me to let me know how obviously stupid I was.

"Fixed! Shit. That ain't nothin' to fix. We was tryin' to get it paved and made *into* a road. Even just some tar. Right now you break a axle if you come 'long wrong. We's still waiting for a road. And some streetlights. We went down to the cou'thouse, all us. But they don' mean right, honey, let me tell you that. They not gon' do shit." I told her we were from the church and all the churches had people out to get folks registered.

"That's good, but I don't even bother with goin' to church no more. Can't make the walk. My legs are too bad for that."

"We'll come get you, ma'm. We'll pick you up and take you down there." She never invited us to sit down but she started to relent when we said somebody would come with a car. Marian told her we would tell the organizers back at the church that the streetlights and the road were very important.

"Well, I guess probably I could."

"What's your name, ma'm?"

"I'll tell you and you write it there."

"And what's your address here, ma'm?"

She laughed. "I bet you girls don't even know where you are, do you?"

"Not really, ma'm," said Marian. We all laughed.

"You go on down three doors, the lady there will sign." We thanked her and headed for the house next door, which was really not even in shouting distance.

"Ain't nobody there," she yelled.

Three doors down the woman inside with two toddlers signed right away.

"Y'all came out here 'bout the civil rights, didn't ya?"

"Yes, ma'm."

"I'll do it. You girls want some lemonade?" Evelyn Turner waved us in past her newspaper-walled parlor loaded up with chairs she was caning, and into her little kitchen that kind of listed toward the ground.

"You see that road out there? Well, first of all no school bus will come out here. The kids from out this way have to walk a mile down to the big road. But when it rains, you can't get in here or out. Can't none of us get out 'cause any kind of car or truck will get stuck in mud up so high it can't move. Folks what has to work has to start an hour early and walk out. It's hard going. Only three or four of us got phones." She led us back into the living room. We talked on as we tried not to swill down the lemonades all at once. She cleared the couch of all her work materials and we sat sweating and squeaking on the plastic covers, and wrote down all the problems she listed. Finally she looked at me hard.

"You must be Leigh Tarrant's daughter," she said matter-of-factly. I was stunned. I hadn't told her my name when she swept us into her house. "Sure you are, aren't you?"

"Yes, ma'm. But how did you know that?"

"You got the very face of her on your face."

"I do?" I'd never thought I had the anything of her on my face.

"Yes indeedy." She was very excited.

"I was very sorry when she died." I felt a knot in my throat, sat up straight.

"You knew my mother?"

"Hell, yes. Excuse me cursing. But yes, yes indeedy I knew her. She was out here a lot. I'll do anything you want, chile, anything. I'll get everybody out here to go down to the courthouse if that's what y'all want. It's no problem. Anybody round here tell you no, you tell 'em I said come ask me about it. I knew yo' mama. She tried to do something for the kids out here. Course the white folk wouldn't let her but she came out here and we all got organized 'cause she wanted to get a Boys Club started." She talked a blue streak and my head was spinning trying to keep up and put it together at the same time. My mother, the oddball everybody talked about as if she were a saint but for no reason in particular. My mother who the women sometimes spoke of with a tone as if they were trying to be nice because they didn't understand something she did. "You don't know what I'm talking about, do you?"

"No. I never heard about it."

"Well, yo' mama was out here, but the white folks wouldn't give her a charter for no Boys Club. Then she said we ought to go down to the City Hall and we went. And she was a mess, too, wouldn't let nobody ride the bus 'cause she said it was wrong to be riding in the back. She was from someplace else, of course, so we just humored her on that one, but look at us now. It's funny, ain't it? We tried to get lights when they put lights out on the county road. We tried to get the road tarred, and named. It's always just been Burleigh's Fields 'cause one of the Burleighs had it oncet. Then they run the railroad right t'ru like we wadn't even here. It's a whole nother bunch of folks over beyond the trees 'cross the tracks. She come out here and got some children that was left when the father disappear one time. The mother had took sick and passed and I guess he couldn't handle it. Or maybe he got killed, we never knowed. And then another boy got killed by the train."

"Yeah, I remember hearing about that."

"Cut the boy in half, threw him a half a mile down the track."

Evelyn Turner told me things I had never heard in my life about my mother, myself, how she carried me around everywhere and left me lying in the grass while she and some boys she got together began plotting out a softball field "out yonder" for the kids.

"It's still there and they're still using it." Marian and I looked at each other. "Something happened to her when she came out here, I thought. She said it reminded her of someplace in her childhood. Well, Leigh walked to her own drummer anyway, but you probably know that. Chile, I usedta see you when you were such a little baby. Let me hug you." And Evelyn Turner took me in her arms littler than mine and gave me one big crush.

She told us whom to see over beyond the tracks, but we considered how long it would take us to walk all the way back to the church and then home and decided to come back another day for that neighborhood. It was easy to see what Leigh Tarrant had found out there though, very easy. And it was easy too to see what the old man had been up against, trying to give what a woman had taken with her to the grave. Listening to her voice telling him about Burleigh's Fields. We stopped at one last house around the bend on the rutted road before heading back. When we knocked no one answered, but we could hear a TV or radio going, so we stepped inside the screen door onto the porch and called. We heard someone answer. Inside the open door we could see six people sitting in the dim living room, three adults, a teenager, and two children. No one looked up, except a teenaged boy who came toward us. Afraid to step in any further, we kept talking. Marian explained why we were there. It was then that we realized that none of them could see us.

"You say you're here about the voter registering?" he asked.

"Yes, we're from our church. If any of the members of your family over twenty-one would like to register, we could arrange for someone to get them and take them downtown. We'll be picking up some other folks out here." We stepped in a little closer. Once our eyes adjusted to the gloom we could see the wide living room was bare except for two couches and an end table. The radio was sitting in a little window onto the kitchen. Beyond, out the back door, we could see the laundry hanging on the line, an outhouse, and all kinds of piles of wood and junk in the yard.

"Well, I don't know if my parents will want to. There's not gon' be any trouble, is there?"

"Oh, no," said Marian, "I don't think so." We really didn't know if there'd be trouble or not.

"If y'all could come back sometime I'll know exactly who wants to go down there." He directed himself toward the sound of Marian's voice.

"What is your family name?" she asked.

"Whatley," he said. "You can put down that the Whatley family will send somebody down to the voting, okay?" We thanked him and left and walked in silence back around the bending track and headed toward the county road.

"Willie?"

"Yeah?"

"They were all blind."

"Yeah."

"How do they make it?"

"I don't know. Maybe somebody lives there who can see."

"How do you think that would happen?"

"I don't know."

"Did you know any of that stuff about your mom?"

"Nope."

"It's weird, isn't it?"

"Yeah. When she was talking, my mom's face came back to me so clear. And then when we walked out I saw the face of that boy."

"Which boy?"

"The one that was killed by the train. His name was Leon. I remembered him exactly."

COLEMAN BOTELER was pretty drunk on the road and he knew it, but he didn't really care. His son had called and said that he was being shipped out from Fort Benning but that that was all he knew. It didn't make sense. Little Cole just kept telling him that they wouldn't tell him where he was going and the old hands had told him that meant it wasn't in the country. The boy had sounded okay, but Coleman knew it wasn't okay. He'd wracked his brain about the thing and had a few drinks. Finally he just got in the car to get some air. He drove out the main highway till it ended and turned into the old two-lane blacktop, Route 1, that ran north through every town on the coast. He was thinking about what they might do with his boy and he kept muttering to himself, "I don't trust 'em, they're still rednecks."

Coleman hadn't trusted them since he'd seen his father hounded by Immigration for being a black man who came from someplace else to this country, hounded by officials for not speaking English, and caned in the street in Brooklyn by an employer who'd heard that's how they handled workers in Haiti. He'd been a reluctant American from then on but an American all the way: English-speaking, book-learned, and always with some dollars in his pocket. When he slowed down for the circle in the center of Gloucester he realized he'd gone pretty far, but what the hell, he didn't have any rush to get home and get to bed. As he passed the village center he picked up his speed. Coleman eased on down the blacktop again, spying on farms, stables, and open fields.

He was doing a pretty good speed when the lights came up behind him. He knew that, but he didn't think he was really speeding. His foot had let up by instinct and he was cruising down toward fifty miles per hour when he looked. The road was sure dark, not another car out there, but still he wasn't too worried. He was used to being stopped at night when he drove up from a trip out of town somewhere. He always made nice, let them see his tweed or seersucker, slowly retrieved his license and told the cops very carefully that he was a college professor on his way home. They usually said something about they just tried to keep an eye on the "bad niggers" or something of that sort. He pulled over to the shoulder. A flashlight shined in his eyes before he could get out.

"Out of the car and careful how you do it." The cops had their guns on him.

"Yes, sir, no problem," Coleman said.

"Naw, there ain't no problem, nigger. Now let's see an ID."

"It's in my pocket." The cop closest to him gestured for the other cop to get his wallet.

"You're pretty tanked up there, partner, speeding out here this time a night. We gonna have to haul you in."

"Here's his license," said the second cop.

"Haul me in where?"

"He's a teacher at that college in Turner."

"We gonna haul you into the jail, nigger, where else?"

"In Turner?"

"You long outta Turner, Professor. I hope you know that much. Where you coming from, one of ya race meetings?" The cop started to laugh. "I believe we'll be doing the white race a favor to get you behind bars. Folks down in Turner put up with a lot more stuff than we do out here." He kept laughing. "You sit-in niggers are scum, you know that?" Coleman didn't know what was happening to him. His head felt as if it were on fire and every hair were burning. His hand swept away the nearest man's gun hand and he lunged for the cop's neck and kicked him in the groin.

"Cracker motherfuckers!" The gunshot was the loudest sound he'd ever heard.

COLEMAN'S CAR was right there on the road when the old farmer's headlights picked it up. In the pitch black just before that spring sunrise he couldn't make out what the other thing was that he saw, so he got out to look. Most of Coleman's body had been shoved into the ditch on the shoulder of the road but for an arm and a leg at the top of the ditch. His wallet was still lying on the side of the road.

By the time Calvin Murfree heard the pickup in his yard he'd gotten a call from the only Negro doctor in the county that a college professor was down at the hospital damn near dead.

The doctor said he'd been able to stop the bleeding and get him a blood transfusion but that he'd smelled trouble when the sheriff came in asking questions.

"Murfree, I don't know, I told the sheriff that I didn't know what happened, but when the sheriff kept asking if the man had said anything I just blurted out that he said a colored man shot him. Then the sheriff looked more relaxed, said he'd be back later. He's got to have surgery right away, yet and still I think somebody better come down here and say they're the family and get him the hell out of the hospital. Take him back down to Turner, or anywhere. Understand what I'm saying?" Murfree said he understood and he had to go because somebody was outside. He swung open the screen door and ran out to greet the old farmer. Listening to the story, he knew something was definitely smelling if whoever did it just left him there, wallet and all, on the road.

"The man couldn'ta been too worried about nobody finding him or following his trail."

"Naw, suh," the farmer said. "And it wadn't no fight, neither. Only the Klan and the sheriff just leave a colored man where they take him down."

"Yup. 'Fraid you're right, man. A colored man would've expected somebody to come lookin' for a high-hat Negro with a nice car."

"Maybe it was the car. Anybody woulda knowed the car won't from roun' here. Maybe that's why he got stopped. Negro in a nice car, must be wrong. Anybody coulda tol' by the car he won't a colored man from roun' here. College professor too. I brung you his wallet." The farmer reached into his overall pocket and handed it to Murfree. "I know you know folks all over; maybe you could try to find his family. Whatever happen, he need to get out of this county 'cause he were left for dead, not to live to tell the story."

"You're quite right, sir. I'll see to it. And I don't need to tell you what you done for that man."

"Done what I could. But I came on to you for the rest 'cause I hear you take an int'rest in folks, thought maybe you could help. I got to get on 'fore the white man be on my back 'bout not being where I'm s'posed to be this mornin'. I'll have my own trouble."

"Yes, sir. I hear ya." Murfree laughed and promised to take it from there. He thanked the man again and watched him pull out of the yard. He opened the wallet in his hand and pulled out the cards. "Oh, man, Coleman." Murfree shook his head. Knowing the name on the driver's license actually made him feel frightened. He couldn't imagine what had put Coleman on the road or put the bullets in Coleman's body. So many crazy thoughts rushed in his head that he decided it was better not to try to find out. He'd just call Lillian and tell her to stand by, not to call the police. The most important thing was to get him out of the county hospital, and worry about the rest after that. If he was almost dead now, he'd surely be dead before much longer. Too many things could go wrong, including Coleman waking up. Once anybody heard what Coleman might have to say, even the way he might ask where the hell he was, there'd be trouble, never mind if some crackers shot him. And there was no point delivering him to the hospital in Turner since whoever did it knew Coleman was from Turner just like he and the farmer and the doctor knew. No, what he needed was an ambulance.

Several hours later a hearse showed up at the hospital instead of an ambulance. The doctor met Murfree, who got dressed in a suit, at the colored entrance to the little hospital near Plum Landing. The doctor was in a real sweat and shook his head at Murfree.

"Man, you've done some crazy stuff, but this beats all. You

got me risking my ass, and I got two nurses with their jobs on the line, but your man here is dead."

Murfree was matter-of-fact. "You told me to get him out of here."

"Here's the certificate. I snuck some blood and a glucose bag in the back of my car. We can hook him up when we're away from here. You got Smith straight?" Murfree nodded his head. "He can just do what he usually does and sign the papers." Murfree nodded again. "Okay, so just go in there and get him the hell out of there quick as you can."

"No problem, man."

"Yeah, yeah, so you say. I'll be waiting in my car till you pull out, then I'll follow till we get somewhere we can stop." Murfree nodded and went in with Smith, the undertaker, to the colored wing. Minutes later they emerged with the body and slid it into the vehicle. Murfree climbed in the back and took off the cover over the man and wrapped him up in blankets stored beside the mattress they'd thrown in the hearse.

"Coleman, you bad-luck bastard you, hold on."

In a hurried stop on a back road, the doctor put the blood and glucose lines in Coleman's arms. With Calvin Murfree holding his two lifelines steady, Coleman Boteler rode north for an hour and a half to a city hospital, stretched in the back of a hearse with the WALKER BROTHERS' FUNERAL HOME marker discreetly covered and two sprays of flowers perched against the back windows. Murfree kept talking to Smith about every detail he had learned about Coleman's condition, the alcohol in his stomach, how much Coleman could drink, how being a writer, the man might have something interesting to say about being so close to the other side, how he'd probably make it up. How he had no idea he was dead and no inkling he was alive. When they later told Coleman the story, through the fog of all the dope and dimness of memory, he laughed. When the laughter in his belly made him scream with pain he knew he wasn't dead because that, he thought, would be funny but it wouldn't hurt.

ALL THROUGH the summer Marian and I made our rounds and in the late afternoons we walked through town. Even in the late afternoon it was still blazing. We walked back through the downtown, past Ralph's barbershop, which was filling up with men getting off work, past Brown's, where folks were getting sodas and hamburgers. We passed Walters' department store and the others, nearly empty stores where only white people now shopped. There were no more pickets, because they were totally unnecessary. Ever since the police sicced dogs on people's mamas on the picket line nobody would go in there, not even people who didn't approve of the boycott. The store owners were regarded as animals for going along with the animals that brought out the animals. People didn't do business with animals. However closed off we might have been from the world other people knew, we regarded our ways as the ways of people.

The town lived in ignorance of our way of life but most of the time that had no bearing on our way of life from one day to the next. We were like South American tribes living deep in the bush whose names for themselves usually translated as "the people," and who called savages those strangers who did not know that the highest good was to say, "I wish for you to survive," and to offer to share their food. The people regarded themselves as simple-living, clean, Christian, and full of the qualities of the God spirit. The people regarded themselves as comfortable in the beauty of their bodies, graceful, with rhythmic and melodic qualities of the God spirit. The people regarded themselves as wishing for others to have life.

But the whites' ignorance that the people were the people and that the highest good was to wish another life had put them up against the will of the humans to live as people. We shut down the town. We never questioned if the way of the people could survive our own actions; our way was created by harshness. And we never questioned if the way of the people could survive if we lived among the others, because it was the way of the people and the fullness of the God spirit. And the other way was the way of animals who sicced dogs on people's mamas and children. It was not the way. At least that was the clarity of the moment in which we walked along our main street and saw the places boarded up, one after another, starved by those who thought the highest good was to say, "I wish for you to survive."

The starvation played no favorites; everybody, except the banks, suffered, and a lot of them went under, like the dress shops, the eyeglass shop, shoe shops, both drugstores, and the other five-and-dime. The Robert E. Lee movie house with its "nigger heaven" and broken machines tried to hang on showing sex movies and then died. Elvis Presley kept the white record store open and the bicycle shop made it because nobody else fixed bikes. No lunch counters were built at all at the Buena Vista shopping center. Confederate flags went up outside every white drive-in hamburger joint, on the antennas of every other car at the white beach, over the bowling alley and other places we never went anyway, and life went on as normal. Maybe a little better than normal some days. The college put on its movies every Friday night. The church youth group had dances almost every Saturday. Ike and Tina Turner were singing, "You're just a fool, you know you're in love," and the Shirelles had put out "This Is Dedicated to the One I Love," a song that made black girls croon in groups on the sidewalk, in the kitchen doing hair, in the basement after school. In the summer of

1960 white folks were a dog but the flip sides were really good. I became a thirteen-year-old. I went back to riding around at night in a car with Dallas, when it would take two hours to drop everybody off at home because we had to stop and get hamburgers and milk shakes or look at the bay.

DURING THE summer Preston stopped getting letters from Little Cole. At first he thought the letters had stopped coming because Cole had moved on to a point of such distance that he wasn't interested in the people anymore since they were so caught up in their American Dream. Preston acted guilty. He kept telling the old man he didn't need clothes for college because he wasn't planning to wear anything but blue jeans anyway. The old man didn't take this lightly—not because he wanted to spend the money, because he didn't—but he kept making reference to how embarrassed he was going to be when he heard tell of his son the bum walking across the campus of Howard University looking like a beatnik. Besides, he'd made Preston get a job as a lifeguard to help pay for the clothes and books. He kept after Preston about whether his problem was that the Negro tailor didn't have the clothes that he wanted. He said they could drive up to Richmond maybe. Preston kept saying no, that wasn't the problem. He didn't want any clothes. He wasn't sure he wanted to go to Howard University period. The old man did not enter rooms marked KID WITH NO COL-LEGE DEGREE, so he acted as if he didn't hear it and went on fussing about loafers and sneakers and Arrow shirts, and the dorm fees. Preston was bugged about Little Cole maybe being right. Preston told the old man he thought maybe he should go down to Nashville, one of the places where the sit-ins still needed bodies; he'd gotten interested in a new organization called the Student Non-violent Coordinating Committee. The

old man said no way. He'd better get all his stuff ready for
college.

WHEN IT came time for the annual picnic there was a debate
about whether or not to venture back into Murfree's county
with our officially dead Negro novelist Coleman, and it was
decided to go instead to Yorktown and picnic on the bluffs
overlooking the river. The schoolteachers liked the symbolism.
Preston didn't come because he said he was too old for it. The
old man invited Jeanne Morrow and Cassie, Pat, Chookie, and
Jeanne's grandson, Jack. The case of Jack Dempsey's murder
was never solved. Everyone knew it wouldn't be. At the picnic
they took up the idea of starting up the school integration suit
again and decided they might as well. Coleman told the story of
his death again and we all laughed, and he also told Charlesetta
she should go into prophecy and forget fiction writing. She
said she'd decided to try her hand at poetry because plots were a
real problem. Maddie told all the women that she was waiting
to go eat lunch in every restaurant in town that was once
segregated, and then she was going to every white ladies'
beauty parlor and sit down and wait for them to do her hair.
Everybody fell out. Bill cracked about how he wasn't going to
pay for all that much integration. Cal Murfree announced that
he and some other Negro farmers were going to try to start up a
cooperative farm up near Plum Landing, and run somebody
else for sheriff one day when they got the vote. Coleman said he
thought he'd drive up to place his ballot. Everyone felt good
even though nothing was over.

Dallas and I disappeared to get away from Tonda, Ronnie,
and Marian, who were swimming in the river. We went to look
out over one of the bluffs and he told me his parents had gotten
him a scholarship to a prep school and he was going to go. He

wasn't sure about it because he thought he might be integrating the place. I thought about ripping my shirt off like Fannie, 'cause I really did like him, but in the end I kept my shirt on and let him show me only one of the many thrills Tonda had listed in her ever-growing catalog of fun things to do with boys.

The boycott took several years, and business just died in the town of Turner. The worst of it for me probably was that I didn't go into a movie house for four and a half years, and Dallas and I, then one or two other boys and I, had to make do with old movies at the college. Everybody in Turner ended up at Buena Vista, black and white, shopping for everything from lawnmowers to lipstick. The first Chinese take out opened there, and by the time they dared to build a restaurant out there the Civil Rights Act had been passed. And I do know that sometime in the sixties, Maddie Alexander ate at the restaurant in Walkers' department store.

LITTLE COLE didn't hear for many weeks about his father getting shot on the road. Almost from that time he had trouble nailing down any facts or certainties. He was dropped out of a helicopter into a fetid jungle without being told its name. In fact, he was told that, technically speaking, he was never there. And he should remember that fact. And when he finally returned to the States it was no longer the fifties and he was utterly mute.

There was no way to account for so many places that didn't exist and things that didn't happen, things that "we" would not do. At least when they dropped him in the Alps he had known it was the Alps when they'd jumped into the snow at night to run radio wires across a border to tie on to Russian lines or to undo lines the Russians had run to army communications lines. The shot that hit him in the dark, the bite out of his leg dug by one of their bullets, would not disappear like the rush from jumping. The rush died immediately, turning into a knot in his stomach the night he looked down on the churning ice water that wasn't supposed to be there hundreds of feet below his boots in the path of his drift. His drift was short. It was dark. His drift was short. The pilot had been off a couple hundred crucial yards. Those guys hit the currents panicked and were lifeless in seconds. Only their chutes kept screaming, kept fighting the water. It was just a job. The bullets in the icy dark. The peaceful border.

His unit disappeared from that place and all the other places the same way, and then they hit the last place. The planes and equipment and faces changed and it was muggier than the worst summer in Virginia and nobody spoke English and it was a helicopter. No passports, no visas, no borders. Just a landing strip. A helicopter. We weren't there and we had no problem there. It was a military camp but there was no wire perimeter. Just jungle. For a miniature base in the middle of nowhere, it was well supplied with something like a PX, a screening room, mess, American trinkets. They said the French weren't a presence in the country anymore, but the people running the operation were French. Asian soldiers speaking French, American Pathfinders and Rangers, all specialists, training in English. There was no war. No perimeter. The jungle was on his skin like thick hair. The young Asian men squatted close to the ground. What they did there clung close to the ground too, and the vegetation closed in on everything that refused to move. There was no perimeter.

SCHOOL INTEGRATION did not come till after I finished high school. It took six more years. Those were years when I tried to run off to the movement rather than go to college, just as

Preston tried. The old man got me loafers, one suit, a dress for dances, and a big trunk. By then I only wore blue jeans too, but the old man didn't put up a fuss. When I asked to go south to do voter registration he thought about it for four days and sat me down and said he wasn't prepared to lose his last child to the war, at least not till I was old enough to decide for myself. My second year in college I heard that jittery Bobby from down the way had been listed as a "noncombat incident" when he lost his life in Vietnam. That spring the old man, who'd become a college official, was taken hostage by the students the same week I called to say I was sleeping on the floor of the dean's office at school. In typical fashion the old man said, "It's fine, really. The administration had it coming."

The sixties didn't really rock Dixon's boat, he just rolled with it and began to express outrageous opinions. He didn't care about Preston's beard, or his becoming a conscientious objector during the war. He decided living together was better than being stupid or being alone. We took him to the opera and turned him on to John Coltrane. His final words on raising children were, "I worried about the wrong things. My children were just born crazy."

THE FACES of those people sitting in my classroom are invisible now, just as invisible as the faces of the family in town who once owned my family and still live there. Once they might have seemed unforgettable, but they retreated and we let them be forgotten. Of course, for our defiance, the invisible faces sought their retribution against the whole lot of us by declaring our southern town in need of urban renewal. But then, like the rest of this story, that would be hard to prove. The fact is that the wrecking balls came two years into the boycott and two years before the Civil Rights Act. To bring back the downtown, most of the old campground—the old neighbor-hood, the black part of town—was condemned and taken down within weeks of the forced abandonment of the bun-galows and two-story houses that we all knew like the backs of our hands. Leaving only two big churches standing, the town cleared itself of any visible signs of our claims to the place. Only the street names remain. We all moved to pockets of black homes tucked here and there, or to the next town, or, like me, kept moving like nomads, scattered to the invisible perimeter.

I was once in a holding cell with a man who told me if he was free he would just sit under a tree. But it would be a different tree than anyone before him had sat under when sitting under a tree. He would never leave the building alive, he told me. "I belong to them," he said of the armed guards outside the barred doors. The way he explained his situation was pretty plain. We both accepted it. He was a dead man, alright. Death hung around his body like lingering smoke from a cigarette. He smoked my whole pack. I let the tape recorder run, took pictures of the rings circling round his head. Shortly thereafter the long rifles collected the debt they felt he owed. When you are one of the survivors you desire to get the tree over with so you can set the stories free from your body. I have to sit under his tree. That job does not pass on. It belongs to the last of the line.

There are a lot of little things that don't mean anything much, but you notice them. I've never been in the public library in Turner, Virginia. I did swim in the water reserved for whites on Turner's beach where they left an African woman to die after being declared a slave. The barbed wire put up to keep us out was left standing in the water. I've never eaten lunch at a Woolworth's counter. It just turned out that way.